1/20

JULIANNA KISS

Also by Hannah MacDonald

The Sun Road

JULIANNA KISS

Hannah MacDonald

LITTLE, BROWN

LITTLE, BROWN

First published in Great Britain in January 2006
by Little, Brown

Copyright © Hannah MacDonald 2005

The moral right of the author has been asserted.

*All characters and events in this publication, other than
those clearly in the public domain, are fictitious
and any resemblance to real persons,
living or dead, is purely coincidental.*

Every effort has been made to trace copyright owners. Please notify
Little, Brown of any omissions and they will be rectified.

A CIP catalogue record for this book
is available from the British Library.

ISBN 0 316 72429 7

Typeset in Times New Roman by Palimpsest Book Production Limited,
Polmont, Stirlingshire
Printed and bound in Great Britain by Clays Ltd, St Ives plc

Little, Brown
An imprint of
Time Warner Book Group UK
Brettenham House
Lancaster Place
London WC2E 7EN

www.twbg.co.uk

For Paul

I have never succumbed to the temptation of self-pity, nor, it may be, to that of true sublimity and divine perspicacity, but I have known from the beginning that my disgrace was not merely a humiliation; it also concealed redemption, if only my heart could be courageous enough to accept this redemption, this peculiarly cruel form of grace, and even to recognise grace at all in such a cruel form. – And if you now ask me what still keeps me here on this earth, what keeps me alive, then, I would answer without any hesitation: love.

Hungarian novelist, Auschwitz survivor and Nobel Prize winner Imre Kertész

PART 1

1990

You say how strange it seems that I never
Write about you, my sons and daughters.
I hear your unspoken reproach: Don't we
matter as much as . . .? And I can't explain.
I can't say, when I heard you at the door,
How eagerly I ran to light the fire
And set places for you and cut the bread.
I had reached that house only days before.
You arrived, pilgrims, wanderers, swallows,
Magi witnessing your own holy birth,
A flock of the wild migrant geese, gypsies.
You took food. The time came when we went on,
Each alone. We had grasped a few phrases
of each other's language, hardy enough
For greetings and goodbyes. Go well now! Look
At the immense distances we travel,
rushing away from each other like stars.

M.R. Peacocke, 'Letters 2'

Chapter One

At Munich the overhead TV flickered and died. A man boarded and without prevarication, as if this were something long agreed, moved through the coach with lowered eyes and sat down next to Julianna. She found the warmth of his foreign body unpleasant. She compressed her arms and legs so that no part of their limbs touched and wished for the luxury of two seats to return. Her alert pleasure at the beginning of the journey had long since faded; the progress of the coach was now agonisingly evident.

He was peculiar in that he sat still the whole way to Calais. He got out at the rest stops, of course, but each time he returned and re-placed himself in exactly the same way. Julianna eyed the other empty seats each time they stopped, but worried that moving to sit next to someone else might cause offence. She was a little afraid of him, yet that didn't stop her from feeling sorry for him. He had no book, no newspaper or magazine to read, and only one plastic bag of possessions. He wore a frayed thin anorak and no socks. He didn't seem to smell, or at least she couldn't smell it if he did, but she was instinctively sure he might. She kept her head turned to the window, leaning her forehead against the smears of others.

Julianna was ashamed of how alert she was to every possible smell on the coach. It was feeble of her. If one lone foreigner disturbed her so, then how was she going to cope in England? But of course it was the proximity of him. So close for so long that, although they never spoke, never looked each other in the eye, when they finally disembarked at Calais the next morning she felt as if they'd shared something, tactfully avoided some issue of mutual embarrassment, when all they'd shared was a view of the road and the sounds and odours from the toilet at the back of the coach.

In those thirty-six hours it took to travel from Budapest to the edge of the English Channel she ate four sandwiches, two sausages, a burger, three portions of potato fries, two bars of chocolate, and drank three cans of Coke, two plastic cups of coffee and one packet of orange-flavoured drink. She stepped out on to the deck of the ferry and felt sick with the pitching Channel and greasy food. Julianna had only seen the sea twice before, on holiday in Poland. She still couldn't summon many adjectives for it. She tried, wanting to be moved by her surroundings on this momentous crossing. Keen to join the cultish worship of waves. Yet it seemed mostly grey, solid and muscular. A large, untrustworthy, unwelcoming surface. Then there was the truth that the carved-away wake, folding at the base of the boat, was the same dirty yellow colour as an old man's moustache.

There weren't many people up on the deck. It was the first ferry and only just becoming light. It was bitterly cold. Each figure folded into itself, shoulders raised, chin down, arms wrapped. Too tempting not to watch the land draw closer as the light seeped into the air. Julianna sat in the brunt of the wind, facing the coast of England. First an indistinct tonal clue, a darker colour ahead, then pale-brown cliffs emerging below a livid slip of pink cloud.

She was glad to have stayed awake for the moment of arrival, glad she hadn't curled up in a carpeted corner or stretched over four plastic seats for some hard sleep. She didn't know how they could – unless of course they weren't all first-timers like her. They certainly looked like it, but then there was no one she'd seen on this ferry who looked like they had any sophistication to them. Perhaps that's the way it always is, she thought, with ferries and coaches that pound on through early mornings and late nights. Airports would certainly be better. Full of all sorts of people, not just this shabby lot, each one as shabby as her.

The journey into London took an age. After luminous green fields, and stretches of unrevealing light industry, they reached streets of sturdy, repetitive houses, roads blocked with shining cars. The coach driver got lost, and there were traffic jams and road works. But Julianna was happy. She was no longer watching for signs of distance passed; she was now watching for her own arrival. She wished that the driver would say, 'Now London begins,' for she was unsure about where the suburbs ended and serious city began. The cars were so luxurious she could happily live in one. It wasn't that she hadn't seen smart cars before, just never this many, had never thought that a new car was a matter of course. There were trees, she noticed. Then smiled at herself: why shouldn't there be trees? And look, a dog, and a child, and an old man, and a fat woman. English dogs and English women. Weary people, crossing the road on the way to the shops, eyed by Julianna as if they were exotic animals in an unsafe reserve.

Finally she stepped down from the coach at Victoria, aching and sticky. The shock of it brought grey chequers before her eyes. She queued for her baggage, then gathered her bags protectively around her and tried to work out what to do next.

She looked like easy prey, waiting there alone in the middle of a thousand arrivals and leave-takings. Around her people ran to the beat of digital seconds, with bags and children spilling out behind them. Others turned on the spot, stuck like ballerinas in a musical box. There were men, young and old, sitting around the edges, one of whom seemed to have taken up habitation in the station. He sat beside a wheeled trolley from which rose a pyramid of tightly tied plastic bags, scarfs, rags and useful tools dangling from the sides.

Julianna scrabbled in the small pink bag that she carried diagonally across her chest. She sat down on the suitcase her father had lent her, thin legs in jeans, splayed over its rigid stuffed bulk, pulled out a brown envelope, unfolded two pieces of paper, turned them the right way up, read, referred back and re-read. *Coach 32, stand at north end of station, twice daily to Brigtown, regular buses thereafter for all stops to Westington, get out fourth stop after station, opposite nursery.* Eventually she grasped the solid facts: she must look for a coach with the number 32, and a sign giving its destination as Brigtown.

However, the translation into action of something read a hundred times for future travel took a Herculean mental effort. As if she had to summon whole coaches into being with her imagination. And when, after nearly an hour, she finally found her coach, she collapsed horizontally on to the back seat and dozed in the magnified sunshine, attracting every trapped fly, until the coach driver sounded his departure with a horn.

She didn't reach Brigtown until after five. By the time she then caught her third and final bus the sun was setting. She'd thought that she was beyond expectation. She'd been travelling for so long. All this way to see fields not so different from Hungary's own. But when she settled into her third stale-smelling vehicle her eyes were wide open, if sore, and the fear of disappointment made her feel edgy. After the teeming city they had retreated further and further away from habitation. She felt the pang of a treat offered, then taken away. She tried to remember why she'd come, for money and language and exploration, that she was finally in the country where her grandmother had been born.

The bus driver told her it would be the next stop, and after crossing a narrow stone bridge they slowed. 'This'll be yours,' he said, with the budget formality of public transport, and she stepped down into the chill, sharply scented evening air. The bus remained stationary, the headlights on, the driver watching her pass through a gate signed Woods Farm. She walked down a concrete driveway, lined by a ditch and wild flowers, faintly coloured in this light. Julianna could hear the engine churning behind her and raised her arm to thank him (he was the first person with whom she had had a proper English conversation). He waited until she and her pale face, her childishly pink bag and her sagging tan-coloured suitcase were an indistinguishable shape and the other passengers had begun to grumble.

She walked, slowly now, up towards the buildings in the distance. The fields stretched away, undulating yellow and brown in the dying light. Ahead she could see different cloud layers: wool-ish wisps moving high and fast across an apricot sky, and a grey mass on the horizon. This she assumed was a mountain range, before it shifted in front of her eyes. She could the speckle of sheep in the distance, hear the rushes on the river bank down to the left. The rushes were tall then bent low, released then swirling; wind materialised. A dog barked and she could see more lights, a house, behind the bulk of a barn. Her head was full, a collision of perception and projection; outdoors, its emergent night sounds and the airiness of being alone, contrasting with the thought of bright interiors peopled and blurred with warmth. She knew the sea was nearby and she thought, perhaps, she who had now seen it several times, that she could smell it in the air.

This is it, she thought. Here I am. And experienced an unfamiliar strength of emotion. The dramatics of this dimming, weather-full day (her poised on the edge of going in) gave her such a soaring feeling that she nearly turned and walked straight back the way she had come. It turned out that Julianna knew freedom when she felt it.

Chapter Two

Julianna had begun her journey from Kisrét on a late afternoon two days earlier. Their village was five miles to the
north of Baskó, a small town in eastern Hungary, where she
lived with her grandmother, her father, her stepmother and
brother. She had said goodbye to her grandmother at the
house, and as they'd embraced, Mila had scolded her. It was
her usual form of affection. This is nonsense, she had said,
as she held Julianna tight. *Buta, buta* she kept saying. *Buta
gyerek*, silly child.

Hugging Mila had always been a lengthy, and hot, affair.
A large part of her bulk was padding; she wore a dress, a
woollen waistcoat, an apron, and then beneath that further
layers; a thin sweater, vest, tights, capacious knickers and a
girdle.

As Julianna's father began to remonstrate about roads and
time, Mila reassured her granddaughter that she would
quickly forget her grandmother, and this seemed to give the
old woman the strength to let go, life's harder truths having
always had an invigorating effect on her. She put her hands
on Julianna's shoulders and pushed her towards the door
saying, 'Be careful who you mix with,' and with the same
severity, 'Give my love to England.' And with that senti-
mental, suspicious combination she sent her out of the front
door.

*

Once the car had started, Mila took herself out into the back yard and sat on one of the old kitchen chairs. The red plastic seat covering peeling back to reveal scraps of yellow foam. She could feel the warmth of the wall pressing against the curve of her spine. Mila's favourite time of day was late afternoon. This was when she and Julianna would go out to feed the rabbits. The first two, exchanged for a pirated cassette of a Paul McCartney album, had been a present for Julianna from her father. These five were the distant descendants. Julianna had bred them and they were sold cheaply to schoolchildren, then even cheaper to women with aprons and stew pots. It had given her a little pocket money.

Afternoons were gentler on old bones. The time of day when everyone slowed a little, coming closer to the hedgehog speed which Mila hardly recognised as her own. She too had little feet and a disproportionate bulk, a dithering set of manoeuvres which kept her busy but did not get her anywhere fast.

It had been Mila's idea that Julianna travel. Why not, now that the child could, now that Europe was open to her? Why not spend the summer in England, making something of her last months of youth? But having waved her goodbye, Mila felt a deep disturbance. Julianna had set off with a face so unprinted by men's fingers it made Mila wince with dark possibilities. She had felt her granddaughter transfer her interest before she'd even left, sensed her head caught in the future tense of another language. But the hole in Mila's daily life would be huge. Everything had been the same for so long, since Julianna's mother had died and her father had remarried; nothing had disrupted their small, self-enclosed family. This rupturing would probably never have happened without the slow domino fall of communism, but Mila knew which event would change her life more.

She shifted her painful joints, tried to remember what

mattered, Julianna's future. Even she, who couldn't remember the weather in England, could remember what it *felt* like to be young. Why was her emotional memory so much better than her factual one? Being young had felt like balancing on a precipice, with a whole new land laid out for her below. Knife-edge and rich. Secretly she thought that she had known her mind better than Julianna, had been more dynamic. But then she had grown up in another time and another place. A place which had been constantly producing new inventions and discoveries. *She* hadn't grown up in a country whose history was of surviving intrusion. Hard for Julianna, Mila knew, what with last year's elections and the dismantling of walls and borders, to realise that it was her will, not her country's, that could open up the future.

Mila's eyes moved slowly around the garden of the farmhouse where her husband had grown up – a home then divided and portioned out after the war, rooms invented out of chastened spaces. She watched the small rabbits making sideways leaps, their twitching kicks and soft landings. Mila thought of the home she had grown up in, of the English town where she was born, of the days before she met her husband János, the man she'd fallen in love with, with such complete surrender that it had shaped every element of her and her life.

Their meeting was a glorious story, a testament to the potential of a single moment. János enclosed Mila still, within an abridged story of their marriage, one that she had told to Julianna thousands of times. She had always told her own story with emphatic completeness, with no room for the uncertainties of the present. Certain details standing sharp as stakes between which to string a simplified storyline. Single moments forced to perform; like the Roman cups found whole, but faded, thousands of years on, their frail form carrying the whole weight of translation for a later civilisation. In its longevity Mila had come to see her story as a cumulative gift to Julianna. A trousseau of sorts.

Mila thought of her stepping off the coach into the wet greenness of England, and wished harder than a prayer that Julianna might be given every one of the joys her grandmother had known and led her to expect, without one moment of the suffering. Then she went back into the house, trying to escape a growing disquiet at all that she had promised her granddaughter.

Julianna had arrived in Kent at the worn-out end of spring. The landscape was so green it was as if the sky and the people were drained of energy by feeding the lushness. That first morning, awaking exhausted after her evening arrival, her impressions were of a heaviness – fat raindrops, mud-slicked outbuildings, saturated air in dense woods, dark caravans, and people speaking in an incomprehensible low, rumbling monotone. If I could just distinguish the words, she thought, I might be able to understand them. Later that morning she accompanied the farm manager, Roy, into the nearby small town of Westington, where he pointed and she acknowledged politely. She saw tightly packed houses, fat wood-pigeons, flooded gutters, cars substantial and armoured, dripping in long, slow snakes. People diffident in gesture, reluctant to look her in the face. That second night, in her caravan, in the small paddock behind the office, beneath a clean but cold sheet, she felt the exhaustion of someone who had been permanently on the alert for weeks. The students normally shared caravans, but since they were an odd number, Julianna was alone. Which she was initially relieved by, then realised was a handicap, as it meant she had no instant ally.

There was a careful imbalance of nationalities this year at Woods Farm: Ukrainian, Hungarian, Polish and Ghanaian.

The 800-acre farm was arable, growing rape, barley and wheat in rotation with strawberries and raspberries. In glasshouses and tunnels they grew little gem and romaine lettuces, and they would also be harvesting elderflower blossom in June. When Julianna had applied to come to England with Rural Alliance, they'd sent her literature explaining that they had been set up after the Second World War 'to encourage friendship between the youth of different nations'. They dealt with a large proportion of the tens of thousands of foreign students that the UK's agricultural work force absorbed each year.

Roy had thought the students from Central and Eastern Europe might form a foursome, apart from the non-Europeans. But for the first few days they were all as wary as one another. Julianna remained silent and absorbed. She watched the others rather than speaking to them. The Ukrainian girls were bolder than her and she had never seen anyone so black as the Ghanaian boys, James and Ngao. The darkest skin colour she'd ever seen in Hungary was that of the *roma*. She tried not to stare but was soon surprised at how ordinary and gentle the boys' movements were.

After the second night Julianna woke to clear skies. It was the first dry awakening the farm had had for weeks. Straight after breakfast they began work picking lettuce in the poly-tunnels that lay on the other side of the road. Once they had picked they would plant, and six weeks later they would pick again. None of them had ever been paid for anything other than manual labour. So it wasn't as if the muscle-cramping work, or the damp warmth of the earth, which travelled over their bodies and into their hair, surprised them. It was the monotony that Julianna found hard. The fact that after what felt like eight hours she'd only been working for two. There was a strong smell of mulch in the tunnels, and another smell, a fuller note above the smell of water, that it took Julianna, ridiculously, the whole morning to identify as lettuce.

They were encouraged to take a full hour at lunchtime – even though they were paid on an hourly rate, so that sitting still felt almost like spending money. Roy said you worked better and longer if you took time to rest halfway through the day. Julianna doubted that she would ever be able to work faster than she had this morning. She felt stiff and a little dizzy.

She wasn't confident that any of the students would talk to her if she sat next to them. So she took her packed lunch and began to walk, and without her they settled into small islands, the two Ukrainian girls and the two Ghanaian boys sitting apart, the other two boys reluctantly twinned. By heading away from the tunnels and off towards the strawberry fields, Julianna sparked a rumour of aloofness that would never quite die.

When she reached the far corner of the field she stopped; she had travelled far enough away to be invisible. She leant on the top bar looking out at the view – the small wood spreading into a dip on the right, a church steeple and houses ahead on the returning swell, then the land mounting towards the Downs. It was a green, rolling, busy landscape – and a more restricted view than she was used to.

Just as she heard footsteps behind her, someone said, 'Hello.' It was a loud but indistinct, just-passing voice, one that opened and ended conversation all at once. Julianna turned sharply and saw a woman she catalogued instantly as harried, then as middle-aged but attractive.

She said hello back.

'Settling in OK, I hope?' the woman managed, opening the gate and stepping back to allow two energetic black and white dogs through.

Julianna didn't know who this woman was. She stuttered slightly and said, 'Thank you.' It wasn't what she had wanted to say, but she had been caught without any language preparation. She watched the woman walk on fast and stumble, proceeded then collected by the two dogs in a bullet-fast chase.

Julianna watched her progress – the dogs manic but never straying out of a certain radius around her feet. She wondered how she was connected to the farm – wondered if she was Mrs Woods, the farmer's wife. Wondered why a woman with nothing more pressing to do than exercise her dogs would seem so rushed.

Mrs Woods walked on fast, feeling her lungs struggle to catch up, the rubbing of her thighs, the wrinkle of her sock in the boot, the dig of an old bra, sensing the student's gaze on the twisting play-fight of the dogs, a young mother and her son.

Miriam Woods had noticed that Julianna was a little flushed, that childish combination of livid white and red that had always spelt trouble with her own son. But perhaps because of the procession of troubled, overcharged, almost disgustingly sexual dreams she'd had last night, perhaps because of the vicious levels of energy she'd felt this morning, she reacted to Julianna's youth more than anything. She noticed the way her eyes shone bright, not tired, out of her slightly sad face, the way her mouth was unhampered by a structure of lines. Something about the sight of this girl gave Miriam pain. As if she were a manifestation of everything she had dreamed of last night and lost with the sunrise.

Summer arrived in the lowlands of England like nature's amnesty, and one morning Julianna stepped out of her caravan into the white glare of a refreshed sun. Her skin tightened with shock, her chest expanded as she breathed in deeply. By lunch break the high slope of her forehead and the ridge of her straight nose were burnt from the yellow glare of heat out in the fields. Her dark hair became streaked with the colour of maple leaves. The transformation was hard to exaggerate, she said in her first letter home.

Now the sun was out there was pungent romance to the work. They had finished in the tunnels and had moved into the strawberry fields, harvesting the Elsanta. The work became rhythmic, almost entranced; they picked unthinkingly, surrounded by the strong smells of straw, red fruit and their own sharp sweat. Around them the light brought everything to life, the fields acid green in the sunlight, the farmhouse itself suddenly picturesque under lilac, dense clots of pink and white blossom in the orchard. The hedgerows now crackled with creatures, not just cascades of raindrops. The roads and paths were lined with tall, repeating stalks of cream cow-parsley, black clouds of insects hovering over each flower head. Painted Ladies and Red Admirals sunning themselves on warm walls, a buzzard circling high in the noon sun, and swifts emerging suddenly at dusk, wreathing around the house.

Julianna and the others worked long and hard under Roy's management, six days a week, but those who came from urban backgrounds were aware for the first time of the seasonal rightness of a working day which began with sunrise and ended with its setting. There was little opportunity for conversation during the day, except at lunch. The students would sit and eat talking sporadically in English, sometimes in five different languages. Lying in the shade of the trees, curls of cheap cigarette smoke dissolving into the scraps of sky, blue between pixelating leaves. But in the evening, when the cut-price meals were cooked, little collectives of like-minded eaters having formed, then there was time to talk in slow broken English, weighted words carried aloft, the flow of their own language beneath.

Julianna was sought out by István, a Polish agricultural student whose mother was Hungarian, as someone he could actually have a conversation with, and suddenly the group seemed less impenetrable. She wasn't bold enough to think of them as new people to whom she could present herself any way she chose, but she did relax into realising they hadn't formed fast friendships without her. There were games after the evening meal, and, above all, a sense of money accumulating, safely, in an unseen vault.

Most of them were glad to be in England and the rest were nevertheless glad to be away from home. There was an energy and interesting tension to the group. Swiftly, Olena, the younger and sexier of the Ukrainian girls, had focused male attention on herself. She basked and revolved in it, as was her genetic due. The other, Sofiya, swiftly realised her role as Olena's bridesmaid. Which left Julianna free of much sexual speculation. She was a strong-featured, brown-haired, quiet-tempered nineteen-year-old, who fitted no one's idea of beauty queen.

Except perhaps for Matthew Woods, who had recently returned, thin and languorous, from retaking his A levels in Cambridge. He first saw Julianna as he sat at his bedroom window, smoking a cigarette. She was walking across the courtyard towards the packing shed. She was tall and long-limbed and purposeful. Tough-looking in a way that he thought quite sexy. Like a young resistance fighter. Or a basketball player on a day off. To describe what she didn't look like was easier; she didn't look like the pretty, compact girls at the crammer. She looked foreign. And Matthew, fresh from a crash course in literature and history and art, had a new appreciation for the unfamiliar. He liked to make his new-found preferences clear, choosing Gauloise over Malboro, Milan Kundera over Wilbur Smith, and French movies with actresses so beautiful he used them as elegant porn.

He had an illicit thirty-a-day habit to support, so over the next few days he spent a lot of time watching her. He saw her stacking boxes in the sheds, fighting with the poly-tunnel materials, bent over strawberry plants, and identified her caravan and watched her light go off at night. He wondered how it was that he had never seen a girl like this before. She fascinated him. Did they not grow that tall or that wiry in England? Or was it just the bourgeois rut of his education? he wondered. Her height and lope and strong-featured face reminded him of Daryl Hannah in *Bladerunner*. (He had a poster of her on his wall. It was a potent comparison.) His stomach clenched when he saw her and he would draw back and watch her from behind his curtains, round corners, as if he were a lascivious old man. In his young life, as an only child, at a boys' grammar school, getting drunk in cliques, passing notes in lessons, he felt as if he had never seen a girl not gaggle or slouch, or sideways slither, fiddling with their hair and the sharp tools they used to snare it.

He loved his mother and felt that he tolerated much for her, and from her, but he loathed the way she called the students the Summer Helpers, as if they were a brand of seasonal fairies. His father called them the Russians, or the Africans, depending on their skin colour, but Matthew would have expected nothing less from him. This would be the first time Matthew had willingly attended the Sunday lunch held in the students' honour, and the night before he chose his shirt with care.

*

20

In the morning Miriam prepared lunch in silence, refusing even Radio 4. A local church rang its bells nearby, but the Woods weren't that sort of family. Miriam worked efficiently but with little pleasure. These were occasions of perennial awkwardness. Matthew was home, so her life had regained shape. But it was funny how she forgot, in the pain of his absence, that he could be as opaque, as maddeningly semi-present as his father.

(Theirs was a confusing relationship; Matthew never saw her joy in him for all her worry, and she never saw the questioning energy in him, because his only reaction to prodding was to grow stiller. In fact, away from her, his drooping, irritating sarcasm became wry and lively.)

While Miriam was a cook of military precision, Gerard was just about capable in charge of a mixing bowl. He had three signature dishes, his favourite being Yorkshire pudding. By now, noon on a warm Sunday, he was well oiled by the second half of the first bottle of probably two eventual bottles of Sunday good claret. So while he made the pudding she cooked the roast beef, cauliflower cheese, carrots and greens, roast potatoes and rhubarb crumble. It seemed a pretty fair division of labour to him. Good Yorkshire took a long time and Gerard was proud of his Yorkshires. Not too proud to be a cooker of good pudding. Not so New Man that he'd contemplate making anything else.

'Shop bought?' he said loudly to his wife, referring to a jar of horseradish on the table. He was on a slow saunter round the kitchen through to the dining room, round the dining room table, and back again, while smoking an excellent fag. Not all of them did the job, taking the throat by surprise. But this one did. The pudding was resting, and meanwhile, on his usual kitchen circuit, he'd noticed the jar of horseradish on the table. He picked it up and inspected the label.

'Yes,' his wife said with her own brand of tartness.

He put the jar down, sensing it was best to let the subject go. 'Nice Russians this year,' he said, starting lap ten.

'They're not Russian. They're Ukrainian and Hungarian and Ghanaian,' said Matthew, arriving in the kitchen to take an apple out of a bowl of manky fruit.

'Have you finally learnt a little geography, Matthew?' said his father.

'Oh piss off,' said Matthew and left the room again.

'Excellent. Excellent. That's what we want. A little display of imbalanced testosterone . . . Just in time for that blonde bombshell to arrive.'

'I thought you'd notice her,' said Miriam. 'She's called Lola. Roy says the boys keep doing all her work for her. She's been doing the tunnels all week and hasn't had to lift a finger, Roy said.'

Gerard looked at her. Sometimes, only infrequently, he wondered if his wife and Roy could be having an affair. In a curious way he was quite at home with the suggestion. His wife was a beauty, a heady beauty – even still, at forty-nine; he'd be almost disappointed if someone wasn't trying to get at her. He allowed his thoughts to return to default. He wasn't a man to brood on people; instead his mind mulched over an intricate plan for an innovative, perhaps unachievable, irrigation system. In the common desire to one day profit from something other than subsidies, he had become a highly imaginative, yet always rather impractical, farmer.

There was a knock on the back door, and a huge black boy loomed in the doorway. It still took Gerard by surprise; traditionally they'd stuck to having Russians on the farm. This was only the third year they'd sent anyone from Africa. Just the extraordinary sight of a black man in his doorway was enough to give him a great global feeling of displacement. This was Kent in May and yet he had a fleeting sense of being transplanted somewhere hot, where he could stalk tigers and be brought gin and tonics on verandas. Instead, here he was, in an overheated kitchen, wearing the old shirt he'd meant to change before Lolita and her gang arrived. Making puddings for them. Perhaps they should go in for a range of farmyard puddings, he thought, fag in hand, failing to remember to invite his guests in.

Julianna came into the kitchen last and stood on the edge of the group. Matthew was lingering at the back of the kitchen, near the fridge, watching for her. She was wearing a loose white nylon shirt, shiny with whorling patterns, and her clean tight jeans. She had washed and brushed her hair for the occasion. The layers of her shoulder-length hair rose and sat on their own static, an inch added to her five foot ten, a pyramid of crackle. Miriam also saw her standing near the door, looking hopeful and lean. Hungry. She felt a little guilty for not having been nicer to the girl when she'd seen her by the gate last week. In previous years and better tempers she'd taken cakes round to each of the students' caravans to try and help them settle in. Miriam wiped her hands on her apron and led Julianna, one hand on her arm, towards the chopping board of rhubarb, suggesting she'd be very kind if she could finish off the job.

'Are you comfortable in the caravans?' Miriam asked while turning roast potatoes. Some of them had been more than par-boiled and were disintegrating into the fat at the touch of her spatula.

'Yes,' said Julianna. 'I have one alone. It is a . . .' She sought for the word. 'A pleasure.' She was unnerved to be chattering in this way with an employer, wielding a blunt knife in the plentiful clutter of their large kitchen.

'Yes,' said Miriam. 'I expect it is. I wouldn't mind a caravan of my own.' She laughed at her own joke. Terribly politely.

'Do you eat rhubarb at home?' asked Miriam.

Julianna looked at Miriam, clearly not understanding.

'That's rhubarb, the thing that you're chopping.'

'Ah,' said Julianna and put a piece in her mouth.

'I wouldn't, it'll be sour.'

Julianna stopped mid-chew, but she was too old and too far from home to spit something into her hand so she just swallowed it with a grimace.

Miriam laughed. Less politely. 'I remember Sally, Sally Bradshaw, they own the farm you can see over there,' she gestured out of the window beyond the blossoming rows of apple trees that climbed up and over the swelling hill, like a highly decorated cavalry, 'telling me how one boy arrived from Poland after getting the coach all the way to London and then another coach straight down to Canterbury, what . . . that must be two days of solid travelling?' She looked at Julianna, who understood half the words, just enough to catch the gist, and nodded.

'More,' Julianna added, reminding this woman that she had done the very same trek through unintelligible towns, driving along in darkness, bedroom lights and foreign shop signs speeding by.

'Anyway,' Miriam continued, 'this boy arrived and went straight out to pick the fruit, desperate to start earning money, without stopping to eat, and from her window Sally could see him starting to eat the Bramleys. Bramleys are cooking apples, sour like the rhubarb.

'And she ran out and said stop, stop, you mustn't eat the apples, they'll give you a terrible, terrible stomach ache, and the boy looked at her and said, in total innocence, why are we picking apples if they cannot be eaten?'

There was a second's silence. It was perhaps an inappropriately angled anecdote for a girl fresh from central Europe, but Julianna's grandmother took pleasure in cooking, and Julianna knew the difference between cookers and eaters and so she and Miriam began to laugh together over the Polish boy who'd never had the luxury of two kinds of apples.

Miriam's laughter never sounded very convincing; she made it sound heavy as shapes on a page, as if she were reading the syllables. She watched Julianna sharply as she resumed chopping. She appreciated the girl's help. But there was something about the silent presumptuousness of her (of all of them, perhaps); filing in, eyeing up the fruit bowls, their flesh rudely firm and shining, shooting off remarks in foreign languages, hanging around uselessly; something about their expectancy and inscrutability made her want to take Julianna in hand, teach her a few home truths. Take off the shine.

She watched Julianna chop slowly, carefully, frayed shirt, long legs, long fingers, hair falling in front of her face, rims of dirt beneath her nails. 'You can go and freshen up if you like,' she said as Julianna finished, the envy leaking out with sharp politeness.

Julianna didn't understand so stood still, looking uncertain. Miriam rolled her eyes in mock humour. 'The bathroom, wash your hands, tuck your shirt in,' and she mimed the gestures patronisingly. Julianna nodded, anxious and a little defensive.

She followed the instructions and went to the chilly lavatory, full of bulging oilskin coats, with an indefinable smell, not of effluents but something colder. She looked in the cracked mirror and wetted her hair, trying to smooth it down. She looked childish and worried, she thought. She tucked her shirt in, even though it wasn't that kind of shirt, and then hesitated, suddenly full of longing for home. Awash with loneliness, she dawdled in the hallway, examining a framed a photograph when she heard footsteps behind her.

Miriam, who was heading off upstairs to apply her own lipstick, did not look thrilled to see Julianna again. As she passed she said, in a challenging voice, 'That's what *I* looked like when I was your age.' Then whisked past her up the stairs, swifter and lighter than if she had been unwatched.

In the dining room Matthew laid the table laboriously. It looked wrong; he often felt dyslexic when it came to manners. But as people were bustled into the dining room he quickly manoeuvred his way round until he was standing next to Julianna, before two empty chairs. People chose places, with murmurs and uncertainty, Matthew grabbed two of the faded blue velvet chairs and gestured to her in an ungainly way. Julianna was surprised. She hadn't noticed this boy before. But she was happy to be told what to do.

After the chaos of all of them in the kitchen and the dogs underfoot, the dining room felt sulky and airless. Everyone was pushed to inhabit their erratically laid space. Some retreated, some grew louder, and in the corner Matthew and Julianna loaded their plates. Matthew trying to broach conversation with over-emphatic exclamations on the passing and taking of vegetables.

Lunch was cooked to different degrees. The carrots hard. The meat bleeding pink. The pudding perfect, soft and stretching in the centre, crisp and golden around the edges. The potatoes collapsing in saturated heaps. The kitchen and now the dining room had steamed up, and the house seemed like a chicken coop, fenced in dark against the bright outdoor light. The men sweated and drank more wine than was intended (Gerard had brought out a good few bottles of his cheapest plonk). Lola grew skittish and black-tongued. István silent and glowering. Only Ngao and James, the Ghanaians, and Miriam held off the wine.

'Where have you come from?' It sounded clumsy in his ears, as if assuming here was a Mecca and the place she had left just a starting point. Matthew's thoughts often machine-gunned like this, rebutting everything he had previously thought or even, rashly, said.

'Kisrét. It is in the east of Hungary. Near to Baskó.' Matthew nodded and then strained to think of something else to say.

'Have you been into Westington yet? Or Brigtown? Or the beach somewhere?'

There was a pause and he saw she was slowly finishing her mouthful before answering. There was a blob of gravied food on her chin which unnerved him. He looked down at his plate and listened as she began, and much to his relief, wiped her chin with her hand and carried on.

'I saw Brigtown,' she said. 'I came on the boat also, not on the plane, so I have seen the sea then.' Her voice was heavily accented. What else had he expected? It sounded strong, slightly nasal. Heavy and emphatic, each word given equal weight. 'I liked looking at the sea. We don't have a . . . a sea, no, that is not the word.' She looked sadly at her plate, and then rallied with recall. 'Like a beach . . . do you understand?'

'A coast,' he said.

'Yes,' she said.

He didn't know that, although perhaps if he'd thought about it he might have worked it out by creating a wonky map of Europe in his head, guessing at the small countries whose names he swore kept changing. 'So it's land-locked.'

She shrugged and smiled because she did not know the word and he obviously did not know her country.

'No sea,' he said. Which was what she'd just said. Her conversations in English often felt like this, circular, lacking in any momentum.

'We have lakes, a large lake called Balaton,' she said.

'Balaton,' he said.

She repeated it, correcting his pronunciation.

'But it's not a sea,' he said. Cajoling.

'No,' she said, 'the sea is larger, but I think it is also more boring.'

And he laughed; it seemed mischievous and he felt a flush of success at the first stanza of their flirtation. But she was only being honest. What made the water interesting was land at the edge, she thought. The grey stretch of the Channel, its gently curved horizon, reminded her of the empty, wind-flattened plains of Hungary more than any liquid.

'Things have, um, changed for you over there then, you know, the Wall and everything,' he said. He and his friends had celebrated the fall of the Berlin Wall by getting drunk on Smirnoff and Budvar. She shrugged and ate in silence for a few moments.

'Hungary allowed people to leave, on the border to Austria, for a long time.' She stopped, and made a gesture to suggest the collapse of a small garden wall, or the closing of a subject. People here kept expecting this from her, as if she was related to Lech Walesa or had removed the first brick in Berlin. She and her friends had envied East Berliners that weekend, in fact. Not for the rush of liberty or the sudden spotlight on their city, but for the fact that each family that crossed from east to west was given £30 to spend in the legendary shops of West Berlin. She'd seen them on the television. They bought a little fruit, maybe a toy for their child. Pushchairs swinging with plastic bags, taking bright slogans back to the old streets.

'How old are you?' she suddenly asked, chewing, still

appraising him with narrowed eyes, reaching for a glass of wine. He was struck by her foreignness. By the sophistication of her movements, by her physical confidence. The way she turned and chewed and looked and drank. It was almost masculine.

Then when she blinked and slowly smiled he was disarmed. Her face came alive. He saw her broad forehead, dark eyebrows, darker glinting eyes, but saw most of all, as if it were the point of its surroundings, the curled ends and duplicate crests of her long wide smile. Her lips glazed with wine and blood. He'd forgotten the question.

'How old?' she asked again.

'Eighteen,' he said. 'And you?'

'Twenty.'

They smiled. It was useful to know. And the more he saw of her face – transformed out of its severity into interest – the more he smiled back. Then she looked back to her food, and continued to eat, perturbed that she could have taken her attention away from the willow-patterned china plate for so long. The boy was sweet and expectant. But she hadn't tasted food like this, richly mixed, for a while. Did he like her? she wondered. She did not think that she liked him in that way. He was sandy-haired, light-boned, with very blue eyes. How she imagined American children raised on milk and popcorn and sunshine would look.

The afternoon slid on. It wasn't that they were slow eaters, the students, just that they kept on going. Seconds, thirds, then final pickings. They were hollow, growing machines. The sun looked into one window then the other, bright and high, working its way towards its longest, finest day still.

Miriam watched Matthew coax Julianna into another lump of cauliflower. The girl's table manners were clumsy, she thought, yet she had to admit a certain grace, even as she shovelled scraps from around the perimeter of the plate

29

on to the wrong side of her fork. She wondered if Matthew was flirting with her. She doubted it; she even hoped not. She would imagine the silly blonde at the other end would hold more appeal than this tomboy with the bad haircut and the synthetic shirt. Lola's doll face and long hair made Miriam think of a children's fairy tale, where women wore veils and gowns – the Sleeping Beauty era. Miriam closed her eyes despite herself. It was so warm in here. She thought of forests and princesses and beasts, an imaginative tapestry of dark dreams and countries, shot through with deer and velvet and bleeding hearts. She breathed in deeply and opened her eyes again. Then turned to Ngao, for some water.

The room was becoming unbearably hot. The sunshine showing the dirt on the windows and the dust on the sideboard. Miriam looked around the room, then down at the begging dog beside her. The skirting was filthy. She was a rotten farmer's wife, she thought, not for the first time, and without much anxiety. Her thighs were sticking together beneath her skirt, and with a sudden movement she left the table for the excuse of the lavatory. Lola followed her, out of curiosity for intimate places, and their feminine excursion precipitated other missions. Gerard and the boys, all except Ngao and Matthew, left to have a smoke in the yard. Ngao cleared plates for Miriam. The crumble could be smelt burning in the oven.

'Have you been to the Waterman? To the pub in the next village?' Matthew asked. They were left alone in the dining room. Like the last couple to leave the cinema.

'No,' she said, swallowing a gentle belch.

'Shall we go this evening?' he said. Casual, as if it might have been discussed before, like a picnic, and they had simply been waiting for a change in the inclement weather.

And because it was her day off, she said yes.

*

30

The walls of the Waterman Inn were lined with high-backed settles. There was a bar billiards table, pictures of foxhounds and ducks on the wall and an aerial photograph of the pub. Outside, kids and sometimes their parents gathered, and at night underage drinkers shivered round wrought-iron tables and chairs. They were very uncomfortable; the hard swirls of iron would leave imprints and bruises, so people often went to sit on the opposite stretch of green. It was a pretty building – decorated with plaques awarding it the Kent In Bloom Best Pub Award for three years running in the eighties. It would be hard to know what had gone wrong since those days of success. Every hanging basket, pot plant, old sink and even bedpan had been taken and jam-packed with bedding plants and climbers. Julianna thought it looked like a municipal park, like the elaborate plantings around Buda Palace on Várhegy. She sat on the green, a little island, twenty feet away from a large group of teenage boys with radios and pints in plastic glasses. She watched them with interest. The red wine at lunch had smudged her usual boundaries; the nervousness Matthew had shown in organising this clandestine trip had amused her. He was obviously scared of his mother. But he was sweet and he had gone to buy her more wine.

The boys in the group were watching her, laughing a little, bursts of excitement. It was all they needed to galvanise their wit, one girl to come and sit near them. It wasn't much to ask for an evening's entertainment.

'Nice evening,' said one, catching her eye and raising his pint glass in her direction. But she didn't hear him well enough to understand so she shrugged at him and turned her head away. A small wash of disapproval spread round the group. 'Stupid cow,' one of them said.

Julianna couldn't understand a word they were saying. They had thick, syrupy voices. But she could easily understand their intent, so when Matthew arrived with the drinks she stood up and put a hand on his arm, to shut them up.

They sat down cross-legged, him aware of how close the points of their knees were to each other. 'Do you have any brothers or sisters?' she asked. She'd been surprised to see pictures of only him in the hallways and toilet.

'No. You?'

'I have a little brother,' she said, and then smiled, 'and I miss him. More than anyone else. Although I like the . . .' She paused again; Matthew was beginning to realise that you had to work harder when listening to someone speaking a second language. 'I like having my own room. It is more private. Tamás did not understand when I shut the door.' She paused and then began again, quietly. She was enjoying the chance to speak English properly. István monopolised her in the evening. She didn't particularly like him, but it precluded the pressure of other conversations.

'When he was young Tamás had dreams and needed to come to my bed in the middle of the night and hold on,' and she made the shape of a sleeping body's protective bracket with her hand. 'I think he forgot who was his mother,' she said, without much edge. 'He fought about the blanket, and he was full of dreams. He was a little animal. Like a baby . . . tiger.' And Matthew laughed.

'Your English is amazing,' he said.

She thought, considering the word 'amazing', and taking it more literally than intended. 'I don't think it is amazing, I know many people speak five languages. Not only two.'

'Not in England there aren't,' he said. 'The British are rubbish.' Julianna didn't understand the distinction people made between England and Britain; she had been taught it was geographical, but people seemed to use the words randomly.

'I learnt when I was a child. My grandmother taught me,'

Julianna carried on, because she was enjoying the sound of herself speaking English (why not British?). It gave those boring facts she'd rehearsed while dragging round Kisrét with her half-brother a new elegance. 'My grandmother, Mila, came from England, from a place called Stratford-upon-Avon.' The place name sounded awkward in her heavy accent, and she looked at Matthew for recognition.

It took him a moment to understand the name, and even then he couldn't have exactly said where Stratford was, any more than Hungary. He knew about Shakespeare but he didn't know where it was. He nodded.

'She used to tell me stories about her beginnings, and her home. It was something different from everyone else. So I liked it. She taught me how to count, and the days and the months, and how to say the easy words, "hello" and,' she paused, '"good morning".'

'Your surname is Kiss, isn't it?' said Matthew, smiling, and Julianna nodded and smiled a little back.

Mila had told Julianna her surname was special, joking sometimes that she'd been seduced by Julianna's grandfather because of it. She'd taught Julianna to think of Britain, another small surrounded country, by water, not land, as a place of neat sweetness and bravery. Of untouchable stability. Hungary had history, but it was clear, even to a child educated towards the tail end of communism, that it had suffered greatly at the hands of others.

'What do your parents do?' asked Matthew. A question he often heard, but not one that Julianna did. She looked a little puzzled. The question of class, careers, the subjective business of social placing, was a tool that Matthew used unconsciously. He had no idea how naive his attempt to locate Julianna on some kind of sliding scale was, as if they all climbed an identical frame, only speaking a different language.

33

While differing priorities were always to be found in a Hungarian town, the subtleties of the English class system were not something Julianna understood. In the same way that the Soviet soldiers had entered Hungary in 1948 and shaken hands with the locals (Russian Jewish soldiers greeting the few remaining Jewish Hungarians with more, with embraces) then turned and looted and burnt their hosts' houses, they had arrived proclaiming that everyone would share a part in this great stage of history, yet rendered people so broken that for many years the key consideration for peasant and bourgeois and intellectual alike was how to survive.

'My stepmother studied,' again she paused, looking frustrated, 'how to watch money, taxes.' Matthew nodded. He couldn't remember the word either. 'But she never had job. She . . . no one gave her a job. But she works in two shops. They work hard. My father works at the hospital. And we have some fields, now. They were returned to us. Now we can grow more.'

'And you're at university?' he asked.

'Yes,' she said. 'I am training to be a teacher. I want to teach English.'

Sometimes Julianna found it hard to believe that she was being asked what she wanted to become and how she wanted her life to end up at the age of eighteen. She had been waiting so long for childhood to finish, been so obedient at performing for each exam, each parade, that she was surprised and suspicious of this gift of having to make decisions. She had somehow expected things, situations to overtake her. Like a reward. She had chosen to study a language because it was a skill that would surely lay a pathway to the future. Because of her grandmother she associated language and travel with the seizing of life.

'Do you like your stepmother?' asked Matthew abruptly. A stepmother was an exotic thing to have. He didn't dare ask what had happened to Julianna's mother.

She shrugged. She found the subject uncomfortable, and rarely told people that her mother had died when she was only four. 'We are friendly, it is OK. She has been a good . . .' She couldn't think of the word. Not even in Hungarian.

She looked uncomfortable so Matthew, attuned to women with sensitivities, changed the subject.

'But you're close to your grandmother?'

Julianna smiled. 'Oh yes. She has always been our mother. She has lived in history, it is amazing. She has stories. It is she who said that I should come here. Because my grandfather was a photographer and before the war he travelled round England and they fell in love and he took her home with him. And she stayed in the same house since then.' Her telling of this story was more fluid than anything before. 'But my grandfather died, it was a very sad time for her, and then strangers came to live in their home, and she had to make money to feed the family, and . . .' She felt shy suddenly, made a gesture of trivia, and said, 'She can tell you her life better than me.'

It was soft evening. The darkness not arriving until well after nine. It crept up on people so that they were suddenly surprised to feel a cooler breeze, to return from the toilets and realise they couldn't make out their group on the green. Matthew was glowing still with wine and pleasure. He had the strongest sensation that these long nights in country pubs were what England was made for and he was proud of the scene, its ease and companionable charm, in front of Julianna. Around them groups moved closer together, kicked glasses over, laughed; a nightingale was heard, and missed by all but a few. From above, the drinkers on the green looked like they were waiting for something, campers at the scene of something predicted.

'What time is it?' Julianna asked when she realised the light had gone from everywhere except the sky – where there was an electric glow to the blue.

'Ten,' said Matthew. 'Are you supposed to be back by a certain time?'

'No,' she said loudly, laughing, thinking of his home. 'Your mother will be waiting though, no?' And when he didn't respond to her teasing she carried right on. 'We are not children, we are your father's employees, not little boys at school.'

'Like me?' he said, looming out of the darkness with an inane grin.

'Yes,' she said and laughed. 'We are not small boys like you.'

He shook his head. He'd always known, since before he even went to school, that the extreme attentions of his mother had made him into something funnier, potentially feebler than others. He began to nod his head instead. There was surely something to be salvaged.

'I *am* a small man, it's true,' he said. 'Still hoping to grow a bit, though. And you,' he looked at her solemnly, 'are a visiting . . . VIP. Bit like a queen. I shall escort you home, and lay cloaks on puddles for you, all the way back to your caravan.'

Julianna understood very little but felt a rush of tribal friendship – something that the playground used to bring.

They walked back from the pub, disturbing the still, warm, scented air of the tunnelled lanes. The black poplars bent their height into each other, vertical streams of gentle movement, ushering the pair onwards, like jittery footmen. There

36

was a strong honey-sweet smell, which Julianna could name in Hungarian but not English. Matthew guessed translations but quickly ran out of plant possibilities. He was a lazy romantic; he liked the idea of star-gazing more than the practice, so he was surprised by the potency of the night landscape. Wood cracks and owl calls, rushes of wind that sounded as if they came from deep within the woods, skiffles of fleshy, new-grown leaves above their heads, the deep blue enclosure of the studded sky.

The three hours in the pub had passed quickly, the darkness finally falling in a second, the surprising difference between a door ajar and a door closed tight. In the tree-hung darkness Julianna became even more lovely to Matthew. Her blunt hair, exotically thick and dark, her bare limbs and alcoholic intensity inviting. He wanted to kiss her but was scared of ridicule. They stopped to look up at the treetops and Matthew felt as if he might topple backwards.

They walked on, not talking much, their voices too loud and human a sound. Matthew became very aware of his hay fever. He suffered badly at this time of year, turned to a red-eyed, rabbity creature. It was worsening as they walked. It must be tree pollen. The pills he took in the morning would be wearing out by now. His breathing quickened and his eyes began to stream. He became convinced he could see the reactive dust, fat green glow-worms of it, eddying around his face. How odd to be walking down the road with a heavily accented girl with an unfamiliar past. It felt entirely natural walking next to her, matching each other's pace, and he thought, with the allergens throbbing in his sinuses, his throat tightening, that he could imagine doing it again and again, their progress down this lane an opening scene.

Suddenly his shallow inhalation cracked and he began to cough, an airless, dry retching. He sat, panicked, on the bank at the side of the road. 'I . . .' but he couldn't talk and breathe, and Julianna, seeing what was wrong (Tamás suffered from asthma), shushed him, placed one hand on his back and tried to help him regulate his breathing with rhythmic instructions. He felt the warmth of her breath on his neck. It reminded him, perversely he felt, of his mother, who had sat with him through black nights – as inconceivably long as the day – and long, raining days off school. Only the breath of Julianna on his neck, the presence of her body smelt and felt different.

After five minutes they stood and started slowly home for his inhalers. They rounded the corner out of the woods, into the open, where the lane widened and cut a swathe through the falling fields. Below, the farm sat sheltered from winds that blew off the coast fifteen miles away.

Julianna stopped for a moment, understanding that this landscape was now a part of her life, an era that she would one day recollect. She was as real a presence on this land as anyone. A small part of its workings. So, this was how it happened – scenes evolving, then disappearing, like courses in a meal. No one from her family, or her collection of college friends, no one knew where she was now. Just Matthew, who had suddenly become that peculiar thing, an intimately known stranger.

Chapter Three

Julianna thought of their days in quarters, like peeled and cored apples. First, awaking in chilled damp air, yawning through breakfast, the muscles warming, earth drying, carrying the smell of night away; then, second, came lunch with its immediate, hot lull tempered by an endless, back-breaking afternoon. Third, physical exhaustion and food and the opaline light of nine p.m., doors swinging in and out of the draining day, stars emerging with the news, flimsy wild flowers shining white, on and on as the night fell with weird light. Then last came sleep. The quarter that was theirs alone, when they would leave themselves behind and dream of confused places, travellers' uncertainties surfacing night after night.

The rape had bloomed and gone, its blaze of commercial colour and rank smell suddenly departing with May. The bluebells and buttercups had long faded with their first flush of spring's release, and now the trumpeting young colours, the whites, yellows, blues, were interrupted by a rash of red poppies. The elderflower harvest had begun; it would only last a month, and Gerard was excited about it this year, as newer trees had now matured. He was keen to see if this could grow into a decent income source. A new company making expensive, traditional cordials had been started in east Kent. Roy was humouring him. Miriam, if asked, would be hard pushed to remember Gerard's plans. He had become easier to tune out each year.

The stillness of the unusually hot days, on the infrequently trodden, almost scrubby dog's-leg strip of land between the farm and the woods, was now broken by the crack of branches and incomprehensible swearwords. The blossoms stood on stretching branches, each individual spray like a miniature acacia tree, great plates of blossom raised to the intense blue sky. The students ended the day covered in a soft yellow pollen, black bins full of a cream froth carried back to the yard for weighing and transporting. Julianna liked the accumulation of the blossoms, the cream level rising up the black plastic bins. There was a temptation to push down and down and see how much of it was just scented air. A load of space and not much substance. The flowers themselves were tiny, each little speck of a flower then divided into a few petals, their individual design the simplest, the most representative of flower shapes possible. They were satisfyingly identical to pictures she had drawn as a child. But all together, thousands on a branch, millions in a black bin, they formed an abstraction as immeasurable as a cloud.

After their long, open-air evening in the Waterman, which had begun a binding of the two of them, Matthew had been to visit Julianna in her caravan every evening. Such was their tentativeness with each other that they would leave the door open and play cards by the bare lightbulb, oversensitised to each other but oblivious to the interest his nocturnal visits might be causing. They drank coffee that he brought in mugs from the farmhouse kitchen. Hers strong, his dilute with milk. Once they drank wine that he stole from his father. They played card games, even dominoes one night. They talked about their families and schools, explained their web of friends. Julianna told him about her best friend Ica who had gone to live in West Germany last year. How much she missed her and how bad she felt that they'd only written twice. They talked about the other students on the farm, and music they liked and films they had seen and books they had nearly read. And they looked at each other frequently, and caught each other momentarily, and she soon grew less likely to blush and he grew less likely to bluster. Then, after a long fortnight of watching each other's movements with anticipation, of replaying moments during the night and next day, just as he was leaving he turned round, narrowly missed the burning bulb and put his lips to the corner of her mouth. An off-centre kiss that caught her and surprised her and made her break into that long, slow-curling smile.

'Go,' she said, embarrassed. 'Go home. I'll see you tomorrow.'

When he'd gone she couldn't sleep so she read more of her novel (whose very title was complicated to understand) and smoked and doze-dreamt below the bright bare bulb late into the night, under the tin-can roof. She opened two little windows by the bed, which was also a sofa, and the air fell on to her body, chill and rich with deep damp earth. She wondered if she and Matthew were falling in love. But then it seemed unlikely that you wouldn't know it if you were. That you wouldn't feel changed, wouldn't appear suddenly more solid in people's eyes. But instead of a transformation, the sense of finally arriving at her adult self, Julianna felt more painfully self-critical than ever before. More conscious of her thoughts and her body. And yet, she thought to herself, the interesting thing was that events seemed to be unfolding before her, nevertheless. Even though she still felt awkward and ugly next to Lola and confused and nervous before Mrs Woods and anxious with Roy, things seemed to be happening. Matthew had kissed her, and even she could see that this hot, fruitful summer brought its own romance.

*

Matthew arrived on the rotting step of Julianna's caravan the next night and every night after that through June. He tiptoed back into his bedroom later and later, and Miriam, who found she could keep quite close tabs on the students if she wished, began to notice the shadows beneath Julianna's tanned skin. She tried to calm a sharp jealousy. Tried to ignore the sexuality of the summer. A summer which burned sharp white outside the kitchen window, bumping the old soft fabric of the curtains with its breezes. Blinding her as she stepped into the yard, hot on her tights (too shy of her varicose veins to go bare-legged any longer). Summer which reminded her of years in which she had had ripe flesh, that rose and filled itself after denting like plump white scallops. It didn't occur to her that these two might be gentler souls than she had been. Years ago she had been complicit in such gratuitous scenes, with someone other than Matthew's father, that she had come to see only danger in the mistakes of the young. Nothing is a more easy mistake to make than sex. It horrified her to think of Matthew as active in that way, so much so that it didn't even occur to her that the two of them might *not* be having sex with each other. Her husband and son were right to sense a restless anxiety in her intense love, it was the anxiety of atonement.

She took Matthew on a shopping trip to London for clothes, in order to try and talk to him. He pretended he didn't care, didn't need them, but she knew he did. It wasn't until they were on their way back from the station that she managed to find the words to begin.

'You are nineteen after all, old enough to do what you want. Get married, or get some girl pregnant. You know, I am aware . . . None of us are saints.' She gave a hollow laugh.

Matthew's face twisted with dismay.

'What kind of girl is she?' asked his mother. She always felt bolder at the wheel. She turned to look at her soft

42

skinned, shallow-breathing, cosseted son, his cheeks flooded by a delta of red anticipation. He had no intention, however, of talking about Julianna.

'Matthew?' she said aggressively.

'I don't know what you mean,' he said, embarrassed and irritated. It was true that he'd never brought a girl home before. He kicked into an old road atlas, so that it wedged further up the nose of the car. His mother was weird. Sometimes it didn't matter and then sometimes it really did.

'She's just . . . she's nice.'

'I shouldn't imagine that you are sneaking into the house at two in the morning because of,' and she moulded her mouth carefully so that 'niceness' came out full of sarcasm.

Julianna was the first thing he'd independently chosen. But he hardly had the vocabulary for opposition. He didn't know how to deal with the new level of malice in his mother's voice so he said nothing at all.

Furious at his silence, at the failure of the conversation to give her the cosy support that she wanted (which would mean a profession of solidarity with her rather than Julianna, not – as it would with some mothers – a profession of affection for the girl and caution when it came to contraception), she changed tack and reached over to pat his knee awkwardly.

'I just don't want you getting over involved and spoiling these best, wonderful years.'

Something in him rallied, perhaps the memory that she had occasionally made these wonderful years rather lonely. 'Jesus, Mum, it's just a girl. That's what blokes my age are meant to do, aren't they? Have girlfriends . . .' he said, and even she realised, because, although she was fraught and unhappy, she wasn't beyond self-protection, that this flippancy was the best reassurance she was going to get.

They drove along in silence, the car vibrating with irritation.

If Julianna had known the power of her absent presence, that it was curdling the atmosphere inside the Woods' family car, she would have been astounded. That kind of concentration was reserved, she thought, for beautiful women. And she wasn't exactly that. Matthew sometimes, no . . . often, wondered in what way and to what extent she was attractive. He was treading new ground each day and needed to encourage himself in everything, even love. There was an angularity, a roughness to Julianna that stopped her from being beautiful. The difference between one angle and another, one expression or another, between morning and night, when she seemed to have settled into her skin, her body still a daily surprise, was more marked than most.

Yet the question of Julianna's looks became irrelevant on Woods Farm that summer. What was more powerful was the fact that people were watching her and wondering about her, made more potent by Julianna having no awareness, no concept even, of this. Miriam, much as she tried to forget it, knew more than anyone that the true mark of a beauty is the curiosity she provokes.

Trying to understand Julianna felt, to Matthew's mother, like trying to fathom a cow. But, then, how was Julianna, even, meant to know what kind of girl she was? She was twenty. And how was Matthew to know? He was in love.

The facts should have been simple. She had a ragged jaw-length haircut, brown almond-shaped eyes, heavy brows, a good strong nose. The nose was perhaps bigger than she might have chosen, but it gave her face gravity, saved it from sweetness for something more powerful. She had a high brow from which her hair rose up an inch in a small sudden cliff. Her skin was fine and small-pored but prone to spots which stood out loud, and (like Matthew, only less often) she would blush aggressively from her neck up, over the tender angle of her jawbone, when embarrassed or exerting herself. Thus her smooth, but reactive, skin invited touch. One wondered, when her blush was at its height, about imprinting a thumb and making a small blanched pool in the vulnerable well of her neck.

Her neck was of average length, her mouth wide and lips elongated, but her shoulders were beautiful. This was Julianna's favourite part of her body. One that could be considered without regret, when wrapped head and torso in worn towels. Nothing much about her struck her as belonging to a proper woman, except the supple, branching outline of her shoulders, like a liquid escape. The bones that ran below, rising out of the gully, bending and curving slightly, were like a stretched reflection of her mouth.

Her arms too were strong and she worked all day in sleeveless T-shirts which gave the far edge of her shoulders, the skin stretching and creasing over the swivelling joints and cartilage, the deepest of tans. She would hunch the shoulder to touch her turned face, the smell of herself, the feel of this burnished, hard, smooth juncture in her body's often remote landscape, strangely comforting. Her clothes brought nothing to her, the vests made badly in forceful colours, her jeans shapeless, wide at the hip, short and narrow at the ankle. Julianna was aware of difference between clothes chosen for beauty and clothes chosen to simply cover and distract, but choice and money had always been limited at home. She could sew a little, with a machine, thanks to her grandmother, so when younger she and Ica had made themselves skirts, from any cheap fabric they could find.

She and her schoolfriends had known their clothes were cheap; it was a mistake to assume that those living through deprivation didn't recognise when they were being peddled rubbish – everyone at home knew Cuban oranges were bad

– and the lack of quality in goods they gave each other as gifts was shaming. Perhaps they used too much make-up, but it brought colour to their skins. As teenagers they swapped and shared whatever they had, the hard-won pairs of Levis for new CDs. An old outfit new on a different girl, even though their Friday-night gatherings at absent parents' houses always included the same boys. She'd been wearing a friend's jeans and Éva's black blouse when she'd first kissed her one and only boyfriend at Ica's nameday *buli*. A mild-mannered young man whose timid touch-and-retreat system for exploring her body had only taken him as far as her bra.

The first thing one thought on seeing Julianna was not, there goes a beautiful young woman, but rather, here is a young woman thinking, or walking, or reading, or eating. There was a directness about her face that made placing a value on her looks unnecessary. She was a young woman who nobody could quite work out, because she did not know much but did not pretend. Waiting, implacably, for life to imprint her and her heart to come into its own.

Julianna Kiss and Matthew Woods finally found and lost each other's virginities one night in early July. It could not have been any other way, for had Julianna displayed one iota of confidence then Matthew would never have got to the stage of removing his trousers. Let alone hers. It was chilly in the caravan, and difficult for Matthew to get enough purchase on the slippery pink sheet to make the impact he thought he ought, before it was too late. A few moments in he stopped, trying to hold off ejaculation, and looked at Julianna, from above, into her eyes, wheezing a little with such exertion in a high asthmatic summer, just at the moment when she opened her eyes, expecting his to still be properly shut. There in the harsh electric light, in the total silence of this English night, in the midst of this surprising, painful penetration of her body, which she now knew had been utterly hers before this ungainly, graceless posting of body parts, which had made no physical sense so far, he looked right at her. He looked into her eyes, which were black with alarm and vulnerability – her, under this boy, who didn't even speak the same language. Then he kissed her, his lips landing clumsily, and caught her off guard. She had been expecting to be allowed to keep her emotional privacy, her fear inside secret in the midst of this naked act. But he caught her, saw the knife-edged trust she was trying to hold on to, and in that momentary visual invasion, rather than the physical one, came intimacy. Their frightful nakedness and the peculiarity of a piece of him inside her became a shared, not a lonely, secret.

The day after, Julianna felt entirely displaced. She wondered if it was because she'd got so little sleep the rest of the night, lying awake, unnerved by this step into a new state, let into the most uncomfortable of secrets, one which everyone else had known of for years. She wanted to talk to her grandmother, but strangely, having always been so sure of Mila's thinking, it felt like a risk. Mila's disapproval was a living, stalking thing and she told the story of her romance with János, Julianna's grandfather, so often that its mixture of patience and eroticism in unimaginable past eras took on an almost religious significance for Julianna. Thinking of how she had now used up one element of her own life already, Julianna felt sad. The handover of her sexual innocence to Matthew had none of the significant symbolism she had so expected. None of the details that sounded like trumpets from Mila's stories: the streetlights and strangers, the adversaries and freak weather. Wasp-stings and plot-turns and cathedral-high views.

Julianna walked across the yard for breakfast light-headed,

certain that her dislocation was as clear to everyone as if she were suddenly walking on air, rather than ground. She was entirely conscious of everything she did, watching her arm reach for a mug, watching herself pour tea, hearing herself answer István. At moments during the day she would suddenly want to cry, then she would berate herself; this was something everyone else had been doing for years before her. Everyone did this. It was a wonder people could concentrate.

She dreaded seeing Matthew. Even once avoided him, when she saw him walking past the sheds. He stayed away until later that night when he came to her step bearing biscuits and hot chocolate. Somehow he'd sensed that what she'd want most was comforting things. One step forward into experience, two steps back into childhood. For his sweet understanding (he didn't know it, but he did instinctively sense the confusion a woman felt when the careful balance of her self-esteem was threatened) she took him in and permitted herself to be hugged. It had to have been him who made the reconnection, by gender she felt, but he might easily have failed in imagination. Julianna took solace in the tightness of his embrace and the feel of his wiry, tough little body around her. When they simply hugged he reminded her of Tamás.

By now the summer's arc had begun the long heat-worn descent. The landscape was waiting, yellowing in the heat, until it could devolve itself of its fruits and then its coverings entirely. The fields were scented, the low-lying plants heavy with pitted red hearts. The students worked solidly, bent or kneeling in the earth, just as Julianna used to watch her grandmother at work behind the house. Caught in the summer's unrolling, mazed by the growth of intimacy and desire, plumped with the secret strength of sexual discovery, the harvest's progress brought staging posts to their new world.

She was now intoxicated, not just with Matthew, but, for the first time, with herself and the distinctness of her days, unravelling at their feet with the rich, interlaced pattern of a Turkish rug. Sometimes when she'd been bent over too long, and stood up, spots swirling in front of her eyes, she had a sense of displaced time. She and Ngao and Lola, and all the others, must look as their ancestors had. Men and women labouring, watched from above by birds with their parabola view of the land. They bent and crouched and moved their limbs unthinkingly as if this kind of shifting, crouching liaison with the ground was innate.

Matthew would come down at lunch sometimes. He would have liked to have worked with them, he said, only his hay fever was now requiring more and more pills to subdue. Julianna noticed with amusement his physical alienness. How little he fitted in with her group physically. How there was no memory of manual work in the farmer's son's limbs. He arrived for lunch and sat on the ground with them, cross-legged and uncomfortable, wriggling around the hard earth on his bony behind. His body didn't work out here, away from the constructs of a house. Sometimes Julianna felt a little embarrassed by his presence. But it was mingled with pride at the clarity of her attractiveness to him. She chose to sit with Ngao or István if Matthew was not around. The students were not divided, but there was no reason why their youth should necessarily prove cohesive.

Matthew grew freckled and Julianna muscular, both supremely aware of their bodies and their different textures – the hardest element of human appeal to pin down. The feel of his skin was sandy and dry, and he smelt thinly of clean soap and cotton. He was so very different to her darker-skinned slickness, her scented hair, her sweat-stained strength. His blue eyes darted, clever. He saw things she didn't and made jokes with words that she struggled to comprehend, but being with him was the best kind of story, ever curious, ever revealing.

Between the two of them there existed a spider's web-delicate world. For the first time both of them became confident in what they had long hoped – since the indeterminate confusion of their early teens – that there was an appeal in their particulars. For so long, as limbs had grown and days recycled, they had felt alone and peculiar in their awareness of their aloneness. Did everyone think so hard on their differences? On their condition of not being anyone else, which was sometimes good, sometimes bad? Surely not? Now, for the first time, they had both found someone to whom they could confess. Sins of thought. And what a powerful chemical this intimacy was; like a litmus test it coloured everything immersed.

What she and Matthew lacked in harbingers and evening gowns was compensated for in the warmth of their rescue, the equality of their absorbed innocence. They would remember the summer they fell in love as if it were their own unmapped island. Within her caravan they were surrounded by protective circles, like a moated camp upon a pebble of land, within a sea that traced the glittering retreats of their guardian suns and moons. For a while, at least, they kept the world at bay.

Chapter Four

Come August, Gerard decided that they needed a quick holiday in France. He chose a nice spot, conveniently near to a nursery specialising in a strain of purple tomatoes. Miriam packed with a roused, if antsy, spirit. She was secretly delighted to be missing the Westington annual summer fête and bribed Matthew to run her stall of home-made jams, chutneys and lumpen candles ('All proceeds towards new mother-and-baby unit in Horden General'). She had vetted the French hotel, and it did at least have a pool and a bar and a tennis court. She pictured evenings spent in a similar vein to the golf club dances of her youth, and would prove to be disappointed by the chilly Parisians with their capsule-wardrobe wives and pervasive children.

Miriam asked Roy to keep an eye on Matthew while she was away, hoping this would limit his contact with Julianna somehow. But the very evening of their departure Roy, who resented being spoken to as if he were an au pair, took pleasure in noting Matthew and Julianna's shadows in the windows of the farmhouse.

Julianna wandered slowly round the quiet house, shoes care-fully removed, her steps silent on the tiles and rugs. It felt odd to be back in a home, after spending so much time outside or in thin-walled, temporary structures like cara-vans and sheds. The absent home-makers' touch was ghostly, sad somehow, as if they were dead, not struggling to make themselves understood on a terrace near Tours. Julianna moved from one piece of framed evidence of their lives to another. It was almost as if it were a museum. All these photographs, certificates, clippings and cartoons; this self-referential decoration was very alien to Julianna. In her home they had had a few generic pictures on the walls, prints of landscapes, a dark scene in a wood by Paul Laszlo that her grandmother was very fond of, so dark that Julianna had always found it hard to understand what was going on. But they had none of this *stuff*. She found it almost maudlin – a deliberate display of nostalgia and memory.

She picked up the heritage trail from the upstairs bath-room, which she preferred to use since it smelt less bad. On the back of the door there was a collage of jokey snapshots of Matthew, wobbling on a three-wheeler, uncomfortable on top of a very fat pony, a red-padded anonymous shape on skis, vivid before white mountains. Julianna looked at each snap carefully, then walked down to a small landing where Gerard's law diploma hung in a thin gilt frame amongst prints of hills and lakes, then down to the sitting room, where a silver-framed wedding photo sat on the mantelpiece, beside a picture of a fat man (Matthew's grandfather) with a circular medallion round his neck, accompanying an elderly woman in a powder-blue suit, one walking foot in mid-air ('The Queen Mother,' Matthew told her with an undecipherable look on his face). At the base of the back stairs there was a very pink oil portrait of a young Matthew, looking sullen, and, of course, that black-and-white photo of a couple on a sofa at a party.

Now that the house was empty Julianna could look more closely at what seemed to be a deeply romantic scene. She knew now that the young man and woman were Miriam and Gerard themselves. They looked relaxed and glamorous, dressed for a grand party, and otherworldly young, but she focused on Gerard's distinctive sharp nose and Miriam's hair, which didn't, in fact, seem to have changed that much. It looked as if it was a summer evening. There was a pale sofa with dark edging, open windows, a walled garden with honeysuckle climbing. The photograph itself seemed very nearly scented, the sense of time, season and temperature was so very strong. But it took Julianna a moment or two to register the oddity of the scene, that which gave it its real charm. The sofa was *outside* the house. Lined up against a back wall, so that the windows looked out on to the sofa, in a neat reversal of the usual arrangement. The sofa was sagging at the front from years of excitable young men who found it hard to sit still, falling off the very edges of drawing-room life. Next to it, almost backed into the climbers on the garden's dividing wall, was an austere wooden chair with arms, probably stolen from the kitchen. Or perhaps the nursery.

This is a very special party, Julianna can tell from Miriam's dress, the ripe flesh it reveals, Gerard's black suit and flouncy white bow-tie. Inside the picture it's clearly late, or perhaps early in the morning. The light is changing. There are wine glasses on the tiles around the sides of the sofa. Behind it there are two wide-open sash windows, and no one to be seen in the comfortable rooms beyond. There is a sense of soft, worn, unobjectionable fabrics, dark wood furniture, cut glass, roses. Solidity and stability. But it's pleasantly tatty, and careless too – in that the windows are wide open at an indefinable time of night and wine glasses remain uncleared. There is that strangely puritanical chair (which was new a long time ago, when someone was first making a home without helpful inheritance). Something has fuelled ease and happiness this evening, something more than alcohol. Youth? Prosperity? There is something intoxi-cating in the air of this walled garden. Is it in the coun-tryside – a quiet corner of a particular wing – or a city house, with a garden whose end you can't see from the attic bedrooms? A garden with a small tangled wood at the end, for making dens.

Miriam and Gerard. Not terribly poetic. Just lucky. At that moment. With fireflies in the borders and table lamps shining flying-saucer circles on to occasional tables. Such rings of bright light.

It made Julianna feel sorry for her own past (which, of course, included events long before she was born) in all its faded colours: her ill-kempt, tired, deserted father, the mother she no longer remembered, her fiercely loving grandmother, whose story was so well told and whose life had then been so hard. The photos that remained of Mila when she was young, and she and János had first travelled round Europe, were tiny and invariably focused on an ornate doorway rather than the young bride to its right.

Although Julianna couldn't instantaneously interpret the British symbolism of the scene, the languid informality of the classic furniture, the distracted poses of the leisured classes, it disturbed her by provoking a sense of longing. But then something weird struck her: these people in the photos suf-fused in ease and perfume and promise, they were Matthew's parents. Matthew who had made love to her and bought her flowers. Thus implicating *her* in its black-and-white magic.

Matthew came up behind her and wrapped his arms around her. 'What are you looking at?'

'This,' she said, 'your mother and father dressed like a big party.'

Matthew peered at it. 'Yes, I suppose they are. I've never really noticed it. It's such a tatty old house. You sort of stop looking.'

Julianna was quiet.

'It's not a house that's very . . .' Matthew thought; clean or tidy were his first thoughts, but that wasn't quite what he meant. 'Luxurious,' he said, and Julianna shrugged, knowing the meaning but not seeing how it connected. Not seeing how Matthew was pointing out one of the things that had been crucial in his life, which elevated him above the richer boys, the clever boys, the Asian and African boys at his school. He understood, although it had never actually been articulated, that the cultured mess of their home, the eccentricity of his father, their easy claim to substantial property and land that Matthew needn't ever work on, needn't ever understand the origins of, was something that gave him inclusion into the upper middle classes of England. He understood this because of his upbringing, which made it very clear that he was a child of his father's way of life. That whatever he had inherited of his mother's stopped there, but that whatever he had inherited of his father could be traced as far as he cared.

Julianna shook her head. She didn't know what that word meant. 'My parents' house is very different. I don't know what you would think.' She sounded a little cold.

Matthew looked uncertain, then laughed, trying to dispel Julianna's melancholy. 'It's not as if you live in India, is it?' Julianna just looked at him. Silent. Foreign suddenly.

'No, not India.' She nodded, considering, and sighed. How could she teach him her childhood in a photo? They had few and she carried none. Why would she, they would make dull viewing. Truly, though, if she were honest, she would like a photo of herself, like that, sometime. There was a vanity inside Julianna; some yearning for effect made her want that kind of attention. It made her now straighten her shoulders and lift her head high, step away from Matthew, making something out of self-consciousness of their difference rather than being subdued by it. She felt, suddenly, charged.

They both stood on the stairs. Her three steps ahead of him. Him looking up at her, like a child to an adult. She was taller than ever, the lines of her body flowing away from him.

He was shy of her, as if it were the first time they'd met. As if she were just as unclassifiable as ever. He took one step up. Julianna, roused from her dream, felt inside her a new impatience, a need for attention linked for the first time to sex. A desire. She took his hand, chilly, dry, and guided it up beneath her shirt, under the elasticated entrapment of her bra, on to her breast, and held it there, her flesh tensing with the coldness of his skin.

Her breast was warm and malleable, his fingers pulsed its softness. Julianna, breathing gently through her mouth, unbuttoned her shirt and watched him watching her body. She undid her bra for him, her torso bare, feeling his fingers circle patterns on her skin.

As was customary, people arrived at Burden's Fields for the Westington summer fête soon after their Sunday lunches had been cleared, if not digested. Everyone appeared relaxed by the ritual of it. Expectations were happily restricted; there would be stalls, none of them very good, and rides, but not that many.

A crowd of several hundred stood in the middle of the first field, before a small stage, the children running into each other like colours. Every year the decorations were pulled out of the vicarage attic. The flags looked brighter inside, in the light of Victoriana, than they did out on the field, fighting against the sharp green of the lime trees, the irregular bursts of sunlight. The posters for this year's fête had promised a celebrity guest, but everyone had known what that meant. The same as last year: a one-time weather girl who had bought a local dairy farm in order to make luxury ice creams.

Matthew and Julianna sat on boxes behind the table trying to anchor the tablecloth down in the breeze. She had laid out all the pots and candles with care. It felt like being a little kid again, playing at owning things. She made many pyramids of jam, and picked some wild flowers to decorate the table.

There was a smell of drying grass in the air, that point in the year when it is hard to physically remember any other season and autumn seems an unlikely idea. The field was peopled in the bright colours of summer clothing, acid drops against delicate skins. Flimsy patterned skirts shifting so lightly in the wind that you could be showing your knickers and not know it. Teenagers wearing jeans of many colours and sweatshirts with hoods. White was popular, Julianna noted. As were drop-shaped pendants of glass, more bafflingly. Many of the teenagers wore them long around their necks, swinging them threateningly.

Sitting there, looking at the crowd, listening to the mayor's speech being swallowed by the wind and the poor sound system, Julianna thought how little she'd seen of this place, its people.

One Saturday night they'd all caught the bus to Brigtown. But they hadn't done much, scared by their Westington pub experiences of spending an hour's work on a single drink. The cost of things shocked them and made them feel isolated from the groups of multi-tongued youth. They felt they were visiting a different, somewhat frivolous planet. They had all, apart from James and Ngao, who were Seventh Day Adventists, bought cans of lager in a shop and sat on the seafront drinking, before catching the last bus home. It was like a circus out there, groups of men and women performing drunken acrobatics and staged fights, floodlit by the endless takeaways and shops.

That night she'd been relieved to return to Woods Farm, as if it were a country of its own. As if she'd caught the bus from Budapest straight to Matthew.

There were a good thirty stalls in the first field and a small fairground in the adjoining one. Some of the stalls were in fact games, where people queued to guess the number of sweets in a jar or tried to move a small ring of wire along a twisting electrical circuit without setting off a red flashing alarm. There was a coconut shy, a strong-man game, and vans selling hotdogs and bins of candy floss. Trays of toffee apples and slabs of thick sweet fudge. Matthew made forays beyond their stall and would return bringing her jaw-clenchingly sweet little cakes.

In his absence Julianna sold a few pots of jam, but truth be told sales were reduced by her accent. Hard to believe something is cosily handmade when the vendor's accent is suggestive of the Cold War. The women tended to suspect a scam. Some kind of uncharitable, black-market jam. Julianna had noticed herself, when in town, that once she opened her mouth, and people heard her accent, they had a tendency to glaze over, to stop listening. She didn't dwell on it.

She was sitting chin in hand, elbow on knee, when a large group, three adults with several young children, walked past. A little girl gave a strong tug on her father's hand and surged away, and now stood, a head above the table, staring at the candles. Julianna could understand that her eye was caught by the pink shapes and ribbons. She could almost feel the child's longing.

'They are pretty? Yes?' Julianna said to the girl. She had a blunt light brown fringe and wide blue eyes. Her ears

58

stuck through her straight hair. She looked at Julianna, and then, after a certain consideration, nodded.

Julianna wanted to give her something, but it wasn't hers to give, and within a few seconds one of the group, a woman with a toddler on her hip and a livid pink birthmark on her jaw and neck, had turned back to gather up the child. She laughed and raised her eyes at Julianna in a familial exchange which she wished had lasted longer. She thought for the first time in weeks of Tamás and watched the woman go, carrying and coaxing children as she walked. She fought a sense of abandonment and pulled herself up straight. If I had that birthmark, she said to herself, I would try to cover it up.

The group walked on towards the beer tent. The small girl, who was called Katie, kept looking back to the table with the candles, and the dark-haired woman selling them. Katie Flood had the isolated concentration of an only child and that woman had been nice to her and had a table of desirable items at her fingertips. Around her the family – her father, her aunt, their friend Bob and her two cousins – made their own noise.

The Flood siblings and their old schoolmate Bob settled into the beer tent. Several pints for the men, Jenny going gently with halves of lager shandy, popping out to walk the littlest ones around. Altogether they made a lopsided family. Two men, one woman, three kids, not a couple between them. But they didn't stand out; families are rarely complete. Jenny, with the birthmark, was mother to two of them, but she extended her mothering easily to include Katie, her brother's only child. Even Bob stretched his presence into something larger and louder and more paternal around Katie. While everyone about him stepped up to the responsibility of an extra child, Richard enjoyed his daughter's presence in a slightly passive way. As if his single-occasional-parent status was a disablement and Katie the wound that he couldn't quite reach.

The elder kids appeared intermittently with friends for money or judgements on arguments. They brought back fair-food: a burger in a sesame bun, a herby sausage in a bit of French stick, a cherry flapjack, a chocolate cornflake crispy, a toffee apple.

Jenny came back looking pleased with herself, Katie on her hip, too big for carrying really, her sticky face burrowed into her aunt's neck.

'I just bought half a cow off a bloke I know,' she said. 'Meat for months.' She saw Bob's face and felt like teasing him. 'You can have some . . . I might need to use your freezer.' He worked for the council, high up in the Department of Trading Standards. 'Oh relax,' she said and announced she was fed up of them sitting in this bloody tent, that she wanted to go and muck around on the rides, and she sounded to Bob just like the teenager he'd adored, the only girl he'd known, let alone been able to talk to.

Jenny kicked Richard into moving, transferring his child into his arms. Katie's disproportionately long bare legs clasped his midriff, and she winched herself up his side. The buckles on her sandles made Richard swear, but he managed to keep hold of the fag in his other hand and pick up his plastic pint glass on the way. As they moved towards the exit of the tent, the older kids springing on the spot, revved up by the surprising movement of the lumbering men, their shambling, many-headed group on the move again, Bob felt a prickle of pleasure, in the sunshine that awaited them outside the tarpaulin, in the nostalgic smell of mown grass and mildewed tent, in the space his friends' unsuccessful marriages left for him in their chaotic lives.

*

Later, Jenny took her two on the dodgems. Bob and Richard sat on a bank, their backs resting on the fence, watching Katie sit, silenced, even slightly puzzled, by her dense cloud of candy floss. The merry-go-round turned, the gaudy sturdiness of the painted horses reminding Bob of fat can-can dancers on an old French poster. Katie watched the carousel with satisfied interest, knowing this was a promised treat.

'D'you remember that year at the Moat House fair?' said Richard.

'The one where you got in that fight?'

Richard nodded. 'That fucker, Steve . . . what was it?'

'He had a point.'

'No he didn't.'

'Well what would you call it if someone picked on your child? All day, every day? What would you call it?'

'School?'

'Bullying. We all bullied him.'

'Nah . . .' said Richard slowly. That would be the last word on the subject. They had their roles.

'I can't believe we're still coming to this.' Bob gestured around him. 'The last twenty years it's been.'

Richard nodded as he lit another cigarette.

'I suppose it depends which way you look at it, doesn't it?' said Bob. 'You could say it's good . . . settled . . . rooted. You know. Or just boring.'

Richard looked at him and sighed.

Bob, so alert today to his status, felt the weight of a life-time of one-sided conversations settle on him. 'I suppose I could just do with a bit of a change.'

'Comes when you least expect it.'

'I know that, but where is the unexpected going to spring from when I know every bloody alleyway in Westington, and every tea-lady in that office?'

Richard didn't say anything. Just shrugged and gestured in the direction of the Downs, their slopes running down to meet Burden's Farm.

Bob wasn't sure if he was listening. Katie, defeated by the candy floss, restless now, walked up the slope. 'Dad,' she said, 'Dad, you know that place, over there, where the things were . . .'

'Daddy's talking, love,' Richard said.

Katie pouted and wandered off.

'You're lucky, you know,' said Bob, almost fiercely. 'You're lucky you've got Katie.'

'What's the matter with you?' asked Richard.

'I don't know,' said Bob, sounding engaged, almost energised, by the question.

'You need a change. A woman.'

'I know, Richard.'

'It's not that hard.'

'It is, until it suddenly isn't. And when it isn't, then it's arrived, hasn't it?'

'They're not trains,' said Richard, laughing.

Bob looked irritated. 'All I mean is that when you're young you assume that if you do all right, then everything will follow on. You think things suddenly come together with your first pay cheque.'

They sat quietly, the dodgems blaring out 'Holiday', Bob's least favourite Madonna. He could see a girl stropping at the coconut shy and toddlers in blobby cars making the heavy, slow circles of giant bees. All the essentials of the fair.

Julianna was reminded of the *majalis* in Kisrét – the May Day celebrations. Although when she was a child the carnival atmosphere had always been mixed with politics. There were balloons and flags, music and games and traditional dances, fights and lovemaking on the fringes, but always the involvement, the images of Lenin carried by those who cared, through the crowds of those who didn't.

Matthew arrived back looking triumphant. On his latest circuit he'd found a new stall.

'I've got a present for you,' he said, and handed her a little piece of orange paper with the number 397 on it. She shook her head, and he explained. It was a raffle ticket. For a prize. A big prize. A trip to New York. Julianna looked so adorably wide-eyed and frightened at the prospect that Matthew had to laugh and he crouched down to kiss her. Which was when they noticed the little girl with the brown fringe had returned to look at all the pretty things.

After a minute Bob noticed Katie had gone and stood up saying they'd better go and find her, and Richard, with a grunt of annoyance, followed him. They headed back to the first field and Bob, who always remembered what Katie did, led the way until they found her holding a stout pink candle.

'Would you like one?' Julianna was saying to her as Bob and Richard arrived. She smiled broadly at them, feeling as if they'd already been introduced, and Bob and Richard both focused quickly on this dark-haired girl, flushed with sun and youth, who was smiling at them.

'They're a pound each,' said Matthew, sounding mean.

'Sorry, sweetheart, no, come on,' said Richard.

She held on tight and said in a quiet voice, 'I want one for my mummy.'

'*I'll* buy it for her,' said Bob, reaching for his wallet. 'A little present,' at which Richard swore and started to say, 'All right, all right, don't worry, Bob, I'll get it for her then.' He put his hand in his right pocket. Then, finding

63

nothing, tried his left one and pulled out some coins that very clearly didn't add up to a pound. At which point he picked up his daughter, who began to wriggle and cry surprisingly loudly, and pulled the gift from her hands.

There was a small pause as Richard carried Katie away. Then Bob pulled out a five-pound note, and as Julianna counted out the pound coins she turned to Matthew and said angrily, 'You could have given it to her for nothing.'

Matthew looked surprised. 'Why?'

'Because she's just a little girl,' she said and went on, 'Because not everyone has . . .' then sighed and closed her mouth firmly, and smiled as she handed back Bob's coins.

Bob had to stop himself from pointing out that they were quite capable of buying the child a present. That she needn't worry. That they had just run out of change.

This afternoon Bob felt as if the past had telescoped closer and more distinct than the present. All around them the teenagers of Westington grouped and drank their way through the afternoon just as he and Jenny and Richard had done, year after year, all through the seventies and eighties.

Then he noticed a poster pinned to one of the tables, something that he'd not noticed before. It was a picture of New York. Manhattan. There was a raffle, and the prize was a trip for two. He felt a surge of relief, almost euphoric. It was as if he'd forgotten there were other places in the world, extravagantly created places where people lived progressive lives. He could go to Manhattan one day. Take a trip that would bring adventure not just booze and sun. Why not? He lifted a tear-stained Katie to look at the poster. The orange sky and black-toothed skyline looked familiar to Bob from the television. Light-strung drawbridges leading on to an island. The stepped skyscrapers a peculiarly isolated competition. *I ♥ New York*, the poster said.

'What does that mean?' Katie asked, pointing at the heart.

'It means I love New York.'

'Is it a word?' she asked. He said he wasn't sure and she looked unimpressed.

'It's the best, most important city in the world,' he said.

'How do you know?' she said.

When they got back to the group he handed two tickets over to Jenny and Richard, saying, 'I've got a good feeling about this.'

Richard raised his eyebrows and said, 'Having one of his premonitions, is he?'

The Grand Prize Draw was held at five, as the stalls were being packed away. The gentle light of a bird-loud evening settling the crowd. The promise of home not so far away, the idea of kettles and baths and mellow Sunday TV, filling the gaps in happiness.

Matthew had bought ten tickets in the end. Wanting suddenly to take Julianna away from damp caravans, greasy kitchens, mousetraps, incidental dog shit, cracked window panes; the thousand corners of a farm. Seeing the two of them, dressed expensively, walking down shining streets.

On the other side of the field, near the road, Jenny, Bob and Richard sat on the ground, waiting. 'Jesus, look at you,' said Richard, taking the piss out of Bob, who was getting Katie to kiss his ticket for luck. 'The tension builds.' He had been in a filthy mood since the incident with the candle and the change.

But it was true that a hush had fallen on the hundred-plus crowd. The manager of the town's new Thomas Cook twirled the tombola drum. Westington's summer fête had never seen such a generous prize, not in the hundreds of years that it had been gathering people from the streets and villages and farms of the borough to spend a day in celebration of summer, losing their money, their inhibitions and their children in a few fields on the edge of town.

The evening sky was scattered with fragments of near-purple cloud. The tombola swung to a standstill. Bob, who was peculiarly convinced that, finally, his number was in, licked his lips. Matthew unconsciously smoothed his hair as the number was called. Number 19. Number 19 and Bob's mood plummeted to despair.

A small woman in brown lifted a hand in the air and quietly gave her name. In his head Bob told himself severely that change only came unanticipated. He and Jenny gathered the kids together, transferring balloons and goldfish between hands. A small ripple of bitter laughter could be heard leaving the ground with Richard, who had perked up considerably at the sight of mass disappointment.

'Luck of the draw,' he said, brightly.

Jenny took Bob's arm, saying, 'Oh bless you, never mind, we'll go to Horden instead, shall we? Drink cocktails on the pier.' So with promises of tea and company and wine Bob finally gave enough of a smile to satisfy the mother of their party and they slowly made their way home. Stepping down pavements, crossing over roads, stepping up, turning left, then right, then right, climbing short slopes; the shape of Westington readable in their footfalls.

Julianna and Matthew sat in the Range Rover in silence. 'Why are you in such a mood?' he asked.

'You can't understand,' she said.

'Can't understand what?' he said.

'This is what I'm saying,' she said. 'You know nothing. Nothing about other people. Other lifes.'

'Lives,' he said, 'not lifes.'

She managed to hold her silence all the way back to the farm. But then they entered the empty house and cooked food together and the comfort of the evening softened her to make amends. She forgot what she'd seen: the little girl's longing, and the embarrassment of a spent-up man.

Chapter Five

Bob Shillabeer had grown up alone with his mother in a two-bedroom flat on an estate on the edge of Westington. When the estate was demolished she'd been relocated. Now that she had a back door and a lawn she would comment every day that the garden would have been more use to her when Bob was three, not thirty-three.

Bob, Richard and Jenny had been neighbours, and for six years the three of them had walked to school together. The Victorian school, still with separate gates for girls and boys, which everyone ignored, was on the main road north out of Westington. Just next to it was a shopping parade, which had white pillars and scalloped awnings, where they had bought their sweets every afternoon.

Westington had felt further from London back then. Now it was only an hour and a half away by train. Since their childhood it had become less a self-sufficient market town and more a dormitory, the main workings of commerce and business taking place far away, in retail and industrial parks, down dual carriageways. The shops in the parade where they'd bought black jacks and pineapple chunks had been closed and boarded up, and only those shops that embraced their marginality remained in the town centre. They sold rose-scented gifts and ethnic trinketry, charity clothes, army wear and second-hand books.

It felt to the older inhabitants of Westington that as the

shops departed the streets were claimed in other ways. Some of the pubs were no better, or worse, than nightclubs. The older kids took over whole sections of estates and the steamy cafés were being replaced by Wimpys. But it was also a forgiving town. It remained charming in places. The city wall ruins had to be protected and it meant that willow trees and cow parsley, holly bushes and sweet chestnuts could be seen around the town. In the morning, when schoolchildren still walked down the hill like laggards, the town sat prettily in the morning mist. The streets narrowed as you got closer to the centre, to the core of its origins, and the St Mary Magdalene church steeple spiked the view. Even the Sue Ryder stores and Southern Fried Chickens couldn't detract from the great swelling hill of the Down's ridge that could be seen from the end of the high street.

Sometime after the Westington summer fête Bob Shillabeer realised he badly needed a new sofa. The springs had gone on the old one and, as with all fancy items gone wrong, once it was broken it was worse than useless. He'd rather have had the space to sit on the floor. One night at the very end of August he decided to take advantage of a skip at the end of the street and called up Richard for some help. The two of them had drunk six cans of Stella before trying to lug it out of the lounge, laughing so badly they could hardly hold it together, getting stuck in the corridor and front door. They'd had a rest halfway down the cul-de-sac. Sitting, staring at the stars, panting hard. It was very surreal, being outside in the middle of the road, on the sofa. They stared up in silence for a few minutes.

'Lucky it's not snowing,' said Bob eventually.

'You're right,' said Richard solemnly. 'We are very lucky it's not snowing in August. We'd be stuck frozen to your nice velvet cushions.'

'Happens in Russia. All the time.'

'What does? Snow in August?'

'No, people freezing to death in the middle of doing things. Taking out the rubbish, queuing for bread, you know. Sitting on sofas in the middle of the street.'

'Warsaw and Westington. Twinned by drunk men.'

There was a pause.

'Warsaw's in Poland, you dick.'

'I fucking know it's in Poland,' Richard said. 'I couldn't think of a Russian place that began with W, could I?'

Bob tried to think of somewhere that began with W. But couldn't.

'Woscow,' he said finally.

Then they began to snigger so badly that someone put their head out on to the street and told them to piss off home.

Richard's sister Jenny had been Bob's first proper friend, a sharp girl with a port-wine stain sliding like a Ribena spill from her hairline to her neck. The two of them came together every break time in the same corner of the playground. The dinner ladies would watch them huddle by the railings, looking on to the disinterested street with longing, but no one ever bothered to bully them. Wasn't it odd, the dinner ladies said to each other, the way kids who were a bit unusual stuck to each other? It was only a matter of skin, of course, but everyone, especially Jenny and Bob, knew they were different.

Richard was the school sprite. He had little concentration, but a wicked charm. Teachers enjoyed his brand of cheek, but ultimately he frustrated them because he was bright and precocious and mouthy, and they knew from experience that they'd be seeing him back at the school gates with his own kids all too soon. Children like that grew up too fast and trapped themselves too early.

Bob's mother would never have considered anything less

than a professional career for her boy. But now that he was thirty-three, still living around Westington, working as a trading standards officer for Westington District Council, and worst of all, still hanging around Richard, she wasn't slow to voice her disappointment. She hadn't brought a child up single-handedly after a night's mistake, withstood comments and aggressive jeers, just so as her beautiful son (and he had been a very beautiful young boy) could waste his life living alone in a semi.

Once or twice, when Bob was still a child, and she had been facing a particularly bad Christmas, Bob's mother had had to visit the town's pawn shop, Silver's. It had been located discreetly in a small road off the high street. Now Silver's was twenty miles away in Horden, but the firm still operated here, offering unsecured loans on small sums around the Brancaster and Kennet Bridge estates, shoring up empty purses in broken flats and houses. Back then pink gold wedding bands and signet rings, with other men's imprimaturs, had twirled in the window, pinned on to plump velvet pads. The jewellery shop displays cushioning Barbara Shillabeer's shame. There'd never been enough to save, not until Bob had gone to secondary school and she'd got a full-time job. Whenever she'd had a bit of spare money she'd spent it on the most visible of luxuries, good clothes. Bob's father had been Brazilian and their son was a beautiful honey-skinned child, all his features softly curved, nothing out of proportion except for his large brown eyes, so deep brown that the contrast between his pupils and the white of his eyes was startling. His mother was a determined, self-contained woman. Bob never knew his father and the subject was off limits. The fact that his skin was not only a different colour to hers, but seemed to be made up of a whole other smoother, more supple fabric, was also not a subject for discussion.

*

Bob loved his job as a trading standards officer with Westington District Council. He set off each morning, an old briefcase in his hand, a copy of the *Independent* inside, with a sense of purpose and rightness. He loved his walk to work, from his neat house in the pricier part of town. Across the playing fields, round the allotments, up in between the old town walls, with their lush cushions of grass, chalk stone outcrops, pretty weeds, trapped cellophane and old condoms. He could see the effect of rain overnight, fragile frost on lichen, summer heat on the fissured playing pitches, a rank smell on the footpaths, overexcited collies and whippets underfoot. On his way in he observed the world naturally at work. Then when he arrived at the office, he observed it at its most false.

With his precision and his unshakeable faith in the process of authority and law Bob drove many of the younger ones in his department round the bend. The air stilled when he arrived at a colleague's desk. He cast a gentle shadow over their papers, his pedantry and kindness indistinguishable. Yet his belief in justice, in the need to pursue it and the properness of permanently invoking its name, got Bob Shillabeer results.

He was a master of fair trading, dressed in baggy trousers and jackets, block-coloured ties and very reasonably priced shoes.

Jenny and Richard, both divorced, both with kids by now, laughed at Bob for his exactitude. They considered him shockingly set in his ways, too used to his own company to ever find himself a girlfriend, let alone a wife. His all-hours accessibility suited them too. Sometimes Jenny wondered whether he was gay, or, more likely, a little in love with her. Why else would he have stuck around here all these years? She and Richard had kids, who tied you down to a place, but he didn't.

In fact, Bob was simply a loyal man. Like many who lose a parent young, to life or death, he took responsibility in relationships very seriously. And it was only now, now that he and his friends were in their muddy mid-thirties, when children learn to speak and love starts to fail, that this pure quality of his stood any chance of being recognised.

Ten miles out of Westington, away from the stained pavements and overheated shops, the pub junketry and garden-fence disputes, it was raining hard on Woods Farm. Julianna and István (who thought a lot about his money, accumulating in the fresh space of his new bank account) were dismantling trestle tables in the packing shed. Woods Farm's packing systems were not hi-tech, and in order for the soft fruit and salad side of the business to become more profitable they needed to increase the turnover – but infra-structure and equipment took extra money, sums that needed to be found from somewhere within the existing calculations, the extended and uneven accounts, perilous like badly stacked wooden boxes. Next year, Roy the manager was thinking, they might have to hire illegal foreign workers who could exist below even the recommended casual worker's wage. Many of the neighbouring farms were forced to do it. Gangmasters delivering silent men, not kids with studies to return to, but with families that needed feeding and no place else to earn money. He figured Gerard probably wouldn't even notice.

It was dark in the shed and cool and smelt slightly of rotting vegetation. But it was pleasantly out of Roy's way at the end of the day, a chance to move slowly and for István to stop and smoke a cigarette in a corner.

The rain thinned and a tower of sunlight fell in through the half-open door then lay shifting on the cement floor. A pattern of leaves, the drip and trickle of recent rain. It was quiet; they could hear a crow, a car in the distance, a radio somewhere in the outhouses. Julianna felt a wave of nostalgia for this moment, here, summer sounds tricking her sense of time. As if she could suddenly imagine being older, in a house, seeing sunlight on the floor and thinking back. During the last week there had been a shift in the atmosphere. Tempers frayed more often, rain had also fallen heavily the day before, on the parched earth, leaving exhausted vegetation saturated. The end of summer was for the first time conceivable.

'Why do you spend so much time with that boy?' István asked. Surprising Julianna, although not himself. He'd been watching her carefully for the last two months. They had only three weeks left until the majority of them went home. Ngao and James would be spending a further three months on the farm in order to get their vehicle-driving and maintenance certificates.

István was increasingly moody but he was the only person to whom Julianna could speak Hungarian, so they talked to each other through the day in a quibbling, impatient way. Also he was protective of her, like a brother, she thought, and his presence combined with that of Matthew's made her feel for the first time like a woman amongst males. Which seemed a glamorous thing. Her shyness was still there, but it acted now as a vault rather than a block to conversation.

The answer to his question was an inappropriate truth. She spent so much time with Matthew because she was trying to work out if she loved him. But she would no more talk of love and sweetness to István than to her distant father.

She acted nonchalant. 'We don't get that much time together.' Then said, 'And why shouldn't I spend time with him? I didn't sign anything when I arrived saying that I wouldn't make friends with English people. You're too defensive, too walled in. You'll never enjoy life, or travel or people, if you don't open up . . .' She was about to continue; a long, florid account of what she felt she had achieved, enjoying the shape of a list in her own language, enjoying articulating how she thought she had come on.

'Because there's very little point,' he interrupted. 'Because we're going home in three weeks. Because he's playing with you – like a new game for the school holidays.' He acted like he was ten years older than her and Matthew, not three. It irritated Julianna.

'And because you're different when he's around, you go coy, and like a little girl. All giggly.' And he waggled his head in a sort of demonstration.

She made a noise of protest. 'That's because my English isn't that good yet,' but he snorted.

'It's not about language; it's about trying to be something you aren't.'

She struggled on, folding the legs up underneath the trestles. Swearing a little to herself at the stiffness of the hinges. She decided to ignore him. He was mean with loneliness. She knew he bit his fingernails until they bled. He was just teasing her out of boredom and frustration. He had no concept of the gentle, happy wholeness she and Matthew felt when alone. Matthew was her creature and neither of them had made much impact on the world until they met each other. As if all along she'd been invisible until someone real touched her. Alone they were perfect; it was what surrounded them that caused problems.

She manoeuvred the table on to its end, walking it slowly on its corners.

'Unless you're trying to get him to marry you so that you can stay.' He said it as though he were solving a problem slowly before a young child. She stopped, shocked, struggling to hold the table upright. István chucked his fag end out into the yard, walked slowly over and picked the table

75

up out of her hands in a deliberate display of strength,

'I guess not,' he said, lining it up against the others. 'You're not that type, are you?'

A flash of feminine curiosity assailed her, the oddity of a man discussing what kind of person she was. 'What kind of girl would you say I was then?'

'A woman. Distracted by a boy.'

He stood in front of her and wiped his face with his arm, then said, 'Lucky him. That's all,' and walked out, leaving her standing, flustered and impressed by the worldliness he seemed to be attributing to her. As if he were talking about some other Julianna. Another one, different even from Matthew's, and a million miles away from the one that belonged in Kisrét.

Bob had tried to buy a replacement sofa, but retail decisions on furniture and clothes were torturous for him. The only thing he had to go by was what his mum's house had contained. These were at least feasible things: the muted, patterned three-piece suites, the white crockery and blue towels. He knew how to live with them. The unfamiliarity of more outlandish modern patterns and designs, which others seemed to admire, made him wonder whether he should distrust all the decisions he made about his lifestyle.

Finally Bob took himself off to a late-night Thursday at MFI, intending to nail the problem on its head. He gave himself a full forty minutes to settle on something, before meeting Richard at eight. He wandered confused, until he saw a pretty salesgirl trying out a cream leather sofa called the Olympiad. The sight gave him the briefest flicker of a fantasy, but it took twenty minutes to persuade her he couldn't afford it.

He arrived at the pub late, to find Richard already drunk and in the mood to pick a fight. Sometimes he got like this, surly and limited as a chained dog. Usually when he was depressed, or when he'd been humiliated. He'd been hard to handle for a couple of months after his wife left. They'd argued themselves, when Richard had told Bob there was no way he was going to the cinema with him, in case people thought Bob was his gay lover. Bob, who had no inclinations of that kind, had still been hurt by the suggestion that he would be an embarrassing boyfriend for a man to have.

'Are you all right?' Bob said meaningfully, after thirty minutes of sniping.

'Yeah, fucking marvellous,' said Richard, so Bob went up to buy another round. He bought some peanuts, watched as the packet was ripped from the cardboard pin-up's breasts. They made his lips tingle, but he didn't care.

With the next pint it became clearer: Richard had been given a court judgement on how much alimony he should be paying.

Bob had always told him how lucky he was to see Katie as often as he wanted. Ordinarily Richard was gentle and almost lyrical in his pub-praise of his little girl. He said that that was when he was happiest, sitting in the sun with a fag, a drink and a kid. A fag to add style, a drink to add poetry, and a kid to give it some purpose – otherwise you'd just be an old fucker drinking during the day.

But this evening he didn't talk about Katie, just about her cost. 'Maria's not the only one that feeds her, buys her things. Spends money on her. And I'm not the only one that can work.'

Bob said, 'But I thought she was trying to get a job. I thought she'd been covering for someone in the travel agent and that they were going to take her on.'

Richard turned his head and met his eyes for just a second, before lighting another cigarette, which gave him the lift, the stepping-stone, the whatever mood-shifting moment that was needed.

'I've got debts, haven't I,' he said. Not a question.

They were quiet. The mettle seemed to have been drawn out of him. He ripped up the beer mat into small pieces, and then pushed the fragments with his finger, matching them back together again.

'Big ones?' said Bob. Wincing as he said it, in a way that must have irritated Richard, like he'd made him touch dog shit.

'Yes, big ones. You tit.'

'Who d'you owe it to? A bank?' It was politic to pretend, Bob felt.

'No, nothing as respectable as that, Bob.' Richard's voice was tight and quiet and venomous. 'The usual, you know, the small loan companies, the people who put pamphlets through the door. Or don't they do that in your street?'

'Silver's?'

Richard got up to buy another round. Which presumably meant yes.

Bob sat, wondered if he shouldn't be buying the drinks, decided to leave it, focused on the brown table, thought about how to handle this for the best. He felt tense but energised. He could help, but Richard could make it hard. He shut off the noise of the pub and tried to feel the fullness of the problem. He had a peculiarly abstract, almost spiritual approach to solving people's problems. He would think himself into the dynamics of the situation, begin to feel the instincts of the people involved, their base motives and their blocks. Then he would try to visualise what the next step should be. It was a creative process, not always easy to explain, especially when his instincts could be peculiarly prophetic.

During the last year Richard, behind on his mortgage payments, had borrowed a total of £2,000 from Silver Services.

But he had got behind on those payments too and had then been forced to reorganise the loan and spread the repayments over a longer period. Last week, thinking he must be getting the total sum down by now, he had phoned up to find out how much he now owed and was told £15,000. Missing payments had triggered the highest levels of interest, he was told. Now he was hardly even covering the cost of his interest in his monthly repayments. This was on top of an over-the-limit overdraft and two credit card debts, which had been handed on to a different set of debt collectors. He also had three further cards which he was using purely to pay off the interest on these other debts. 'It's so easy,' he said to Bob almost wistfully. 'I get five offers a day through the post. They know who I am. They know that I need it. They lend it and they seem to know they'll make their money three times over out of me. I can get credit cards like that.' And he clicked his fingers in Bob's face.

He agreed to let Bob look over all his paperwork at the weekend. He said with anger, some of it definitely directed at Bob, that it'd be 'fucking humiliating', but he had faced up to his enslavement enough to know he needed help.

The interest on Silver's loan would now be obscene but perfectly legal, Bob knew. Any level of interest was legal here in the UK, something he had pointed out many times to the staff in his office. Getting in debt, he liked to say, was tantamount to giving your freedom away. Which, now he came to think of it, nursing an alka seltzer at his kitchen table the next morning, was probably why Richard hadn't told him before. And perhaps why he'd taken to calling him a tosser recently. While Bob liked the word tantamount, and didn't mind tosser, he did not like being described as self-righteous. He was sensitive about his obsession with right and wrong.

People were getting richer, Bob's mum liked to say,

remembering the thirties. But what she meant was it was easier to get hold of money. Some of the people who borrowed money from Silver's could do little to avoid it. Unemployed, unwell or unable, through bad luck of a complex kind, to live life within its conventional bureaucracies. Others used it like a punitive treat; an accessible but expensive way to buy a new fridge or cooker. But others, like Richard, had overstretched and overspent, aspiration mistaking itself for need, until they were desperate enough to be taken advantage of. A mortgage, an ex-wife, maxed credit cards, and then something, a bad back, or an old bill, came calling and they'd used up the resources for respectable debt. Suddenly the bank, having judged their income by their postcode, having targeted their weaknesses specifically, having been so seductive and promising, would withdraw its favours and begin to phone at night. Having spent the whole relationship promising discretion, ease and peace of mind, the bank begins instead to behave like a stalker. So you turn to the local lender, who at least has a representative who speaks your language on your doorstep.

If you were confident in tomorrow, you'd have saved. If you'd ever had any money it might have been easier to know how to resolve your finances. Bob, raised frugally but reliably by his mother – living in his modest house, on a reasonable mortgage – could see that. There was such desperation, sewn through agitated lives. He could see that.

Chapter Six

Julianna and Matthew sat in silence outside the Waterman Inn. It was nearly closing time and an owl could be heard, as well as the tiny roar of a distant phalanx of bikers.

'What would have happened if you hadn't come this summer?' asked Matthew finally, the randomness of romance so disturbing. 'If instead of Julianna there had been a great big scary . . . what is, what would a monster be called in Hungary?'

'Anya,' she said. It was a joke. *Anya* was a word for mother. But only she understood it.

'A hairy woman called Anya, then. What would I have done this summer?'

'You could perhaps read a good book.' She was irritated by his description of her as a pleasant summer activity. She felt uneasy tonight, anticipating the end of summer, the return home, the end of her and Matthew. She already felt reminiscent for that point in midsummer when they had been so unassailable and protected. Innocent, she thought now, just seven weeks later. She could imagine letters and phone calls, him regaling her with costly, jubilant adventures, a barrage at the beginning, dwindling as the year turned. Spring arriving without post. Her watching the trees ugly in their early sprouting, ugly herself with the lack of every-thing.

Until now they'd avoided the subject of how hard it would

be after. Only spoken of each other in some kind of play-time future, that even took them through children and old age. The truth was they were both scared of discussing the difficulties. So they talked of how they would meet in the Christmas holidays, in Paris . . . no, Berlin . . . no . . . without him explaining he would have to lie to get there and without her explaining that the money might never be found. She tried to convince herself that if their feelings for each other were as strong as they should be, could be, then they would last and survive, just as her grandparents' had done, and somehow, in a strange hybrid land, they'd find each other again.

Matthew didn't register the gathered weekenders and louder locals, nor the geraniums nor the Golf convertibles, and would have been astonished if Julianna had explained it was all part of something to which she didn't belong. He was stuck trying to imagine what was going on inside her head, just by watching her face. It felt like trying to imagine Hungary. He was map-less, penniless, going in old, deflective directions. 'I don't want you to go back.' He sounded suddenly petulant. 'Do you?'

'We will write,' she said, sidestepping.

'I don't think so.' While she sounded flat, he sounded strangely excited, overwrought. 'You'll forget about me, find someone else,' he said.

'No. Why do you say this?' she asked.

'Because everything's changing. We'll be in different places. It won't be the same again. Ever. That always makes me feel sad. I hate it. I think you want to get back to something. Be back at home. I can tell.'

'I think this is your mother saying this to you. Doesn't she? I am sure that she does. She wants you back in her kitchen all for her,' and she laughed to deflect the despair she felt and then began to tease him as if she were his mother instead. 'I don't want to leave you alone either. London is a big city. You'll disappear and no one will be able to find you.'

He looks a little indignant. He has rather higher-profile plans for his future. He is thinking of journalism. Of Paris. Or New York. Julianna's tenderness and her interest in the small machinations of his uneventful past and self-conscious thoughts have given him new confidence. He is looking forward to the rest of his life. But he cannot imagine being without Julianna. Literally. She brought his imagination to life. Her arrival made so much that he had read, heard, watched and doubted seem possible. So he simply cannot imagine without her now.

'Come with me,' he said.

'No.' She made a shushing noise. 'I can't. I have college. Stop.' He was like a child.

'To London. Come and live with me. I've told you about the flat. It makes no difference to Tone and Jonny, it'll just help them with the rent. They won't mind.' She was looking at him in amazement. He seemed to be serious. Her mouth was slack, and her eyebrows raised. He breathed, then steamed on.

'You don't want to go back to Hungary. I know you don't. You can't bear living at home any longer. I know it's difficult for you to make money and have a proper life where you live. It's all fucked up there. Dad says it's only going to get worse. Dad says it'll get worse for your family before it gets better. He says you can't just change government and expect it all to happen smoothly. And here, there's everything you need. You can get a job. Or go to college, do a degree here. And we can share a bed every night. Julianna? Please think. You'd love it. You'd love London.'

She tried not to cry. She suddenly felt tired, with relief at his wanting her in his future, with the ludicrousness of his suggestions. She laughed as she refused him. She felt so much better for having been asked.

'I have to go home. You know that I don't want to leave you.'

'If you don't come it's because you don't want to. I know you, you're not scared. You're not scared of anything.'

She thought again how childish he sounded.

'You don't understand,' she said.

He suddenly thumped his fist down. 'You always say that. Why am I prepared to go for it, to try it, when you aren't?'

She laughed at him. 'You have no risk. What are you risking? I am the one not returning to college. Staying where I shouldn't.'

He felt confused. Was her present tense deliberate? And how could she say that to him? Julianna, who with her still presence had noticed everything in that house, everything about the way the farm was run. Noticed every crack in their family. How could she dismiss the enormity of what he was suggesting? It was just possible that by choosing Julianna his mother would punish him for ever.

The distance between them was suddenly clear in the way they sat, the places they looked. There was no longer a communality in the air around them, just an occupation, trenchant, of their own spaces.

The pitch inside the pub grew louder, the activity on the green outside more frenetic. Someone was playing cricket with a plastic beer glass and an umbrella. Cars came and went with radios blaring. Crisp packets collected in corners and on flower bushes, bright pillows of colour. Julianna thought forwards; the peace of her home, her grandmother, the wide-spreading fields beyond the garden, a landscape on the edge of wilderness.

She finished her drink and said, 'I want to go now.' She felt ready to go home right there and then. Unspeaking, she and Matthew, his hands in his pockets, his face sullen, walked down the gravel driveway on to the road back home.

They continued to walk in silence for about five minutes, following the usual road that ran deep into the woods then came out into the clean sweep of hillside below which Woods Farm sheltered. Julianna wanted to say, 'I love you but what did you think would happen? That we would face no problems? This sadness is a part of it all,' but when she glanced sideways at his fresh face, it looked so petulant that she knew her heavy sense of romance, one that took some sustenance from the drama, was not shared.

They stepped on and on until up ahead they saw a minibus, stopped as if in an accident, halfway up the bank. Its back lights flashed. It was quiet, not even the usual calls and wood creaks of the night. Everything must have been jarred by the noise of the sudden halt.

They carried on walking, quickly, and when they were about twenty yards away it became clear that the minibus had crashed, not dramatically, there were no flames, but enough to mash the front left corner, buckle the bonnet and leave the engine steaming. All was weirdly quiet and Julianna and Matthew broke into a run, thinking that the driver might be silently bleeding, stuck behind the wheel. They reached the front of the bus, saw the doors were open but no one was in the front. They looked around, breathing fast. It was only as Julianna's heart rate began to drop again and she had calmed enough to see her surroundings carefully that she realised she could see heads inside the bus. Dark scalps leaning against the windows. Necks awkwardly crooked, eyes closed. She paled instantly, stepped back – there were several of these slumped forms, their heads lolling.

'Oh God,' she whispered, turning from the still scene, her hands going to her mouth. Suddenly a figure appeared from round the back of the minibus. She sensed him before seeing him, but the fact of him being alive shocked her and she screamed with that delayed realisation of a horror movie. He was a small dark-skinned man in a striped T-shirt and baggy trousers. He smiled nervously.

In the minibus, one of the heads moved. It tilted slowly upright, a toy coming to life in the dark, blinked, turned to look out of the window, focused on Julianna and yawned at her. Next to him a man coughed without moving.

They were asleep. The little white bus must have held at least fifteen of them, squeezed in next to each other, tipping to the right. The engine still steaming, the ten yards ahead illuminated by one remaining light.

All those men exhausted. Such a strange tableau. They were like animals in transportation. That tiny space full of the possible strength of fifteen men; they could have burst through it with their hands but instead it was a tilted, ticking cradle.

The man was still smiling. 'Do you need help?' said Matthew. The man smiled and shook his head. He wore slip-on shoes, too big by the looks of it. A child's style of T-shirt with a small collar and three buttons hanging off, a man who must have been at least forty.

'Has someone gone for help? We can go and call the AA if you like.'

He shook his head again. Less smiling, and more nervous.

'Where are you from?' asked Julianna. He shook his head once more, as if he didn't understand. She was sure he did. 'Where' is one of the first words you learn.

'I am Hungarian,' she said.

'Romania,' he said, in English.

'Have you been working?' she said. She knew about these men, who escaped from the instability and poverty of their rural homes and smuggled themselves into Britain, working in factories and on farms, for people who paid them too little and worked them too hard. He hesitated, which gave her the answer she needed. It was the most dangerous question of all.

Is someone bringing help? she asked again. Yes, he said. Is anyone hurt? No, he said. She paused, her heart thudding at the fear accepted by this man. Should we go? she asked. He nodded yes.

She looked at him, cornered and scared, on an unused side road, at midnight, edging back towards the secrecy of the woods. In a backwater of prosperous England. Transport in the half-light, fathoms from Matthew's world of parental kitchens and free universities, easy cash-cards and bright pizzerias. She felt this man's humiliation in his stained clothing, in his cattle-truck transport, his illicit work for a farming pimp. His bloodshot eyes flickered at the sound of a car, and Julianna, wanting to say something to establish her understanding and kinship for this bus full of displaced men, said what her grandmother would have said. 'God bless you.'

Matthew and Julianna held hands as they walked off quickly, following the dark edge of the road, treading in the dip where tarmac gives way to weeds, now feeling it important to be close. They had probably never been more apart, not even when they'd first spoken at that Sunday lunch. Then they had at least both been alike in their curiosity. But now, disturbed by this glimpse of other journeys and lives, she needed the safety of someone else's hand. She felt, intrinsically, an understanding of the displaced but she also felt Matthew's discomfort. She saw then how their separation would go, the next little tear in the crease.

It was time she went home. This might all have been a false start. She could always return some other time as another person. Her affinity with that man disturbed her. Better to be a part of things at home than edging along a road in darkness.

István stood in the kitchen examining a letter addressed to Julianna. She tried to take it but he snatched it back, and again, and again, until she shouted his name as if he were a disobedient dog. When she saw the handwriting she was surprised. She would be home within the week. Why write now? There must be purpose to this letter from Éva, so she procrastinated by making tea, carefully. She took her mug and her letter outside, sat cross-legged in the concrete right-angle of the building and forecourt, facing the fields and climbing sun, and began to read.

A kestrel hovered overhead on swiftly fanning wings, waiting for a mouse to reveal its minuscule self, a mouse as blind as Julianna to the feathered cursor in the sky. Anyone watching would have seen nothing to suggest that the letter contained news of her grandmother's heart failure and death.

Julianna was a person whose sadness turned inwards. If anything she got stiller.

I am sure you'll think I should have telephoned, or written before the funeral, but, to be honest, wrote Éva dishonestly, *I have been so busy that I have had to focus on the important things.*

Julianna finished the letter. Wanted tears to flow instantaneously. She felt sick instead. She had not thought that her grandmother would die. She was wholly shocked. The no-longer-existence of someone who carried the entire shelter of her home. She had always been there. Mila's whereabouts was the measure by which Julianna's days had passed. It was just not possible to remove her from the world, within a moment, after a letter. She had lived so many years, carried so much history inside her, and she had – importantly, the fact reverberating in Julianna's head – Mila had never, ever shown herself to be frail. To die when Julianna was not there seemed so entirely impossible that she felt angry too. But of course it was she, Julianna, who had left Mila. Left her in a way Mila had never done, months ago, with a nervous happiness in her eyes.

She remained motionless on the ground. Julianna knew Mila's death could not be described as tragic. She was eighty. Éva said it hadn't been painful. Logically she knew, whatever her grief, that it belonged to the proper order of things, but it didn't feel like it, it felt wrong, something quite murderous.

A side-thought penetrated and she wondered at her own mind's self-regard. (How I don't stop, she thought disgustedly.) How had she felt when her mother died? Mila had been her mother for so much longer now. She couldn't remember, she just remembered how she had always thought of it as a thing that had had to happen. Something divine. But her grandmother's death reconfirmed the truth. People did leave her. The death of her grandparent was the end of a state of grace, of a blamelessness. All that childish nonsense Mila had told her, which suggested her life would have a natural rightness to its events. Just look, in the end Mila had died without her. Without Julianna having told her the things a person should know before they died: how and why they were loved.

Her grandmother's history had often seemed nearer than her parents', perhaps because she continued to wear strange garters below her skirts, and maintained the sanctity of a tie on a man and the importance of the proper usage of cutlery long after her father and stepmother had begun to occupy the uncomfortable, humiliating middle ground between old and young. Mila's hectic past and sepia photos were more real to Julianna, because unlike her parents, she could imagine her thirty years ago. She had changed so little. Grandparents bring the past with them, and encourage you to taste it, smell it, recite it. Julianna knew Mila's story better than her own. She was sure of it. But her parents were obscured, her mother lost and her father all unexplained sighs and uncomfortable braggadocio.

Julianna's grief was pure; there had been no confusion or resentment or guilt in their relationship while Mila was alive. A good grandparent rarely outlives their grandchild's welcome. To their grandchildren they die early, sealing their myths with their death. She was astonished that her grandmother could have died without her knowing – not that her stepmother hadn't contacted her, that didn't exactly surprise her – but that she hadn't known within herself. Nothing in the air, in this foreign place, had informed her.

Within minutes of reading the letter Julianna felt herself and everything in her sphere to be changed. But Mila's death had no impact here in England, on Woods Farm. Nothing had altered. Her grandmother had suffered so (whatever romantic storytelling light Mila had shone on events, Julianna knew that she had been struck by loss at each of politics' turns, not least that of a beloved husband in the 1956 Revolution, at the hands of a Russian soldier), and it seemed ungrateful of the modern world not to sense and mourn her death. Julianna was shocked by how easily the day continued to turn, and more personally by how, hours later, she found herself hungry for something to eat and longing to be held by Matthew.

Later that night, wide awake, her arms and legs stretched over a dozing Matthew, clinging to him even though there was no chance of either of their prone bodies going far on this narrow mattress, Julianna suddenly wanted very much to not go home. The thought of the house without Mila, with just Éva and adolescent Tamás and her quiet, quiet father made her feel cold. She and her friends had always enjoyed classifying Europeans, in town, on holiday – Poles with their Fiats and customised clothes, Czechs in canvas shoes and Skodas, Soviet girls with ribbons in their hair – and the thought of swapping sides again, becoming the stationary one, made her feel panicky and trapped. Her friends and her family could wait; Matthew could not. Her working holiday visa still had another two months to run. Perhaps she could stay for just two more months. It would make no difference. A small procrastinatory space. Who in her life would care to object, now Mila was gone?

She remembered the man with his minibus full of sleeping figures, living illegally and secretly. Why had he come, not stayed with his family, sought food and money in prayer? It wasn't as obvious a question as it sounded. Your land is your land. Some will not leave at any cost. Why was he here – beyond the need to feed hungry people? Because he refused to accept the future someone else was making for him. He wanted to try to create something of his own, for himself and his children. Or the children he hoped to have, for they are as present in the minds of poor men as anyone.

She was reckless, imaginative with grief. That blessed future, the one her grandmother had promised would guide her, seemed to in fact require a decision, and with that came the full, radical possibility of behaving badly for the very first time. She thought of waking for two more months to Matthew, his slim twining warmth always with her. In her projection she felt a flicker of her grandmother's own brand of determination. She had lost for ever one of her ties with her home, and sensed a perilous freedom. Mila had been her only source of wisdom and advice; she couldn't wait any longer for guidance. She would make her own, first choice. She would go to London.

She turned out the light, leaving herself breathing fast in the dark. The caravan instantly extinguished in the eyes of the farmhouse.

Chapter Seven

The next evening two men from Silver Services arrived on Richard's doorstep. They stood shifting, listening to Richard descend the stairs.

It was his weekend to have Katie to stay. She'd been dropped off the night before. Already in her Barbie night-dress, quilted pink dressing gown, a small white bear (who had been bought complete with a name and his own birth-date) held in the crook of her neck, her thumb in her mouth. She cried quietly for an hour after her mother left, which was familiar to Richard, but hard. It wasn't that she rejected her father as she cried – no, she clung to him – it was just because her parents wouldn't stay together in the same room for longer than a greeting. The brisk comings and goings were tiring and anxious for her and she felt a little guilty at her pleasure in her dad – which was why she often stole presents like pink candles for her mum. When the doorbell went she was upstairs, mucking around with an old flat-bed cassette player Richard had found for her.

They could hear Richard swearing at something which was cluttering the hallway. One of them did up his bomber jacket; the other belched.

If Richard had known who was behind the door he might not have opened it so swiftly, or let it swing wide as he scooped up the post. He was a man of easy movements and he was happy to be here, playing music with his kid on a Saturday.

Out of the two of them Richard only recognised Pete, the small fat one in the leather jacket. His first reaction to the two of them, shiny with rain and out of breath, was amusement.

'All right?' then, 'I sorted everything out a few days ago. I said I'd put it straight next week.'

But by the time he finished, they'd already walked in, through the wide open door. The other one was new and clearly meant to be threatening. He was harder and larger and wearing a blue blouson jacket.

'We've been through this already,' Richard said. 'On Thursday. Don't you remember?' and he gave a sarky little grin. The newcomer, Frank, looked at him with a growing smile on his face. The prat actually presumed they'd got it wrong.

It started with Pete barging, but in a strangely gentle and polite way, a small fat hand on Richard's chest, into the front room.

'What are you doing?' said Richard. 'Get out.' Following them into the front room, irritated more than anything, spitting out the t. 'I'll get you what I owe you on Thursday. I've told you, I'll have the money, definite.'

Frank didn't say anything. Pete said, 'I'm guessing that you haven't got that money today then.'

'No, 'cause we agreed Thursday,' Richard said arsily. And he muttered something under his breath. Which was a mistake, the pushing-it-just-too-far mistake he'd made since back in school.

Frank wasn't a comic criminal. He wasn't a criminal at all. He simply believed in a bit of force. If pushed, he might have even agreed that he was a little bit old-fashioned. He didn't have a character or a repartee in this kind of situation.

But Richard shouldn't have called him a wanker. It depressed him, which given that he'd also already drunk too much today wasn't good news.

Pete smiled as you do when you see someone stepping just where you want them, and said flatly to Frank, 'I'll see what's around. Leave you to it.' He gave a wave, strangely feminine, and left what his mother would have called the parlour, like a lady leaving a servant to clean up the floor. He shut the door behind him, and heard the scrape and thump of a quiet person making contact with the furniture.

Pete wandered into the kitchen and looked around. Clutter on the surfaces, bits of tools and cutlery and pizza packets. A half-empty roll of Polos. Paper curls of sweet wrappers on the floor. He took a Polo, then two more, and sucked them noisily. There was an oven, no microwave, a cheap portable radio, flecked with paint. Plain china in the cupboards, blue-spotted tumblers. A child's drinking cup, with the two handles like cartoon elephant's ears.

There was a quiet, dull shunt, a muted grunt.

He wasn't protesting much, thought Pete, a little disappointed, like a large wet dog who knew he deserved a kick. He came out of the kitchen and walked upstairs, checking out what the house held, stopping to catch his breath halfway up. He had heartburn and the Polos hadn't helped. He suddenly felt weary rather than full-of-it drunk.

The first room was a child's bedroom, pink. Full of toys. Nothing of any interest. A piece-of-shit tape recorder on the floor. He walked away without crossing the threshold. Up two steps into the second room, where he finally found the television. Richard had already sold the one in the living room to meet the last payment he made.

'Frank,' he shouted over the staircase. 'Leave off and get up here. There's a telly.' Then to himself, 'Crap telly, but it's a telly.'

The door to the front room opened with a sudden sucking sound. Frank came up the stairs breathing heavily.

'Quiet fuck he was.'

'Get the telly. It's in here. I can't carry it, I've got real pains in my chest after that steak.'

They fussed with plugs, a fiddly, unfit duo. 'Down there, you twat.'

'Hardly worth it,' said Frank, carrying it downstairs.

'I never had a telly till I was working. Black and white it was. D'you remember that, Frank . . . black and white? Crappy picture it was . . .'

Their voices drifted down the stairs. Upstairs in her bedroom, under the bed, Katie heard them descending, still talking in a loud, back and forth kind of way. She was very still, she'd been very still ever since she heard her dad say 'get out' in that way. They hadn't got out. Then she'd heard another door shut. Then she'd heard someone walking around downstairs and then she'd hidden under her bed. Quiet and still.

Under the bed there were great clumps of hairy dust. More dry than dirty. Clingish. She was frightened and knew it by the way she wanted to cry. When she had heard the man coming up the stairs something inside her had tightened; she'd curled her body tighter and wriggled back until she could feel the wall against her back. The hardness of it helped her. Safe on one side. But Katie was worried that they would still find her. She knew she always came to stay on Second Saturdays. Second Saturdays were Dad days and they were coloured blue blocks in her mind. Substantially different from the Other Saturdays, which belonged to her mother and were pink blocks. Whoever these burglars were, they might know that too. That today was the day she spent with her dad. The man came up the stairs and stopped in the doorway of her room. It said *Katie's Room* on her door. She took only tiny quick sips of breath.

It wasn't until he'd moved away into her dad's room upstairs that she remembered how much she needed a wee. Because she didn't know what to do, and could hear this man shouting, and then another one, who sounded bigger and heavier, coming up the stairs, she let her pee out. She could feel the constricted flood seep between her legs, over her thigh, down into the dusty carpet. It was hot and she could smell the familiar odour of urine, and sure that someone could hear or smell her under the bed she began to cry very quietly. Her face hot, and damp too now, and after a few minutes her body hurting to be allowed to move. Where was her dad? Then she suddenly realised what she needed to do. She needed to find her white bear. His small, complete, soft form always brought her a living comfort. She listened to the men descend the stairs, bickering foully at each other, then heard the front door close, and then began to wriggle out from under the bed, bravery driven by need of the bear.

Down in the sitting room Richard heard the door close, and driven by the thought of Katie upstairs, dragged himself to the door.

From the moment Pete had left the front room Richard had known what was coming: a kicking that would hurt rather than hospitalise him. He had wondered about taking Frank on. But Frank, although older, uglier and obviously less fit, was taller, broader and bulkier than Pete, and then suddenly, in the way fat men can be, surprisingly swift, so that he had Richard against the door before Richard had had time to formulate his plan. Frank specialised in not giving people time to make plans. From that point on Richard knew he'd have to get it over with and keep quiet, rather than making the situation worse and letting Katie hear that anything was up. Frank had punched him quickly in the stomach, and then when Richard had bent over, his mouth wide although no sound was coming out, Frank threw him down to the floor and began to kick at his stomach, catching his arms and legs, and once his face. Richard curled into a ball to protect himself. Still he made no noise. He pulled himself in so tight he could hardly breathe, and could, even despite the pain, smell his own sweat, and over and over in his head he said, 'Don't come down, don't find her, don't find her.' It wasn't that he thought they would actually harm her, they weren't paedophiles, just small-town heavies, it was just he knew Pete would implicate her somehow. Richard couldn't risk Katie seeing him like this, bloodied like an animal, otherwise he knew Maria would never let her come and stay again.

He'd heard the shout from Pete with extreme relief. Once the front door had shut and a minute or two had passed, Richard dragged himself to the door on all fours and reaching up, opened it. The pain was of a recognisable, although extreme level. He tried to call out to Katie but his voice wouldn't come.

He heard a small movement upstairs. The very faintest of carpet brushes and padding of small feet. And this, this slight, delicate sound, a tentative emerging after the storm had passed, was what broke Richard. His breath caught in his clagged-up throat; he could taste blood, dripping down the back of his gullet from his nose. He breathed deeply, felt the pain grow louder in his rib cage, coughed feebly and tried again.

'Katie.' His voice cracked and the noise upstairs stopped. 'Katie. It's all right. Can you hear?' There was no noise. Katie stopped, waiting, as so often, for this adult drama to play itself out, the bear cradled in her left hand, below her chin, her right thumb in her mouth.

'Katie. It's fine now. Just someone come to get someth . . .

Can you hear? Are you OK?' Suddenly, for the first time, he panicked. They might have touched her.

'Katie? Katie? Tell me if you're there,' he shouted this time. Hearing his worry, she stepped out on to the top stair and said, 'Yes.' Very quietly.

'Jesus,' he said, gulping his breath. 'Don't come down, Katie, I've just got to clear up a bit. It's a bit of a mess. You stay up there. I'm going to get Bob round. You stay there until he comes. I'm fine. Just tidying up. Will you stay there, Katie?'

'Yes,' she said. Less quietly.

'Good. You're a good girl. We'll have a treat after this. We'll get a pizza and have a treat. Go to Uncle Bob's, watch a video. You think about your video. Think about what you want.' He kept talking as he crawled to the telephone in the kitchen and called Bob.

Bob had arrived home about five. He'd been hanging around MFI and the Olympiad suite again. God, he needed a girl-friend.

The house felt empty. Outside the street was quiet. It had begun to rain more heavily; a car went past in a wet roar, windscreen wipers working recklessly hard. He felt a familiar focusing, an awareness of insight, right now, into how this, this familiar lull, was a distillation of his life in this town. Even though it was far from cold he lit his fake coal gas fire and flicked the telly on, trying to turn lonely into cosy with the application of a few luxuries. If he'd had a sweet tooth he'd have got a tin of Quality Street out. The babble of *Blind Date* began. Despite himself he pictured his mum in her house, doing the same, just a mile away, and he suddenly felt a little bit desperate, and thought of the one conversation they'd ever had about his South American father, an engineering student, who'd appeared in a jazz club in London in 1959 and, she'd said, showed her that there was more to life than this bloody country. He suddenly felt a peculiar longing for heat and colour and the pulse of something exotic. Or erotic. Just something.

To Bob's relief (he was usually a very chipper man) the phone rang. It was Richard.

Bob arrived at the house five minutes later. Katie answered the door. Standing on her very tiptoes to turn the latch. He bent down to pick her up. She had tear tracks on her flushed cheeks and pressed her face hard against his shoulder. Together they packed her things into a small red suitcase, which had a pink quilted lining and baggy elasticated pockets in the lid. Her ability to concentrate very hard on these small feminine items impressed Bob. 'My hairbrush and toothbrush go in there,' and she pointed impatiently. 'And I need my pants. Not those. Those.' Then he took her round to Jenny's.

He returned within twenty minutes and found Richard sitting on the floor of the bathroom trying to wash his face. Bob had to swallow a vomiting reflex when he saw him. He wasn't good on blood. 'Jesus Christ,' he said, turning away. Angry at Richard. 'What the fuck have you done?'

Richard looked at him and over his rapidly swelling lower lip said, 'Thanks for the vote of confidence.'

'What were they after? What did they take?' asked Bob, who wondered what they could have thought they were going to find in this tatty little rented house. 'Have you called the police?'

'They weren't burglars, you twat. It was Silver's, after their money. So no, I'm not calling the police.'

'But didn't you tell them, we're going to sort the money out, we agreed I was going to come round and help.'

'Yeah, funnily enough, Bob,' Richard could do this, remain coolly superior even with blood dripping out of his nose and a swelling eye, 'funnily enough they didn't really have time for a chat. They just fancied a bit of a go. And obviously they know they'll get their money now.'

Looking back, Bob realised he had felt a very peculiar twinge of something like pleasure when Richard had begun to cry. It was just so unexpected, so unlike Richard, that it was like discovering Father Christmas does actually exist. Having spent his life a little in awe of this normally robust, insanely relaxed man, Bob felt touched to be there with him in his moment of crisis. He was privileged to be allowed to see it, let alone to help.

The next day Bob picked up Katie and cooked dinner for the three of them. She was tired and clingy, reassured that her father seemed to be the same person as before, but disturbed by the highly coloured bruises and the sore faces he made. That he felt pain was a strange and uncomfortable discovery for her, like finding what lay beneath a tortoise's shell. She hadn't thought adult men did and she was unhappily aware that now this had happened her days contained a new element.

After Katie went to bed they talked. Bob was insisting that he could add the full sum to his mortgage, lend Richard the money, and that Richard could then pay him back, in reasonable instalments, over time. Richard was reluctant, but ultimately agreed, for the sake of Katie. Her being in the house yesterday afternoon had frightened him more than anything before. It had made him feel like pissing his pants, like some eight-year-old. In charge of a five-year-old.

Richard said thank you, into the silence and knew he should go on, say more, but Bob just held up his hand and smiled. He looked a bit embarrassed too, although blustering like a mate, rather than absolving like a priest, might have been better.

Richard's pride was very badly hurt. He watched Bob, who was looking at his shoes, out of the corner of his eye, aware that he should be full of gratitude and affection. But sometimes Bob could really get on your nerves, so silent and neat and amiable, healthy brown and self-sufficient. A little Buddha in his own little semi-detached. Sometimes he was so infallible he was fucking alien. Richard was beginning to wonder whether he should have accepted Bob's offer, whether a kind debtor wasn't actually worse.

Into the silence of the sitting room Bob said, 'Will you let me see the agreements you signed?'

'Jesus. Do we have to? Can't we just talk about something else?'

'I know you don't really get what I do at work. You take the piss because you think I just check out kitchens for rats all day.'

Richard's head tilted back on to the sofa. 'Bob Shillabeer, International Rat-Catcher,' he said in a bored rather than funny voice.

Bob ignored him. 'I get people's licences to trade, in whatever their business is, taken away. I can get this shit closed down, if I have evidence.'

'I told you, I'm not going to go to the police.'

'You don't have to press charges. You just have to give me a statement and,' he began to speak quickly, as if a timer were about to go off, 'presuming they are acting outside the Consumer Credit Agreement in a number of ways, then we can hopefully get their licence revoked without even going to court, without even taking a civil action against them. They'll understand that you were too frightened to press charges.'

Richard, initially distracted by hearing Bob talk professional, was then riled at being described as frightened. 'I'm not fucking frightened, I'm just not stupid.'

'I know you're not, I'm just saying that's why you don't have to press charges with the police.'

'Well, either way if I end up in court, I'm going to get my head kicked in again.'

'A statement would almost certainly be enough, then you wouldn't have to go. It might take six months, at least. By which time this would have all blown over. He needn't know who gave the statement.'

There was silence.

'You think it's all right that he carries on doing that? Taking advantage of people, then beating the shit out of them when they can't fulfil their agreements?'

Richard shrugged. There were things to consider. He didn't like the idea of owing Bob something, of having to be grateful to him. This civil thing, though, Richard could tell he wanted it, and that it would get him some saintly feather in his cap. Richard sighed, as if he were about to say something with a certain assertion, then said, 'Whatever.' He felt tired and a bit sick, and sincerely doubted Bob's ability to make anything much happen.

A fortnight later Richard's debts were paid and he came into Bob's office. He made a statement and left convinced that it would come to nothing. After that Richard and Bob saw less and less of each other. Only meeting once a month for Richard to hand over the warm, greasy notes that went towards paying Bob's loan back.

Bob bought the Olympiad cream leather sofa, confused at his friend's distance, depressed by the depletion of his life each time he came home. The settee sat against the radiator, and as the autumn grew colder and the central heating came on, it began to fill the room with the smell of warm animal, the ultimate white elephant, too large for the space and slippery to sit on.

*

When Matthew and Julianna said goodbye, behind the packing sheds, they had held each other in the tightest of grips. Even though they would be seeing each other in a week's time, neither of them doubted the drama of the scene. She was leaving, just as planned, as if she were going to catch the coach from Victoria back to Budapest that afternoon. Instead she would wait for Matthew in the Earls Court youth hostel. Julianna felt the power of a woman in the midst of a romantic revelation.

So she was only fleetingly disturbed when Matthew took her face in his hands, and said, 'Whatever happens, wherever we end up, I'll always be thinking of you.' The tone struck her instinctively as wrong, but as the engine of the Land Rover started, out of sight, her mind skittered away from doubt into passion.

The car began to cook the concrete hot, thrumming as Roy waited for the two of them to disentangle themselves, somewhere hidden. They emerged, lips swollen, faces blotched, and Julianna waited maidenly as Matthew loaded her case into the boot. She felt every beat of the activity, this churning of the still, summer-worn air around them. During the season they had all settled into their separate strata, like packed layers of earth and clay. The permanence of the landscape and the farmhouse, the repetitiveness of their tasks, everything had begun to seem infinite to Julianna. As the unfit monster of a car made a shunting gear change and pulled off fast down the driveway, she felt the fresh wind on her face, and longed to be able to cry. Now that she and her shallow roots had been removed, all of them would settle back in on themselves, compacting down, once more, as if she'd never, ever been.

PART 2

1991–2

We were riding through frozen fields in a wagon at dawn.
A red wing rose in the darkness.

And suddenly a hare ran across the road.
One of us pointed to it with his hand.

That was long ago. Today neither of them is alive,
Not the hare, nor the man who made the gesture.

O my love, where are they, where are they going
The flash of hand, streak of movement, rustle of pebbles.
I ask not out of sorrow, but in wonder.

Czeslaw Milosz,
'Encounter', translated by Czeslaw Milosz
and Lillian Vallee

Chapter Eight

Mila had always begun the story of the day she met Julianna's grandfather with the same sentence: 'It was the tenth of September 1936, and I had a brand-new hat.' She would settle herself more comfortably, her palms flat on her lap, or when Julianna was young enough to put to bed before the sun had set, she would encase a single, light hand in hers. 'It was purple tweed, with the tiniest little black and white speckled feathers, and a velvet band. It was on a hunting theme, and I knew I looked fine when I'd stood in front of the mirror that morning.' Mila didn't say – or had chosen to forget – that she had also worn her highest heels to the Briggs and Brothers offices that day. At that stage in her life, high heels were the closest Mila had yet come to independence. She loved the enforced, impudent elegance of them. She felt as if she were walking down the road with her silk underwear on show.

'I had two friends at work. Doris and Rose,' she would continue. 'Of course I was called Millicent then – or Milly by my mother.' She'd lived with her parents and been glad every morning to step out from the still house-air into the phone-ringing, cigarette-smoking world of law and men and commerce. She and Doris and Rose spent much time discussing how and what their final escape from home might be. Although they all hankered for love – Rose with her boyfriend, still hankering for some indefinable other – they talked of jobs, of travelling. They talked of America, of colonies, and sea travel, and if they were at all cautious none of the three of them dared show it to each other.

Yet, in the end, a husband was the only way they knew to get moving out of Stratford-upon-Avon. There were young lads at the office who tried to woo them, so many of them that in Mila's memory they soon blended into one generically eager face, its hair slicked back like a seal. But those boys weren't the only men to be seen by Millicent, Doris and Rose. Their horizons were broadened by the fact that they lived in one of the world's better-known small towns. There were endless charabancs of tourists, American couples in tea shops, school parties of kids, even purple-black African men – all of them streaming in and out of Shakespeare's house. The house seemed to absorb them all. Millicent used to wonder at its tolerance. It was beyond ancient, a stalwart red-brown, myth-perfect house. It seemed to sag and bow happily into one new decade after the other, while all around the shops got rebuilt and painted, the cars got faster, and electrical items came on sale, noisily competing for interest with the livestock market.

Aged twenty-five, she and Doris and Rose hadn't admitted to needing to be rescued by men, but the facts were self-evident. They weren't the kind of girls who had the kind of education or the kind of careers that would allow them to go anywhere, other than into town, alone. They were from anxiously respectable families, mostly in trade. Not quite professional but a cut above the working class. The girls' days were busy, and they didn't yet know how much they relied on their mothers to cook, clean and care for them. They talked longingly of single girls' flats but they did not mend their own tights or cook their own food. They were more like their fathers than the helpful daughters that had been expected.

In a few years war would come and liberate Doris and Rose from marriage and spinsterhood, give them uniforms and status and RAF officers. But Millicent didn't wait for that and fell for a Hungarian instead.

She and János first saw each other late one night in September 1936. It was 10.30, and she and Doris were walking home from a meeting of the local choral society. Millicent noticed him and said to Doris that she thought it was clever to photograph Shakespeare's house at night, when it was silent and resting in the past. Reflections of lamp-light wavering in the leaded windows, as if candles still burnt inside. It was cold, and quiet, and all they could hear were Doris's steel-capped shoes scraping the cobbles (Doris's mother did it so they would last longer). There was something unnerving, though, about a man trying to take photos at night in an empty street. Neither of them had seen it done before and the magnesium flash, when it came, drained the world of all substance – the ever-reliable relic, the lustred shop fronts, the ironmongery of the street, their very legs and feet reduced to sudden monotone thinness. Then it was over, as abruptly as a cloud clearing from a full moon, leaving a spookish burn hovering before their eye-balls.

Shock had halted them, but they started walking again, quicker, Doris's shoes a cast-iron guarantee against silence and secrecy (one other reason to always cap your daughter's toes, perhaps). The photographer turned and watched them hurry past, a smile growing on his face. He lifted his hat – to show he was at least a gentlemanly predator – and Millicent turned to watch him as Doris hurried her, arm in arm, away from the embarrassment of her shoes and a single man.

Millicent twisted her neck to keep him in view, enjoying the way he watched them travel up the road. An unashamed

111

stare. Enjoying the very risky nature of coming across him alone. Later that night she wondered whether, if she'd been walking the streets (she swiftly, with high excitement, corrected the syntax of her thoughts; not walking the streets, but on her way home) alone, she might have dared to be drawn into conversation, whether they might have embraced beneath the lights of William Shakespeare's bedroom.

The next day, at lunchtime, he sat down next to her on a bench by the river. She was eating her sandwiches. He made her jump, and then when she recognised the hat and the camera, she blushed. There was an impertinence in the air; it was a rude, blustering, skirt-lifting, duck-quacking, early autumn day. There was a band playing somewhere, and the sound of applause.

'Have you ever been to Bonn?' the man said.

She thought, and then, after a delay that suggested a slight memory lapse, some shuffling of forgotten places, said, 'No.'

'Your river reminds me of the countryside around Bonn.' His voice was quite clear, but heavily accented, the words broken into a different shape. As if he were a creature suddenly given a voice and a box of words with no instructions.

She smiled politely, wanting him to talk more but too well-mannered to know what to say next, so saying nothing.

He was silent for a while. She couldn't look at him properly, but got the impression of a man of good height and sturdy build, hair a little long, messy even. Bright eyes, mobile mouth. An expressive sort of figure. A presence. The silence continued until she thought she might as well finish her sandwich, and began to chew resignedly. Then he spoke.

'Have you ever been to Budapest?'

She shook her head with annoyance; at that moment she was struggling with a soft slice of tomato, suspended between the bread and her lips.

'It's not so like Stratford.' He smiled, a little wickedly, and she looked away and wiped her mouth.

'Have you ever been to Luxor?' he said.

'Of course I haven't,' she said, unable to stop herself from laughing. Tumbling out of composure.

'No. Neither have I,' he said, then introduced himself.

He must have used that patter before, with young girls on park benches. Mila hadn't minded, though, because she knew what had made her different. The difference was that she wanted to go. Anywhere, everywhere. The remoter the better. She was impatient for it. You didn't always get that on a park bench. (The irony of ending up in a country she was never able to leave had not been lost on her. She'd frequently found it worth remarking on, past expectations being fresher than one might have thought.)

It wasn't a love affair like in the films, though, one predictable chord following another, harmony followed by requisite disharmony, on to the happy fragility of the closing note. It was awkward and full of uncertainty. But also of urgent excitement. Mila was greedy for her real life to begin and, importantly, she and János very, very badly wanted to explore each other's bodies. The fact that she was still a virgin when they married represented the triumph of her parents' wakefulness and the discomfort of a Midlands town in winter.

He was photographing the major historic sites of Europe for an Austro-Hungarian publisher. He had travelled through Germany, Austria, Switzerland and Belgium and was meant to move on to France in October. Spain in November. Italy in December. But he lingered, waiting, until, somehow, Milly assured him, it would suddenly seem proper to her parents for them to marry. No, she said sternly to his exasperated teasing, it wasn't that there was a correct number

113

of meetings, or a requisite time span; there was just a certain grace needed for her happiness on her wedding day. She would know when it came.

He wrote to his employers and blamed the British weather for his delay.

When the day finally came that he and Milly married it rained for seven solid hours and the banks of the River Avon burst. Serves you right for lying, said Milly, wife-ish. The fields where they'd walked were flooded and the trees they'd hidden beneath were shrunken and immersed. The drama of it silenced even János.

'I wept as we left for our honeymoon,' Mila would say to Julianna with an ear for the dramatics of it. 'We took the train to London, a taxi across the city, the boat train to Calais, then went on to Rouen. And the prospect of one cheap hotel, one foreign country after another – well, I couldn't help feeling as if the end of the world had come, and I had brought it on.'

Forty-eight hours after Matthew was meant to have arrived, a letter came for Julianna instead.

She'd been sitting in the same chair, looking out on to the street, watching for Matthew for two days. Compact with fear, of abandonment and humiliation. So on Monday, when one of the hostel staff shouted out her name, she jumped up, heart pounding, assuming he'd finally come. Then one of the Australian girls who ran the hostel with a haphazard bossiness handed her a letter instead. Her heart dipped but there was still room to think that everything could be salvaged, that the answer lay within. Then she saw that it was a letter from her father. Forwarded from the farm in Matthew's hand. She opened it, looking for a message from him, but found none.

A procession of breathtaking disappointments.

114

She ignored the two pages from her father and her eyes searched the envelope for a sign from Matthew. But she could find nothing. Not a word.

She knew now what was meant by a broken heart. She'd heard people talk of the condition before, heard Mila describe the long nights after János died, and hadn't known whether she would ever manage to reach that pitch of emotion. She'd been such an imperturbable child that she would never have believed that she could feel so furious and frightened. But now it turned out that words of passion could be confirming, not just aspirational. Her heart was broken and the clarity of the condition was some consolation.

She spent the rest of the day and the whole of the night lying under the duvet, shivering, broken to such a state that she felt only shock and a certain remove from what seemed to be her body, her abandonment, her life. There was no mystery to what had happened; he had simply decided he didn't want her with him. She wondered whether he had known that when he'd said goodbye.

She went out early the next morning, retraced her steps from a few days before and walked into Kensington Park as the gates were being unlocked. For that hour, a cool, quiet lawn of dogs and joggers, she felt a flat acceptance of the realities of her situation. This was the way it had gone. She was a small figure on a bench in an empty park. Unknown by anyone, left by her rescuer. She had assumed that later she would pack her belongings and head back to the coach station. Slowly rewind the looping length of her journey, back to an unimpressed, empty house, without Mila. To college in Baskó, to a recognisable future, surrounded by the same hills. But it occurred to her, sitting on the bench, that she would feel worse if she were sitting at the kitchen table

115

of her home. Just as insignificant and alone. But even mor
hopeless. Swallowed by the inevitable.

Here was at least somewhere else. Being in London ha
to mean something. Even if its scale frightened her. She ha
money, after all, and six weeks on her visa. Six weeks t
make something of this accidental independence and los
her fear. Instead of looking for a coach today she woul
busy herself trying to find cheap, temporary accommoda
tion. She left the park and wished Matthew could see he
in all her resolve. If she stayed in London there was afte
all a chance that he would see her suddenly, be struck b
his cruelty and mistakenness.

Now, two weeks later, sitting on the edge of her bed, Julianna
looked at the mauled envelope – her father's and Matthew'
handwriting meeting. She remembered her moments of des
peration, her phone calls to the farmhouse, with pain. Gerard
graciously deflecting her, 'I'm terribly sorry, he's gone
Gone to London. No, we have no number. No address. No
as yet.'

This room she now sat in, the one she also slept and
dressed and often ate in, was very cold. She had wrappe
herself in the duvet, a stiff rather than pliant and feather
one, making a shell of herself.

She had half an hour before she had to leave for the firs
shift of her second job. She'd been living in this room
sharing this house, in the East End of London, for a weel
now and she had found solace in exhaustion. It was an effec
tive distraction from panic.

She tried to follow the words of her father's letter, thinking
they would bring her calm, but she was finding them hard
to absorb. Her mind kept returning to the complex issue o
public transport.

Julianna had planned the route to the office she wa

cleaning that night but there were so many variables to buses that it was hard to know how long it would take to travel from Bromley-by-Bow to Notting Hill. She found the transport system terrifying in its multiple options and similar-sounding stops. She tried again. Focus helped to keep out the cold.

You must write and reassure me that everything is in order. I want to be reassured that this Matthew looks after you. I expect you to return to take up your university course. But even before then – if things are not going well – then it is always better to be at home. Always, always.

She put the letter down, irritated, remembering why she hadn't caught the first coach home after Matthew's desertion. She wasn't prepared to boost her father's belittling pessimism even further by admitting Matthew's abandonment.

Later, at work, she changed into her Vital Cleaners staff T-shirt and caught sight of herself in the full-length mirror. Her skin surprised her with its darkness; she'd almost forgotten how hot it had been. She considered her appearance with an unprecedented detachment and thought how young she looked. How, in this T-shirt, hair scraped into a pony-tail, she was made unremarkable. She clenched her fists. She could feel the sharp curves of her fingernails cutting in. It was reviving, the clarity and intimacy of the hurt.

She found her locker and struggled to open the door. It came unstuck suddenly, releasing a sour smell. Inside was a dented orange and a grey sock with purple stars on it. On the inside of the door was a flimsy, magazine-clipped picture of a long-haired man with tight trousers singing into a mike, a heavy-metal singer.

She wondered if it still belonged to someone, whether she'd been told the wrong locker. She worried about the sock. Should she just leave it there and put her stuff in?

Because together they didn't smell good. Tentatively she tried the locker to the right, then the one after that, but they were all tight shut.

She had a sudden awareness, one that halted her, all over again, of each locker. A tremendous sensitivity to the rows of closed metal boxes holding paltry, soiled examples of each individual. Julianna was learning this new landscape and its components quickly; the dirty surfaces and hard-fought items.

All over again, she gathered herself together and left the room.

She'd been told where to find the cleaning stores, and besieged by uncertainty at each detergent decision, she struggled to remember what was necessary. First she had to hoover, an action which seemed to have no noticeable effect on the felt-like carpet squares. Then she cleaned the mini-kitchen, washed up cracked mugs, chipped at an encrusted soap dish and swabbed at the exposed areas of desk. She wondered if she were ill, she found each and every empty seat so unnerving. Framed photos and half-eaten rolls of sweets. There were collections of battered black shoes under many of the desks, as if this place had been abandoned in haste, by people in need of their hands, not their possessions.

She could find no clue to the work that was done here.

They were allowed a fifteen-minute break in the staff room by the lockers, although Julianna later found out that they docked a whole half-hour from the pay. She sat opposite a silent black man who chain-smoked through the period. The supervisor, whose name Julianna couldn't quite catch, teased him in what she soon came to learn was a West Indian accent. Julianna liked the lilt of it, the rather camp theatricality it gave every sentence. 'You never eat or drink?' the supervisor asked him, and he shrugged, saying smoke filled him up better. Then suddenly he reached across the table and held out his large, warm, rough palm for Julianna to shake. 'You're a wide-eyed new girl,' he said. 'I am Amos. I am studying for a PhD in economics.' Then he settled back again and seemed to show no further desire to talk. Others arrived into the small staff room and poured themselves glasses of tap water. One small middle-aged woman took out a thermos flask from a bag, and the smell of sugar that came from her tea made Julianna feel envious. She wouldn't have thought she'd ever have found herself regarding a thermos as an item of covetable luxury. Another young woman sat next to Julianna. She was pale brown, perhaps Middle Eastern. (Julianna recognised she was guessing half the time. She wondered what they had been teaching her at school, ignoring all the subtly shaded people of the world.) She seemed disappointed to discover that Julianna was not studying, unable to understand why she was here. 'You have a husband here, perhaps,' she said after a while. Julianna shook her head, thinking once more that she would never have expected to wish that she had such things to boast of, an academic achievement, a husband, a thermos. It was hardly the stuff of *Dynasty*.

By the time she had finished cleaning her floor it was midnight and someone had turned off the lights in the locker room. Perhaps assuming everyone had finished, perhaps assuming no one could take that long to perform an unwatched job. She found the blackness frightening; there were twenty floors of this building, each one butted up to its glassy edges, ghosts of furniture sliding into the electric night. Miles of empty dark corridor.

*

She left the office fifteen minutes later, having been discovered in the dark and ballsed out by the supervisor for being slow. Julianna stood alone on a quiet, empty street. She looked left and right warily, street lamps shining on yellow and red road markings. A moonless orange light to the night. She was awash with pity – sadness not purely for herself. Then a car crossed at the junction to the right, then another, then more and more, faster and faster, showing her as London would again and again that it wasn't nearly so late as she thought, nor nearly so empty. It was only the traffic lights changing, only the imposed stop-start rhythm of this high-density living.

Her house, her home, her room. It looked better by night. Tall and understandable in the peace of two a.m. By day its red-brick grandeur was embarrassed by the noise and filth of the four-lane road. It was such an angry road, that running easily across it now felt illicit. Julianna climbed the stairs to bed, walked quietly along the corridor past the half-open door of Radmila's room. She did not wish to talk to her at this time in the night, when she would surely be even worse-tempered than during the day. Julianna had to get up in four hours. She would have to do this again for the next four nights. Then begin again one day later. She lay in bed in pyjamas and a jumper, beneath the sliding bulk of duvet, coat and blanket. Something was troubling her, beyond the ever-present lacking of Matthew. It was, she realised, the amount of distance she had travelled in a night, the amount she had seen and done, compared to her lack of witnesses. No one knew where she'd been.

Her room was at the back of the house and she slept fitfully, waking often, hearing the traffic thicken until it was light.

*

She'd found both the room and the cleaning job in the *Evening Standard*. Her day-time job she'd seen advertised in the dry-cleaner's window, on her way back from viewing the room. It was a young American woman at the hostel, called Kelly, who prefaced all her sentences with a 'You know what', who had told her about the *Evening Standard*. Julianna, who had gone through a fervently obedient period of pre-teen socialism and anti-Americanism, and had then been seduced by America, by shows with all the realism of her beloved *Dynasty*, was surprised to meet an American behaving so simply and generously. But it was indeed the New Yorker who had handed her the paper and pointed out the numerous boxed adverts for cleaning staff, waiting staff and labourers. Then it was the Vital Cleaning Services supervisor, Jamal, who had promised her work immediately and instructed her to be back the next day at four for an induction course, who had asked her if she also needed somewhere to live. Jamal seemed to be an all-purpose fixer. At the end of the induction he asked people who needed help with accommodation to come and see him. A crowd quickly formed around him. It was almost as if they were back at school – unhealthy, overgrown children slouching on the sidelines, in search of guidance in an impenetrable world. Julianna saw how much power this man's knowledge of lettings and wages and offices and shops gave him. He talked as if he were running a conspiracy, something designed to work against or under the rules. Not at all like one of her party-proper school teachers in substance, but every bit as officious in style.

Within a day the jovial Jamal had fixed her income and her rent. Not purely out of kindness, she discovered. She would be paid £2.50 an hour. She would have to give up a night for the induction course and then the first night of work for Vital would be unpaid, as it was deemed a trial session of employment. A £7 deposit was taken as security against her uniform. It would then take two weeks for her wages to be processed, as a cheque, which Jamal could ensure would be cashed, at a small charge. He would also, he explained separately, require ten per cent of her weekly rent as a payment for having found her the flat. The rent would be £40 a week. They would also require two weeks' rent up front, and two weeks as a deposit. Julianna, cushioned at this stage by her summer savings, accepted every instruction because she could afford it. But she wondered how some of the others in the room could. Frankly, they looked impoverished to her. 'My mother gave me her savings to come,' explained a boy who had been sitting next to her at the induction. 'I was promised a home and work by some Afghanis who met me at the bus station where I had to sleep. I gave them £150. They found me nothing. There is not so much money left. Enough, I hope. It took her thirty years to save. And I lost that much in five minutes.'

It wasn't until after they'd left the induction, ready to meet him at the flat the next morning, that she wondered if it was in fact Jamal's property, if he was the owner of the flats, and if it was therefore fair to pay him extra. But to be fair to herself (and someone had to be), what did she know of this world of bargaining? The slow entitled process towards the dreary Soviet housing of her home seemed simpler.

As with most of her schoolfriends, Julianna's period of dutiful socialism had not lasted long. They gritted their teeth, bent their backs to the rucksack and ploughed their way through a competitive, prize-obsessed education, and soon forgot their Young Pioneer, pre-teen disgust at the lazy licentiousness of the West. But perhaps some of the community in communism, the sense that you were part of an army of would-be heros, competing against a wider world, remained

122

in them. She had thought not – her parents had made their irritation at their social duties very clear. The attending of cultural circles, workers' days, children's days, the queuing outside shops, the sharing of luxuries, the pretending to belong. They had taught her to keep below attention's eye-level, avoid anything unusual, even children of single-parent families and clothes that were too fine. Chocolate that was too Western. After Nagy's proper burial, she had gathered in Baskó square with her family and her friends' families in celebration. The lights of the town hall, the old, high town houses, the training college, and, most beautifully, the baroque church, blazing full around them. Then they had all felt the cold light of a suspiciously familiar dawn. When asked, she would say in honesty, having seen the deprivations it could effect, that she was no longer interested in politics. Thank you. Communism was a nice idea, but not one that could ever work, not while human nature stayed the way it was.

Six weeks came and went. She watched the day when her visa expired come closer. She told herself that she could leave whenever she wanted, pack in five minutes. Be gone within ten. But no one had ever asked to see her visa anyway. The day passed. She couldn't leave now, now that she was just beginning to understand the layout of the city, the buses that would transport her. She'd paid the full month's rent. In short, she was paralysed in the present. Why leave when no one knew where she was anyway? Was she not paying her way? Doing jobs that no British person seemed to want to do? There seemed to be more than enough London to go round. The week passed and she still hadn't left. She watched her passivity with interest.

If she went home she would certainly never see Matthew again. It would be like handing him the city to roam in.

Sometimes she went into phone boxes and used Directory Enquiries to try to find an M. Woods in west London. The number of M. Woodses increased at a fascinating rate. When she first did it there were 257. Two months later there were 290. She didn't have time to call all of them.

The dry cleaner's where she worked during the day was forty minutes' walk from the house. She got up at six, to be there for half past seven, and was grateful to not have to catch buses to both jobs. She would walk up Farley Road, in the shadows of the high-walled Victorian factory, until one day skips and scaffolding arrived and she was forced to walk on the other side of the street. Only when signs began to advertise new executive apartments did she learn that this had once been a match factory.

This dense chunk of city, so full of different races, bore the stamp of many centuries of habitation. But the building work moved relentlessly on, as if it were keeping pace with Julianna's relentless above-ground travelling. She never went on the tube, it was too expensive.

In the distance a skyscraper was being built. That was the Docklands, she was told. A wasteland being transformed, the brand new facing the decrepit. 'It's going to be fantastic,' Jamal said. 'Like Manhattan,' he said. And Julianna tried to remember that she was witnessing the future as she walked towards her job as a needlewoman, a mender and alterer of clothes. She struggled to see it as she stepped up on to pavements where match-girls had once vomited poison in fluorescent puddles. She could see washing hanging from windows and milk kept on the ledge. Bearded Indian men in loose white outfits, surely designed for hotter climates, compromised by patterned jumpers and green anoraks, gossiping on street corners. Old women bent double, walking slowly round rubbish and broken glass, no different from old women in Poland, thought Julianna. Occasional white professionals, rushing out of estate agents, into the safety of cars, or standing, looking tired, smoking at the edges of cheap offices. Or at the gates to sprawling hospital sites – complicated signery, old Portakabins, ugly outcrops, as if the new illnesses just kept coming.

Walking down Straight Mile, through the opening market, past men who had been up since three, she dodged the trolleys of vegetable crates and metal trees swinging with handbags. Just one or two of them could be relied on to flip suddenly out of construction absorption at the sight of her, the one bare-headed, loose-haired young woman they'd seen by seven in the morning. The potato man liked to sing, a different tribute each morning, 'Foxy Lady', 'More Than a Woman', 'Lady in Red'. His neighbour swore at him, but she liked him; she thought he would have a big family and grandchildren and a good heart. It was nice to have a few people she saw enough of to imagine a home life.

Over the road from the potato stall the same young Asian shopkeeper watched her every day. Julianna didn't know where he came from. Radmila, who was from what had once been Yugoslavia, and was now Croatia, but called herself Serbian, said with a shrug that you could tell they were Bangladeshi by looking, just as it was obvious from Julianna's face that she came from Eastern Europe.

'Central, not Eastern,' Julianna had replied.

'You think it makes any difference here?' she had snorted. 'If it is so central, then go home again.'

And Julianna spent her first months in London not entirely sure why she hadn't. The fact that it wasn't her inside looking out as the coaches hammered down to the tunnel under the Thames was a source of constant surprise. She wondered if she fooled them into thinking she was at home here.

Some mornings she bought a few things in the market

on her way to work, carrying bruised fruit and veg, cheap tins or discounted soap in thin, striped plastic bags. Her handbag was cheap and collapsing too. She frequently resewed its fake leather at the machine, examining its straining straps, terminally useless, bound to end up like the peculiar tat that littered the streets of the East End. A shoe here. A belt there. A toasted sandwich maker on the corner.

She'd become hyper-aware of the dirt on the streets. The dull greasiness of door fronts and handles. Rotting market produce fetid even in the autumn air. Rain falling on the entrails of meaty rubbish.

She would walk on through Victoria Park, a great philanthropic expanse of green that exhilarated and frightened her with its morning emptiness. Then finally to Homerton where her situation awaited her – the formica table, the sewing machine, the mound of fabrics.

Someone in the late seventies or early eighties had obviously spent a bit of money on opening up the dry cleaner's. It was called Laundry Heaven and the sign above the door had a red rose. All the fittings were red, there was a good strong racking system and the industrial washing machines and pressers out the back were old but sturdy. The owner, his two daughters, one son, wife and mother lived in the flat above, which was accessible through a door at the back of the shop.

The first thing that struck you on entering were the many piles of dirty clothes. Clean clothes just don't collapse in the same soft, defeated way. There was such a proliferation of hillocks that they seemed quite organic. Julianna soon took the dirt for granted – the look of clothes worn hard and over-long, the way dirt collects in a regular rippling pattern on a shirt cuff. The stiffness of a blouse's armpit. The coarsened texture of a stain on silk. Spreading darknesses on crotches and ties, snail trails down special-occasion lapels.

The floor too was decorated with accident and detritus – spilt pins, plastic tags, loo-roll pulled, trailing, from pockets. Below that lay something more adhesive, ten years of unwashed floor. Zahib, the owner's seven-year-old son, who hung about the shop before and after school, wore scruffy Nikes which made schtick-schtick noises on the lino. Above him, on the till, the machines and balanced on the shaving-foam pinnacle of a duvet sat little foil ashtrays full of stubby bent butts. The ash lifting and falling each time the door was opened on to the road outside.

She could have swapped her jobs twenty times over, there were jobs everywhere, but the pay wouldn't have been much different. Vital Cleaning Services were always asking her to recruit people, and the teams were permanently short two or three bodies. She had seven pounds a week left over after her rent, bills and food. She still had her savings, but having subtracted the deposit for the room, she was certain she would not need to touch them again. The money was her escape route, it meant that any time she had to, she could go.

After three months of doing two jobs, Julianna was beyond tiredness. She was living and working illegally, yet she didn't have the energy for a decision. Presenting herself for accommodation and employment in front of strangers was, it turned out, not as draining as the thought of returning home. She rarely got into her bed before 1.30 a.m. and often woke in her sleep, as if the strength that made her alert during the day, and her sleep heavy at night, had gone. She lay thinking of Matthew, wondering at how she had been left by someone she had once been going to leave. Sometimes she was still awake by the time the road began to get noisy, trucks screaming to a halt like wounded dinosaurs.

Bus stops were where she felt unhappiest. Plastic wind shelters clinging on to the edge of the pavement. Her and the rest of the publicly untransported queue being deafened by long lorries. As it got colder and the mornings darker, she imagined going home, back to the familiar, but the fear of what might happen as she left the country only added to her paralysis. She wasn't sure what they might do, because by that stage she'd be leaving, but still, she was frightened of the consequences.

Julianna knew she could work as hard as this in Budapest, and feel less alone as she did it. She had told her father that she was simply taking an extra year out of college. He had written again, grumpily acquiescing. As if there was anything else he could do. It might yet be true, she could go back to college, study and become something useful. But right now she was more frightened of being stuck there than of being here. At least here she didn't know what might happen. Her future in Kisrét was all too predictable. A job teaching in Baskó, mealtimes in small kitchens, smoking in cafés, the same collection of frequently inebriated men, sniping with Éva, trying to provoke Tamás out of puberty into conversation, always wondering whether she would feel happier somewhere else.

Julianna was too proud to go home until she had a better story to tell. In the meantime she was harming no one; feeding herself by doing jobs that somebody needed to do, and paying rent for a room that she'd only felt able to sleep in after having scrubbed its floors and walls until the water ran clear.

Through the winter of 1990 and 1991 Vital moved her from office to office. Then, in March, the week after her twenty-first birthday, which she celebrated by getting drunk under Radmila's instruction at a stranger's house in Finsbury Park, she was moved to a restaurant called East Coast. The day she first entered the lobby of the tower and rose up to the twentieth floor, she felt, for the first time, as if being here, in this city, might actually be the achievement she sought. The restaurant was brand new, a glassy, harsh white sign of a new nineties aesthetic. Here Julianna glimpsed the insides of a different London, decorated and scented as it was. She found it so beautiful that she didn't even associate it with money. It seemed altruistic in its loveliness. She was surprised that they had even allowed such a motley collection as the Vital cleaners through its elevator doors. That early-morning shift she cleaned with a fanaticism, as if this were a temple and her passage and purity depended on its cleanliness. She enjoyed it. The manageress noticed her polishing the fixtures with extraordinary vigour and the next day requested that the tall dark girl be a permanent member of Vital's team.

At night the diners left deposits beyond the obvious in the white marble lavatories. Small stains that were almost indelible, a smudged whorl on a mirror, a small slick of skin oil on a wall, a black scrape on the skirting. Soft shards of toilet paper and small dark hairs sinking in the air of the Ladies', cigarette ash rising in the heat of the bar, collecting on the ledge above the windows, and in the morning a concentrated Julianna damped down the stale, debauched air with bottles of Flash steaming water.

She wore gloves when doing the toilets, when on her hands and knees retrieving Tampax tubes from corners, but she had lost her sensitivity to the detritus of human waste many months ago. At first she had wondered how a woman could manage to spread her urine so far from the bowl, or how flecks of something congealed could find their way on to the walls, but the forensics of cleaning soon palled.

She looked paler and thinner than when she had arrived in London, six months ago. Her hair had grown, and not in any particular shape. The two crescents that ran from the upper inside corner of her eyes then down into the dark smudges of sleeplessness below, were anaemically white. Yet she looked alert again, her eyes more rapid, her movements more certain, as if somewhere in the last few weeks she had found an ambition.

After finishing the Ladies', she worked her way through the reception, cloakroom and offices. Most of the arriving kitchen staff ignored her, looked around her swift-moving, silhouetted figure to the river view, always glinting with low promise beyond. But not all of them. Those who had spoken to her were surprised at the accuracy and subtlety of her accented English. They looked, once that was established, with new interest at her thick-browed, round yet hollowed face. But she didn't offer much, or ask anything more and nearly everyone gave up sooner or later. Since she could speak English well enough, her reticence obviously meant she was either dull or shy. Or illegal, and there was nothing new about that in a restaurant in London, but certainly illegal enough to be scared. There was no point in pushing, in investing friendship or flirtation with her, as she would undoubtedly be gone soon.

But the staff of East Coast were wrong on both counts. Julianna was both hard-working and bright, and the manageress, who was grateful for her lack of attitude, had plans for her.

Secondly Julianna wasn't scared. Illegal, yes, but scared, no. Not any more. Back home in Kisrét, it might have taken her thirty years to learn what she'd had to these last six months. And even then she wouldn't have been able to experience that which she knew. She would have accumulated wisdom the small-town way, by learning of what happens to others, sagacity meaning that no story surprises you any more, not that you've lived any of them. Julianna was twenty-one, and she had lost herself to adult life overnight. Within the space of six months she had encountered every construction of living, every desperation and aspiration under England's indifferent sun.

Julianna wasn't scared, she was concentrating.

The night Julianna was offered the job of cloakroom girl for the evening shifts, she realised that her savings had been stolen from her room. She hadn't checked on them for a week or so and she took her travel bag down from the top of the doorless wardrobe in the corner of her room. Inside the sour vinyl cavity there was a pair of pink socks and inside that she kept the roll of cash. She felt complete disbelief at the money's disappearance. She thought that she must simply have changed the hiding place and then forgotten, because who could possibly have found their way past her locked door, to a pair of socks?

She walked into the kitchen, at the end of the corridor. Around the table sat her flatmates Radmila, Dragan and Josif. Leaning against the kitchen surface were three other men – who she recognised as Josif and Radmila's friends. They all turned to look at her. She stood speechless on the edge of the small, fogged room. They had been sitting in there, smoking all night. There was no other room to settle in beyond the bedrooms. The television was perched on the sideboard near the sink, the sound on low.

Julianna looked at them and realised any one of them could have taken her money and they would never tell her. It excluded her, the way they had formed a solid mass sometime before her arrival, the way they treated her like an ignorant child, their aura of tragedy and their enforced stagnancy. They weren't able to work, since they were all three waiting to be granted asylum, and so there was never a time when Julianna didn't come home and one of them was there.

She walked out as Radmila said, 'Here, sit here, here's a chair.' Julianna held the door shut behind her and looked down the stairs, at the patterned carpet, which collected infills of dirt at the base of each step, at the mustard walls and old banisters, rods missing at intervals. There was no front door to the flat; they simply shared a floor, and since everyone was at home, all the bedroom doors were ajar. She walked into Radmila's room. The air smelt stale and her bed was covered in papers. She looked at the chest of drawers, at the deodorant, the dirty hairbrush. A hairclip, a lipstick, all of which surprised Julianna; she had never seen Radmila in any way adorned. Julianna was intimidated by her but tried to hide it. A little brick of grey eyeshadow had almost been used up; what remained was shiny and hard. There was a photo propped up, and Julianna picked it up. A family around a table. Julianna recognised Radmila, one of three long-haired girls, all staggered on the verge of becoming young women, like bathers queuing to dive. There was a middle-aged man and woman and a bald-headed old man, in the centre of the table, raising a glass, a cake in front of him, with the broadest smile of all.

One sister was dead. Julianna knew this. Radmila had told her the day Julianna moved in. She hadn't known what to say. 'How?' she'd said, and Radmila had looked at her with genuine surprise. 'Do you mean to say why? Or actually how? Because I don't think you want to know the how,' she'd said before going on to tell her, just exactly, her eyes locked hard to Julianna's.

Julianna walked out of Radmila's room quickly. One of those sisters was no longer alive and it seemed indecent not to know which one. As she closed her bedroom door someone else could be heard climbing the stairs. Another friend of Radmila's emerged at the top, out of breath, and he nodded at Julianna then entered the kitchen.

Julianna sat on the bed. She could have been in the bathroom when they took her money. It could have been anyone. So many people passed through. Could it even have been one of her flatmates? And where else would you start looking for money but in a bag?

She was ashamed to go and talk to them of money. Radmila would look at her with that mixture of pity and anger, at her ignorance and her purity. ('They shot her after raping her,' Radmila had said. 'Her husband was one of the rebels of Knin. They took retaliation on her instead. They said they shot her in self-defence. But she'd always refused to hold a gun. My family, they have stayed, they are barricaded into their house. They say they are part of Krajina. But myself, when I find "Chetnik" written on my door, this word is a Nazi word, this is when I decide to leave.')

Julianna's savings had been her secret, her prize. A mark of her ambition, and she thought it best not to talk to Radmila of things like ambition. Radmila could not possibly have anything left for ambition of her own, thought Julianna. She was so glassy-hard that Julianna could not imagine what went on in her head. It frightened her to try.

She sat on her bed and felt the distance between her and everything else. Without her savings it would be harder to ever find her way home. She felt the distance between her and Radmila, their own distances between their homes. The absences in their distant villages. The distance between her and the English car drivers on the road outside, between the small height of her flat and the tower of commerce that she could see breaking through the sky. She felt as if she were in the midst of a cyclone of irreconcilables – survival and money, love and family. She felt herself sitting very still at its heart, as if someone had once told her that the best thing

133

to do at the sign of a storm is to curl up somewhere small and hidden and hold your plans close to your heart.

What she had been planning, to move up from the lowest rung of employment and find a flat with a front door, was now dependent on making a success of her new job. The next evening she travelled to East Coast (the kind of restaurant which Matthew might perhaps aspire to), to her proper, public job, with a tight feeling in her stomach. This was a rope dangled into a pit and she knew she had to use it to haul herself out.

She had set off too early and so stopped on Waterloo Bridge to look at the river. The scene was alive with a polyphony of sounds and textures. The light caught the river's choppy dips with white flashes, the water flowed beneath, in shadow, a black rippling slick. Bathtime boats made their way downriver in a froth of importance, two police cars crossed a far bridge, their blue lights playing quick like fireflies. And the traffic never ceased. The incessant movement meant she was ignored. The loss of her money had reduced her, made her utterly dependent, and for this reason, she handed herself over fully to the city (a construction with a great many enclosures for the small).

Chapter Nine

It was a cold Tuesday night in October, thirteen months after she'd left Westington, and Julianna sat neatly, anticipatory, on her stool, waiting for the restaurant's first customers of the night to arrive.

The cloakroom was a small space, and, however she felt about herself, she wasn't a little woman. After bashing her funny bone against the wooden flap, her hip against the door frame once too often, she had learnt to keep her movements minimal. She was reading a book one of the customers had left behind. It was good to read. She was aware her English wasn't improving at anything like the rate it had when she'd first arrived at Woods Farm. Most of her friends spoke worse English than her. Her best conversations in English were held with Zahib, the young son of the owner of Laundry Heaven.

The first dinner guests began to arrive at 6.15. They were called the 'Pre-theatres'. After this they would go and watch plays in the grey block by the river that looked like an old piece of Soviet delusion. Others would then come late, after a show, from the rubbish and red lights of the West End, in a cab, from one stage set to another. She liked to be ultra-polite, but in a different way on different nights. She changed the way she did her hair each night and it would make a difference in the liberties she would allow herself. If her hair was loose she found herself more demure. If it were tied back into a tight ponytail she was a little brighter, bolder in movement and voice. They were the minutest of adjustments, but her cloakroom was the smallest of environments. And with no one to go home to, even the slightest of smiles, the smallest coquettish flick of a wrist, was daring. She sat and watched them come and go, smelt their coats and read their labels, peered into their shopping bags – the tissue-wrapped shapes mysterious. East Coast was a stage set, so unlike the world she saw outside that the noticeably rich seemed caricatures, and they impinged on her imagination much less than unconfident guests. She watched these unlikely couples more carefully. They were unnerved at first by the sharply styled reception, but would shed their skins when warmed by her gentleness. Their coats were thinner, made out of synthetics, their hair and skin less glossy, and they were visibly worried by the issue of her tip. She had begun to feel very protective towards the uncomfortable.

The book she was reading this evening was as mystifying as the pop lyrics Zahib tried to teach her. A woman called Lydia seemed to be worrying about her faith and seeing a lot of the local vicar. The vicar, who had a twinkle in his eye, which baffled Julianna, told Lydia that her husband Roger was depressed. Julianna wasn't surprised. She shut the book. It was quiet tonight. Tuesdays often were; the restaurant, and the whole of the city, picked up speed on Wednesday, rolling quickly towards the weekend, and then out again on Monday with a sore head.

She couldn't see the windows from here, peculiarly, since there were so many of them in East Coast. Its shiny white floor was an acoustic disaster, but the floor-to-ceiling windows gave expansive views north and south. So expansive that many of London's concrete mistakes were revealed, many more than one might have otherwise known. Julianna's cloakroom was off the walkway from the lifts to the reception desk. She could tell how hard it was raining tonight by the saturated coats and dripping umbrellas as the guests came in. The water began to run up her forearms into the crook of her elbow, rubbing her skin red where her sleeves were rolled up threefold. Puddles began to collect on the floor and it was a struggle to stop the bottoms of the leather shoulder bags, brief-cases and paper shopping bags from getting damp. She began to stack everything on the upper racks, and it was while bending down that she heard a cough behind her, at the door.

'Hello. Nice view,' said a small man. He had a red nose and a moustache.

Julianna held out her hand to take his coat. The talkative older men made her wary these days. They assumed she was paid to flirt, and she was very rarely inclined to do so. The evening guests were mostly too old to be attractive, but occasionally she saw younger men in suits and ties so immaculate and angular that their young flesh was rubbed red at the neck. Just a few of them had a reckless enough smile to suggest they could have made friends.

This kind of man, though, unnerved her – with his clammy fingers that enclosed hers as she held out his tag – as if she were colluding in some fantasy with him.

'Bet you get bored in there?' he said, leaning over, getting his fill of her figure.

She said nothing, and he saw her disapproval and said, with the sudden hatred of the drunk, 'Well, aren't you a stuck-up bitch of a thing? Don't they pay you to fucking smile?' then pushed himself away. She sat down on her stool, shocked by his words, and, trying to compose herself, closed her eyes.

*

Jack Harvey, although six foot, with a tendency to heft, was a light-footed man. He had a table booked for seven p.m., where he and his financial director were meeting an American who ran a financial services company in Chicago, the Stateside equivalent of Jack's own. He was running late but his walk was still deliberate and quiet. He moved down the white corridor, towards Julianna's inset black cloakroom, designed to have the tantalising contrast of a boudoir off a stately landing. Julianna's eyes were still closed as he arrived in front of the cloakroom. With his usual contained haste he shrugged out of his raincoat, not thinking of which individual might be here, in the dark cubby hole, handling his goods today. He slung the raincoat over his arm, tweaked at his tie and looked up to see – with that strange trick which freezes time and makes the opening of a butterfly's wings a beautiful, considered stretch – Julianna, eyes closed, feeling the damp enclosure of her cloakroom. Her profile was of such clean lines. A young woman in a disappointed pose, a down-sliding mouth and three distinct, sculpted points – her chin, her lips, her nose. Had he never noticed the exactness of a woman's profile before?

Then, quickly, after the longest time, with a smooth switch of her neck, she turned to face him, eyes wide and unblinking. A face of unusual clarity. As if it were the first unspoilt face he'd seen in months, the first unfudged by powder or professional politeness. It wasn't beauty, or anything so qualified, that struck him, he wasn't given to aesthetic judgements; rather the surprise of a pure presence, here in the lacquered insides of a wardrobe.

She stood up, unnerved at having been caught unawares, tears threatening, and he was able to look directly at her face, at the oval in which the brown pupils fluctuated, the swathe of pale, silvery skin, fanning out from the inner corner of her eyes, the delta that begins the cheekbone's swell.

She was grateful that this was a more patient, less drunk man, and her face broke into a warmth and amusement, as if he'd seen something adult that he shouldn't. Her hand was reached out, a large bony hand, to take his coat, a polite gesture of demand, as composed as a marble Grace, one finger stretched further out from the stepping curl of the others, as if she were intending nothing but the drawing of attention to her form.

With the slightest of nods, an encouragement to give her his coat and leave her behind, she invited him back to real time. He became aware again of himself, his name, his responsibilities and the presence of people, queuing, undressing behind him.

He handed over his overcoat and walked away.

Later on, as he was struggling through his starter (this place always fucked with his appetite), he discovered a cloakroom tag had been placed, silently, at his elbow. He looked behind him, expecting to see the girl walking away, but there was nothing, just that same hard, shining tunnel of wall and floor. It seemed unlikely that she could have been and gone without him noticing.

Julianna sat waiting (what else?). She examined her fingernails. They were dirty. She would have liked to go to the toilet and dig her nails into the soap, extract the half-moons of dirt on to the hard, scented white squares. She was aware of her grubbiness all the time. If she looked closely in the mirror she could see specks of black all over her pale skin. When she rubbed her face they smudged, leaving shooting soot trails across her cheeks. She'd developed red patches on her back and her belly. She wasn't sure what they were, but her stomach now resembled nothing more than a map of the world. Each fungal patch on her skin (the result of too many damp towels and sheets) had the crenellated outline of a coast. Her clothes smelt sour too, from drying too slow, too close together, hung off table edges, weak radiators and chairs. She could have handled the leering sexual comments better if she hadn't felt so uselessly unappealing. The warty man had disturbed her, dented her charming evening carapace. That man afterwards who had found her nearly crying must have caught her sadness, but *he* had not played with it. He'd said nothing and let her compose herself. She was grateful.

All evening long she waited for the kind tall man to come back with the tag she'd delivered. For after all there wasn't much else to do. Manual jobs leave plenty of time for the brain to meander, examining past struggles, imagining future victories. She said to herself that she wanted to thank him and she was happy to wait for him because that was what she was paid to do, but she was so bored, and he had done such an unusual thing, standing waiting for her to open her eyes, that it was not hard to turn it into an adventure.

Her grandmother had been a great one for signs: birds arriving early, peach sunsets, a politician's birthmark. Everything meant something. She had told Julianna that one evening in Baskó in 1956, after she had just buried Julianna's grandfather, she had turned a corner and seen a woman playing a harp in a window – obviously practising. But, equally obviously, sent as a message from János, with a reliably kitsch sense of humour. To still have the humour for jokes when you'd been killed in the 1956 revolution (in the 'events', as the old women of Kisrét would say with a certain air of mystery) and for Mila to still have the humour to receive those jokes had struck Julianna as miraculous.

Jack Harvey and his three guests stayed at their table until

10.15, whereupon they stood, replaced their suit jackets, hitched their uncomfortable waistbands and felt the three wines (and brandy) in their legs. The change of altitude sobered them a little and they hushed as they crossed the restaurant. The tables were mostly cleared and a few waiters leaned, like potted bamboo, in corners. But back in the corridor Jack's colleague remembered a joke and they burst into Julianna's sightline in an eruption of laughter.

They made her jump – after all that anticipation! She fumbled with their tickets and bags, shy of him. He was turned away and she had to say, 'Your coat' above the other men's snorting and shifting. He turned and took the long coat from her hands, and as she handed it over she smiled at him and said, 'Thank you.'

He had been prepared this time, and should have just looked away, ignored the sign. But her smile caught him and he couldn't but receive her blessing. And he had so rarely, if ever, been blessed by a woman that the effect was more religious than pleasant.

He felt a drunken escalation, a desire to press his face to her breast, where her white shirt was unbuttoned to a modest level, but took his coat and walked out instead. None of them left a tip.

Her stepmother had written, with the last photo of her grandmother, who sat looking vacant in sagging tights, odd shoes and two scarves. Julianna had a sudden, unexpected flashback to the way her own mother had tied scarves very tight around her neck, as if she were a leaky package and the scarf were a piece of string.

In the photo Mila looked as if she'd caught her reflection in the mirror and taken flight from her body in shame some hours ago. Julianna did not appreciate the picture but felt that it would do something sad to Mila's soul if she were to leave it floating on top of the full bin. She put it in with her underwear.

Her stepmother wanted to know how her studies were going, whether she was eating properly and making friends. Julianna's father had lost his job, she wrote; in fact many people were losing their jobs. Everything felt uncertain, she wrote, and people seemed to have even less money than ever before. It was good, she wrote, to think of Julianna making a new life in a country where there was a little more to go round. Whatever, she wrote in capitals, whatever happened, Julianna was not to consider sending them spare money home. What spare money? thought Julianna. Irritated by the flimsy hint, she folded the letter away.

Not yet, she thought to herself, I've nothing yet. What could you think I have for you yet? She wished her father would write again instead. If she'd seen him she might have told him the truth about her life in London. She'd have been able to handle his censure in a way that she could not have borne Mila's. Even though she was no longer alive, Julianna feared her grandmother's disapproval. She knew Mila would have thought her granddaughter's existence no better than a labourer's. Having had to fight to do nothing more and nothing less than survive over the last fifty years, Mila had earned her right to hypocrisy. Julianna knew that more was expected of her. History's poor luck had fallen on Mila, whereas Julianna felt she now had nothing worse to blame for her tired, cheap life than the chance of freedom and money itself. Nor did she have a sweet story of love to justify the freezing flat she lived in. Only Matthew's betrayal, which still humiliated her if she kept still long enough for it to catch up.

Julianna had too much future in her head, not enough experience of how to effect change in its unravelling by herself. All that she carried with her at the moment, her only luxury, was an increasing certainty that she could look after herself and that something might yet happen. Before she'd come to Britain she'd worried that nothing ever would. She smiled like an old timer at the memory of her anxiety. Just sometimes, when the sun shone, or she got lucky and could nudge her commute on to a beautiful route, she felt excited.

'Is a shit job, you know. They give you no money, they work you too hard, the chef, he's a prick, the head waiter is mad. He is . . .' Gianni thought for a moment, looked at Julianna, 'you know . . . a . . . how d'you say?'

Julianna shook her head. She wished he wouldn't always come and lean into the cloakroom, over the shelf. He smelt strong, of aftershave and rank kitchens. The smell of dying food couldn't be avoided even in a place as modern as this. The kitchen air was always infected by bin bags farting foul smells. Strangely, what with there being so many windows, only a few could be opened.

'He is a homo!' Gianni said with a eureka gesture.

'Oh,' said Julianna and sighed.

'You are tired,' he said, pouting a little. 'You need some holiday. We should go to Leicester Square.'

'Why?'

'To walk round, to see the sights. Then we go back to Newington, where I have a friend in a little bar, where they give me a lot of free alcohol.'

Julianna did the same sweet declining that women seem to learn in school. A shake of the head, a gentle emphasis, patronage – as if friendship will salve. They are the only ones who come enhanced out of such an exchange. But Gianni was a pro, and left with a wink. 'You lose,' he said. 'You lose a good time.'

Julianna had not been kissed since Matthew had said goodbye and she had no urge to be touched by anyone. No one had tried very hard to get beyond her force field of reserve and caution. She saw London through a filter of him too often. Earls Court was where she had stayed when waiting for him. Ealing was where he might be. This was a place he might like, and that, he might not . . .

It was a slow night so she read her new book. She'd finished the story of Lydia and the vicar. This one was a little denser and the language older, and harder for her to understand. They sold old paperbacks cheaply in the charity shop by the bus stop. It was a charity shop for animals, which puzzled Julianna. She had an image of a cat counting out money. A dog at the bank. The soft orange paperback smelt like old banknotes, and advertised itself on the back as a classic of romantic literature. She'd seen a film of it once. In black and white. She had no idea it was a book by a woman, and found it hard to believe it was the same story. She was ten pages in when Jack and his guests arrived.

Julianna, having discovered it was indeed the same *Frankenstein*, was engrossed and once again failed to notice Jack Harvey's arrival at her counter.

'Excuse me,' he said, quite gently.

She started, stood up, tucking away a strand of hair, straightening her skirt. Then she recognised him as the man she had liked weeks before and blushed. He was not so old as she remembered, forty perhaps. He had a serious face.

She went through her usual routine, but her movements seemed exaggerated to her own eyes, her hands far away, her clasp of the coat clumsy, her stretch for the coat hanger overdone, her rip of the cloakroom ticket fumbled.

She didn't think – you don't, not right in the middle of an exchange, not unless you can take hold of it and slow it down.

Instead she found herself saying, 'It is nice to see you

144

again,' with such clarity that she had to quickly sit down again, taken aback by her own effrontery.

Two hours and a strategy decision later, he arrived at Julianna's door to collect his coat. They smiled at each other and she took his ticket, but without bothering to look at the number took his coat, one amongst many grey overcoats, from its hanger.

He took the coat and smiled some more and didn't know what to do. He wanted to talk to her. Find out her name. But Derek, his business manager, stood beside him, shuffling, and the maître d' was holding the door for them at the end of the corridor. He took out his wallet and pulled out the largest note he could find and left it on the small pewter saucer for tips. She looked down and then when she saw the fifty-pound note stopped smiling, her fingers fanned flat on the edge of the wooden flap, thumbs below, a capable, ready stance.

'You must not leave this,' she said, 'Please. It is too much.' Her accent, Polish or something, gave a heavy emphasis to each word, but was also a little sibilant. A touch of the East.

'Don't be silly,' he said. 'Take it.'

'No, I don't think I can . . .'

He picked it up and, from the awkwardness, with no fore-thought or preparation, or even awareness that that was what he wanted, he said, 'Then may I take you out for a drink one day?'

There was a second's pause, then she said, 'Yes' quickly, as if he might change his mind. Then, sounding helpful, as if every offer were about employment, 'I have Sunday and Monday evenings free.'

He nodded, said, 'Fine,' and then walked right off. He gave the note to the maître d' for the staff, and reached the lift with a rush of energy, untouched even by Derek calling him a flash git.

To be honest, it seemed unlikely that he would ring a restaurant and ask for the cloakroom girl and reach her, in her cubby hole. But he liked having asked, having shocked her. It was up to him after all . . . Entirely up to him. She was a stranger, someone who didn't even know his name. She would be waiting and he could call.

Chapter Ten

ack rang Julianna exactly ten days after he'd asked her for
a drink. She sounded tentative, as if she didn't often use the
telephone. He felt a surge of heroism, for finding her,
reaching her, the young woman he'd discovered mutely coat-
sitting.

He suggested a drink on her next Monday off, and that
they meet in a bar in Covent Garden. There was an avun-
cular tone to his voice (was he taking her for tea?). She
murmured an incomprehensible response. He put down the
phone uncertain as to whether she'd understood anything or
indeed agreed to it. Impossible for him to have slowed down
to check. A different woman, yes, but the same him.

Four nights later she arrived at the bar in a tight skirt and
too much make-up. She walked towards him, while tugging
at her skirt. She was nervous, and she was reasonably tall,
like him. Those were the things that struck him the most.
He should have been pleased at the effort she'd made, but
he was upset. He remembered her differently. She had looked
better in her white work shirt, he thought. There she had
seemed purer and more open. Perversely, less stamped by
circumstance.

People's voices buzzed, and the dangerous chink and
clatter of glass notched the energy within the bar higher. He
was both struck by her and embarrassed by her. She lacked
the confident slouch, the sheeny wealth of the other women

in here. She looked more like the toilet attendant than his date. But then he noticed an expensively dressed man staring at her. This man, an adult, not a kid, was sitting on one of the stupid low red pouffes, his ankles and thin socks rudely revealed (we are not Bedouins, thought Jack, why must they make us always pay so much to look stupid?). The man watched Julianna cross the room with open admiration and Jack felt encouraged.

He stood up to greet her. She looked as surprised to find herself here as he was. Obviously there was no kissing to be done. They didn't know each other. She was a cloakroom girl. He was buying the drinks.

'What would you like?' and he gestured at the bar, which was mirrored and back-lit, an electric syrup wonderland. She didn't know so she asked him what he was drinking and he ordered her a gin and tonic.

They stood at the bar talking about where she lived. It was not a part of London he knew. He wished she hadn't told him about the day job at the dry cleaner's. It toppled the imbalance too far. But she was clearly sensitive to social awkwardness, as she immediately turned the conversation off her life and on to his. Which embarrassed him much less, because work was one of the few things he did know how to talk about. Yet it was more difficult being a prince to a showgirl than you might have imagined.

'I'm a businessman. It's very dull if you don't understand it.'

'Do you think I would not understand?'

Which was exactly what he'd meant.

'No, not at all. Just not everyone is interested in the financial industry.' There was a pause. 'I like it, though.'

She nodded.

Then, without knowing why, in a disgraceful escape of

148

honesty, an explanation which he normally kept wrapped in humour, 'It's made me very rich.'

Her head jolted at the vulgarity of him. This was not a sentence she'd ever heard said before, not in reality. He looked a little shocked himself, a surprised half-smile on his face. She thought him distasteful but she did not want to seem immature, so she said, 'How very rich?' her eyebrows raised, perhaps enjoying the boldness of her play.

'Rich enough,' he said, not knowing how to explain.

She didn't know what to say either. He swirled his drink with the plastic stick and then took it out and dropped it on to the bar, whereupon it rolled off on to his shoe. He wiped his shoe against the back of his trouser leg. She could tell from his confusion, from his lack of calm, that this conversation was not planned, or practised, or easy for him. She sensed the mistake in the air and felt for him suddenly. A fleeting insight into the particular embarrassments of being male and the brinkmanship it required.

'Do your family live in London?' she asked, beginning again with the subjects she understood.

'No, no,' he said, fiddling, looking around. 'I grew up in a town called Horden, near the south coast. Do you know it? Probably not. Best not.'

'I know it. I stayed on a farm near Westington last year.'

He was surprised, but did not wish to discuss his childhood. So said nothing more.

She watched him carefully, tried to get a clear view of him. Wondered if he was attractive. She'd not been able to remember his face this morning – only his height and solemn presence. She'd never wondered whether she found Matthew good-looking; they'd fallen into love because they found themselves doing better than friendship. This man . . . it was all so rigid. His face was not expressive, but he had very dark eyes and a thin nose. White skin,

149

with patches of irritated pink, a top coat of short grey hairs at his temples.

'I picked fruit,' she said, 'with other students, from other countries.'

'Apples? Hops? What?'

'Lettuce, strawberries, raspberries and elderflower. Why do you laugh?'

'Elderflower . . .' He shrugged. It sounded medieval.

'For the . . . the,' she had forgotten the word, 'the drink.'

'Cordial,' he said, looking surprised at himself.

'Yes,' she said.

'An old-fashioned word,' he said.

'It is?'

'Where are you from?' he asked, wondering why he hadn't before. He almost expected her to say 1810.

'Hungary,' she said, and explained some more.

Julianna was not so naive that she didn't imagine a sexual imperative behind Jack's arrangements, but she didn't imagine any more. She didn't understand that his impulse was a romantic one, so she had gone out wearing a new persona. She wouldn't sleep with him, a middle-aged man who boasted about his money, but she would enter the spirit of the encounter by charming him, enjoying him, playing at a game she had no intention of closing. She was twenty-one, and she had read about things like this. It would be an adventure, and she would like to taste life as lived in the books she had been reading for so long. It was the closest to a business meeting she'd ever come.

They found a table to sit down at and Jack went to the toilet. When he returned, he noticed Julianna poking at the single flower in a vase with her little finger.

'Is it real?' she asked, smiling, pointing at the scarlet flower, its yellow stamen at right angles to the waxy, veined tranche. A spade of flower flesh.

'I think so,' he said. 'Do you like them?'

She grimaced slightly. 'They do not seem like flowers to me.'

'They look like aliens to me,' he said.

'Alien?'

'Umm.' The fact that she was Hungarian meant little to him, which was good in a way. He wouldn't have been able to translate the word into French, Italian or Spanish either.

'Like people from another planet.' There was a pause while he looked at her intently working over the words, sounding them for a meaning, rearranging their shapes to fit a sense in her head. He liked her accent. It reminded him of wood. There was something heavy and rhythmic in her emphasis.

'Ahhh,' she said slowly, languidly, and mimed a space-ship with her fingers. He looked at her oddly. A girl making a spaceship from the squashed lozenge of air between a forefinger and thumb.

There was a pause and he wanted to say something complimentary.

'You look very elegant,' he said in the end, which wasn't true, but which made Julianna smile, and which magically, instantaneously galvanised their pleasure. It made her think of movie stars and cigarette holders, strapless dresses and hotels. She had never been told that before. It was a polite compliment, a nostalgic one, and she liked that. There was something interestingly controlled and experienced about him.

She took a sip of her drink, uncrossed then recrossed her legs, relaxed a little. He watched her legs surreptitiously, through the glass table, moving his glass on its coaster. Her legs were the colour of ghosts beneath the black nylon. Synthetic, flammable, morgue-ish.

He liked legs. The first woman who'd taken him to bed

(and it had wonderfully, totally been that way round; even with hindsight it had undoubtedly been Deborah who had unbuttoned her own shirt and put his hand under her bra, had had pop socks on.

Julianna was wearing ten-denier black tights, because that was what she thought appropriate when having drinks with restaurant-going, suit-wearing men. She could see and then soon he could see the dark hairs on her thighs, where she hadn't thought to shave; the no-man's-land of her body.

They looked up at the same moment, caught each other's eye and laughed, complicit.

Julianna watched him, throwing his head back. His teeth stained at the back, a silver filling glinting, a dirty, private part of his mouth. Suddenly yawning and seeming a little restless. Not quite so precise a man any more.

She began to feel unsure of why she was here, noticed the increasing noise in the bar and an extravagantly flirtatious woman at a table opposite, a waitress dropping a glass, the volume of the previously subtle music being ratcheted up.

'You like it here?' she said gently, but still impolitely.

He stopped smiling suddenly and looked around, offended. It was an upscale place for a certain generation. As such, it did its job. He looked back to Julianna, her wide open face, and understood that she might not like it, when it made her look so badly dressed and out of place.

'Do you?' he said.

'I would like to go for a walk, I think.'

'Would you?' he said, and smiled. Actually surprised.

For the first time in as long as Jack could remember he walked the streets of central London without a particular purpose. They walked side by side, slowly, not touching, which reminded her of that first walk with Matthew along

152

the road through the woods. Their last walk too, with that broken, smoking minibus.

They were quiet at first, her and Jack, him placing himself carefully on the outside of the pavement, her with her hands in her jacket pocket, her scarf tied tightly, comfortingly round her neck. She heard more foreign languages being spoken than English. She saw one or two people sitting in doorways, begging, people more tired and beaten than she ever wanted to be, Roma mother and children on a corner, a square of carpet beneath them. Her grandmother had been rare in their home town in sometimes shopping from Roma families, in treating them just as if they were her neighbours.

Jack looked at Julianna as she walked, interested by himself as part of a walking couple. For the last decade he had seen a series of different women, but he had avoided intimacy. He hadn't walked down a street with a woman, further than a cab's stopping distance that was, for a long time. It was a whole other form of companionship; it meant reacting to others, negotiating pigeons, turds, gaggles of unwashed alcoholics. (Was the city pissed every night? he wondered.) He took quick stares at her. She looked exotic, wrapped in her scarf, her dark hair caught at the back. She moved with long, slow strides, walking round cars and along the pavement to cross roads, stopping rarely. It was almost a lope, her head rising then falling a little with each stretch. He didn't remember noticing a woman's walk before. He enjoyed their proximity, the flush that had appeared in her cheeks. He wondered how he walked. He'd never thought about it. He just did. One foot in front of the other, nothing particular to remark. He remembered, though, like finding something he didn't know he'd lost, that his brother Mike had teased him for being pigeon-toed when he was a kid. He did wear down the insides of his shoes quicker than the outside. He remembered too when his shoes and socks were too cheap not to stink. He'd hated that.

They walked past a pub and saw an arguing couple, red-faced and high-pitched like Punch and Judy.

'She should take him home, put him to bed,' Jack said.

'She should leave him,' Julianna said, 'find a boyfriend who does not shout at her.'

'You're quite right,' said Jack. 'I have been told.'

They'd almost reached the National Gallery before either of them uttered another word. They crossed the road and walked down the steps into the arena of Trafalgar Square. Tourists played in the fountain. Jack felt as if he were in an old spy film. Standing in front of a fountain with a dark European girl at his side. Of all the movie genres that could have come to mind, he thought it was one of the sexiest.

'Here we are,' he said. There was silence as they listened to indulgent screams. The group in the fountain were all teenagers. Boys and girls. They were either drunk, or just young. Their exuberance made Julianna and Jack's awkwardness, however full of potential it was, noticeable. She was beginning to find his seriousness dignified and his concentration, his deliberation, flattering. The conversation wasn't easy, yet it suggested a progression of women before, which made her feel desirably chosen. But she worried whether this was going well – whether she was getting it right. Perhaps beneath the impressive exterior he was shy. She felt strangely sorry for the two of them. For herself for having been abandoned by the boy she was in love with – who might have brought her to a group of friends like those in front of them – and for Jack for having acted on a half-lustful, half-altruistic whim and ending up with an awkward girl, whose English made conversation as slow as fishing. She felt grateful for his kindness in trying to make this evening still pleasant.

154

She turned and smiled at him, a warm smile, full of sympathy for the mismatched package that was the pair of them, and he was charmed, once more, by the openness of her. He smiled back and very briefly, in an inspired gesture that suddenly made both of them feel richer, put his hand upon her shoulder blades and let it rest, touching her bones with his thumb.

Jack was used to feeling outside scenes, but reaching out and finding someone who understood that feeling was something quite new.

'When did you come to England?' he asked.

Still they stood, side by side.

She hesitated. She was so used to answering these questions obliquely.

'Not so long ago.'

This *is* a spy thriller, he thought to himself, a rusty reflex for self-amusement coming back to life.

'But why did you come? You could have picked fruit here.'

'For the money. For something new.'

'Good for you,' he said, turning to look at her. 'I call that brave.'

'Not really,' she said. 'My grandmother was English. She was brave, she left in 1936. My grandfather was Hungarian, and she went to live in his home. And then there was the war, and the occupation, and the fear, and then afterwards the Russians. Then he died, in the revolution, when my father was young. So she was all alone. So she was more brave.'

'I think everyone was braver then. We only have to worry about ourselves now.'

'Well, you do,' she said, gesturing at the lavishness of central London, and he thought he understood what she meant.

'What's Hungary like, then? Has it changed these last two years?'

She turned to face him, laughing. 'Do you always ask a lot of questions?'

'No,' he said, shaking his head. 'Only you.'

They watched each other. 'Is this good?' she asked, narrowing her eyes. 'Is this why you asked me?'

'I don't know,' he said. 'Are you enjoying it?' Strangely Jack thought he would understand if she said no. And that it wouldn't anger him, wouldn't humiliate him. Would perhaps provoke him into greater forethought the next time. She, like him, wasn't one of life's easy, settled souls. Already he understood something of the way other people's lives echoed through her, isolated her. Because, he thought, it was the same for him.

'You know,' she said, her head on one side, looking playful for the first time in the evening, 'what I thought I do not know, but I think I am. I think I think,' she laughed, 'this is fun.' She smiled widely, which made him smile back. If he was careful, he thought with a flourish of hope, this might be different.

They caught a bus to a pub in Green Park ('My first bus in years,' he said, and in her head Julianna formed this picture of a boy not allowed out, rather than a man refusing to get out). They stood close in the corner of the pub's green velvet interior, squeezed between a cigarette machine and the window, and she told him about all the waiters and staff in the restaurant. Just as they both were becoming aware of how close they were standing, and she had noticed that his eyes sometimes looked dark grey, and he had thought how nice it was she was so slim, she suddenly said she had to go, as she had to get up at six. 'Me too,' he said, and outside he hailed a cab. She demurred, said she had a bus pass, but he said, 'I'll take you to your bus stop.' Three minutes later he leapt out, saying, 'I've given the cab the fare, just sit back, enjoy the ride home.' And he left her, yet again, confused, the scent of bank notes in the air.

He walked back down Piccadilly, not really looking for a cab for himself. He hadn't touched her, which felt right, but nor had he said he'd wanted to see her again, which didn't. He'd been concerned by the thought of her, who had been so his for the last three hours, on a bus.

He was walking past a bus stop when a double-decker pulled up promising his area, so he thought, why not? He got on, paid with a twenty-pound note, oblivious to the driver's grumbling, keen, somehow, for the adventure to go on. He sat at the back, squashed between a woman with bulging bags and a crew of underdressed teenagers, hair scraped to the top of their heads, heavy jewellery in their ears. They looked like warriors, not girls. It was hot and he unloosened his scarf. He felt them watching him, nudging each other, laughing at him. Having money meant you never had to put yourself in a situation where you wouldn't be welcomed. It was the first time he'd seen himself being laughed at in years. On the other side of the road was a hotel where he'd drunk champagne the week before. It was like looking through the wrong end of a telescope.

The bus girded its loins, pumped its doors shut and trundled on, out into the road. Carrying its city protectively inside, unpredictable and impenetrable as an old red rhinoceros.

Julianna had Monday evening and all day Sunday off each week. Gaps in a blocked-out timetable. By their third meeting they had progressed to kissing quickly hello on the cheek, a bob and a reach from both of them, swift but jerky like garden birds.

She chose what they did, a gallery or a park or the movies, and then she waited on street corners in the cold while he decided on exactly the right place to eat or drink. She looked longingly at the McDonald's. Why was it so incredible that she might suggest eating there? The ability to visit McDonald's whenever you wanted seemed to her one of the privileges of living in Britain. As it was, she ate bread for breakfast, chocolate and instant coffee for lunch at Laundry Heaven, and then she, the waiters, barmen and kitchen staff all ate at 5.30 in the restaurant.

Out of all her jobs before, she preferred East Coast, for the food mostly, but also for the sometimes vicious speed of the humour, the jibing solidarity between them. It was freewheeling; staff came and went, lured by the promise of better pay and more respect, which never materialised, and the humour was risky. The chefs in particular were quick to take offence, even quicker to take revenge. Their pans were hot and their behaviour manic. 'Cocaine,' said Gianni. 'What?' said Julianna with a sigh. It was tedious always being the last to understand.

Somehow they'd got wind of Julianna's sugar daddy, as they called him. How? she wondered. Somehow it, he, the phone calls, were in the air, up for passing around, like the pastry chef's choux failures.

At East Coast, or in dark restaurants with Jack, it was possible to forget the coldness of her room in Bow. Until she returned, stumbling up the stairs, hollow with tiredness, following the clammy, stained walls. Unsurprisingly, Julianna had never asked Jack back to Bromley-by-Bow for coffee. It was a physical impossibility – the thought of Jack climbing the stairs, shaking hands with Radmila, Josif and whoever happened to be gathered smoking in their kitchen. Like snow in Africa. She longed for their meetings, for the glamour of the venues, the boost in confidence that being his companion gave her, for his attention to her thoughts and his gracious care in her pleasure, but she often found herself silent, almost sleep-walking through the first few hours. It took some adjustment to find yourself amongst the scent of lilies in Kensington.

'Can't I come to pick you up?' he said after a month, after they'd only just begun kissing. Light as ordinary greeting kisses but different because of their placing, two mouths leaning slightly to their right, a cross-shaped placing, come and gone faster than telling the time.

'No, you can't,' she said.

'Will you come to my house for a meal then?' he said.

'Do you cook?' she said, looking so astonished that he laughed, loudly, the way he never did with anyone except her.

'It's a fair question,' he said. 'Put it this way, I promise you won't starve.'

'No,' she said, more seriously, 'I don't want to.'

He said he didn't understand, and she looked almost cross. 'I have pride,' she said. 'I am scared of the . . .' she sought for the word, 'difference.'

So am I, he thought. But he had his pride too; he couldn't only ever meet Julianna in public places. It wasn't so much about sex, or at least it wasn't just about sex. He wanted to see her in his own context. He was beginning to feel as if he had hired her as an escort.

'Please,' he tried again. 'For God's sake, I just want to sit on a sofa with you,' and she was pleased that he'd expressed an emotion towards her. She could understand that need to sit on a sofa in peace so well that she agreed to come for supper on her next night off.

Jack lived in Kensington, in a house that he'd bought before the failure of his first company, ITSystems Inc. After that company had been forced to close, nearly half a million in debt, a hundred people made redundant – by him personally, one by one, his stomach churning below his desk – he remortgaged the house to fund the capital for Associated Financial Holdings, negotiating with the bank to consolidate the debts. Founding a financial services firm was not what he'd intended when he'd left university, but after his first failure he'd realised that what mattered to him was running a business that worked.

Money was a state of mind, he'd realised. Not a real thing. If you accepted that the purpose of bankers was to see the world with its trousers down, that debt was a commodity they needed as much as you, that the economy could only ever grow through debt, then and only then did you have the confidence to see the world as waiting and wanting and ready for you to make money out of it. But he'd learnt his lessons with ITSystems, grown AFH slowly, while all the time pulling in extant information favours and investing his profits in the early worldwide web.

He knew he'd inherited a certain courage and cunning from his father. A financial fearlessness. That and his grey-brown eyes, thin nose and thick, coarse brown hair, which was trimmed fortnightly into two flat wings. They were probably the safest things to have inherited. He saw his other attributes as a result of a poor childhood, a good brain, a grammar school education followed by a decent university. And more work, more attention to detail than he assumed his father had ever conceived of. He had sympathy for scientists, surgeons, traders, classical pianists, people who frazzled their brains each day with vessel-blowing concentration.

The house was large and mostly white. It was half a large mock-Georgian – actually Edwardian – white house in between South Kensington and Earls Court. Ironically it was only twenty doors down from the youth hostel where

Julianna had spent a week. Weeping. In summer he had only to open the French doors to step out into his own little garden which then led to the central gardens behind. He had had it decorated by someone who knew about these things, so that the walls were an iridescent pearly white, and the furniture too, apart from a black leather armchair and a matching red velvet one. He had aggressively large prints, authentic in that they only had 299 brothers, on the wall. A Warhol, that he now regretted, was in the toilet. The only way to atone for his unoriginality. The floors throughout were pale shiny wood and rugs were dotted around. He wasn't sure he liked it. But it was his; the lighting was neat, the bedrooms were as luxurious as a hotel's, and an illusion of cosiness could be created in the sitting room by sitting in the far corner of the tank-sized sofa, with a drink and the television on quietly and the faux fire that turned on at the flick of a switch. The fire seemed to float in a shallow basin, like a flower in a finger bowl, set back in an alcove. It reminded him of the black-and-white illustrations of Romans and vestal virgins in his grammar school textbooks. *Amo, amas, amat.* Underfloor heating, baths so steamy they could hide assassins, sheep's entrails and young women chosen for sacrifice because they had lived so little.

Despite such classical reveries he gave his background away, he knew, by his tendency to turn the telly on as soon as he came home. He couldn't stand the quiet, and he hadn't ever spent long enough listening to music to work out what he liked more than the self-complete chatter of a television.

Last time they'd been out she'd said to him, with her gloomy surprise that so amused him, 'Sometimes it seems very odd that I am sitting here in a restaurant like this. We don't have restaurants like this in Kisrét. And I don't think even in Budapest they are like this.'

161

'What are they like?' he'd asked.

'Darker, I think, and older, with men playing violins. Real people don't go to restaurants. Not even now. Party people went; we could now, I suppose, but still there is the problem of how to pay for it.'

'Shall I tell you a secret?' he'd said, and smiled his lop-sided grin. 'Sometimes it seems just as odd to me.'

'You?' She arranged her face to clearly spell doubt. 'No. This is here for you as much as them or them . . .' She gestured around the restaurant.

'I didn't grow up with money, Julianna,' he said, closing the menu with a snap.

Julianna arrived at his house early on Sunday evening. Jack found himself almost breaking into a jog to let her in. When he opened the front door, the wind carried through and a window somewhere inside slammed. He could feel its force as he held the heavy door. There she was, pulling hair out of her mouth, wearing the same scarf and thin denim jacket as ever. She was wearing her black work trousers, though, not a skirt, and a black jumper that she'd bought from Whitechapel market, soft like lambswool although actually viscose, round-necked and close-fitting. She had thought that since she was eating at a person's house it would be better to be less dressed than usual. A little more relaxed. For the first time her clothes did not show her circumstances; the little earrings that glittered were made from the same paste as any young woman's. She had bought them from the Indian stall, an extravagance, but at 50p a bearable one. Besides, her supper would be free.

He took her into the kitchen first and poured wine into a ridiculously oversized glass for her. She had to tip it high to be able to drink. Jack felt touched by her. He had had two vodka and tonics before she got here, between the unacountable hours of six and seven, but even Stolichnya couldn't explain the great rush the sight of her gave him. He was clumsy and overexcited and smiled at her broadly as they chinked glasses and he showed her through to the sitting room, where the lights blared and colours occupied hostile camps in different corners.

Julianna, having approached the house and stood at the front door, thinking that to live at a house such as this would be something to live up to, was now uncertain. It reminded her of the restaurant, only without all the tables. A home should not be like a restaurant, however beautiful. The ceilings were state-room high. It would be impossible for a person to sit comfortably in this colour-splatted vacuum. It didn't seem so much modern as scientific. She stood leaning against the sofa, one arm resting on its white bulk, worried to let go in case she be forced to choose where and how to sit in this place. The armchairs were huge, the sofa so deep that it would be impossible to lean back.

'Wow,' she said.

'Sit,' he said, 'anywhere,' he added.

'Where?' she said. 'There's too much choice.'

He went and fiddled with the sound system, leaving Julianna to perch on the edge of the low sofa. He tweaked the lights to make things appear softer-edged. She sat, arms on knees, looking at a book of paintings on the coffee table, her legs splaying outwards from the knees, her scuffed boots and tight trousers making him think of girls on horses.

She smiled as he sat down next to her, feeling slightly hysterical. How could she like him and the idea of his home so, and yet think it so wrong inside? What did she know of these things?

He looked at her.

'You don't like my flat, do you?'

She laughed very, very loudly with relief and pleasure.

Now she had permission she lay right back on the sofa, her head just touching the back of it, and pointed to the ceiling. 'No, it is beautiful – but so grand, so empty,' her arm stretched out either side. Now she looked like she'd fallen on her back from a great height, a James Bond villainess on to the snow.

She turned her head to look at him; he watched her from five feet further down the sofa.

'Do *you* really like it?' she asked.

He was lost for words. How was he supposed to know?

'Frankly, it's the least of my concerns. If you really want to know . . . I don't care. It's a place to come home to.'

'If you care so little,' she said, 'maybe one day I will show you where I live.'

'I'd like that.'

'No, I don't think you would.' She laughed again. 'It is not a nice area like this.'

She sat up, sighing, smiling, the aftermath of laughter and reached for her drink.

He watched her, wanted to kiss her hard, decided against it, thought he might go play with the food instead, then thought, with the force of twenty years of accumulated mismanagement of such situations, fuck it, fucking-fuckingfuck it, and said, 'I want to kiss you.'

At which she laughed again, rudely, then told him he'd need to come closer than that. He got up and knelt in front of her, his knees cracking, her giggling again, and he took her face in his hands, more to steady himself and make it easier than because he knew that the boldness of encircling her face would silence her, but it did, and he kissed her.

It was an exterior kiss and he broke off quickly, leaving her still reaching. She drew back, looked at his serious face, then kissed him gently once again, the soft, slippery inside of her lower lip catching the top of his. Clumsily they lay down together in the narrow space between the sofa and the coffee table on the abrasive wool of a red patterned rug. They lay there for what seemed like a long time, concentrating on each other's faces, him stroking again and again the full length of her back, wallowing in the reality of her.

Down there on the floor, surrounded by the chrome legs of his negligently chosen furniture, their warmth grew. He could feel her saliva around her mouth, touch her chin and ears, embrace the whole of her, hear a crack in her voice, kiss her nose, press the length of himself flat against her. He followed again and again the lines of her flesh encased in her overheating black fabrics. He thought to himself, why has it been so hard to get here, to a place where I feel warm? And that was his overriding sensation, the warmth that pervaded his body, of her breath, of her hands, of her face. He felt like a child in the sun down here. Playing and experimenting, pushing flesh and his luck, marvelling at this long-haired, smooth-skinned young woman (the kind of girl he'd so longed for all those lonely, achieving years of school and university). All the stiffness of his handmade shoes, leather belts, pressed suits, neat hair, abandoned and discarded, as if he really had never believed in it, all of it forgotten for a rummage of flesh, the burrowing of his head, her face, a childish batting and pushing and playing of bodies. He held her so tight it hurt, and laughed, he wasn't quite sure why, at the thought of himself down here, shoeless, untucked, rumpled. At the view from here, the balls of fluff below the sofa, the edge of the rug, the toenail he had ripped off the night before caught in the rug's fibres, the underbelly of the coffee table. He hugged her and thought of where he had to be tomorrow, at the head of a table, and he knew that at that point in the future he could look back and think of now with pleasure and secrecy. Tomorrow he would have something else to think on.

They finally emerged above beverage level, red-faced and swollen-lipped. Her make-up had been erased with spit and friction, but she was flushed and bright-eyed.

He cooked for Julianna that night, or at least he opened and chopped and laid things out. Oily pots and paper packages from Harrods food hall, rare beef, artichoke hearts, apricot tarts and chocolates.

He brought the food in and, avoiding the long dining table, placed it all on the coffee table and they ate it on the floor with the television on so low that it couldn't be understood but could be relied upon. It felt as if they had made a den.

'I wasn't sure that you wanted me, it's taken so long,' she said. She felt bold with desirability. So looked after and so wanted.

'Why? Why do you think I asked you for a drink that first time?'

'I couldn't tell. You didn't talk easily. I didn't know why we were meeting at all.'

'I suppose,' he put his plate down and cleaned his mouth carefully with a white fake linen napkin, 'I'm not very good at this kind of thing.'

He looked a little old and tired as he said that. Her need to keep kissing him, touching him, was surprising; he was so different to the hard-bodied, sprite-like Matthew. Sometimes he reminded her of a bear, lumbering and a little mournful. Not handsome. Something different, though, broad-chested and certain. Powerful in both obvious and less obvious ways. She wanted to climb far inside him. Own him. Grab his attention and not let it go.

'Tell me about your day tomorrow. What do you do every day? From beginning to end.'

'I don't want to talk work with you. I want to talk about new things.' But she just waited, so he said, 'I go to an office and I sit behind a desk and I run a company. A company that sells money. And I am good at it.'

'You sell money?'

'We lend it, like a bank.'

Julianna thought. She had no vocabulary for institutions such as banks; she thought of them as unavoidable and inexplicable. Like mountains. Like governments – no, more permanent and impersonal. She'd never really thought about them before.

'You enjoy it?' It seemed unlikely.

'It's not a question of enjoying it really; it's everything, it's what I am. It's a company I've built. It's the main thing in my life.' There was a pause. He watched a commercial with a duck in it. Into the silence he said, 'You probably think that's rather tragic.'

'It means then everything for you is about money.'

'Most things are about money, Julianna.'

There was silence apart from the very slight murmur of the television.

'Does that disturb you?' he asked.

Julianna thought that this was probably what the real world was all about, unclear, unpalatable truths. Truths that she as a child and a hostage to communism had never learnt before. She swallowed, and smiled. 'No, I am only eating,' but just then they were both distracted by a roar from the television, a cartoon duck being eaten by a dragon. 'Is there more in the kitchen?' she asked.

'Stay,' he said at 11.30. 'I have to be in the office by seven – I'll get you to work on time. I'll get you to Laundry Love or whatever it's called.' His shirt had come untucked and he wasn't wearing any shoes. It's not possible, he had just discovered, to sit cross-legged comfortably if you're wearing shoes.

'Where will I sleep?' she asked.

She wanted him to want to take her to bed, make love to her, although she was scared of it. She had only ever slept with Matthew, had often found that painful, although necessary in a way that she presumed was desire but found hard to imagine afterwards. Matthew had been tentative and vocal, inexperienced and excited, and had made her feel calmer in comparison. Standing in the middle of the room, she waited for Jack to reply. She picked up one of her shoes with her feet, reached behind to pull it over the heel, bent to tie it up. She thought of her own room, and the house that smelt and the cold walls that she could feel emanating dampness on her face as she lay in bed.

He watched Julianna make ballerina postures from the doorway.

'To be honest,' he said, pushing it, enjoying this new development, the invention of him saying what he wanted, so that there wasn't the usual great chasm between his head and events, 'to be honest I'd like to share my bed with you. But just to sleep. I'm tired. We're tired.' I could do with the company, he nearly said. Some things had to be held back. How much could you admit to a beautiful young woman? There was no longer a chasm between them – but still a gully. He could never share everything in his head. But to share his sleep would be something. Quite a thing.

She borrowed a T-shirt of his – enjoyed the smell and feel of it. The outsize, boyish logoed nature of it made her feel feminine, like an American on a TV show. He lent her a new toothbrush – gave her the spare bathroom. She scrubbed her face with soap and water, and by the time he came into the bedroom and found her sitting up, making her own comedy face to match the situation, she looked about fifteen.

He was wearing pyjama bottoms, but nothing else. She

was more embarrassed for him than by him. They made small talk about sleeping positions – as he folded the duvet back and climbed carefully in, a gesture which touched her with its elderly caution – until he turned off the lights, and shifted in the pitch black to whisper to her. He, more confident in the dark, without so many clothes on, played with the childishness of their chasteness, and whispered sweet things about the dreams she should have, and stroked her hair, then her face with the back of his hand.

She could feel the warmth of his body even though nothing more than his hand was connected; she kissed her own fingertips and asked him where his mouth was, and he could hear her limbs against the sheets. 'Here,' he whispered and felt her fingers land on his lips. He took her hand and held it tightly by his chest. They lay like that, facing one another, until sleep and the night took over and they forgot where they were. The sky darkened and the streets quietened at pavement level. The clear depths of night fell down to the closed houses, and they rolled nearer, then away, then back. A dreamed fall shuddered through her body. The deep blue outside intensified then diluted and they slept on beneath the sky's cover, until the cycle was done.

Further south and east the New Covent Garden market opened and flowers were selected for the next week in East Coast. Cracks of dawn in the sky, the weak half-light revealing massive strip-lit hangers filled with bright roses and lilies, poinsettias and gladioli.

Chapter Eleven

Over Christmas and on through the cold spring of 1992, Julianna's own life was so divergent from the time she spent with Jack that she sometimes woke unsure whether she was in a dream or really in his bed. It wasn't even as simple as the luxury of her evenings and Sundays with Jack feeling unreal. The days at Laundry Heaven and the hours passed in her cubby hole at the restaurant felt as surreally unreliable as his glass furniture and expensive tit-bitty food. The nature of her own life meant that she was there to be un-evident. So it was easy for a young woman on an erratic diet and not enough sleep to begin to doubt at midnight or midday whether she was really there.

She was used as a postbox in East Coast and in return she began to blur faces, forget them from one minute to the next. Her perception lowering to match the consideration she was given. Behind the sewing machine in Laundry Heaven she was spoken to only by Zahib.

Usually he asked impertinent questions about her romantic life, and tried to show off about his friends. Julianna humoured him because she thought he must be a rather lonely child. She loathed his father, but was not fright-ened of him in the way that his son was. Just occasionally Zahib would come to Julianna asking, in a coded, off-hand way, for a little adult kindness. That morning it had been raining so hard that Julianna could see the raindrops, fat as utter drips, fall the length of the window to the pavement. As she hemmed a batch of cheap curtains, she could see rubbish tumbling down the street, carried along the gutters in a growing stream of grubby rainwater. Zahib had said, forlornly, 'It's raining really hard,' and she instantly felt the problem and his confusion. It would, of course, seem to him that umbrellas were the kind of thing that other, more organ-ised families than his had.

'You need an umbrella,' she said to him, stilling the sewing machine for a moment. He had no hood on his anorak, after all.

He shook his head, pursed his lips, then said, 'I don't have one. Should I have one? Rashid has one. I think.'

'You can borrow mine,' said Julianna. 'I found it on a bus. It is a smart black one.' Then she thought and added, 'But you must bring it back, I will need it tonight.'

Zahib shrugged, as if to say, of course, nothing ever comes without a qualification.

His father came into the shop on the end of this exchange. He was a dishevelled man and his stare disturbed Julianna. He reminded her of a friend of her father's – one of the ones her stepmother hated, who had once or twice encour-aged her father into late nights and games of cards. Something about the way he licked his lips and pouted his lower lip up and over his facial hair to suck and chew at it. He watched her hand over the umbrella, staring at her breasts. Julianna disliked giving him the impression that she was shy of him, but it was best never to lock concentration with his red-stained eyes.

Zahib arrived back at 4.30, bearing Julianna's umbrella proudly.

'I kept it with me all day.'

'You did? Even in lessons?'

'Especially in lessons. The boys in my school are all bad thieves.'

'The girls too?'

'No,' he said, taking his weary eight-year-old self through the back door and up the stairs to watch cartoons on television. 'The girls are just whores.'

That evening Julianna needed to get to East Coast early. There was a special function on. She didn't normally finish at Laundry Heaven until 5.30, but would have to leave at 4.45, take the bus to Whitechapel, change and catch another. That way she stood a chance of being in her cubby hole by six, as requested. But she was at the mercy of the buses. If she was late she knew very well she would find herself back with the cleaning agency. She would have to join again the ranks of doctors, dentists and academics who cleaned for a living because immigration laws made it difficult for them to do something as simple, but legislatively complex, as practise their skills. It seemed England needed cleaners and pickers and packers more than it said it needed engineers. 'The sadness is,' one of the kitchen porters said to her, 'my country needs them most of all.'

Julianna had no reason to complain, said Radmila, whose form of friendship had grown even more aggressive with the news that Julianna had a British boyfriend who owned his own company. She would question Julianna in the early mornings and late nights. Why didn't she go home? She wasn't in any danger, Hungary was a safe country, a prosperous one, compared to hers. Julianna had a family, a place at college. Radmila too came from an educated family, she had been training to be a doctor, but now there was nothing left for her. But Julianna, she had everything to return to. What was she doing here? It was hard for Julianna to explain when sat around a small low table with four people seeking

172

asylum from a level of persecution that belonged to her grandmother's era. The atmosphere that Radmila and her Croatian Serb countrymen imported to the house was brittle. Loss always threatened to overwhelm. They told Julianna things that she simply couldn't relate to a country which wasn't far from her own, in terms of geography and recent history. Radmila's father had been a teacher. Now he was hiding in a forest. Julianna had absorbed her stepmother's cynicism and assumed that politics made no difference to the lives of ordinary people. These purges, which her grandmother had always described as 'people made pawns', were proof of Éva's wrongness. Julianna was learning that there was much worse suffering than poverty.

The bureaucratic uncertainty and boredom of Radmila's situation did not help her, and Julianna might have previously imagined that one could do nothing for a woman who had suffered as much as Radmila, except welcome her. What was so dreadful to discover was that it was quite possible to periodically feel dislike of her only friend, to feel her to be unreasonable, hysterical and unkind. Though, of course, Julianna would tell herself, breathing hard in the peace of a locked bathroom, she had every right to be. And she herself should perhaps be less combative on the subject of noise and the lending of milk. Yet the fact remained (how to admit it with such disparities between them?) that although sometimes she was glad of a female friend, sometimes she didn't like Radmila's company very much.

Perhaps Radmila frightened her. Julianna felt Radmila's past in her own nightmares. Her permanent presence (she couldn't work and didn't choose to do so illegally given that she was seeking political asylum from persecution and the authorities provided her with a weekly benefit) was a door to a quite other world. Her figure by the window was a portrait of pain exhausted to passivity, of sanctity in suffering, an icon which should be observed daily with a religious devotion. Lest we ever forget. And just as she had been by the tableau of those dead-tired men on the crumpled minibus, Julianna was disturbed daily by the human potential to survive anything.

It wasn't that Julianna's flatmates or colleagues told their stories willingly, or that there was a competition to their and their families suffering, just that it leaked out in small ways, with anecdotes, clues and gestures. In her dreams Julianna fleshed out the skeleton of these exhausted lives and lay awake until six wondering which particular mistake, or piece of luck, had brought each of them to this place.

There was no denying that the comfort of being with Jack brought her happier days.

Zahib's father watched Julianna fold the curtain she had finished. This kind of work was easy, it was all about running the machine true and fast as waves of fabric gathered and bunched in the stabbing needle's wake. Very little skill was involved, just some concentration. She tidied the spools of cotton – paintbox colours lined up in the window. Her small pink Tupperware box with pins, poppers and buttons at the end of the row.

'It's not five thirty,' he said, seeing her put on her coat.

'No, but I have finished.'

'I pay you until five thirty,' he said. There was silence as she picked up her bag, pulled her hair out from under her collar.

'Then you can fire me,' she finally said and walked out of the door. There was pleasure to be found in the smallest gestures.

He watched amazed as she slowly shook out the umbrella, put it up and threw him a smile of such beaming audacity that he almost forgave her. He lit a cigarette instead. A woman like that should be kept behind closed doors.

'You should be careful,' he shouted as she walked away, 'I am good to you. There are many people who won't take illegal people like you. You need me.'

But it didn't work. His tone might have done were she at home in Hungary, twenty years ago, when they were all compromised by survival, but what power did this man have in her life? It took turns that surprised even her. Instead she smiled right at him and walked out of his sight.

She'd seen enough to know that this entire layer of London, this kind of invisible job, the mending and handling, cleaning and guarding, depended on those who had next to nothing. Poets made the worst floor polishers but the British were no threat. She thought that there were probably more jobs in London than mushrooms in the world. Just that they were all the same. But she wasn't the same, because Jack had found her and claimed her as his.

The private party at East Coast ended early, so she went to Jack's afterwards. He was still working and she said, 'Don't stop, I'll watch TV till you are finished.' In fact she liked to watch him do ordinary things. He was physically awkward, and having found it embarrassing at first, almost catching, she was beginning to find it endearing. She recognised that the soft unobtrusiveness of his clothes, the neatness of his surroundings were important to him, because he always looked as if he felt out of place. Except when he looked at her. It was very odd. She found it hard to work out. He seemed to gravitate towards her, and when he stood in front of her and held her he spoke with such earnestness, such direction and purpose, that she felt both safe and scared, all at once.

Which was why she liked simply watching him, as she

was doing now, sat in front of the computer, the phone tucked beneath his chin.

It was quite odd, Julianna decided, knowing things about a person, how they smelled and what they said in their sleep, and what irritated them or turned them on enough to let a groan escape in a place it shouldn't . . . It was quite odd knowing these things and thinking them, while looking at a man while he spoke to someone else about proper things. Their intimacy was a portal; a parallel universe lay in their knowledge of each other.

Just as she was thinking this, bang on cue, he turned and saw her watching him.

She was leaning against the doorframe. Her legs were crossed (like many tall women she was rarely seen straight), and she was holding her coffee cup with both hands. The sight of her did what it always did, it distracted him.

'Hang on, Derek, sorry, can I . . .' He put Derek on hold. 'Go away,' he said.

Once she saw he was being funny, she said, 'No. Why?'

'Because I can't concentrate with you around.' She dismissed his old-fashioned nonsense with her hand and settled into the crook of the white sofa so she could watch him better.

He sighed, and got back on the phone. 'Derek . . . sorry. What were you . . .? Right.'

He wrote something on a piece of paper, stopped, looked at the computer, pressed different keys, so a graph grew then fell, then began folding the piece of paper. Still talking, he finished his paper aeroplane to his liking then swivelled and sent it flying to Julianna's feet. She opened it, smiled. Then slowly, reluctantly, she removed her shoes. Then her socks too, because she couldn't imagine they were an attractive element of a woman. She was examining the baby-white unfamiliarity of her toes, her overlong toenails, when another paper aeroplane landed at the far end of the sofa. She scrambled to reach it, and read it on her belly, and then with one gymnastic movement reared back on to her knees and removed her top.

She moved around the sofa now, trying to find a way to feel comfortable in her jeans and a bra, trying not to feel shy. She took a look at him. More typing and a faster exchange with Derek. He didn't see her and there was no new sheet of paper before him, and she felt disappointed, until, sensing her, he swung round and said, in the middle of a sentence about some third quarter, 'Jeans,' so loud and plainly to both her and Derek that she laughed right out loud.

In the end she was sure he was refusing to let Derek go, purely so he could have the pleasure of watching her sit naked on the sofa. Surely Derek had other things to do, gestures towards an independent life. Perhaps even he had a woman quivering with cold and anticipation on the sofa. Although Julianna had learnt enough about what Jack expected of his workforce to think it unlikely.

Julianna's body was leaner than it had been a year ago. That Kent summer had fed her and browned her and worked her so she was muscular. But now she had the body of a young urban woman, pale, thin, with some loose flesh above the bones, on her thighs, her belly, at the top of her arms. But her rib cage was narrow and her breasts high and Jack wasn't sure he'd ever been able to look so long, so properly, so without shame at his reaction, at a real woman.

Finally he finished his conversation and made his way slowly across the room towards her. Who would have thought that, even at the age of nearly forty, nakedness could be such a surprise? It was like having a sun rise in the corner of your room.

He did lay his hands on her, but by then both of them

were trembling and just the feel of his mouth on her side made her squeal with oversensitivity so that she drew his warm, furred head into her lap and folded herself over him. Whispering the word *lassan* slowly, over and over, in his ear.

'How do you make such good aeroplanes?' she said to his head, in her lap.

He twisted so that he talked up at her, the position of a restless but possessive child. It wasn't very comfortable, but his desire for Julianna often wasn't.

'My father taught me how to make them,' he said, watching her closely, hearing her digesting belly, which sounded like furniture being dragged and crashed inside institutional rooms. 'You learn all sorts of things in prison,' and then he smiled to feel her quake with laughter.

Until that point he hadn't told her much about his past. They spoke more about the present, Julianna slowly telling, after glasses of warm red wine, about Radmila and her family, so that he could embrace her and distance her from it all. Jack balanced Radmila's excluded, obsessive despair in a way that comforted Julianna. Explaining the progress of conflicts in Yugoslavia, then Bosnia, as if his view could clarify all, and it did salve her conscience and bring her calm to have an Englishman interpreting Eastern Europe for her ears. She forgave his lack of horror; in fact she didn't need to forgive it at all. It was too close and yet very far.

They only looted their respective histories with permission, after an opening anecdote. They were limited moments, not hugely revealing. Neither Julianna nor Jack knew what to ask, as they had no concept of each other's families or childhoods or education. She came from a Soviet state. He came from Horden. He was good on politics and economics, poor on life's details.

Neither Julianna nor Jack saw themselves as products of their parents; in fact they saw themselves almost as being who they were in spite of their parents. They both had a strong sense of their lives as a narrative, as a story with potential. Jack had a tight grip on his personal plot, but no one to share it with. Julianna was young enough to believe in the future as a dance orchestrated by some unseen force. Not ready to recognise her own role in shaping it, not given to the self-examination that would take. This was perhaps why they came together twice a week with so little dissembling. It was dramatic, urgent, dynamic, she his witness, he her rescuer.

His father was a hard man, he said, who had aspirations, who had made and lost small fortunes with extraordinary frequency. Who carried the charm of a magician around him, because he always managed to pull a coin hot from the ashes with which to save the machinery of a small-town business from failing.

'Do they have a class system in Hungary?' he asked her, not knowing how to explain the main thing to her without.

But she didn't quite understand and said, stranded in the middle of this man's confession, 'I don't know.'

'My father is a pawnbroker. He runs a company called Silver Services.' He used a mock-baritone. A voice he would never use to describe AFH, his own company, a hundred times the size, a thousand times the profitability, but a money-lender for all that. A law-abiding, brochure-producing financial services company employing ex-Cabinet ministers and BBC governors, but, yes, still a money-lender. 'Do you understand?' Julianna nodded. Of course. They had them all over. It sounded old-fashioned, but not untouchable. 'When I was eight he went to prison for assault; it was an argument over a debt. We'd always lived in this one house, which was all right, but when he went in we had to sell it and move away, to Horden. And . . .' he paused, 'there wasn't a lot of money, which was fine, you know, the general state of affairs for most of the planet, except that I, being a precocious little sod, really minded. I *really* minded. I was sent to a grammar school, because I worked hard. I wanted the teachers not to think I was some scum kid because school was full of people who lived on a different planet to us. With money and security and, I don't know, culture and a future. And that was . . . is . . . all about class.'

'We had our own . . .' said Julianna, trying to understand, wanting to be seen to understand; she gestured with her hand, strata of air up towards the ceiling.

'Strata,' he said, sardonically. 'Well, we were at the lower end.'

'And now you're not,' she said, uncomfortable at being so underdressed for this kind of talk, feeling intimacy slip and her need to be touched going to frustrating waste. She wriggled out from underneath him. She didn't care what his father did; she happily accepted the economics that provided for the life she tasted with Jack. The trick was to keep it separate, to unlearn her youth and accept the realities of the world. Her life in Kisrét, her summer at the farm, her room in the East End of London, this lavish house all obeyed their separate imperatives. They were individual planets, and she was flexible, singled out, stepping from one to the other.

Julianna sat up and covered her chest with her arms. Jack sensed he'd ruined the moment and wanted so much not to have. None of that mattered any more. Everyone had a preface, after all.

'I want to have a family, you know,' he heard himself saying in a fast, embarrassed voice. 'Do it differently, get it right.' He watched her smile at him, and thought he could feel the lukewarm wash of pity, which was not what he'd wanted at all.

He stood suddenly and told her to put on her clothes. They were going to buy late-night treats and oysters down the road. Then they'd come back, having cleansed themselves on sea tastes and distanced themselves with cold wine (wine that evaporated in the mouth then burst into elderflower in the swallowing), and begin the undressing all over again.

Chapter Twelve

It was well over a year since Bob Shillabeer had watched Richard drip blood in the bathroom and nearly a year since he had signed the first letter of advice, essentially a first warning, to Jack Harvey's father Stephen. Bob recently had been promoted to head of the inspection team within the Westington District Department of Trading Standards, and one of his first acts was to issue the formal caution. A final warning to obey the Consumer Credit Act of 1974 or face prosecution by the council. Justice had begun the slow circling wield of its heavy sword, above the head of a man who had lost Bob his oldest friend. But Bob was beginning to realise he actually wanted the battle, not just the capitulation.

The grounds Bob had presented for a formal caution were indisputable. Silver's were a licensed credit broker and as such should know perfectly well what the required contents of the agreement were, and specifically that notices of the lendee's five-day right to cancellation should be sent after signature. Silver's were simply failing to send these notices out. Bob hadn't even had to use Richard's statement, or try to find others to corroborate his experiences of doorstepping and violent extortion. Doorstepping and violence, it went without saying (but often went without being heeded), were one of the few elements of the traditional extortioner's game that the Consumer Credit Act had outlawed.

Bob was willing Silver's not to clean up their act. He was

willing them to carry on in the same cruelly lazy, small-town manner as before – so that he could initiate prosecution. It would probably take years, it was a project stretching into the future in the way he'd always assumed his friendship with Richard would. He had been so sadly certain that the future held no change for him, just the familiar triumvirate of him, Richard and Jenny. With his comfortable low-level dissatisfaction he had made the mistake of taking his essentials for granted.

Even though short-term unsecured lenders' interest rates usually were high (they charged anywhere from 20 to 300 per cent annually), Bob reckoned that once it came to court even the doziest judge would also find Silver's guilty of extortion. Faced with the statements Bob had taken, the judge would have to condemn the way in which debtors were forced into top-up loans and penalised for late payments, then made to pay further interest on all the fees and penalties they were told they had incurred. One family who had contacted the DTS were so deep in debt (a chronic back problem had left the husband unemployed and his wife, who was diabetic, had never worked) that they had already paid back five times what they'd originally borrowed and still owed another £25,000 more. 'It's like waking up with the full weight of the house on your chest,' the man had said. 'Every day for eight years. It's a life spent worrying.'

But the stories of violence would almost certainly go unheard. Would Bob be able to promise that there would be no comeback on them or their family? No. So witness statements would probably never be given in court. As well as fear of the lender, there was fear of the court process. Why involve yourself in institutions such as that when all that the Department of Trading Standards could exact was punishment? Why surround yourself with professionals and lawyers who treated you with that demeaning distance, as if they were vets and you a pig.

There was a waiting list to be declared bankrupt these days, to be rid of debt and have it lifted from your life. Bob too underwent a sudden shift. He put more and more money into repaying his mortgage, making one-off payments as often as they allowed him. It was a one-man protest that no one would notice. The literal translation of mortgage, he'd been told, was 'the grip of death', and a small flame of anarchy was born in him with the total understanding, as opposed to the knowledge, that this was how the world made its money – by lending it. Each new loan from his bank advanced a new sum to be spent. And each new debt created interest, brand-new money created out of nothing, cash minted out of hope. It saddened him, worried him even, the thought of a world bound by chains of its own making, hungry because of its greed.

The pressure to make strategic decisions, rather than just inspect traders and enforce legislations, had grown with the promotion, but then so had his zeal. Seeing him eat over his paperwork at the weekends, his mother despaired of him finding a wife or having a family. She worried, secretly but more fundamentally, about his love life. She never saw him with a woman, so where would he be getting any fun from? It wasn't right for a young man not to have an outlet. She knew what men who chatted you up successfully were like, and they tended to have . . . it felt disloyal to admit it . . . they tended to have a bit more zing than him.

However, Bob's mum had never worked in an office, so she didn't know the multitude of arrangements that could be found behind frosted-glass doors. For months now Bob had been liaising, in considerable depth, with one of the younger members of the inspection team, Alison. He took surprisingly subversive pleasure in knowing what underwear she was wearing beneath her skirt suit. They maintained a vigilant secrecy – relationships within the department were far from encouraged. Bob was sweetly oblivious to the gossip around them, the enjoyment (possibly on a level even with the knowledge of underwear) everyone else in the department got from listening to the two of them talk, with their overenunciated normality and briskness.

Alison knew of Bob's particular crusade: the Consumer Credit Act and money-lenders who were acting at the limits of it, but Bob hadn't discussed Richard. It bothered him too much. The excitement in his liaison with Alison came from the secrecy, and the sweetness from the contrasting normality of the mornings after. They met in a quiet Italian away from the office for pizza and a bottle of red wine, illicit pleasures dissolving overnight into the coy efficiency of a standing breakfast. It wasn't a confessional relationship; Bob loved the burbling pitch of their chatter.

Bob and Richard hadn't met up properly for months. Richard didn't return his calls any more, was always on his way out when Bob popped by. He'd been repaying Bob, in pretty regular instalments, even though Bob hadn't wanted it, could have afforded it himself. Bob had watched Richard get more bitter and seen how with each repayment, each meeting in the pub, he drank and sneered at Bob even more. Finally, forced to admit his hurt to himself, Bob went round to Maria, Katie's mother, who said Richard hadn't seen Katie for a fortnight. Which was unheard of before. Maria said Katie was crying herself to sleep every night, and that if she'd known what a fuckwit he'd turn out to be, she'd have given Katie a different father. She said this quite loud at the front door. Bob could see Katie sitting at the top of the stairs sucking two fingers, so after waving at her (she unclasped her small fist just quickly, her hand starfish wide for a second), he turned and left.

Bob began to wonder if this hadn't all begun with a failure of his. He was Richard's friend, he should have been able to help him much, much earlier on. Sitting in Jenny's front room, the two of them talking on the sofa beneath the noise of children's television, she also said she hadn't heard from him for weeks. She was ashamed, she said, stubbing her cigarette out, smelling the tar on her fingers with a nervous, instinctive gesture. Ashamed of what? asked Bob, for whom the word had an upsetting strength. Ashamed of her pessimism, she said, that she wasn't more surprised by Richard, ashamed of the fact that he'd not visited his child for a fortnight. 'And you,' she said, more thoughtful, less confessional. She felt protective towards Bob, she always had, she didn't know why; his shining caramel skin had brought him enough abuse in his time and he'd survived just fine. He was impervious to the world, it seemed, so why did she feel the need to protect him?

There was something so very hopeful about Bob, and Jenny hoped Richard wouldn't be the one to break it. She'd long ago stopped trusting in human nature; it remained as complicated as it had seemed to be as a child, when they'd all presumed it would become clearer. The elliptic silences of marriage, the impenetrable assumptions and defences of friendship, the damned inability of any man to sense what was inside her on evenings when she felt lonely and nostalgic for an ease or grace of life that she would never have.

He had so little in some ways, Bob. So few connections and complications. His job, his mum, Jenny, and before he opted out, Richard. That was all. It had made him innocent, she thought to herself, although Richard was obviously doing his best to show Bob some disappointment of his own.

*

186

He'd been dreaming when the alarm went off, and it wasn't the kind of dream you'd want to repeat in the canteen. With the split-second creativity that always astonished Bob, the beep of the alarm was incorporated into the events. It became an alarm going off in the building they'd snuck into, its controlled electronic cheeping suggesting something more nuclear than a burglar. He woke with a jerk. For a moment he wasn't sure who was in the bed with him. He tried to focus, and saw white flesh, a back with a spot on it, and short blonde hair, curled and crested like a sheepskin rug. Not Richard. But Alison. Bob came to a little more and wondered at himself for wondering who he was in bed with. He tried to blink away the dream dregs (begging Richard to let him suck his cock at the office, promising to do all his geography homework if only he just would). He felt a great downward shunt of lust, and shifted over to Alison's back and began to kiss her spine, lower and lower until he got low enough to want to roll her over and lift her pelvis, catching a strong smell of semen as she divided her legs with the slow, stoned pleasure of being awoken. He licked at her until he felt a little as if he might suffocate here between her thighs, face pressed into her sticky, ticklish genitalia. He emerged from the duvet breathing heavily, kissing her, tasting of her, pushing hard into her, his eyes closed. She closed hers, turned her head to the right, towards the window, into a fantasy. The two of them, away in their own worlds, groaned and pushed themselves quickly to their separate orgasms.

He had a general sense of their lovemaking later that day. Inelegant, greedy, deep. He caught sight of Alison in the office, walking past his window, hoisting her handbag on to her shoulder, not an elegant move, but one which reminded him of her body, of the different parts of her that he had touched. He felt strangely moved by the sight of her pale face, the scarf that she always wore, whose label said *St Michael 50% real wool*. She was made up of very ordinary things, yet entirely mysterious to him.

His phone rang. It was Cheryl in reception.

'I've got a lady here for you,' she said with all the disdain of a good receptionist. 'Maria,' she added. 'I asked her whether she had an appointment, but she doesn't seem to think she needs one.' Bob heard a sharp, dissenting voice in the background and went straight down.

He got to the bottom of the stairs and turned into the lobby, catching sight of Maria and Katie before they could see him. He was used to thinking of those people he was friends with, those he worked with or was related to, as being the lucky ones. The solid ones, who were entirely separate from the souls he saw pounding the stairs day in and day out to the benefit investigation office on the first floor; the families he saw in court, or on the rougher estates, so full of random hostility that he was always, shamefully, surprised by the articulacy in their aggression. Even Richard, with the debts, and the violence, even then – that had clearly been a mistake. But now, for the first time in his life, for the first time in the thirteen years he'd been with the DTS, looking at his friend's wife, bristling with challenged pride and anger, the child, scrunched into a chair far away from her mother, Bob thought to himself that it was all mutable. These two looked as excluded as any of them. It could go one way or the other, at any given moment. That there was no specific kind of person who ended up on one floor of the council offices or another.

Katie sucked the fingers of one hand, while the other fiddled with an abandoned pamphlet. Her mother stared out of the window, jangling her keys in her pocket, and as he walked towards them he wondered where the fuck Richard was, his friend, who was supposed to be supporting this thin

188

woman and their young child. He felt a rush of anger, then a pang of betrayal.

'Katie,' he said, out loud.

She turned and saw him, hesitated for a moment until he crouched down and opened his arms, then walked over to him smiling shyly. She identified him with her father, so was always happy to see him, who had always been gentle and respectfully adult with her. Spoken to her in full sentences, explained things with the time and patience of a non-parent. Ever since her parents had split up, she'd had a strong sense of the impropriety of her own household. It was unbalanced, and she minded that with all the conservative disapproval of Westington's MP. But in front of Uncle Bob, who had bought her that candle at the fair, and whose calm always made everything so very clear and reasonable, her anxiety faded. She stood grinning inside the circle of his arms, and struck by the smallness and vulnerability of her he picked her up and hugged her as if there were danger in the air, just as her father would have done if he'd been there.

Maria did not run or smile. But puffed out her cheeks, pursed out the air, showing her resentment at being here, at her sodding luck which had landed her here, begging for a babysitter.

'I'm sorry to do this, but Richard's called, he's in Portsmouth. Don't ask me why. He sounds in a right state. He says he needs to see me, without the little one,' she said, 'so I've got to drive over and my mum's ill and won't have her. Or can't have her. Whatever . . . and I can't go to Jenny. She's at work, in that nursing home. So . . . well . . . I thought you might . . . Can you?'

'That's fine,' he said quickly. 'What's he doing in Portsmouth, though? I mean, I haven't seen him for weeks, but I just thought he was about but busy. I didn't realise he'd gone.'

'I don't know what the fuck he's up to. He says he's go no money to pay my alimony, that he had to get away, tha he'd been drinking too much. Says he's living in a shithol and needs to see me without Katie. I'm supposed to g today. And I'm tempted to tell him to fuck off. But yo know, he's her father. He was my husband.' She stopped an looked away. 'You've got to have some loyalty, haven't you? she finished, on a quieter note. They were both silent for moment.

Bob and Katie watched her mum go, then he picked he up again and kissed her on the head. He thought she migh want comforting. *He* certainly did. Everything seemed t be slipping. Then he put her down because she was actu ally quite heavy. He took her back up to his office. It wa lunchtime and there was no one around. Bob thought, as h frequently did, how odd it was that there was no one to b seen. He lived in a town and worked in an office, but ho often did he sit on his sofa, look out of his window, wall down streets, across football pitches and car parks and ye see no one at all? Except of course here, now, was Katie Way below his eyeline and running to catch up, holding pink plastic doll by its foot. They went into his office an he told her he just needed to sort out a few things. Sh looked at him blankly. 'And then,' he said, struggling for reward, 'we'll go to the Wimpy?' She smiled, took a deep breath and began.

'My daddy used to take me to the Wimpy sometimes But sometimes he didn't. He said it was expensive. He use to take me to the café at the end of his street and I'd hav cheeseontoast.' She said it in a rush. 'I liked the chees better than the toast. I liked the Coca-Cola, but I didn't lik the funny men in there. There was one,' she walked roun the desk to where he was sitting and inveigled herself on t his lap, 'and he smelt.'

Bob was trying to work out how to reshuffle his meetings so as to be able to take some emergency time. Strictly classified as family time.

Katie said quietly, 'My mummy's gone to see my daddy.'

Bob sighed. Oh God. It was so inevitable, the heartbreak of it all. He sat her on the edge of his desk. When she'd been younger Richard had told Bob how she had had problems with words, forgotten them and got them muddled up, and her alternatives had so charmed the adults around her that she had got labelled somehow as a little extra special, a little extra sparkling than the next small girl. Remembering how she'd described the pins and needles in her leg as sprinkles, Bob looked straight into her eye promising her Coca-Cola and a multitude of other sweet treats. As if both their lives depended on it.

A few minutes later, he knocked on Frank's door. Frank was his boss, the Chief Weights and Measures Officer, an archaic term for a fairly unreconstructed man. Bob stood on the threshold.

'Frank, I'm going to have to take the afternoon out, so I won't be at the operations meeting this afternoon.'

Frank's face expressed surprise. 'OK . . . you all right? Not well or something?'

The door opened further. Frank's eyes made a sudden drop down to the small child that had appeared at Bob's legs.

Bob looked a little embarrassed. 'She's not mine, obviously, just helping a friend in a bit of an emergency.'

Frank watched Bob walk away, stooping slightly to hear what the child was saying, then a few minutes later saw him retrace his steps, struggling to get a red coat on to the miniature girl.

Frank was amused. He had nothing but respect for Bob. That was what he'd always say. What was more, it was almost true; Bob was the hardest-working, most ruthlessly honest man he'd come across in his thirty-year career. He wasn't high-flying, he was too careful, too fair for that. But sometimes Frank would take home to his wife tit-bits of Bob's naivety, anecdotes in which Bob would try to reason with the unreasonable, and though he tried to be fair to Bob, Frank's tone as they sat in the conservatory with their 6.30 Cinzano was a little less than respectful. So it amused him to see Bob flustered, having to bend the rules a little. He liked him all the more for it. The man did the job of two men. One afternoon was a drop in the ocean. I just hope, Frank thought lightly, licking his thumb to flick through a report, that he's not being taken advantage of.

That morning Bob had received a call from a woman who said she would be in debt to Silver's for ever. She said it had begun two years ago with a £200 loan for a new fridge for her daughter. Soon after taking out the loan, she said, she'd got ill and had been unable to work. They'd scared her the way they came round at all hours and she'd signed a new agreement that gave her a little extra for Christmas for a bit more cash each week. She'd thought the agreement would run out after two years in the same way, though, and this spring, after some bad news, spent money planning a little holiday. When she'd asked, assuming the payments were nearly over, they'd told her she had another two years left. She'd got sicker with worry, missed more payments, until they'd made her sign a third contract, paying a little less every week for another five years. But this time when they'd gone she plucked up the courage to talk to a neighbour about it and try to understand the contract. She'd found out that she now owed £6,000, all in, and her neighbour's husband had told her to contact the DTS.

As he sat in the Wimpy and watched Katie quietly prodding the fizzing island of ice cream in her Coke float, reduced from princess to parcel, Bob treasured this latest complaint. It might be enough to provoke the prosecution. The correct end to a story of exploitation and violence. The end Bob's moral compass demanded, his sense of loss and debt to Richard and his daughter focused on a single bearable outcome. Bob had never been an aggressive man, but he stoked it, thinking about Richard, drunk, in a pub, by himself in Portsmouth, his daughter here in the lap of another man.

Later that afternoon he drove Katie through the rain round to his mother's house, because if he'd had a dad he would have wanted to see him right then, would have liked the reassuring solidity of an older male. But his mum was in, playing cards with friends and sherry and the table lamps all on, making a merry blaze against the loneliness of a Thursday afternoon. To his relief she ushered Bob and the child in with all the bluff pleasure and unspoken quizzicalness you could have asked for from a man.

Both Julianna and Jack had watched their relationship lengthen and their involvement deepen with equal surprise. Julianna couldn't believe that she still interested him. Each week she became more confident in the sex, and each week she became more scared it would end. The difference in their circumstances only seemed to grow, even though every meeting brought a new revelation of his fallibility and humanity for her to treasure.

Jack couldn't believe that he had finally arrived at this experience, from which he'd been excluded for so long. It was like the first time you learn to ride a bike; there comes a point when you are actually doing it, and from the sidelines you look as if you might be the kind of person who's been riding a two-wheeler all along. The two of them, he had discovered, had their own momentum. The unpredictability of investing so much in one single other frightened him, but his lifestyle was so dominant, and Julianna so pliant in his hands, that he never really thought of it as two separate worlds coming together. More that he was allowing her into his.

Julianna had calculated that today was the anniversary of six months since they'd first met. She was calendar vigilant; it was nearly eighteen months since her work permit ran out. To distract herself she spent the early evening at East Coast making Jack a card. She knew he would be pleased – he was childish, even embarrassing sometimes, the way he played with the 'we' they made. She sometimes thought she and Matthew had behaved in a more adult way than she and Jack. Sometimes he talked to her like an old man to a grandchild; sometimes she spoke to him as if she were his mother. Julianna found it a strange combination of comforting and sexy, he and his golden interiors, safe houses in that dark, wintering city. But summer was coming, he promised, and the evenings would get long again. All the more light to see you with, he went on, and mock-bit her on the bum.

The card was meant to be their own map of London. She'd cut the tube stations South Kensington and Bromley-by-Bow out of an underground map and then stuck them at diagonals from each other. Then in between she'd stuck discs containing the yellow streets they'd visited together. All of them held together in the net of a lop-sided heart. She enjoyed making it, the sticking and cutting reminding her of being a child, in the kitchen with her grandmother. Being a woman, mapping their story, reminded her of Mila too and the lines her forefinger would draw on an old map of

194

Europe. Saying, we went there, then there, then, I forget, perhaps there.

As she was finishing off his card he arrived. 'A surprise,' he said to her, putting his finger to his lips. He'd come in to eat late and alone that night so that he could take her home. It was not a treat he had ever allowed himself before. He wasn't entirely happy being the man waiting for the cloakroom girl to come. But he wanted her with him tonight.

She seemed peculiarly attached to her job. It was a trait which he admired; it reassured him of what he suspected, that Julianna had no concept of the money he was worth, but he hated the fact that she did two such menial jobs. It brought him closer again to people he thought he'd left behind, back nearer to the margins. He wanted her to always be free when he was, to come home and find her waiting barefoot and absorbed in a paperback, picking her toes on his expensive sofa like a teenager.

It was eleven before Jack was finished. Taking his time over a decaf espresso (hard but not impossible), re-reading the papers. By the time his coffee was gone, the last table was just leaving and he'd read every single one of the classifieds. He looked around for a waiter to order the bill, and could see Julianna handing over the last table's coats. He'd found it hard to avoid staring at her throughout his entire meal. He could just see her if she leant forward, her chin in her hands, waiting for time to pass. He'd wanted to be the last to leave so that he wouldn't have to sit outside in the car for too long, like some pimp.

As he was being instructed by some astrologer prick with a double-barrelled name to think carefully before severing ties that he might regret (which meant precisely what?), he heard raised voices. They seemed to be coming from the kitchen, behind the white swinging doors. A waiter came bursting out, followed by a man in a raincoat and then a policewoman. The waiter came to the table quickly, smiling too flamboyantly, and said, 'Your bill, sir, shall we fetch your bill?' and then turned to the policewoman and said, 'He still has to pay, he is a guest, we cannot lose the money just because you are here.'

Jack asked what was going on.

The waiter shrugged. 'It happens. They like to hunt,' he said, and went to the bar to run up the bill.

More and more staff were escorted out of the kitchen, accompanied by policemen as well as other greyly dressed types. Jack looked round towards Julianna. He couldn't see her.

'The two in the kitchen said it was empty, said they'd finished for the night, we'd no idea there was someone left,' the plain-clothes man was saying to the policewoman. She said something Jack couldn't hear and then went back to the kitchen. The raincoat followed the waiter, who clearly wasn't hurrying with the bill.

It was only when Jack saw the contrast between the waiter's skin colour and the man beside him that he realised this was actually an immigration raid. He glanced towards the cloakroom again, tried to think what he knew about Julianna's situation. He didn't know – she'd always been vague about how long she'd been here, why she'd stayed on after she'd finished fruit-picking. He'd asked about how she'd been able to stay, and she'd said they had been sorted out by the charity that matched farms to students. But that was a long time ago, surely? Why hadn't he found out? The fact that he'd shied from the knowledge was not a good omen.

Where was she? He felt high with the tension. Had they taken her somewhere? He couldn't see if she was still there. They'd obviously rounded everyone else up. They must have thought the restaurant was empty; he hadn't ordered anything for a while. He hadn't seen the police arrive, they must have come through the kitchens. Where was she?

Tapping the tablecloth with his credit card, he was trying to move his chair back surreptitiously, get a better view of the cloakroom, when he suddenly saw her saunter slowly from the ladies' lavatories across the walkway to the cloakroom. They must not have checked, thought Jack, exhaling with relief. He looked quickly at the bar, the immigration officer and the waiter, but they wouldn't have been able to see her from where they were standing.

Jack suddenly thought that, in fact, he knew nothing. He'd been told nothing and neither of them, knowing nothing, would be doing anything wrong if they were just to leave quite quickly and quietly together. He stood up from the table and walked over to the waiter, who was neatly folding his bill and putting it on a small silver platter with a cocoa-dusted truffle, deliberately irritating the officer.

'Here,' said Jack, flicking open the bill, 'here's my card. I'm just going to get my coat.' The waiter took it, his eyes dark and hard.

Jack rounded the corner and stepped inside the cloakroom; Julianna opened her mouth in surprise at him, but he hissed at her, 'Shut up. There's police here, with immigration officers, they're obviously after illegal workers. Tell me honestly, are you going to be OK, or is this going to be, I mean, I don't know, are you? You never told me.'

The look on her face answered his question instantly, though. She just stood, silent and still.

Jack looked around the cloakroom. There was just his coat and a few others, including a fur-collared cream coat which belonged to the manageress.

'Put that on,' he said. She shook her head. It wasn't hers. 'Put it on, you're my girlfriend, we've been having supper together here. Just keep your mouth shut. All right? You don't work here. You're with me. Now just wait.'

He rounded the corner with his coat, turned into the restaurant and signed the credit card slip, then said goodbye. In what he hoped was a nonchalantly concerned way, he added, 'Good luck' to the immigration officer, who said nothing except, 'Right, come on' to the waiter.

Jack went back into the corridor and took Julianna's arm. She looked as if she was half ready to faint anyway. They walked quickly through the doors into the corridor where the lifts were. The waiter, perhaps sensing something, maybe a little too much movement for one single man, shrugged off the officer's hand, walked round the corner into the cloak-room corridor. The immigration officer followed, just in time to see the swing doors close. He put the waiter into an arm-lock and forced him back towards the kitchen, where he belonged.

Jack and Julianna walked swiftly, their footsteps in time with each other as they moved down the corridor towards the lift. Their reflections in the windows thin and ghostly, hovering above the light patterns of London. Clumps of golden interiors, streams of red rear lights, flickering white headlights covering the ground. Their shoes clattered loudly against the shiny ceramic floor tiles. Jack caught sight of them, looking strangely dated. A couple in long coats, escaping. The woman with her hair in a bun.

There was a policeman by the lift, to stop poor buggers like that waiter escaping, Jack supposed. Not them, though. Julianna was his, and he was on his way home.

'Excuse me,' said Jack, 'We need to leave, we were having supper in the restaurant and we were just paying for our meal, then all of this kicked off.'

The policeman looked at him. They had been told the restaurant was empty, that was why they'd planted the two kitchen staff, to make sure they came in before the staff left but after the guests had gone. Fucking immigration officers. They always screwed up.

'Do you have a receipt or anything, sir, just so I can have a quick check? I'm afraid we were told that the restaurant was closed.' Jack sighed and took the credit card slip out of his wallet. The podgy-faced policeman smiled at Julianna. 'Sorry about this.' She smiled back faintly. He looked at the signed slip. Restaurant must be cheaper than he thought. He might bring his girlfriend here after all. He stepped aside, and pressed the lift button for them. 'Sorry to disturb your evening.'

As they waited for the lift to come, the police radio began to crackle. He called in. Julianna felt as if she was going to be sick. They'd know she was missing. They would all see she wasn't there. No one would lie for her. Why should they? She and Jack held hands so tight that she would feel it in her fingers for days to come.

They were on floor 20. The lift was at floor 6 and climbing.

'We're missing two,' the radio said. The lift reached floor 10. 'One male, Miko Janovitch, Polish, mid-twenties, white overalls, and one female.' Floor 18. 'Julianna Kiss, the cloak-room girl.' The lift, 19, 20, sounded, opened and they stepped in. Jack pressed Ground. And then again. And had to stop himself from doing it again. Julianna turned away from the open doors, saw herself in the bronzed glass, saw her wide eyes, the shadows of her face, her panic. She saw her youth, suddenly, and what could be done to her by large, impersonal forces. I should be at home, she thought. How did it come to this? Out of the stillness there came a shout on the radio. 'Jesus Christ,' the voice said, 'he's gone out the window, fuck, back-up, get in here, one of them's climbed out the window,' and the policeman by the lift began to run towards the restaurant.

The doors finally closed, terribly, terribly slowly, and Jack breathed out as if he'd been holding it in all along. They began to descend.

Jack took Julianna in his arms, held her, saying, 'It's all right, it's all right,' and plastercast stiff she swore in her own tongue over and over again. He pulled away and looked at her. 'Breathe deeply. We've just got one more bit. Just got to get out of the building, then we'll be in the car. Breathe. It's going to be OK.' She was breathing quickly, shallow. So as the lift landed pneumatically, and settled on itself, he said, quite harshly, 'Julianna, look at me, look at me.' She looked at him. 'Stop it. You have to stop it. You have to keep calm. You're with me, everything is going to be fine. No one is going to stop us. Not us.' She was as white as a sheet. Anyone, even the dimmest of policewomen, would be able to see how distressed she was.

They stepped out into the lobby. It was brightly lit, but empty. They walked quickly through, expecting someone to step out from behind a marbled pillar at any moment, then round the revolving doors into the cold, damp night. Over to the right was a collection of police cars, and at least five officers huddled together. Their voices indistinguishable, communicating with the radio, furry but loud. None of them noticed Jack or Julianna as they walked quickly away, towards the main road and Jack's car.

He had parked on the other side of the road. He had to restrain Julianna from running to the car. 'It's OK now,' he kept saying quietly. 'It's OK, sweetheart. It's OK.' Endearments came from his mouth that he had never used before. He wanted to wrap her tightly in the darkness of his overcoat. He opened the passenger door and helped her in.

As he shut the door and walked round the front of the car he saw the growing crowd of cars and men in the fore-court. He saw a couple standing on the pavement looking up, one of them pointing towards the top of the building he and Julianna had just left. He followed their eyeline, only now remembering what they had heard as the lift arrived. He looked up and isolated the restaurant by the blaring block of white lights, high up in the tower. That must be it. The man, the one who had escaped out of the window, must be outside still. And then the woman on the pavement cried out, and Jack's brain was slower than his senses, so he felt sick before the snap of understanding came. For a fleeting portion of a second he saw the figure, a small, dark matchstick form against the pale, glittering building, fall. It was obscenely quick, a filament floating over the eyeball and then blinked away.

But leaving an imprint. Jesus Christ. He had watched the man fall, controlled, resting on his front on the resistance, arms and legs wide – and then hard and fast, sucked down through the length of a second, on his back, until they heard the thud of his body on the ground.

The woman was saying, oh God, oh God, oh God, oh my God, over and over again. An ambulance siren could be heard. A screaming high sound coming closer. Jack stood in the freezing cold. The pattern of the fall imprinted still on his eyes. Then he opened the front door of the car, his fingers so cold they hardly worked, and drove off without remembering to turn on his lights.

They drove for five minutes or so in silence, and Julianna felt her breathing calm and her heart settle, no longer flailing against her ribcage. He reassured her that no one was following, that no one would care that she'd gone. Julianna thought that right here and now, with Jack, in his car or his house, she was probably safe. But the safest place of all, she knew, would be home. Kisrét. This was the price she had paid.

She realised she'd left the card for Jack in the cloakroom and began to cry, because she realised this period, like a movement in music, was over. The thought of that carefully plotted, naive little card made her cry even more.

Jack stopped the car and turned the key, so they were sitting in a quiet and murky darkness. Raindrops streamed down the windscreen; a car passed, taking air with it, another following in its vacuum.

He took her hands and kissed them and said, 'Don't cry. Please don't. It's OK. I can make everything OK.' He wanted to say so much, yet his words were such flat choices. He could think of nothing elaborate.

She stammered and excused herself and took away her hand to wipe her eyes; she couldn't quite explain that it was sadness, not fear. She was being moved on and she could feel him peeling away. She knew how it went, and where she would have to go. She knew what it would feel like when she left.

'I want you to marry me,' he said. 'I need you here, so marry me, and all this,' he gestured outside, 'goes away,' and she looked at him in shock, round eyes, a furrowed brow, and her tears suddenly stopped. Her look of amazement, and gratitude, was like an exhalation, an outpouring of emotion, from her to him. Love carried from one to the other, borne suddenly and received, with terrifying need. Breathing in, out, the same air, side by side, inside their small safety locked world. Outside, people and rain falling without them.

Chapter Thirteen

Nor did the weather favour Jack and Julianna's wedding. Four weeks on and every May wedding in London photographed under an umbrella. There was the odd exception: one Saturday a bride exited the porch of a church in Marylebone and the sun broke through with such precision that it was like an audible blessing. But there was nothing like that on Julianna's day. Nor were there small children for her to foster, hold hands with, basking in mutual charm, stunned with attention.

So there were no small children, and there was no sunshine, but there were bemused parents, suspicious siblings and then, quite suddenly, *peculiarly* suddenly, with the waving of a word and a pen, a husband and wife, wired with bravery and want. There was a white dress, an elegant grey suit, a collection of strangers and then a passing drunk who threw obscenities into the already uncertain crowd on the registry office steps. Only Jack's mother had remembered to bring confetti, which she flung in petulant fistfuls at their midriffs. There were too few for cheers, only Radmila and Julianna's father for the bride; Stephen and Rose Harvey and their middle son Mike, and Derek, Jack's old friend and associate, for him. So the weaving drunk, with impressive acuity, must have sensed a weakness, an opening. He joined their group at the base of the steps, and continued, without ever having begun, an anecdote which had the large generality of bad luck. He talked about a man, with a sum unspecified, and the Lord (or a lord) who had insulted him and had then . . . and on and on.

At that point Jack moved the small party on, round the corner, into the cars, irritated out of adoration by the way capable adults, frozen and self-conscious at such public eventfulness, seemed to have lost the ability to work in a group. His mother kept shearing off, doing something with the strap of her pink shoe. His father, standing by her side, smoking a cigarette with vigour. Julianna's father, a small man, had pre-empted action and now stood on the wrong side of the street. That peculiar friend of hers, Radmila, getting into the wrong car. His wedding and they a collection of misfitting parts.

It wasn't meant to be like this, he thought, in their car, waiting for his wife to follow. Not his wedding to Julianna – this would probably have always been like this, she hadn't yet discovered her potential for celebration – but his wedding. The one he'd held in the future, which bore so little resemblance to this day.

But then there was Julianna, now sat beside him, alone finally, in the back of the cab. Turning and smiling nervously to him, this woman his wife. A mediocre day giving soft edges to the world, her form blurred in his eyes with silk and decoration. And unlikeliness. He felt the flood of feeling she always invoked, at the fact of her face turned to his, and also at the pathos of the two of them stuck at this peculiar wedding which seemed to be theirs.

'Is this all right?' he asked, wanting her happy. 'Is this what you wanted?'

She smiled and kissed him luxuriously. Desire could always be counted on.

*

As the lunch passed, Julianna watched the guests talk politely. It was expensive and stiff, a room in a hotel with waiters and marble. She could have coped without seeing waiters or marble ever again, but this was her wedding. Julianna had a vision of a different kind of party, which lay submerged beneath the real view. They would have been sat around a long table, under a tree, in a garden or a field, where people would have behaved in quite a different way. Colours stark with sunlight, an Eden for a day. But in this large red-brick hotel, which looked just like a Victorian foot hospital, their small party occupied only one room out of hundreds. Off the carpeted corridor, behind a cream door, it felt as if they were acting, and also hiding – the windows draped in thick nets, London traffic somewhere far away.

Halfway through the wedding breakfast she went to the Ladies', and took a wrong turning into the hotel lobby, which was full of light and noise and the sudden arrival of a large southern European family. The women in the family saw her and stopped each other and pointed admiringly. For the first time that day Julianna felt her symbolic loveliness. She looked long and fluid in the draped silk, even, finally, elegant. Her hair was loose, pinned up in places with bay leaves and small star-shaped white flowers. She was a little uncertain of how to walk in this disturbingly light outfit, so her presence was charming rather than statuesque and the men in the lobby were distracted and clapped. Julianna was shocked by how much the sudden feeling of being beautiful made her happy.

She sat on the lavatory feeling very odd. Unreal. Disassociated from the legs and fabric below her. This was her wedding day, stupid to pretend it didn't matter, that she hadn't thought of it as a child. Yet she had been disingenuous, had pretended, had allowed her husband to organise everything except the dress, and that Radmila had organised with

205

the vicious zeal of an unattached older sister. But how stupid . . . because here she sat, separated from the day, like an exotic escaped from the zoo, an object of awe, and untouchable. What she really wanted was to go back in and proclaim, reclaim, make it very, very clear how much she wanted to do this. She now had a life rooted, begun in passion, a story to tell to her own grandchildren. Hardship, and its loneliness, was over and her awaited life could now begin. Everything ahead was unknown, as if, like Mila, she had left her past under water. But that was the nature of the exchange. Marriage between two would bring comfort and purpose to each insufficient one.

She had felt at the moment she had said yes to the shiny-suited registrar an exultation of spirits, the high altitude of a promise. She'd missed the music she hadn't thought to plan, as they'd kissed and finished and walked away from the man. She held on to that spacious moment, when her breathing could be heard in the still room, and Jack was watching her intently and the quietness had been momentous, and she felt a flood of emotion, as certain as the spread of colour in a clear, full glass. That moment hung suspended in her mind, in contrast to the peculiarity of this hotel and the muddle of feelings that Jack's assumptive proposal had later brought. That moment of marriage, when she'd said yes and named him and her in front of an audience, had felt like her own.

She returned to the Gershwin Room, nodding and smiling to the dark-suited family at the base of the stairs, and went to her father. (This was only the second wedding Julianna had ever attended. The first had been his.) He was a short man, dressed in a thin grey suit and a wide patterned tie. It was only a matter of fabric but it managed to set him apart from everyone else. He had his mother Mila's serious blue eyes, and close-cut hair, flecked with grey, and a heavily grooved face. Within his suit, though, he looked more substantial than she remembered. He was smoking a cigarette (the only stipulation she had made about the meal; her father had to be able to smoke) by the window. He took her hand between his. Smoke spiralling from their combined fist. Held her hand tightly and then released her.

She wanted to say something graceful, adult, something to mark the transition, and to thank him for making the long journey to her wedding, but even she felt her youth, and felt the need to reassure. They had never found it easy to talk; he was shy of affection.

'You must tell Tamás how happy we are, and how I want him to come and stay with us. And how I'll come and stay too. Soon.' She had hardly spoken Hungarian for months.

'That was a good meal,' he said to Julianna, side-stepping. He had been quiet since he arrived; worried, she thought.

'Be happy,' she said, almost pleading.

He sighed. 'This is very . . .' Then he stopped. 'I would have liked to have known him. Just for a week. Before you married him.'

'I know.'

'This was a big surprise, Julianna. I was still expecting you to come home. To finish college. Where your family are. And you won't be coming back now. Not in any permanent way.'

'I'll go to college here.'

'You leave with such ease,' he said, looking down, as if he almost wished her gone and it all done with. 'It's hard to explain, hard to explain why it's so hard. You must have your own life, of course.' Then he smiled, and said evasively, with levity, 'Your mother would have been pleased. You look beautiful, and you will have a good life.' He gestured at the

207

wealth around him. 'And Mila, she'd have been pleased too. He will look after you, and all this is every bit as grand as she would have wanted.'

'I know,' she said.

I haven't left you, was what Julianna felt like saying. I've simply found a place to begin. But she knew that to say that, having just said her wedding vows of love, would be to suggest she didn't believe in her husband so much as herself. She was suddenly, powerfully aware of all that could happen without a decision, and as she stood there prevaricating over how to comfort her father she felt her husband's arms round her waist, and the distracting bulk and strength of him at her back.

He whispered hello into her ear, and he was not sorry to see his father-in-law move away. Jack had tried to find the right level of formality to speak to his new father-in-law but had found György Kiss discomfortingly direct.

Julianna swivelled in his arms so her front lay along his, her torso sliding in the unstructured shift. Their faces so close to each other that he could smell the greenness of the tamed leaves in her hair.

On the other side of the room, Stephen Harvey, proprietor of the long-running Silver Services, watched his son Jack embrace his new wife. He watched the length and firmness of the woman under his son's hands, and he said to his wife, ever the unwilling repository of his comment, 'I can see why he married her.'

He sat with his legs wide apart, a skinny frame and a protuberant pot belly straining at the bottom buttons of a slightly shiny blue shirt. His face was impassive and, very slowly, with considerable finesse, his little finger curled delicately, he worked his way round the crevices of his mouth with a pink plastic toothpick. Beside him his wife, Rose, fussed with her shoe again. The pink strap was too stiff and tiny to be manoeuvred into its little gold buckle, and it was rubbing the knobble of her ankle, making a hole in her tights. Stephen looked round the room. He wasn't a man given to throwing cocktail parties, to worrying about social smoothness, but even he could see this was a peculiar ragbag of people, an expensive affair attended by people who didn't know how to make the most of it. Next to him Jack's brother Mike chatted to Radmila. She was good-looking in a frightening way, but then Mike was a boisterous man who'd been ignoring threats for much of his life, so he carried on.

All told, Stephen thought to himself, this must have cost a good three thousand. He poured himself another glass of wine, presuming it was good. He was allowing himself a moment of reflective pride – a man is so much a result of his father – when his wife, suddenly rearing back up from her ankle strap, knocked his arm. Stephen's wine slopped on the white linen, and he hissed at her as if he'd paid for every drop himself.

They'd decided no speeches, so when Julianna's father moved forwards, his hand on his chest, and cleared his throat loudly, Julianna thought perhaps he felt ill. But, it seemed, he wanted to speak. 'You'll have to translate,' he said to his daughter.

Jack looked at her, annoyed by this flouting of the planned proceedings. Julianna took his hand and made him stand beside her and her father. She was smiling, and as ever the animation softened her face, and it struck everyone for the first time, from the guests to the waiters, how very young twenty-two was.

People readied themselves; Stephen poured himself a fresh glass of beer. The waiters looked nervous and scuttled suddenly, champagne bottles aloft. But György wasn't simply making a toast. '*Apám családjában van egy szokás . . .*' They waited while he spoke words of a heavy, peculiar shape – it was hard to know what to do with their faces when they didn't understand the meaning. It made some of them feel rude, and certainly on the back foot.

After a minute he stopped, and Julianna, who had coloured during her father's words, began to translate, frequently looking downwards, one arm clasped behind her back.

'My father says that in his father's family there is a tradition. When two people get married we drink to each one of the parents and grandparents, because they are the ones who gave . . . birth to the married couple.' Jack thought again how weird their language was, hard and slurring at once. '*Nemeik eljegyzés hosszadalmas . . . nemeik nem,*' he continued, his voice becoming more emphatic.

'He says some engagements are long and some are not.' Light laughter. 'Jack never met my . . .' she prevaricated, not knowing how to refer to herself, deciding in the end to speak as if she wasn't there, '. . . Julianna's grandmother, Mila. She was born in England, and so she is perhaps the reason Julianna has come to live here. And for that reason I should be angry with her. But I could never be angry with my mother, in the same way I could never be angry with Julianna, because they are,' here Julianna floundered again, 'good women.' Which wasn't what he'd said at all. 'And although both are now very far away, Julianna is at least on a telephone, and I hope to see more of Jack than the old man who carried off my mother.' Translation hadn't helped the joke. He raised his glass, to Mila; they all followed. Then to Julianna and Jack.

It was silent once they'd sat down, and almost as if to smooth the uncomfortableness, Jack stood up.

'I wasn't going to make a speech,' he said, 'but since Julianna's father couldn't resist, I feel suddenly emboldened.' The fulsome confidence of Jack infected the others.

and they loosened and smiled in anticipation. It was a timely reminder of who this man they were toasting was. Now that he unpacked his charm, you saw how very forceful he was.

'I first met Julianna in the restaurant where she was working. I was with Derek, and Derek must have been rather surprised at my poor grasp of anyone's figure except Julianna's.' There was a hearty laugh, except perhaps from Julianna, who looked amused but rueful. Derek laughed the loudest because, however much Jack might have been entranced by Julianna, as he was now claiming, it hadn't for one moment distracted him from the discussions of that night. But then, while Derek did not expect Jack to tell people what he knew to be the truth, nor would it occur to Jack to even consider what Derek thought. Derek's interest had so long been assumed by Jack as his own.

'Entranced,' he repeated, and here for the first time he seemed on less sure ground. And Julianna continued to look at her hand, twisting her new ring around her finger. 'She is a very unique, beautiful woman, infuriating sometimes, but someone I know I can,' and again there was a loss of steam, a slowing that Derek rarely saw, 'be myself with.' He nodded to himself and the others, saw Derek nodding back, had memories of meeting rooms, and realised an occasion such as this required generosity rather than self-revelation. 'To the parents and grandparents that brought us here,' he said abruptly, swinging a glass into the air, spilling champagne on his hand, where it trickled slowly beneath his cuff and up his forearm. Julianna, who'd thought he was going to toast her beauty, stood up with a mix of disappointment and relief.

The afternoon progressed, although it seemed to take an awfully long time. By five p.m. the waiters had waned and bottles stood empty and sticky on the table. Stephen and

György had found mutual ground on the subject of tobacco, brands and smoking habits of the past, while everyone else wondered whether they were having repetitive conversations with the same person or a different one.

Then, suddenly, there was one of those moments of very ordinary drama that make you wonder how the world ever runs smoothly at all. Or how the body keeps working when there is so much to go wrong. A waiter dropped the tray of glasses that he was carrying and began to have a fit, on the floor. From another room, alerted by some inaudible grapevine, a woman came running, another waitress, similarly slight of build, so that they seemed to be related, or perhaps married, and fell to her knees at his side.

'Don't worry, it's fine,' said Jack to Julianna, turning to another member of staff, asking of doctors, while Julianna sat watching the group of people around the waiter. She could just see the man's leg judder violently, as if electrically charged. She wondered how his sister or wife or friend had known. She had come running so fast through the doors. Mila had always said she knew the exact moment that János had been killed. She'd been working in the kitchen; her son – Julianna's father, now standing grey-haired at her own wedding – was at school, and Mila had suddenly known something was wrong. 'How?' Julianna had always asked as a child, gripped by love's mystery, the glamour of death. 'How?'

'It was like somebody had suddenly stolen all the oxygen in the air,' Mila would say, with more drama than communication. Given that everyone knew what day he had died, and why, Julianna had never been told more about the actual method of his death.

In the car, on the way to the hotel in the countryside, Julianna tried not to think of her father, setting off with his battered bag to the airport. She wondered if he'd find his way. She could imagine him lost and too proud to ask. She'd picked him up in the car two days ago, and she knew he'd not understood her instructions about returning to Heathrow on the tube. She wondered if she'd ever be able to think about her home again without guilt. Her father had never provoked much poignancy, had never encouraged Julianna to feel it for him, until now, when she was irredeemably gone. Why, when two men had stood and pronounced on her loveliness, did Julianna feel so errant tonight? As if her real self, the kernel, that despite all her conflicting experiences and her conflicting longings she trusted to know what was right, had disappeared on her wedding night. She had thought she would feel released, after the act of marrying. Freed to finally live with the fullness she'd been so long awaiting. But she wasn't sure if here, in this heavy built car, with a man whose moods she sometimes struggled to define, she didn't feel a little helpless. As if liberty were too large an element to be sieved effectively into the act of marriage. Freedom focused into a fine point of law could only ever be unreliable.

Tears seeped, and she turned away from Jack in his beautiful suit, to look out of the window at London's suburbs, and focused on dilapidated things. Mila, she knew, would have said she was overtired. She felt a pang, a need for someone like her grandmother, who had led the way from one country to another, like a pioneer. Someone to tell her how to pull herself together, and when. A mother, even, to bolster and reassure. How slow I am sometimes, she thought, to work out what's missing. Everyone was meant to have a mother on their wedding day. She tried to imagine how it would have been to have a mother to share the very feminine, mysterious inevitability of the day, and couldn't.

Still, as the car drove on and on, Julianna knew it was heading towards events of a not unimportant nature. She was about to arrive at one of her storyline's pivots, departing into isolation with her husband, dressed in the most beautiful underwear she'd ever owned. Cream lace, trimmed with deep red, velvet bows and bands. She was thin and pampered and interested by her own body in these clearly sexy times.

Their bed was being carefully turned down as they reached the end of the hotel's grand drive, and she and he would lie on it, for lengths and lengths of time, eating caviar and cake, and further combinations of lubricious extremes. Port Salut and pears, duck with loganberries and lavender ice cream. Vodka cracking ice cubes with petrified flowers and steaks dripping blood and butter with thyme. Everything in those first few days of their married life was about strange combinations and the sex beneath. So that by the end of the week, everything they did, from eating to walking to swimming to sleeping, could only be done with their limbs touching. Their bodies too coldly exposed without the other moulded on.

PART 3

Spring 1995

Remember, brother soul, that day spent cleaving
Nothing from nothing, like a thrown knife?
Then there was no arriving and no leaving,
Just a dream of the disintricated life –
Crucified and free, the still man moving,
The balancing his work, the wind his wife.

Don Paterson, 'Sliding on Loch Ogil'

Chapter Fourteen

By the time Julianna was a teenager Mila had no longer been able to remember how whole decades had passed, or what people's names had once been, but she could still tell picture-perfect anecdotes of her early years of marriage. The pain of her new shoes as they ascended the Eiffel Tower, for instance. She hadn't been able to tell János they were agonising; they were surviving off expenses meant for one and these elegant French shoes had been a rare concession to her femininity.

She'd been stung repeatedly by a wasp in Granada. That she could remember too. It had got stuck in her hair, which was loose and long. She'd become a little hysterical and he'd danced behind her, huge and ineffectual. An old woman swaddled in dark layers, with a lumpen black back, had extricated the wasp and killed it between her forefinger and thumb.

'Really,' Mila had said, 'János, please. Go away. I will get better much quicker if you leave me alone,' and she sat down outside the old woman's house, on a small hard chair, trying not to vomit.

The old woman had reappeared from her house, through strands of beads that divided, bustled then settled, with lotion in a jar and an enamel bowl of water, and tended to Mila's head gently. The small street was quiet; it was early after-noon, and Mila could hear more benign insects hovering around the coloured tin cans, planted with red and pink flowers, that were lined along the bottom of the house wall. Once the pain's din had muted Mila thanked her, in the few words of Spanish she'd learnt, and smiling, relieved the old woman of the one task which had befuddled her curled fingers, the replacement of the fancy butterfly hair clip. She'd gone to find János in a café, full of affection for the Spanish which she was never, not even by 1990, to lose.

She had told Julianna these stories again and again but never about the shock of marriage. You don't tell a young girl such things. Mila had discovered just a little of János in those first few months, yet he had already renamed her. He found the 'y' in Milly childish; Mila would make more sense when they reached home, he said. She was renamed and given a new nationality without him ever questioning whether she minded. Much that was assumed as traditional was suddenly revealed as peculiar to the newly married Mila.

She had quickly discovered how unhappy unhappiness made him. Her tears physically pained him. Her constant weeping during their first week of marriage made him go quite pale with exhaustion and she ended up tending to him instead, in the dim light of a shuttered room in a rainy French cathedral town. A damp cloth and his forehead hot, even though it was not a warm October in France.

In the New Year of 1937 they'd reached Italy. Now, Italy had done something most peculiar. It had turned her into a reader. János had laughed at how unintellectual his new wife was. He had good knowledge of English writers, much better than her. 'I've had more time alone than you,' he said. It was true that when they were still (not that often), he frequently opened a book, and she, masking disappointment, lay and watched and thought. When they were travelling (more often) she felt she should watch it unfold. 'I've never seen abroad before,' she'd say when he teased her.

'A field is a field. A peasant a peasant. A cow a cow,' he'd say, and she'd thought this shocking and profligate, so when the time came that she realised that not all the world needed to be watched, she'd been reluctant to finally admit to boredom.

But then Italy came and he (horrified, almost embarrassed, to hear she'd never knowingly seen or read a Shakespearean play; 'Oh, probably, at school,' she said, and marriage struck *him* for the first time as a peculiarly tight thing) decided to read their own matchmaking poet aloud to his wife. The extraordinary wonder of this man who she'd only ever thought of as ancient and dead, having breathed and smelt and seen things so sharply, hit her. And him having been born just down the road from her and Rose and Doris. János bought her a collection of his plays, set in the tiniest type, from a panelled and sombre second-hand bookshop in Florence. He inscribed it, *All the worlds we have to discover, you and I, Mila and János Kiss*, which she thought sounded like poetry too. Already the frightened young woman in Paris that she had once been seemed inexperienced and unworldly compared to herself. She talked to her younger sister in her head all the time, giving her helpful advice on marriage and life and the broad pleasures of travel.

Whether it was Shakespeare or growing assurance, for the first time she felt infected by the spirit of the place they were travelling through. Stark hills with high towns, sharp blue winter skies pierced by dark trees, paintings in churches – delicate, smoky, painedly human, with clothing painted in livid patches of a private red. The beauty of northern Italy subdued her, involved her, made her want to understand more so that she could be drawn in further. Instead of fearing the glittering church interiors as morbid, with their dripping Christs and weeping widows, she decided they were spectacular. She had wondered where women congregated, how

221

they lived, there were so few to be seen doing anything other than working, and at church she discovered them.

Every week János would send new film back to Budapest for developing. Julianna took over the task of packaging and posting the risky little spools. She loved that János now trusted her to do this, to *assist* him, and she liked to explain to the post office in general that her husband was a *photographer*. It still seemed to her a very modern thing to be.

She had become quite frugal, and organised. She told her mother in letters home that she would be shocked. While her letters to her sister still had an unfortunate lecturing, boasting tone, her sister knew that this meant she was enjoying herself. Milly had always got bossy when there was fun going on. She didn't tell her sister how little time and money she had now for old luxuries like nail polish and face cream. János understood extravagance in bookshops and stationers better than in pharmacies. Mila had slowly abandoned possessions en route, and now only a few remained. Having once been a girl who treated her belongings poorly, she began to feel quite passionately and protectively about the few she packed and repacked into her small suitcase. Their familiarity gave her such a rush of feeling that she once or twice had to remind herself they were only *things*. She knew them so intimately now – her hairbrush, bracelet, hair clip. For some reason János had sanctioned hand cream, although Mila felt, with some irritation, that it was an odd concession. He had not married her for her hands. But one night, before bed, he'd lain watching her navigate her way round a new, yet utterly familiar, room and said he had watched his mother put on hand cream every night of his childhood. Mila had understood, for the first time, that this business of marriage,

222

familiar to everyone in appearance but not in content, was frightening for a man too.

What most scared Mila was reaching Budapest, and the static domesticity of a home. Eternally travelling was one thing. Arriving would be another. Children would come (for some reason she thought continued exposure to trains would protect her from pregnancy; she didn't realise that that was why János withdrew himself at the end of their lovemaking. As with many things, including Italian food and now poetry, Mila had decided she liked sex, and did not choose to reveal her ignorance by asking backdated questions).

In Budapest, she realised, she would be expected to enter into the next sphere: mothering and homemaking. Having only just escaped from her own mother! Travelling meant in her head that they were only ever a few trains from England, but permanence scared her. On nights when she couldn't sleep she thought of Doris and Rose and how they'd idly boasted of how much they'd like to see the world. But none of them had ever meant that they'd actually like to live out there, in it, for ever.

They'd assumed love would rescue them, but Mila-Milly was beginning to wonder if the dynamic, the exchange wasn't rather more subtle and complicated than that. Rescue meant being taken from entrapment and set free. Or did it? Did it not also mean being saved from risk and placed somewhere safe? Did safety not come from limitations? Still, she adored being with János. Neither she nor her girlfriends had even suspected the sense of freedom, the sense of the world unfolding, that sitting quiet and relaxed in a café at dusk with her husband could bring. She was proud of him in public and fascinated by his being such a *man* in private. The bedroom she supposed was the one place where she did feel both romance and risk. So perhaps this was the way it was meant to be.

It was from such circular thoughts that Mila began to turn, more and more, to the linear narratives of books. She devoured over twenty novels those last few months before they returned to Budapest. That too was a new thing. All those other plots swimming inside her head, bringing colour to schoolbook histories and wars. Her own limited past merging with a hundred potential stories and the tools of story-telling newly to hand.

The *kisgazdaság* János called home was a modest five-roomed house surrounded by open land, their own farm-land. It was an unobtrusive building. Just two storeys high, three rooms below, two on top. A lavatory out the back. It had a flat white exterior, shutters and a pretty white wrought-iron door. The couple who had been looking after the house and land in János's absence had obviously tended the garden of his childhood home carefully. Out here, where everything seemed far away, butting up against the first folds of the Bükk hills, there was little decoration to the buildings, but there were strong red geraniums growing on the steps and in the window boxes of almost every house in Kisrét. If not in the architecture, there was a grand beauty in the wilder-ness. The single-gauge train track on which they had arrived had cut through endless stretches of beech woods. Then granite cliffs had broken through, lurching over and above the train. The peaks higher and closer than she could see out of the little train window. János had said there were wolves and wild boar beyond.

She opened the front gate, and saw that the house was sur-rounded by an inner garden, although garden was possibly the wrong word for it. It was an outdoor workshop – as if all the piles and rags and odd-ends of her father's shed had been spread out on a trodden earth floor. There were neat piles of wood up against the bark of a fruit tree. A deconstructed bicycle. A rusting fruit press. Wooden crates and several white enamel bowls and buckets. Then she noticed, as it leaned into sight, rooting at the base of a decrepit tree, its nose snorting at the barren ground, a big brown horse.

She was putting off the moment when she would have to enter the house. (It was like being asked to look into a crystal ball and see all of her future at once.) She went instead up the side of the house, which was painted down to a point a couple of feet above the ground, so it looked as if it were raised up on red bricks. The horse and a companionable pig were paddocked with wire fencing into a square patch to the left of the garden. Up ahead there were more fruit trees, a patch of vines, beans growing up posts. She wove between them until she reached the bar of wood that ran round the edge of this domesticated plot. At the end of the garden the land began to slope upwards, and at the top of the hill . . . and here her heart began to beat faster at the surprise of it. At the top of the ridge, clear and distinct, grey silhouettes against the flat white of the late-afternoon sky, was a herd of grey horses. The group seemed to sprawl off the ridge of the hill – leaking to the far corners of her vision, gathered erratic but close, slowly shifting, necks channelled down, nostrils moving over the grass. They shifted imperceptibly, like a dense cloud.

This view she was prepared to live with, she decided. It had romance. Pressing her hands against her stomach, bringing them round on to her hips, taking a deep breath of the rich animal air, she went in to meet her home.

It was a small town, smaller even than Stratford, which amused Mila's sister when she read the first letter that Mila sent from her new home. 'All that way!' she said, and felt the secretarial banality of her own life brighten slightly. Mila, however, found that spring frighteningly surreal. Life was so much more primitive, the temperature and the people so much coarser than at home. Budapest had promised something slightly more civilised; even Baskó (the nearest large town) had offered something baroque, a little more ornate. This tiny town was more of a village. A rural pit stop before the land rolled into Czechoslovakia. The main preoccupation of her youth, her own decorativeness, was now rendered pointless.

János had cannily wrapped the task of learning Hungarian in the tissue of lovemaking (she was now a Kiss, and she had learnt the word for lips – *ajkak*, which like most of the language sounded both breathy and hard – before all others). But now, marooned in a sea of it, language had become a source of misery to her. She could buy things and count, but not much more. He had tried during their first week at home to make her speak Hungarian in the evenings with him. But she had cried and said if she couldn't talk properly, fully, and feel understood for at least a few hours every day, she was sure she would go mad. János said she needed some friends, which sounded curiously insulting in her ears, although she tended to agree with him.

'Where will I find English-speaking friends?' she asked. She was occasionally surprised at her boldness and rudeness to a person whom she loved and respected, and who clearly knew so much more than her about everything. Except, perhaps, about her.

'I don't know,' he said. 'I will find some for you. At the university there will be many English speakers.'

She made a disbelieving face and picked up her English magazine again.

'I should have taught you German, probably,' he said.

'Why?'

'Because plenty of people speak German here, you know that. You hear it.'

'No,' she said, 'I don't think I'd like that. It's even more ugly than your language,' she finished, but this time with a smile. She pushed at his thigh with her toe.

He grabbed her foot, a woollen chunk of warmth.

'I think German will become more and more useful for you, as they grow in power,' he said, in English, clumsily. 'They have become Hungary's brother. We are joined with them. Through history. Geography. There are always arguments and divides and we have chosen our side.' Mila smiled at him sadly, then went back to her magazine. János watched her, and wondered if his wife had any idea of the way the world worked, and the importance of birthplace and land. He would never have given up his nationality for a woman. Yet he couldn't have borne leaving Mila behind in that water-logged town.

He believed change would come, but along different lines to the past. They had all lost so much, all of Europe, that from now on things would have to be fought in a different way. He and his friends' concerns were with the poor, the uneducated, the feudally downtrodden of their own land. The families leaving rural villages to feed the industrial boom and living in black filth on the edges of their gracious cities. His quarrel was not along the old distinctions of territory. It was not a vertical divide, between countries or continents, east or west, that mattered. The real issues, he believed, were horizontal; they lay in class and wealth. His family had always had a little land, his father had been a doctor, they were educated, bourgeois. He paid for that privilege in worry. He saw the sufferings of Mila, the language isolation and the family separation, as the price she had to pay for following her heart. What worried him was how he would be forced to pay for following his in bringing her here.

*

Mila found some solace in her surroundings. On a large scale, there was a ruined castle on a rocky promontory nearby with a view that reminded her of the landscapes in the paintings they had seen in Italy. The horses, too, brought their own drama, men almost like cowboys rounding them up and leading them across the hills, soft broad hats on their heads, cigarettes in their mouths. The horses weren't normally coloured, she didn't think. Some were white, silvery, with pale cream manes, and these ones she reckoned moved in a different way, knowingly, deliberately, like the most beautiful girl in a village. Then the spectrum ran from pale greys – iron freckles on the rumps, their manes still pale – until they were a dark, soft colour, the ring collar of a dove. Yet the more perfectly dark their velvet skins, the paler cream their manes became.

János set off for his teaching job in Baskó every morning at 7.30 a.m. He had taken a temporary job teaching geography at the school where he himself had been taught and had so excelled. Just until the next commission arrives, he said. Mila wondered what she was meant to do when he got another commission, which would mean leaving and travelling again. But so far there had only been excursions of a few days, to Budapest to photograph a group of political writers, for nothing. To Vienna to capture the historically rich home of a recently rich woman, for more.

Mila treated these days like holidays; there was less need for household work with János gone, and she would catch the bus to Baskó and visit the churches, drink coffee in one of the hotel cafés by the fortress walls or the prettily bridged river. The teacher-training college ran the length of one side of the town's main square. The place fascinated her. All of them young, lingering outside, clutching books and sheaves of paper, talking as if what they said mattered and might

228

influence, yet only the same age as her. One empty day she paid for her coffee, picked up her gloves, crossed the square and went right in. Through the heavy wooden doors, below the symmetrical windows that were shaped like rhomboids, meeting and then sliding with a Viennese flourish down to lower points. Through the heavy velvet curtain that kept the draughts out of the entrance hall, large, white and echoing with hundreds of fast steps on stone floors and stairs. No one seemed in the slightest interested by her arrival. There was a reception desk, but no one at it. She looked at the signs, recognised the meaning of one – library – and began to follow. The stairwell circled up to the first then second floor and the sign then directed her along a long corridor of large closed doors. Each door gave a name and a long list of what she presumed were different classes that could be attended within.

The college was obviously very old, even though its massive, sturdy stone style was unfamiliar to Mila. It was constructed as if it were a thick square frame around a large courtyard – which received the sunlight in strict divisions. Mila heard a clock chime, the same chime as her father's carriage clock had had (Big Ben's own song, he'd pointed out to every new visitor). The eleventh hour chimed and simultaneously six or seven doors opened and people began to file out, feed into a growing train of walkers. Down below, the courtyard was being used as a rushed short cut, as it probably was on the hour, every hour. Up here, on the second floor, there were two streams, those on the left travelling anti-clockwise, those on the right heading the way Mila had come. She allowed herself to be carried along, admiring the women's serious, capacious leather satchels. A young man attracted comments as he fought like a fish against the current.

The library door was made of dark wood, and the matt-gold

handle stuck a little as she pushed it down. She stepped into complete darkness, then light flooded in, and someone stood before her. There were two doors and no light in the airlock between. The woman moved aside to let Mila enter. She stepped forward and then, feeling herself surrounded by something extraordinary, she gasped. The first thing she was aware of was the colour, a deep, warm, pinkish-red wood. It was a library, built floor to ceiling from this living, soft wood. Books of old burnished bronze bindings, and others of pure white leather, were shelved from ceiling to floor. It was a big room, people working quietly at tables in the window recesses, and it was divided into two storeys, so that halfway up there was a wooden balcony and walkway to access this higher level of shelves. On the ground floor, doors in the corner of the room gave access to the stairs, and doors or windows were inset into the flow of shelves. Bookshelves were squeezed into corners, into pediments above doors, and these were then stacked with perfectly shaped books that decreased in size, so that not an inch of the room was unused.

It took Mila a little while before she registered the ceiling. Then when she did look up and see it she actually said out loud, 'Good God,' and the woman who had let her in laughed and said, in English, 'Beautiful, yes?'

'Just beautiful,' said Mila. 'You're absolutely right.'

That was the day Mila made her first Hungarian friend. It was Mila who suggested they have coffee, yet years later they would argue over who initiated their relationship. With the perspective of time Mila was certain she'd never have had the bravery to suggest a coffee to an unknown woman. All she remembered about those early days in Kisrét was the fear. Her fear feeding itself with empty time. That was when she simply didn't have enough to do, so she remembered that lonely fear much more than anything she felt in later years, when she and her family and friends had had a real reason to confront danger. By then she'd found despair could be distracted, adults keeping each other busy, the principle no different from babies.

Over that first coffee, side by side on a velvet sofa, sharing a cake piled with cream, she and Krisztina agreed to exchange lessons in each other's language. Krisztina was not planning to go to England at any particular time soon, but she was keen to expand her knowledge and was more than realistic about her home town. One day she took Mila up to the top of the teaching college tower, where in the eighteenth century an astronomer had corresponded with Greenwich and spent every night plotting the stars. There was a flat-topped roof from which you could see for miles. Krisztina pointed to the north, south, east and west. Gesturing vaguely to borders. 'Here is Ukraine. Yugoslavia. Czechoslovakia.'

They turned slowly on the spot. The town was in a bowl and hills surrounded them, higher to the north and east.

'Where is my house? Where's Kisrét?' Mila asked, then recognised a large yellow-painted church on the road out. 'There,' she said, pleased at long last to be able to locate something.

'The man who built this,' Krisztina pointed to the stone beneath her feet, 'wanted it to be a university. A place like . . . a great university.'

'Like Oxford?' said Mila.

'Yes, a place where great people studied. But Austria, when we were part of their empire, did not like it.'

Mila thought suddenly of Siena, where she and János had climbed to the top of a church and looked at the hills of Italy disappearing into an orange sky. That was a small, rich, wonderful city. Full of great art and buildings. Baskó, with the best will in the world, wasn't. She felt sorry for the dreamer. How people invested in places so.

They continued to look out, her and Krisztina, in silence.

'I think, sometimes,' said Krisztina, who, Mila was rapidly discovering, thought quite hard about things, and who was a daughter and sibling to others who talked in a more involved way than Mila had ever heard before about politics and ideas and writers, as if they were actually a part of such things, 'if you can see a long view,' she gestured out far with her arm, 'you feel more,' and again she stopped, and made a clenched shape out of her hands.

'Trapped,' said Mila.

'Yes,' said Krisztina.

They stood looking at the horizon for a while and then turned to go down.

It was Krisztina who explained to Mila that the soft charcoal-coloured horses with the weird creamy-white manes were actually youngsters, taking their time to adjust. Foals were born dark then lightened to meet the silvery genetics of their breed as they matured. And even when fully grown their coat was still in the process of changing. 'Just think,' Mila said to János, 'no one might ever have got round to telling me. I could have remained that ignorant for the rest of my life.'

Chapter Fifteen

These *fin de siècle* days Jack Harvey felt as if he were super-human. His days would blossom just as he had visualised while being driven to work at 6.30 a.m. His impressive car negotiating the city, travelling unimpeded, nosing swiftly round corners, padding over speed bumps like a zoo-escape cat. Jack in the back, plotting the way the day would work, the formal dance of each meeting, driving AFH's future with his will. AFH was the realisation of his strength, like seeing your own intelligence take physical form. It was the shape of him, and it was the best of him; it was born of him and it grew and grew and created money each day. And if this was not a very clear-headed, economic way to assess his own business he would have to be excused on the basis that it was only his stamina and energy that gave his excitement away. To outsiders he seemed the model of success well-handled.

As the years had passed AFH had taken on all the necessary facets of what one would describe as a well-rounded man. It counselled and pensioned and negotiated fairly, and regularly gave to charity without prompt. It had advice leaflets for those who had taken advantage of its services a little too much, as if debt was as discreet an embarrassment as thrush, and now it was sponsoring after-school clubs in urban areas to distract and encourage the children of those below the poverty line, those who were beyond aspiration's arms. Thus the children of the very adults who borrowed money from the respectably marketed AFH were taught to trust AFH, even if only through recognition of the syllables painted on community centre walls and stuck on to book covers in their primary schools.

All of these good things AFH practised. No wonder Jack was so absorbed that he failed to practise such tolerance and compassion himself. *His* job was turnover. His company was the living thing and must choose its actions even more carefully than himself. Sustainability was rooted in society. He'd seen businesses fall at the hands of angry protestors, newspaper articles, questions in parliament. He knew that. But him? Well *he* was as sustainable as his pulse. Free to act as he alone wished. His company was the accountable thing. The feelings that had driven him to rescue Julianna three years ago, to marry her with such hope and demand her presence so wholly, to plot her switch from an illegal to legal resident as if it were a time of war (with all the fever of Julianna's frequently evoked grandparents), were being slowly buried. As if he were kicking earth over his own weakly human scent.

The physical proximity of marriage unnerved him, let alone the emotional.

The first two years had been novel. They both understood the strangeness that two such different people should have come to this. That strangeness was a protective blanket under which they could both still call up love. But somewhere in the year after their son Luke's birth the gap between them began to dominate, rather than enchant. Jack turned on his heels and ran from the self-conscious attempts at understanding that it would have required to bridge it.

He was aware he spent little time with their child. He knew that. It hardly needed pointing out. But he was himself, and he was a man who worked. No one, including even

234

his child, was born with everything. The two of them, Julianna and the child, had a way of looking at him, a combination of yearning and disinterest, which was too unpredictable for him to know how to address. He loved them, he supposed. But they frightened him. Both of them seemed barely under control, and he saw the photos of boring-looking blonde women with hairbands and fat children in school uniforms on his directors' desks and thought that that was the kind of conventional family he would have liked. Somewhere where they'd understand that he was his business. Not ask any more of him. Understand that he was giving the very best he could, and that AFH was part of him, part of them, and that it was a more valuable asset than some middle-management dad.

He was aware, perhaps too aware, of the benefits of an attractive and passionate young wife. But her youth only highlighted him. He aged as soon as he stepped through the front door, suddenly twice her age. In the years since they'd been married she'd grown even slimmer, her hands seeming even larger at the end of her tiny wrists and long, unchanging arms. She wore her hair up, unless they were going out, or she was going to bed (they rarely went together, but he would not have countenanced separate rooms. It was one thing to wonder quite how he had been so magicked by Julianna one winter, but quite another to stop needing to feel her body in the middle of the night. *Sex* he still needed. How could he not, when she was so lithe during the day and limpid in sleep?).

She slept facing towards him. He had found the fragility that position gave her touching for several years; before the baby was born he sometimes arrived and left before she ever opened her eyes to see him. Now she awoke easily, he and his son the disturbers, her always the disturbed. When he emerged from the shower in the morning, he would see

Julianna feeding Luke, her body still sloping with sleep, his son's feet scrunching and releasing with pleasure. He frequently fell asleep at the bottle – which gave Jack the impression of his son as a self-indulgent, sensuous little bugger. He felt both an unwelcome pressure and a certain pride when he looked at the child.

They had started having sex again a few months after Luke was born. Despite the wheeze of the baby's breathing down the monitor, which felt much more intrusive and aggressive than a product of a similar act should have done. Sometimes he suspected Julianna did it just to please him. He wondered if he was meant to feel bad about that too. He would remember the sex during the following day, at the urinal, in the car watching the women of the city walk by. And the thought of her neck and her long hair and weighted breasts recurred and he was suddenly filled with a memory of her skin, not just a taste or a smell, but a texture learnt and loved with his lips. These moments were as intense as the emotional generosity he'd felt that first winter with Julianna. Then he would remember how little he could bring himself to speak to her, how her lack of understanding about everything made him plain angry. He wondered what other people's marriages were like. Where they the same? Smothered resentment, distances between you stretching like weeks ahead, suddenly punctuated by such mute, intense, dark patches of night that the contrast was disturbing. He found it impossible to speak of who they sometimes turned into at night. He knew her body well now – he'd seen it grow with the baby and then return – and when they were out in company or coming back in the car he found the knowledge arousing. He knew where things began, and how her rhythm worked, and when her body reacted. But he had no idea what was going on in her head.

Next month AFH would go public. He had felt empowered by the first two years of their marriage, permitted even

236

more energy and confidence, as if the gaining of a wife had closed a certain, draining channel. He had achieved extra-ordinary things without even seeking further investment, taking over two competitors, merging customers and offices, doubling pure profit. The roadshow had begun, the round of presentations to fund managers and analysts, and already he was racking up several mentions a day in the business pages of the broadsheets. He'd been invited to speak, chair, contribute, dine, invest, view, hear . . . These things meant one thing to him. He was being invited to spend his money all over the place. All the legislative discussions, political phone calls, personal string-pulls and marketing campaigns were worth nothing if they did not help AFH to thrive. He thought he was canny in not falling for the lie that because his time was being sought *he* belonged. He didn't belong, but as long as AFH continued to grow, he had respect. He would be welcomed, but they would never be easy with him, in the way they were with many of his more junior directors.

The date of the AFH flotation was even marked on the kitchen calendar, Jack noticed. He'd been irritated by Julianna for doing that, as if it were a dentist's appointment. All roads were leading to this; the fact that she needed reminding made him feel as if he'd married a simpleton. He'd watched her jig the baby, talk her very straight (not cooing or concessionary) sentences to the infant in her light accent, and after all the urgent activities of his powerful days, it felt like catching sight of a hidden, shameful and very foreign relative.

'What will you do with this money that comes from selling all these shares?' Jack's mother had asked the last time he'd seen her, at Christmas. Jack had realised then that having a grandchild had changed her. She was generally sturdier and more present, and was transformed into actual animation when with the baby. He watched her gleefully dancing Luke, and despite himself, loathing himself, he wondered why he never remembered her being like that when *he* was a child. She boldly asked things she would never normally have done, like the purpose of floating his company. He'd laughed out loud, as an initial response. Then said, 'Well I never,' which earned him a sharp look.

'We'll grow,' he said. 'Maybe we'll buy a bank. What d'you think? It'd be interesting to have a legitimate high street bank in the family. What d'you reckon?' he said, wanting a reaction. 'By the time he's teenage and spotty it'll be a whole other ball game.' But all Rose said was, 'He won't have spots. He takes after his mother.' And while this exchange was taking place his father was talking with Julianna, sat in the chair with the mechanical footstool that folded itself outwards if you leant far enough back. As if nothing mattered. As if everyone's business was as risky as a pawn shop on a shopping parade, files of dodgy agreements out the back. Every parade in Horden now came complete with a video shop, corner shop, Chinese takeaway, hairdresser, £1 shop, and if you were lucky and thriving, a post office, and if you weren't, his dad, still leeching off the bottom rungs. Sitting smoking in his shop with its soiled, curling carpet and hard plastic chairs.

'Yes, but you haven't seen what I've seen,' Jack heard Stephen say to Julianna from the end of the room. Stephen always spoke to her as if she were slightly stupid, in a loud, slow voice, enunciating the words carefully. Julianna didn't seem to mind. She was laughing now. It was extraordinary how quickly she had capitulated from a reserved, disapproving politeness into familiarity with the old git. It humiliated Jack now to think of all the self-pitying crap he had told Julianna in the first year of their marriage. At first, discomfited by the luxury of her home, and the ease of her life, she'd questioned him hard about his father's business and AFH. But then she seemed to have accepted the status quo of their family in a way that made him feel as if the one person who could have brought justice to all the tyrannies of his childhood had defected to the other side. Jack sighed. They were all so fucking unruly. His mother asking daft questions, his father flirt-fighting with his daughter-in-law, and his wife, plenty moral when she wanted to be, laughing with the nasty old sod. This was what not leaving your past behind did for you. He dreaded to think what Julianna had left behind. Her family were coming to visit at some point this spring; it had been threatened for years, and now that the child had arrived, it could hardly be avoided.

Jack got off the sofa and went behind the crazy paving bar Stephen had built himself. In amongst the Mallorcan tat was a great deal of duty-free. His mum and dad had been to the same hotel for the last ten years, and met the same other couples there. His dad moaned each February when the time for booking came, but they always went. His mother said much less on the subject; the treat was precarious enough already, but she always came back looking a decade younger.

Jack stood at the French windows, looking beyond the reflection of the Christmas tree, multicoloured lights on slow, fast, fast, slow, into the leaf-deep garden. He could smell the winter air on the draught.

He heard Julianna laugh again and strained to listen to their conversation.

'Where was he born then?'

'I think it was somewhere near the sea, in Poland.'

Stephen snorted. 'Well that doesn't help much . . .'

'No but to me, as a child, that was extraordinary, I hardly ever saw the sea until I came to England.'

'No sea!' Stephen looked delighted. 'No way . . . no sea? This summer we'll be down at the beach every weekend with Luke and you. Leave the boring bugger at his desk.' He winked at Julianna. 'First time I saw the sea was when we was evacuated from London. We went to Portsmouth, saw these massive boats come and go. The first time there was this huge warship leaving. And it was packed on the boat, all you could see was white, thousands of men standing shoulder to shoulder saluting. And the crowd was there to wave them off and they went all quiet as they left the dock. There was that many people on the boat, and on the shore, and you didn't hear voices, just the boat churning in the water.

'You'll never have seen a boat carrying that many people; you don't except in wars, big boats of soldiers, big boats of refugees. But you want to hope you don't, all those people, 'cause one bomb, and then whoosh, that's the lot. A boat full of people standing shoulder to shoulder is like a prayer – it's that powerful. And that stupid.'

Julianna was smiling. Jack clenched his teeth. His father could get quite lyrical after a few whiskies.

'He died,' Julianna ploughed on, talking of her grand-father, 'in 1956, in the revolution against the Russians, in Budapest. They fell in love in 1936, you know this I expect, but I am always still curious about how it was for them. They fell in love and she went back to his home, with no idea what was coming. Just a few years before the Nazi occupation, they were just two young people and then there she was. An Englishwoman, suddenly in the very worst place at the worst time. And then they survive, she has forged papers, they lie and they bribe and they make it through. Only then the Russians arrive and they kill my grandfather when he was still not fifty.

'I just always wonder how could she not have known there

240

was a war coming. How did she cope with being so . . . without control? So at the mercy of governments and armies? No money or food or land, everything beating them. But even twenty years after he was gone you could tell how much they were in love.'

Jack raised his eyebrows. This again. She talked about their lives with such longing. Almost envy, he thought. It was the fucking Second World War . . .

'He must have been a brave man,' said Stephen, raising his glass in a toast. He's drunk, thought Jack.

'I don't know,' said Julianna, and for a second Jack was pleased with her. 'I never knew him.'

'What d'you mean, you don't know? Of course he was bloody brave. I don't think women really know about physical bravery.'

Julianna laughed abruptly. 'That child,' and she pointed to Luke, 'ripped my body. You should never, *ever* say that to a mother,' and she wagged her finger at Stephen.

He belched to cover a slight embarrassment, but not for long. 'I'm talking about history, not babies. You all think security is your God-given right, and you've no idea, not one of you, how history has made you what you are. You don't understand that you're just rolling along, in the wake of everything we've done. Your grandfather knew about history, he tried to buck it, to fight it. And you lot think you're all incredibly individual . . .' he said with a sneer in his voice.

Julianna opened her mouth to protest. Then closed it. Stephen was unshakeable in his hatred of the modern world, and she'd quickly learnt that arguing with him was pointless. Recently she'd begun to feel these flashes of panic. Different from the panic of new motherhood; an intense, trapped anxiety that the future was done. She hoped it was a temporary pessimism, not a premonition.

'Although I've got to hand it to you, Julianna,' Stephen

continued, ignoring objections as ever, pouring himself another glass. 'You could have stayed in one place and you didn't. You've got to have balls to do that.'

You collection of stupid fucking frauds, thought Jack. He turned to see his own son, arms above his head in his grandmother's hands, take two rare, distinct steps on the carpet. Jack watched, surprised. He'd never witnessed the mechanics of his child's development before. It wasn't quite an independent movement but his son looked incredibly pleased with himself. Jack had never seen anything so self-celebratory. The round-balled foot was lifted a little, held for a fraction of a second and then placed down with wobbling concentration. His arms held in triumphant, pneumatic crescents. His body rocked as he took another step, the whole of his padded form on the verge of collapse. He looked like a plump child, but he wasn't. That morning, unusually, he'd seen Julianna change him, and he'd been surprised by the thin length of his legs and torso. He had his mother's dark hair and, Jack realised, watching them now, his own mother's smile. It was a distinctive smile, because the right half of their lower lip went a little lower and wider than the other.

'He's got your smile,' said Jack to his mother, astonished at the simplicity of the biology. His mother suddenly looked so pleased that Jack wished he had a camera.

He sat down and briefly tried to play with his son.

Chapter Sixteen

Jack and Julianna's son, Luke János Harvey, was nearly twelve months old. He had dark hair that shone and curled as if he were a happy, wicked seed in a bunch of bland and blond cherubs. He had a pert nose, a large forehead and a tendency to keep quiet for many days, and then to produce a move of such mischief that Julianna was convinced her child would become something very important, or find himself in jail, early on.

She was amazed how he thrived and demanded of her, regardless of the fact, impatiently uncaring of the fact, that she had been totally unprepared to become a mother. With his birth had come a roaring certainty, the instinct to protect her son, but also an equally strong uncertainty as to whether she was doing the best for him. She thought of Luke as having the capacity for limitless forgiveness, which was fanciful, but then she remembered so little of her early childhood that who knew what she had forgiven. In any case it was no more incredible than the idea that she was a mother. She was now doing something she could be certain her own mother had done too, which gave Julianna a new way to imagine her, an expanded knowledge of her life, which she liked.

Routine was rarely broken in 36 Leicester Gardens. She shopped, dealt with the house, paid the bills. Twice a week she took Luke to local baby groups. They had had a cleaner for a year, but Julianna had found the dynamic of employment so uncomfortable that when the woman had left she hadn't bothered to find a new one. Ordinarily Jack worked seven days a week, five of them in the office until seven p.m., but recently he had been staying even later. He worked in his office at home on Saturdays. Only on a Sunday did he sleep a little later, until 8.30 maybe, read newspapers, eat and go for a walk in Richmond Park with his wife and child, then return home to read work papers in the sitting room, under pools of subtle lighting, almost voluptuous in the mess of information with which he surrounded himself. He poured himself steady quantities of red wine, occasionally changed a CD, felt the afternoon light giving up on him and welcomed the night and the week coming in. This was when he seemed to Julianna happiest. Not that he didn't want her there, or Luke, if he wasn't crying. He liked to look up and see them. She could see how they would make a nice tableau.

She had grown more self-conscious, as she became more invisible to the outside world. As if she were an old woman fighting a losing battle, or a creature becoming unaccustomed to the light. Sometimes she felt so unengaged with the world around her that she could quite see how her mother might have died and left everyone uninclined to remember her.

Jack had only become aware of the county council court case against Silver Services a fortnight before it was due to be heard. David Golding, his communications director (they joked that his real title should be Minister without Portfolio), had come into his office with an unusually cautious air. He was a large, bearded man who was surprisingly delicate in his movements and manners. Everyone trusted him; something about the glasses and the gut, the obvious physical drawbacks, allayed any competitive or fearful agendas.

Those who came to him with only self-serving matters found themselves welcomed, hugged, given a great many opinions, a couple of jokes, were spun round and round, wrapped dizzyingly in his train of thought and sent on their way. Later they would find it hard to explain what exactly they'd been told, but it only increased their appreciation of him. He was widely respected and spoken of as being clever and on the right side of honest. But only Jack knew quite how brilliant he was, and quite how deceptive.

He sat down on the edge of Jack's desk. 'Had a call from a Jim Kirstoff,' he began. Jim was a financial journalist – he'd recently left the *FT* to start his own PR agency, and he was someone with whom David had a reciprocally helpful relationship. 'He's heard something and wanted to let us know that it was on the wind, as it were.' He handed Jack his handwritten notes from the conversation. He always wrote everything down in his scratchy handwriting. It was old-fashioned, but as the rest of the world got faster and sloppier with its conversations, as the slipped sense and elliptic grammar of the email began to infest all copy – so that a stream of consciousness style was no longer the preserve of old people and novelists, and began to be found even in mortgage pamphlets – David's careful, contempo-raneous notes were an effective weapon.

'Harvey Snr, Silver Services, civil prosecution, harass-ment, extortion, Westington District Council, CCA 1974, 21 Feb, *FT* diarist on trail.'

Jack finished reading and said nothing for a moment. He put the piece of paper carefully on his desk, aligned it with the edge, and thought to himself, I will fucking kill him.

'I presume we can deal with it,' he said instead.

David watched him and wondered to himself why men without a background were rarely successful. A mental note in his head, an opening sentence for the political thriller he

245

intended to start writing once his late-in-life children, Toby and Sophie, had learnt to sleep through the night.

'Yes,' said David, 'as long as you're happy to leave it to me.'

Jack nodded.

'What are you going to do?' he asked in an unconvincingly detached way.

'Well. Generally speaking, there's usually a man with a crusade in any court case. This one works for Westington District Council. Which is good news,' he said, in his flattest voice, 'because we can do some good for the town, at the same time as freeing up valuable court time.'

It was quiet in the office. Jack's left hand began to pull at the flesh of his chin and jowls.

David became more intimate. 'My point being that this is really quite unnecessary. There's no need for your father to carry on working.'

Usually the chasm between Jack's past and present didn't show, didn't matter here in his pristine, steel-clad office block. But something in the weird peace of the office alerted Jack to the fact that his discomfort was seeping out. David was waiting.

'I am quite sure,' and in that word he invested a great deal of emphasis, 'there's nothing Dad would rather do than retire.'

David nodded and left the room. The exchange had lasted no longer than a few minutes, but he knew how much Jack would have hated it. But David wasn't a powerful man for nothing, more powerful than the men he worked for because he was the one person who could receive, deliver and solve such events. He was never the person to fall.

After David left the office Jack sat very still for five minutes, before picking up the phone to his father. What was happening inside him felt so out of control that the only thing he could do was sit very still. He felt at first nothing more than a tremendous roaring rage, and if he'd been far away from everyone he would have bellowed, head back, mouth wide to the sky, arms rigid and fists clenched. But here he was behind his mahogany desk, thirty feet up from the ground, at the end of one long open-plan office after another.

He stood up, and walked to the window, trying to ease the tension in his stomach and chest. What would he have done if his father had been there? But his father would never be here. The two of them hadn't been in a room alone together for decades. Had Stephen any idea what this place was, what his life was? Did his father even know what he'd built? All those ignorant years – playing petty gangster, breaking people's arms, thinking he was a hard man. He was fucking pathetic. And he was his father.

How could that be?

Julianna never knew where Jack was or what he was doing, just the estimated time of his return. But he phoned on his way to Westington that night, from the Alfa Romeo. Julianna was just putting Luke to bed and sensed something in Jack's voice, some extra, added layer of distance, some spillage of anger, which was unusual. She heard a small jubilant voice inside her – she could be in bed by the time he returned.

Their marriage had once felt like their own independent adventure, and now she cheered when he didn't come home.

She told herself she was tired. In fact she *was* tired. She had a lot to do. Her family were coming to stay soon and she'd decided to redecorate the spare rooms. There was obviously no need for her to save or stockpile or borrow for celebration – not as there had been in Kisrét when a party for returning family involved loaning from and inviting in everyone. There was nothing for Julianna to do but to keep the house ticking over, the three of them fed, occasionally replacing elements of the house, using an endlessly refilling bank account. Redecorating was the least she felt she could do for her family, and tomorrow she had the baby group coming for lunch. She comforted herself with the thought. Some of the women were nearly friends, even if they spoke in shades of introspection that Julianna could not recognise. There was a film on telly too – she was sure it would distract her, it was about a wife taken hostage. Together the movie and the educated, unworking mothers would remind Julianna that marital problems were just hiccups in a lifetime.

He didn't leave the office until 8.30, so the roads were clearer by the time he left and he was able to drive through east London to the M25 with aggression, a style which appreciated a certain space and lassitude. The Kent A-roads were interspersed with irritatingly small roundabouts, ones which required little or no rounding and so there was no point in slowing down, just driving over the little rounded domes at the centre, fast. Like hitting and running each time.

But by the time he arrived he had lost some of the violence inside him. He was calm and distanced enough to notice once again the distinct smell of leaf mould in the cold air.

Rose was surprised to see Jack at this time of night. She answered the door in her dressing gown.

'You ill, Mum?' he said, walking past her without an embrace.

'No, dear,' she said, not wishing to describe her domestic habits to her grown-up son. She always changed into her nightgown at nine, had a cup of tea and went to bed at ten. He didn't wait for the answer.

'I need to talk to Dad for a while,' he said, and she nodded. She could tell this was not a social visit. She shut herself into the kitchen where she made him a coffee. She left it on the counter, hoping he'd find the floral mug by instinct, and went to bed.

Jack had worked it out in the car. What he hadn't done, and what he now needed to do, was take control of the family. Ignoring and disowning wouldn't solve the problem. His father was out of control, and his brothers knew it but didn't care much. They saw their parents no less than Jack (perhaps three times a year each), but they weren't burdened with the wealth or success that confers responsibility in families. He understood this now. He was disturbed to have realised, somewhere beyond Bromley, that he hadn't grown up in relation to his parents. He was still thinking of them as if he were a son, not a father. A young man, not a substantial one.

His father came down the stairs slowly, smoothing his hair. Jack wondered briefly if he too had been dressed in his pyjamas, until he saw Stephen's face and he remembered. That, unlike his mother, this was not someone who was softening into old age and quaint behaviour. If Stephen was doing anything, Jack thought, confronted by his coarse-skinned, red-nosed face, he was getting worse.

'It's late,' Stephen said. 'Something up?'

Once, when he was very young, when he'd been on the up and had been proud of himself and his family, Stephen had had the head and the inclination for affection. But not within his sons' memories. The closest he had ever come was moments when he'd been able to provide them with things they needed. A car for Mike, a loan for Tony to start his building business. It was harder with Jack because he'd never needed anything.

Now that he had his audience Jack didn't know how to

begin, and the living room was silent for many seconds. They stood facing each other, Stephen next to the fireplace, Jack in the centre of the thickly carpeted room. It was hard to think in here at the best of times, it was so swagged and plush and textured. The overriding colour was a rich red, and as Stephen bent to flick the gas for the fake fire Jack saw the redness in the small starter-flames swimming in front of his dizzy eyes. With that distraction Jack found himself loosened to talk. He sounded less powerful to himself than he had intended. More tired. But he was, at least, in control.

'I don't want to know the ins and outs of it. We've all ignored it for years, Mum and Mike and Tony and me. But you are too much of a liability to be working any more. Were you going to tell me about the court case at any point, or just, you know, wait until it ruined me? I don't even really want to talk about it. The less I know about it the better. But you need to know several things. We will sort it out. It will be dealt with . . .' He wasn't looking at his father. He must have known that it was best not to because Stephen was looking at his son with a still, hollow-cheeked disdain. Something about his mouth suggested that an only mildly funny joke had recently been made. 'But you have to stop. You have to close up and stop. Retire, for Christ's sake. AFH is being floated next month and you . . .' he faltered; he felt suddenly very close to choking, not crying or coughing, but seizing up, and hardened his tone to quash the reaction, 'have no conception, no idea of the amounts of money, the implication, the size of what is about to happen with AFH. This is,' and again, the same childish instinct to scream from frustration at a parent who refuses to understand, 'this is my company, this is my family. You threaten every single one of us with the way you behave.' Finally he looked at his father. Who was watching him, not

250

moving an inch under the focus of his son's life anger. 'You always have.'

'You sound like a bloody teenager,' Stephen said, finally. 'Get out.' Words like spitting.

Suddenly Jack was released and angry and able to say it, gone beyond frustration into adrenalin. 'You ruined our fucking family when you went to prison, and you never, ever learnt. That woman has waited on you for years, and we've kept quiet for years. And you are an old man, a pathetic old man, holding on to some tiny, crappy racket. And you think you can still cut it. You think it still matters whose door you kick in in this fucking backwater. Well it doesn't. Not any longer. It's done. It's finished.'

'You think I can't deal with a court case?' Stephen said, flat and calm as you like. 'Where d'you think I spent all those years? Butlins?'

Jack watched him, held his breath and then said with visible constraint, 'What do you want? A fucking war? What? Yes? Are you going to win? If I walk away, you'll lose your licence and then you'll lose this house. Or you give it up, let me deal with it and then you can spend the rest of your life playing golf. And my mum gets to see her grandchild from time to time.'

There was a pause, and then Stephen breathed in, and said, 'Yeah, well,' as if a little bored, 'you've said what you wanted, so you can go now.' He bent to turn off the fire, and when he pulled up he looked hard into his son's face, his eyes frightening, as if they'd absorbed the burn. 'You still can't see that you and I are just the same. You think the money you lend is cleaner than mine? You think you're a better father than I was? I can't see it yet, Jack. You've got even less time for your wife and kid than I had.' Then he sighed, as if even he found the next sentence a little sad. 'I've got customers, so you can't close me down that easily.

251

And since it's got to be all above board, hasn't it,' and his angry eyes almost twinkled, 'you're going to have to buy me out. And . . . and you should know this by now, you ungrateful little sod, I'm not that cheap.'

Chapter Seventeen

In the lobby of the county court Bob Shillabeer edged his finger in between his collar and his neck, wincing as he caught raw skin. He wondered whether his new shirt wasn't too tight; his flesh seemed to be bulging. But he was too nervous and too sensible to really trust anything that he was thinking. Alison had phoned him before he left, wished him luck, and asked wistfully whether he might get off the subject of Stephen Harvey once and for all if they won the civil action against him this morning.

'Have I been boring about it?'

'A bit.'

'Oh.' He was surprised. 'I didn't know.'

'Hmnn.'

'You should have said.'

'I did.'

'Oh.'

Alison sighed, and said stoically, 'Never mind. I hope it works. He bloody deserves everything he gets.'

'Alison . . .' Bob didn't like her swearing.

'Oh for God's sake.' A sound of exasperation exploded. She'd been a friend, who slept with him, for several years now. She'd never seemed to want more of him. There was an ex-boyfriend lurking, and the two of them were now too stuck in the aspic of casual behaviour to ever seem to move on.

'All those complaints, all that work you've done, no one having the balls to stand up in court. The crying shame,' her voice was quite loud now and Bob had had to hold the receiver away from his ear, 'the tragedy of it is that you couldn't get any more than one lousy witness statement. People don't care; once they've worked out they can't be forced to pay, they can't be bothered to go out of their way and do anything to stop him from trapping other people . . .'

'You don't sound bored now,' said Bob, interrupting her.

Whereupon she had growled at him, in a friendly way, and put the phone down.

He loved it here at the court. It wasn't an imposing building, just a 1970s two-storey, horseshoe-shaped, red-brick construction that could have been a funeral parlour or family planning clinic. But it did have raised flowerbeds all around, eight steps up to the main entrance and a red and blue stucco crown above the door. Once inside its bland, sand-coloured interior, there was an atmosphere of contained dynamism.

Bob had great reverence for this seat of municipal power. He, even if most of the town didn't, knew the decisions that were made in here, and the effects they had. Decisions that made the difference between good and bad children's homes, the difference between the town's bins being emptied and not, between whether you got sick from a takeaway or not, whether the drunk man who knocked your grandad off his bike got points, fines or a licence to do it again.

Westington felt to Bob as if it were in a state of flux. Structures and prices were on the move, bureaucracy shifting, and certain parts of town and certain parts of its population running away with the turn-of-the-century prize for life satisfaction. Depending where you lived it was either an offshoot from the notoriously rough Horden, or a delight-fully rural little city. The divide, as benefits changed names, slipped out of the reach of a normal person's comprehension and patience, made public days – Saturdays in Westington high street, sunny days in the salty air of Brigtown – seem more like battles than shared habitation. Car parking, shops, prices, sales, estate agents, supermarkets with colour-coded ranges for luxury and basic. It was beginning to seem to Bob as if everyone should wear a T-shirt coloured according to their income bracket.

But he still believed in the power of the law to reset the misdirected, redirect a crawling child away from the live socket, again and again and again till they learnt.

At 9.30 in the morning the courts were still quiet, but Bob had that sense of jobs being done all around, oblivious to his awe, as if he were submerged, wearing goggles, watching fish. Phones rang, people walked, doors opened and closed, conversations, so simple, thought Bob, and yet, without the key, incomprehensible. Bob's thoughts slowed, he watched and absorbed the people all around. Here came a man.

'Given the circumstances, and well you know what it's been like, I've asked that they simply hold off . . .'

A walking man in too short trousers spouting, while his companion waited his turn or held his tongue or dreamt of Caribbean seas. Bob watched them go, heard a shriek of laughter and turned to watch two girls come down the stairs, their shorthand speak conspiratorial, so their words were unintelligible but their attention was clear.

There's a family, or at least a collection of people of different ages, sitting on the bench to the left. It is only the fact that they are prepared to share bench space that gives them away as related. Bob knows himself that unless under duress, a bench is really only made for two strangers. These four sit in a glum row, awaiting a court order of a domestic kind, Bob suspects. Not poverty stricken or untouchably ill, not grubby or mad, just depressed, Bob thinks. The lot of them. Not at all pleased, unlike him, by this building they find themselves in. The bureaucracy of social services, he knows, has a tendency to lose the people it's helping en route to the targets for helping that they have been set. Whenever he sees someone down on their luck these days he sees Richard in his head. There are even young people sleeping rough in quiet little Westington these days, and beggars in Brigtown. And whenever Bob sees them, worrying whether to hand over money, and if so how much, he wonders if Richard's all right, remembers him pissing himself with laughter at Bob's bulk supplies of toilet rolls, the time he came round to mend Bob's plumbing. Richard, who went from Portsmouth to London, who has managed to slip through the net and has vanished. But is probably absolutely all right, new garage, new woman, new town . . . probably. Bob is sure he isn't a man to be beaten. Yet he is both sure and full of fear.

Bob looked at his watch: 9.45. He had arranged to meet Frank, Chief Weights and Measures Officer, here as well as the council's prosecutor, Mark Bollam. He was early, but someone needed to be first.

It's no wonder I'm on edge, he thought, using his precious ability to self-soothe; this has been so long in the brewing. He felt such triumph at just being here, at having driven the prosecution forwards, that he was worried about jinxing the result.

They hadn't been able to bring a criminal prosecution against Stephen Harvey, as no one was prepared to press charges against him personally for assault. However, one man had provided them with a lengthy witness statement which had given them a case against Silver Services to take to the civil courts. This, combined with a history of complaints, would enable them to argue he was clearly in

256

breach of three regulations of the 1974 Consumer Credit Act. First, he was still failing (despite letters of advice and a formal caution) to send clear cancellation notices within the statutory five days. Second, they were charging Silver Services with doorstepping, approaching people in their homes, offering them loans without having been invited in (the usual tack was to say they were trying to speak to the neighbour; did they know when he was likely to be back? Or was his bell perhaps broken? Then, with a canny, nonchalant patter, drop the subject of loans so softly into the ping-pong of their face-to-face conversation that they seemed to be mind-readers, a gift from the gods, because who, on a street like this one, in a block of flats such as this, didn't need more?). Finally, they were accusing Silver's of harassment. Of using threatening bailiffs and of violence.

The reason Stan Walker, out of the twenty others who had made complaints, varying from assault to extortionate interest, was prepared to put his name to a witness statement, and give evidence in front of the magistrate if required, was that he was ill. He had been diagnosed as having a degenerative disease which he had said to Bob took the threat out of thugs like Harvey.

At some point Stephen Harvey would walk in here (was this really why Bob had arrived early?) and he would be able to look at the little man. He thought he'd be little, everyone made a point of saying how ordinary he looked, a bit sharp perhaps, but regular enough. Would Harvey know Bob's face? No, he'd know his name but not his form. Why would he? Bob's will be one of the faces he passes but doesn't notice on his way into the panelled room that will remove his ability to trade ever again. More fool him, thinks Bob (who realises getting here this early gives him far too much time to think), more fool him indeed. If he paid more attention to the people of this world, Bob thinks (the volume of his own voice loud in his head), if he worried a little more about the effects of his behaviour, he might not have ended up here.

Bob went out to the front for some fresh air, where he saw Frank coming up the steps. He was ridiculously pleased to see him. 'Frank, Frank, hi, hi, I was early.' He grinned at Frank, irrepressible. They'd known each other a long time, him and Frank. Bob felt a surge of affection, in a seemly team-ish way.

But Frank didn't return the smile.

'We need to have a chat,' he said.

Bob said that that was fine, but Frank didn't answer and continued to walk round to the right of the courthouse. Down the side of the building, past beds of brown, cripple-sticked roses.

'Has something come up?' Bob asked Frank's retreating back. He was worried that Mark Bollam, the prosecutor, wouldn't be able to find them round here.

Frank held up a hand, forestalling any further enquiries.

Not until they'd walked round to the back of the building did Frank stop, put his briefcase on the floor and light a fag. Bob had only ever seen him smoke in the pub or at Christmas parties. He pulled hard on the cigarette, pursing his lips and holding the cigarette so delicately that his gestures gave him the stance of a woman. The smoke hung at their heads. It was a still day.

In the seconds that followed, before Frank spoke, Bob thought nothing very coherent, predicted not at all what was to happen. The clearest way to describe what was inside was to say that he felt like a reprimanded child again, one waiting inconspicuously for the humiliation to begin, and that for the first time he instinctively recognised that this must be his default in times of fear.

'How long have you worked for the DTS?' said Frank.

'Thirteen years. You know that. What's going on?'

'How many prosecutions have you been involved with?'

'I don't know, I don't have a number. What's going on?'

'So you would say you know the procedure for eliciting admissible witness statements?'

'What?' But he understood the meaning if not the words so said, 'Yes.'

'He's withdrawn it.'

Bob put his hand to his head, aware of the stagey nature of the gesture just as he did it. So this is what people really do when things fall apart, he thought. They gasp and put their hands on their scalps, just as if the sky were actually falling in.

'Why?'

'Because, he says, you pressurised him when he was ill and unstable.'

'But that's just not true, you know it's not. You met him.'

'Whatever the truth is, he's withdrawn his statement. And I'm afraid, Bob, I have no choice but to suspend you, pending further discussions.'

'Pending discussions . . . ?' Frank never normally talked like this, he was known for his bluntness, for his spade-calling tactics. 'Are you saying I'm being fired?'

Now that Bob, helpful to the end, had used the word himself, Frank seemed to have found his feet again. 'In a word,' he said, 'yes.'

Neither of them said anything else. Frank drew on his cigarette one more time and then dropped it. Bob watched it fall, saw the white cylinder roll, still burning and smoking, until it rested against the wall of a flowerbed.

Frank might as well have told Bob he didn't exist. Might as well have removed his life with two words. It simply wasn't feasible to take away his job. It was what he did. What else was he?

'You can't fire me,' said Bob. 'That's my job. It's what I do.'

Frank said nothing. He looked at the floor. When he looked up his face had slackened, now showed appeal. 'I . . .' he began. And then stopped again. He turned away. 'Go home,' he said blandly. 'I'll be in touch. I have to go and sort this mess out.'

Through the windows in the busy lobby the two men, dressed in shades of grey and dun, could be seen shifting their feet in the midst of the concrete flowerbeds. Frank took a deep breath, and with the same robust language of assertion, which did instead of compassion, and which would continue to hold him in excellent stead for the next two decades, he said, 'We'll talk, as soon as I'm a bit clearer.'

Then that was it. He was gone and Bob was left standing there. Where Frank had stood was now just an empty space. Bob just standing still, opposite no one now. His heart hammering.

Thirteen years he'd worked there. He was good. They'd always got on. They'd always respected each other. He'd been promoted again and again. You can't just sack people like that. That is not a proper way of dismissing someone. You can't be fired for no reason. Or for a reason that's not right. No one forced him. He's changed his mind. He's frightened and blaming people. They can't sack someone because of that. They can't do that to me. They can't.

Standing there, just at the time when the business of the day gets underway, he felt exposed. As if he were in a dream wearing no clothes. All around people worked and belonged, and now he had nowhere to go but home. His office full of him and empty of him, his PC screen black.

*

He stood there until it began to rain. As he walked out on to the street a young man, a court reporter for the local paper, who had been watching Bob and Frank from the window in the lobby, fell in line with Bob.

'Are you all right?' he asked, lightly touching Bob's arm.

A car drew up in front of the courthouse, music flooding out of its open door. Bob seemed woken by the sound and turned and registered the stranger.

'Oh,' he said. 'Sorry?'

'Are you all right? Has something happened? You looked . . .' he didn't want to say upset, because that did nothing for a man's pride, 'rather unwell back there.' He gestured towards the garden.

Bob considered for a moment, rain dripping off his nose, then said, 'Well, normally I wouldn't be quite so open. But no. No. Thank you. I'm not all right. I've been sacked. And I don't know why.' And to their mutual horror Bob's face began to crumple into crying. He took a staggered breath, as if he'd been punched, and managed to contain himself.

'The worst thing of all,' continued Bob, trying to laugh, 'is that I've spent nearly four years trying to make this day happen. And now I'm just meant to go home.'

The stranger said nothing. 'I'm sorry,' said Bob, smiling thinly. 'Bad day. But thank you.' He stepped back and held out his hand, taking his leave from the brightly lit courthouse behind him, full of people planning their elevenses, answering the phone, looking forward to the moment when they finally reached their nocturnal home.

The young man shook it. 'Bob Shillabeer, one-time DTS inspector,' Bob said.

'Matthew,' responded the young man, 'Matthew Woods. From the *East Kent Gazette*.'

*

261

When Matthew got his first proper job (after a series of pub shifts) as a junior reporter at the *Brigtown Gazette* and announced he was moving into a flat on the seafront, everyone at Woods Farm was rather relieved. Including Roy, who'd ensured Matthew got the job by pulling a couple of Masonic strings.

Straight after finishing his degree in history at London University, achieving a 2:1 with sporadic effort, Matthew Woods had gone on a trip to south-east Asia. The span and the sum of it expanded, and when he finally returned to Woods Farm he was broke and red-brown as a diseased leaf. He showed no gratitude at the warmth of his mother's welcome; he seemed too tired and undernourished for anything much. But he commented on the new bed linen (freshly bought at John Lewis in his honour) and thanked her for developing his fifteen films of photographs. Miriam, who had just embarked on an Open University degree in anthropology, was shocked by the paradisical scenes that her callow, beautiful little boy had passed through so easily, his offhand conquering of Third World buses and beach huts. But Matthew, who felt more strongly than ever that by downplaying his excitements they would be given more privacy, was fascinated by his mother's decision to do a degree of her own. He championed her unnoticed genius to a degree she found both seductive and embarrassing. Somewhere along the line, over the last four years, her son had become someone whose attention she was grateful for. She wasn't quite sure where or when this had happened.

On the evening of the aborted court case Matthew sat opposite his mother in a pizzeria in the regency back streets of Brigtown. They were high in the town's climb, and outside you could smell the sea, but not hear it or see it. At this time of year it was a restless, forbidding barrier for the people of the town. No longer an interactive element, but something to be wary of, an ugly brown grey through its unloved months. Inside the dated Italian restaurant it was humid and smelt of heated bodies and coats. They were eating pizzas with creative topping combinations and names of Italian old masters. Matthew's was a Titian, his mother's a Raphael. She'd taken some time to choose between that and the Rubens, which had pineapple and mangos with parma ham.

'So,' she was saying, 'I asked the local bookshop whether they had it, and you'd have thought that I was asking them to fix me up with a Ghanaian rent boy, not actually looking for a book on sex tourism. The narrow-mindedness, you know, that place. I sometimes feel very stifled by it. I try not to. But . . . well, anyway.' She drank a little wine. 'I did get hold of the book. And ohh,' she hooted with laughter, 'it was rubbish. I wrote her a letter. So funny. Me, writing letters, but honestly, Matthew . . . She can't write. And half the facts are wrong. There's a lot of fraudsters, you know, in this field.'

She was animated and red-cheeked, her shoulder-length hair a little crazy now that half of it was grey, her sleeve dangling in the pizza, not one but three necklaces of organic colours and shapes sitting on top of her navy sweater. He liked her like this, outraged and funny, antsy and active. Off the subject of him, on to the subject of her own life. His mother had not suspended interference in the slightest, but she was at least finding her own ways to fill her time. She had yoga classes, and her degree, and drinks parties with local Amnesty International members. Her life seemed entirely separate from his father, but, anyway, he found the concept of his parents' marriage both too familiar and too peculiar to consider much. The word fraud reminded Matthew of something.

'Mum, have you heard of someone called Stephen Harvey, a pawnbroker in Westington Silver Services. I thought you might have known something about him.'

It was the silence that made him look up from his careful folding of the undercooked pizza base. He had constructed an ideal mouthful of cheese, pepperoni and mushroom. She never normally stayed quiet for very long. She drank a little wine and Matthew suddenly thought that she looked a bit old, the frown gully between her eyebrows deep.

'No,' she said, in the voice of a different mood altogether, but just as recognisable, 'should I?'

Chapter Eighteen

Stephen Harvey had had Miriam Bingham marked the first time he saw her in town. The tight neatness of her was provocative, and she was well dressed enough to pass for upmarket in this provincial town. He'd wondered about the layers of silk and nylon that must be holding her in, giving that slight rustle to her movements.

The second time he came upon her, she was standing there pawning a brooch in his shop. Small spots of pink in her cheeks, dangerously glittering eyes. She seemed defiant. Which he liked. But it struck Stephen as a shame that she should be in here, risking a reputation. He knew how the small town talked. As the church bells counted slowly to twelve and young Larry thumbed out the notes, Stephen came out from the office, and careful not to look directly at the woman, took a business card out of a delicately engraved silver cigarette case and laid it on the glass counter. 'If you would prefer, madam, we do offer a personal service. Within the privacy of your own home, as it were.'

Miriam was the youngest daughter of a wealthy retailer, a man who had turned his own father's saddle sales and repairs business into a chain (Westington, Horden, Brigtown and Mordon) of successful hardware and electronic shops. It was television that made Ted Bingham rich, turned his figure portly and his daughter's hands soft. But his wife never quite adapted to the wealth. You don't turn middle class in one generation. At the age of eighteen Miriam was going to parties (via the tennis club, the country club and the solicitors' girls) where the guests would have referred to her mother as 'salt of the earth'. Or at least they would have done if they'd ever met her. But they never did because Thelma Bingham inhabited only the world of the house. It was an orange-toned existence, a battle with synthetic weapons against problematic elements like sunlight, dust, rainwater, flies and moths. There was little chance that Thelma would ever break out on a blustery day in a pleated skirt for the tennis courts.

Three years after a local photographer had snapped Gerard and Miriam together on a sofa at the tennis club summer ball (Miriam giggling as he whispered in her ear, 'Gerard. Don't. Don't be awful'), the couple were married. He qualified as a lawyer and Miriam had every kitchen accessory a new wife could need. Her father bought her a blender, a meat thermometer, a rotisserie oven, a new present every time she popped back for her dinner. He was proud of his daughter and his son-in-law. They were attractive, and successful, good for his business and good for his heart.

Even Ted could tell his daughter was a sexy creature. He liked that. Not in a funny way, but no one wants a daughter that's not pretty, that doesn't lighten your old friends' days with a smile. She wore tight skirts that stretched over her bottom as she reached in and out of her own blue Hillman for her shopping basket. She liked to visit her husband in his office. Sit briefly on his knee at his desk, push her luck with a quick kiss, be rewarded with a smack on her rump. But, being bored and young and in need of attention, she wished he would push her face down over his desk and force himself upon her. Right there and then in the middle of

266

Westington on a Tuesday lunchtime. She'd have given anything for life to surprise her.

Her mother was alone in recognising the danger her daughter was in, forcing her spirit to be satisfied by a kitchen. She'd been brought up in tenements, on streets that were much closer and more intimate than Laurel Avenue, so Thelma knew that with an appetite like that, it wouldn't take Miriam long to get the surprise of her precious life. And it didn't – not at all. Not once everything had begun to go wrong.

Gerard resigned from Baker and Berridge five years after he had joined and on the same day that Miriam suffered her fourth miscarriage. His father, Peter Woods, had died a month before and they had been waiting for Gerard's elder brother to return to the farm and take up management of the five hundred acres. However he hadn't been seen or heard from since the funeral. In the circumstances it seemed the only thing to be done. Only for a while, Gerard said, certainly not for more than six months, which was fine, as law was not a profession that disappeared. Not a profession that he couldn't return to easily in time. 'You see,' he said, 'I don't intend to be a farmer. Not even a gentleman farmer. Because I do not intend you to be a farmer's wife.' And he'd stroked his wife's forehead. She'd winced. Laid flat out on the sofa with a hot-water bottle under her jumper instead of a baby.

They moved into Woods Farm, the oak banisters, stone floors, dirt-bound tables no longer unnoticeable, almost organic, as they had been through Gerard's childhood, but now hopelessly old-fashioned and dirty. For the first time in her life Miriam got down on her hands and knees, and her mother even ventured out to help her. Thelma enjoyed the low, close rhythm of cleaning floors with her daughter. Miriam did not.

The early years of Miriam's marriage were spent in a permanent state of possible pregnancy or recent miscarriage. She longed for the status but also the companionship a baby would bring her; she wanted to be the mother she'd wanted. Cheery. Up-to-date. But each month made her resent the supposed inevitability of a child. There was less money for distracting shopping, and somehow less point, now that she could go days without the twenty-minute trip to town, without seeing anyone except her husband and the farm workers. So one morning something in her rebelled and made her gather a silver brooch and a pearl necklace out of her dressing table. Presents from her father. They were hers to do with as she wanted, and they were useless, so she would sell them. It was a display of displeasure at the fall of their professional status. But also, in a kind of perverse way, a sensible move, now that money was tight, ridding herself of the pointless presents. It made perfect sense to her angry, speeding mind.

Her char, Lucy, had told her about Silver's. This, she thought – with all her youth, not yet even thirty – was what her husband had reduced her to.

Miriam deliberately dressed drably for her first visit to Silver's, but when Stephen emerged offering her privacy and personal visits she instantly regretted that decision. She flushed with confusion, then anger, then humiliation. He was challenging her on the propriety of her risk. To be pulled up on behaviour by a pawnbroker, to be visited by a man like him, in her own home, would be far from thrilling. It would represent a considerable fall. She was her father's child, particularly in her hypersensitivity to the town's social hierarchies. This man didn't even have the nous to know what he represented to her on that sliding scale of men.

She made a slight noise, as if tasting something nasty.

He looked up, his head slightly to one side like a bird. They looked at each other, her heart thudding with vexation, at everything, him, her husband, her childlessness, the farm, her father, this bloody town. He bit his lip slightly in consideration, as if he were sizing her up, she thought. How dare he, she thought, does he not know who is in charge of this situation? That they had *land*, that she didn't really need this money? That they could afford food and bills and a car just fine; that she would spend it on creams and lotions to calm her and restore fertility to her brittle heart?

She cannot ask for her brooch back, she does not want to concede that she shouldn't be here; she does not however want to make an enemy of a man who frightens her, belonging as he does to a class she has departed.

But, as Stephen Harvey shifts, clasps his hands behind his back, continuing to look at her, something in her recognises this manipulation, offensive and interfering as it is, as a masculine appreciation of herself. The inappropriateness of the idea gives it power. So she takes the card without a word, scrabbling like a small animal to pick it up off the flat surface in her leather gloves, and leaves.

Stephen watched her go, quick down the steps, hand to her throat, left, left, right, back into her world.

Stephen Harvey had begun life with everything. A mother, a father, a home, a hearth with wood in it when needed, a cot, plenty of siblings, a rag-taggle soft stuffed dog to suck and maul and a fine head of black hair. The way he told it, though, meant approaching the myth from a different angle. They were, it was true, not wealthy. His father shovelled shit for a living, it was also true, but it was horse shit, and the horse and the shits belonged to the Duke of Norfolk. The flat where they lived, theirs as long as Stephen's father stayed in the Norfolk Estate's employment, was in the cobbled back streets of Regent's Park. It meant that the rats that ran with the ostler's children were better fed than most in London. Stephen was the sixth and final child. By the time he arrived his mother had worn right through her maternal emotions, and his father retreated to a routine that only allowed for six hours out of twenty-four at home – every minute of them, except perhaps a few each week in which he'd bother his wife, spent asleep. Motor cars revving dangerously through his dreams.

His upbringing gave Stephen an education in the labour and muck that supported the lifestyles of the rich. The horses were now mostly for pleasure, and the motor cars kept just up the street were polished and loved like the horses. Stephen knew how the cars smelt after parties; he picked up tissues, found undergarments, bloodied handkerchiefs, dog shit walked into the carpet, lipstick on the window panes. He knew that their status and sophistication was dependent on the likes of him finding their detritus and disposing of it carefully.

He'd become a driver at fifteen, trolleying the duke's second daughter around most of the time. She had a couple of expensive habits and an unnecessarily modest allowance so she would steal things – useless knickknackery in precious metals and stones. She would secrete them in her little clasped handbags (only small, quite valuable things would fit, in fact) and shove them into the passenger seat as they turned out of the drive, telling him to pop by a little shop where he could sell these bits of nonsense for her. At first Stephen thought it was her nonsense to sell, then after a while he realised (having examined some of the pre-war engravings) that they couldn't be. So the next time he hesitated, Felicity panicked and offered him something for her trouble. After accompanying her to several discreet jewellery brokers in the West End, it occurred to him that these establishments were one of the few where her kind needed the help of his. Most of those running the shops were foreigners and Jews, but not all. And who cared? It was money that he was after. So at the age of twenty-one he found himself a position in a small broker's in Westington, Kent, which he later bought cheaply from the old childless man who had taken him in and taught him everything he knew.

By the time he met Miriam Bingham in 1967, Stephen Harvey was thirty-four, married, with three sons – Jack, Mike and Tony – the eldest of whom was twelve. He had a blue Rover, they had a charwoman, a new washing machine purchased outright from Bingham's, none of this instalment trickery (Stephen recognised debt when he saw it), and best of all, he had plans for expansion. He was part of the new world order. So when, one hateful Tuesday afternoon, a week after her trip to the shop, Miriam phoned him saying with shaky offhandedness, 'Do you know much about silverware; trays, teapots, that sort of thing?' he offered to come up the very next day, sensing an opening of various kinds. A different class of customer; at the very least, a new avenue of work.

The next day was colder and Stephen drove out wearing his new suit, dark grey with shine to it, a thinnish spotted tie, carefully polished black shoes. Before he turned up the track to Woods Farm he pulled over and applied some expensive cologne and ran a comb through his thickly oiled hair. He pulled in his pot belly, then leaned to check himself in his rearview mirror and was struck by the familiarity of the neck-craning, tie-tweaking gesture. It took him right back to his days as a driver, and suddenly angry with himself, as if he'd admitted a weakness in the wrong company, he sneered at his own reflection and anxiety, and accelerated fast off the verge, wheels spinning in the mud.

*

He had put his hand on her arse as she walked upstairs to fetch something. Stephen Harvey reached out and just put his fat-fingered hand on her arse. She stopped instantly and stood very still; the flat placing of his palm was like an electric shock. In her imagination she'd willed it, but now it was here, now the physical move had been made, she was frightened.

'Get your hand off me,' she said. He knew he hadn't miscalculated, though. He slid his hand lower round the curve of her buttocks. She felt taut.

'I said take it off.' She emphasised every word. She didn't move at first. She'd forgotten that she could – just walk off out of his reach. Then she sort of remembered, and when he didn't remove it began to step carefully away, her heart mashing against her ribs. But he moved quickly and grabbed her ankle, so that her shoe fell, clattering against the wooden banisters, and she twisted and struggled and landed on her hip.

There was a hiatus. Breathing heavily, Miriam looked at this man. Scared of what she'd brought about. He was sweating, bent over, above her, still holding her ankle. His grip tightened. She was cornered, on her back, on the stairs. Her skirt rucked. Waiting to see what he did next. What now – what effect could she have against a man like this, alone in the house? She was aware of her body. Her skirt crumpled, riding up beneath her. She could feel the place between her legs. Her skin prickling with anticipation. The fear remained, holding her still. How would he do this?

Suddenly flaring out of the tension and his scrutiny, fleetingly scared of being hurt, she kicked up and hard with her free foot. Her heel caught his face, gouged the thin skin beneath his eyes and a drop of blood quickly welled. He laughed and in a sudden scrimmage of movement, like animals, he grabbed her forearms.

'What do you want?' she said. As angry as the first time he had ever spoken to her in that shop.

'Whatever you want,' he said with a smile. 'All you have to do is ask nicely,' more playful than mean.

'Then get off me.'

'No,' he said slowly, 'I don't think that's what you want.'

She struggled again, but he just held her arms and smiled. And she felt a great burn of physicality, a need to be touched, pushed hard, brought up against the edges of herself.

'Please,' she said.

'Please what?' he said.

'Let go.' She didn't whimper it, though; she said it again as a challenge. He didn't answer. He just looked at her. She felt herself burning red before him.

Seconds passed, then he said, 'Do you want me to? To let you go? I will if you want,' and he spoke softly, intensely.

She shook her head slightly. 'Then what?' he said, not playing but needing to know.

'Touch me,' she said, ashamed of herself. Caught in the pulse of her twisted body. She could feel her heartbeat where he gripped her wrist. Everything stopped except for what he did next. The photographs and pictures glassy squares on the walls. The carpet running like lava, below and under them. The radiators warming with sporadic, effortful clicks.

Very slowly, and with great gentleness, he released her hands, laid them down and lifted up her skirt, beyond the top of her stockings, pushing it up to the hinge of her hips, so that he could see her pale green underwear, the curve and the dark padding – her silk-cushioned cunt.

He surprised her when, with rare honesty, unbuttoning her blouse, still not touching her, he almost winced at the sight of her, laid out, skinned beneath him, and said, the top of his hand smoothing her stomach, 'You have everything I've ever wanted.'

273

He spread her thighs, so that they hung slackly open, and her flesh collected and sat at the side of her, and looked at her, white, opened, limbs contorted, sharp joints and meaty bits. She lay back, saying quietly, 'Oh God.'

And moving swiftly he felt her and then crammed himself inside.

It hurt her and didn't satisfy. He withdrew and ejaculated on the carpet, murky blobs holding their shape on the new, liquid-resistant carpet fibres. He might have fallen in love with her. The first and last time that could have happened to him, if it wasn't for the fact that after the act was done, and they were both dressed, and he turned to say he now had to go, an expression of uncertainty on his face, as if trying to thank a temperamental woman for a perfect present, she said, covering for the pain, 'I presume I have some time to get them back, before you sell them.'

She had cast him as an extortioner, and so he would remain. She would give him her possessions and her body on other occasions over the next three months, but never her courtesy.

He was frustrated and addicted to the turn of events. He desired her more than anything he'd ever come across, more even than money. If she'd ever given him room for a gesture or the time for a single moment of emotional abandon, he would have found sacrifice somewhere in himself for this woman. But she wouldn't even give him the respect of a tradesman; the way she treated him was as if he, not she, were indebted. It was a far cry from his early imagination of life as a businessman, where a man could keep control of his world, whatever issues of class might arise. He realised his power only extended so far, that his kingdom was limited. He could rely on himself to always coax a phoenix from the flames, create money out of disaster; he could rely on debtors to cringe, and he could rely on his family to absorb what remained of his energies at the end of the day. Each of his children, but most particularly his first-born, Jack, felt the force of his angry disappointment.

Miriam would realise she was lucky not to have got pregnant by him. She didn't think so at the time. She willed it at the time. Imagine carrying the child of this man, with his flash car and shit-shovelling background, his hard softness, his mutable power. They would have had to leave. Just the two of them in the dark night, in his fast car. Heading to Dover, her belly warm with energy, her body sore with use.

She didn't get pregnant, though, not for another five years. When Matthew was conceived, so very properly, by her own cuckolded husband, as if the hard exchanges with Stephen had never happened.

Chapter Nineteen

Julianna had walked and walked the streets of London when Luke was first born – taken tubes to far suburbs – she thought perhaps she knew the limits of it better than any of the Londoners she passed. She had a strong sense of the city as an individual personality, something that knew of the attention she paid to it, of the knowledge of the streets that she was storing. Like a cab driver, she discovered canny cut-throughs with neat names like Middle Row and Love Lane. She could visualise how Kilburn ran down to Camden, how Amersham gave in to the countryside, how Wimbledon merged in greenness with Putney.

Once a month, at least, they went to the zoo. She had a season ticket, an indulgence that amused Jack no end. 'He doesn't know an elephant from his grandmother,' he said rudely. But Julianna liked it; on a quiet weekday it was like a secret. A place where wandering was encouraged.

'How lovely,' said the woman behind the counter in the café, one sunny day. 'How lovely to be free to spend all day here with your kid.'

She was lucky, it was true, to be free to do whatever she wanted between seven and seven. They liked (that is Julianna liked and Luke was hardly in a position to argue) the exotic creatures. Giraffes and big cats, elephants and penguins.

'One day,' she said to Luke on her knee, who was intent on opening a red plastic pot of raisins and apple bits, to be shared later, and not entirely happily, between him and the animals in pet corner, 'we will go to Africa together and see lions and flamingos.' She liked the idea of him older and amused and protective. Her smaller than him, proud of a son who was teasing her. They usually reached home about four, when the streets were spotted with clumps of trailing schoolkids. Luke tired and the house quiet. The walls refracting the music on the radio. Windows open, air still, squirrels in the garden, the sound of them descending a tree just like running water, and Luke, who'd finished squelching his way through orange pulp in a red bowl. Happy now to simply be holding a toy car in his sticky hands.

In less than two weeks her family would come to stay. But tonight it was just fish, late, with Jack. Which he wouldn't like, would dissect more than eat. Tomorrow, play-group, where all the slightly wrong babies, the too greedy, too pretty, too big, Tabitha, Harry and Kyle, and their condescending mothers, would prod the benign Luke to tears. Whereupon Julianna would exercise her freedom again and move on.

She'd made a resolution today to try not to think too hard on the future. She was wondering instead about a second child, to increase the noise around her and lessen the time.

Yesterday Matthew Woods had interviewed Bob Shillabeer. It had felt like painting with glue. They'd sat in his front room on that peculiar white leather sofa for hours. By the end of the afternoon Bob had eaten an entire packet of biscuits and perversely Matthew was sure the sofa had become even more bloated. It was impossible not to sympathise with Bob's confusion and obvious misery; it was like meeting an exile. But it did teach Matthew to temper his excitement at the prospect of a story, at least in front of its subject.

As far as Matthew could divine, Bob Shillabeer's friend

Richard Flood had left town because of his debt with Silver's, having been assaulted some months before by Harvey's heavies. (He repeated Harvey's Heavies to himself and laughed. He was enjoying this.) The assault had led to Bob's involvement and it had kicked off a clearly personal campaign to have Silver's licence removed. Matthew's editor agreed that a situation with a suspended DTS worker, a cancelled court case and a violent loan shark might very well be worth sniffing around. Since Matthew had found it, he could have it, as long as he updated the editor daily. He'd take Matthew off it the moment he thought it was going nowhere, he said, and Matthew had felt for the first time like he was doing an actual job. Yesterday, as Matthew was leaving, Bob had asked him, a little desperately, if he really was going to write something in the paper, and had offered to help him in any way he could. It was Bob who suggested he go and see Richard's sister Jenny, for a different account of Richard's debt and the assault.

The atmosphere when he arrived at Jenny Flood's was very different. It was a long, long time since Matthew had been in a house full of children. It was the first thing he noticed on entering the house – the noise. Up the cream-carpeted stairs there seemed to be a fight of catastrophic proportions raging, girls' and boys' voices, and the slamming of heavy things against wood.

Jenny ushered him in, muttering, 'Christ almighty,' under her breath. She went and stood at the bottom of the stairs, hands on hips, and took a deep breath before starting to shout, in an enormous voice for a small woman. Matthew, lingering, hands in pockets in the hall, winced at the decibels.

'WILL YOU STOP THAT NOISE . . .' There was a sudden lull; the woman looked like she was summoning the gods,

278

or denouncing the government, as if the stairs were the Parthenon and she a rebellion.

Three kids appeared at the top of the staircase, grinning and shoving. The boy slipped down a step, squeezed out by the jostling. Then the girls stepped and squeezed him down another.

He told them to get off, to piss off, but the girls continued to bat him between them and down the stairs, smooching rude things in his ears, squirming their faces in his hair.

'Leave him alone,' Jenny said, grabbing him from the girls' tentacle arms and trailing hair. Matthew was kind of scared by these Nereids; he had an old fear that they would come and steal his trousers, leave him hopping in the playground. He remembered how young girls were just as strong as boys, but with the underhand bonus of breasts. He grinned a little nervously, and the girls, as if they'd smelt the fear, stopped at the bottom of the stairs and looked right at him. One of them straightened her mussed-up cardigan with a precociously tidy gesture. The other levitated on to the bulbs of her feet, then audibly slid her heels back down the carpeted step.

'Go and do your homework,' Jenny said as if there was nothing extraordinary about these two intertwined girls, nothing electric about their sudden stillness and attention at the bottom of the stairs, and she showed Matthew into the front room and shut the door firmly on all of them.

'It's a tip, sorry,' she said tightly. 'I only just got in from work. Since I split up with my boyfriend I've realised that some things, like hoovering, have to suffer a bit.' She lit a cigarette and sighed smoke rather than exhaling, and for the first time Matthew noticed the large port-wine stain on her cheek and neck. She moved things around a little and fetched tea before really speaking properly. She was used to keeping busy until people had settled in and accommodated her trademark. Some never did. He sat bright-eyed on her sofa, like some little pedigree terrier.

'How old are you?' she asked, once they'd both finally got their tea and an ashtray apiece.

'Older than I look,' he said.

'Oh me too,' she said and laughed. 'It's like doctors and policemen; even journalists now look the same age as my son. You're meant to look grey and boozed up, aren't you?'

'Shouldn't think it'll take long,' he said. He had a comic, slightly teasing way of talking. More interesting than she might have expected from a terrier. Like a teacher that you might have fancied at school. The conversation flirted a little like this until he eased her slowly into the present. He asked her about Bob, a better place to start, he thought, than a disappeared brother.

'Did Bob tell you that we've always been friends? Since primary school?' she asked, and then as he was about to reply, yes, she went on, 'He made friends with Richard through me, we were friends first.'

Then just as he was about to ask her whether Bob had told her his suspicions on why the council halted the case, she came straight to the point of her own pre-emption. (Small wonder Bob had never made love to her; she would have got to the heart of the matter and frightened him half to death before he had even got the words out.)

'Richard left here because of the debts. Bob took them on. Richard paid some of it back, but one day he didn't have what he owed Bob and he just left town. He'd never have admitted it, but I think he was scared. Not like scared of being beaten up again, he was always a fighter anyway. Not scared like that, scared like reaching rock bottom, giving up on making something of himself. It's a crappy town really, you know, this one . . .' Matthew wondered why she presumed he was from somewhere else, 'unless you're living in a nice bit, or outside and you've got a big house and countryside for kids.' He kept quiet. 'There's not much work for people who aren't trained – I mean, you know, I'm a nursing assistant, there's always plenty of ill people, but Richard, well, he was a self-taught mechanic, with no talent for money.

'He's all right, you know,' she said, noticing Matthew's concern at the past tense, and then she cackled with laughter. It was a good laugh, he thought, womanly, full of understanding. Capable of seeing right through his pretence of experience. 'He just dumped his past and all his debts and started again. No one'll find him now who he doesn't want to.' Then she stopped and looked worried. 'Jesus, you're not going to put that in, are you? He'd kill me. You just want to know about the assault, don't you?' and then she got them some cans of lager and told him about that night four years ago.

When she'd got to the point at which Bob had left Katie with her, there was a ring on Jenny's front door. 'I'm looking after next door's,' she explained. Then another, and another which lasted until she got to the door and opened it. Matthew felt the fresh air rush in and heard the voice of another child, high-pitched and imperious,

'I done a picture, look, LOOK AT MY PICTURE, it's a horse, a horse with SEVENTEEN legs.' Then suddenly a small boy appeared in front of Matthew. Just about the most comical thing he'd ever seen. A rucksack, with a lion's head on the top, slopped off his arms, a raincoat with frog's eyes and ears on its hood, a piece of white paper in his hand. He was like a highly decorated troll. The boy came up to Matthew and stood very close. Matthew drew back a little.

'I drawn a horse and it's got seventeen legs.'

'Seventeen,' Matthew rejoined politely. Suddenly the child

leapt into the crouching, grimacing position of a mini-sumo wrestler. Then he roared, he actually roared, at Matthew, who laughed a little. The child was obviously disturbed.

Then as calmly as he'd begun, the child stopped roaring. 'What was that?' he asked Matthew. Who thought 'fuck knows' to himself, but shook his head instead.

'A tiger,' the boy said.

'Gosh,' said Matthew, putting his jacket on. He thought this was when he was probably meant to leave, although he didn't want to. Jenny had told him the story of that evening, on tape, and was prepared to stand by it, although she'd asked not to be named in the newspaper.

Matthew's attempts to speak to Stephen Harvey were getting nowhere; the business seemed to have closed and numbers changed. Yesterday, he'd discovered, existing loan clients had simply received paperwork from a company that even Matthew recognised from its adverts, called AFH. It had explained that they'd taken over Silver Services, that the interest on their personal loan would be adjusted to AFH's standard rate (somewhat lower than Silver's) and new agreements would be presented at a time suitable to them. Matthew had made some enquiries about AFH this morning, but hadn't got far before he had to leave. There was one computer with access to the internet in the office and he'd found no official site but had printed out some articles that were floating around this back-of-beyond bank of information. AFH, it seemed, were a rather larger, rather more ambitious company than Silver's. There was an article about a man who was on the board, previously an MP, and another about a sponsorship deal for a home counties rugby club.

'Gosh,' said the child, mimicking Matthew, and his accent. 'Gosh,' and he began to prance round the room like a show pony, one footfall to each gosh. Was gosh a defunct word now? Matthew wondered. His father had used it all the time in a bored, cynical way.

Matthew stood up, made for the kitchen, where Jenny was negotiating with the three other kids over a packet of biscuits and two hot-cross buns. He wanted to ask her if she knew where Stephen Harvey's house was. The children stilled as he walked in. Jenny was old-fashioned enough to expect formal visitors to stay out of the kitchen, and arranged the biscuits between four plates without looking up.

'Think I'd better be off,' he said. 'Just wondering if you knew at all where Stephen Harvey lived.'

'This is Katie . . . Flood, my niece,' Jenny said, to somehow remind him of his manners. She wasn't going to discuss this in front of Richard's own daughter.

Matthew looked at the girl, one of the two who had wriggled the boy down the stairs. She looked back, interested by this not unattractive, very young man in the kitchen. It took Matthew a good few seconds to work out what was happening inside his head. It felt like something resurfacing, like remembering something he'd forgotten long ago. She had wide-apart dark brown eyes and heavy brown hair, a big mouth and strong nose, and the pumped, shining flesh of a young girl.

She looked just a little like Julianna. He didn't know how old this girl was, ten perhaps? She was half the size of Julianna but with the same dark, waiting presence. The effect of her serious-eyed stare on Matthew, for whom so much emotion translated into the restriction of oxygen, was physical. He felt a sudden emptiness, a lack beneath his ribs, and his breathing began to tighten.

Jenny showed him out of the house, promising shortly that she would have a go at finding where Harvey lived, and left him bemused on the pavement. Something about the house, about Jenny Flood's home, had undone him. It reminded him of how he had felt when he travelled through Asia. A straight-backed, sweating foreigner watching local families laugh at him in a foreign language.

Matthew walked until he saw a pub and sat head bowed over a pint. He tried to filter his thoughts. He thought how he had abandoned Julianna, and wondered how he managed to shovel away the guilt most of the time. He thought about how he had loved being beside her – it had made him feel that the world had been laid out for his visit in particular – about how little she had presumed. As if she were interested to see how he would turn out, but had no claim. She had expected him to make his own decisions, and had even given him the space for it, so much so that he managed to avoid all risk of independence by letting his mother make them instead.

At the age of twenty-five Matthew was only just beginning to discern how little he knew of other people's lives. The gap in understanding was rather more daunting than any gap in knowledge. That household today had drawn him out like a far-flung traveller who arrives in a community that seems to make a very simple sense. The children . . . who'd have thought there was such distinct charm in a house full of ordinary, battling kids. Jenny watching him with the experience of real truths and necessary lies, smoke meeting between their heads.

He felt charged and restless, the summoning up of Julianna activating and hurting him, but not depressing him. He couldn't imagine her home, in Hungary, and he didn't know whether it was his inability to see into the centre of Europe with a sixth sense that made him sure she wasn't gone. That she was somewhere, not that far, stepping on to streets just as he had left, present but never to be seen again. He wanted to walk straight back the way he'd come, back into Jenny Flood's house again, where everyone's oddities

284

cancelled themselves out and more was said in an afternoon than in a year at his parents' house.

Julianna had been Jack Harvey's own new-found land. He had explored her with amazement and trepidation, like a man landing on an undiscovered coastline. To him she came from nothing and nowhere, only existing under his gaze, born for that moment, waiting silent for him. And she was always so taken aback by the turn of things – by their relationship, then his proposal, then her pregnancy – that it was easy to assume that she had lived the pure life of a novice waiting for him all along. Given Julianna's pliancy and her acceptance of the material elements of their life, one might have thought that she'd surrendered her will entirely by now.

But she hadn't quite; her isolation had recently become more active, less modest, her background hovered noisily and her foreign history was now symptomatic, to both of them, of the way she didn't fit in his world at all well. Something was making Julianna very unhappy and she wasn't prepared to accept the state – but both of them were unable to communicate how they made each other feel. Julianna could really only communicate her intimacy with sex. Neither the words nor the mechanics of lovemaking had been taught to her as a child. The women of her childhood were expected to work and manage, but also to submit. While her grandmother had given her expectations rather than the intimate language of affection.

'Why on earth would I want to go and visit your home town?' Jack asked after a fractious meal out with Derek and his wife, who, Jack noted, had been polite enough to pretend to be interested by Julianna's childhood.

Julianna had been home once since they married. A ferociously expensive set of barristers succeeded in getting her indefinite leave to remain in the UK. Which allowed her to leave it for Hungary occasionally.

'Because Hungary is a beautiful country. Some of it is very . . .' she shoved the swinging bathroom door away with exasperation, 'wild and . . . and empty,' she told him, chucking a pair of balled tights into the corner of their bedroom.

'I have wilderness here.' He gestured as if Ben Nevis lay somewhere just east of Maida Vale. He was lying on the marital bed (he called it that a lot, with a cynical tone; he thought it was funny). His shirt was undone and he still wore one sock.

Julianna, out of sorts with cystitis, indefinably angry now that the sex was over, at having given in to his quick, effective moves after he'd been so dismissive of her all evening, said, 'You know nothing about it. After all this time. Where I come from. You make fun of my family.'

'I didn't marry you for your family.' He smiled. 'I didn't marry you for your potatoes or your party credentials or your revolutionary pedigree.' That night he'd heard the same anecdotes about Julianna's family history that he always had to sit through. How the blessed Mila and János had bought a forged passport, how she'd had to speak the language like a native, always fearing the Nazis, how János died trying to save his country from the Russians. And so on and so drearily forth.

'Anyway I've been finding out quite a lot about Eastern Europe. Their economies for a start. Business opportunities.'

He watched her walk around the bed. She had a small waist, even though she seemed to always be eating. He liked to rest his head in the curve of her. He had always loved her flesh in a really quite consuming, absorbing way. Hers was the only body he'd ever really thought perfect. He still did, when aroused or just undone; lying with his furred length pressed against the smooth juts of her body's profile made him feel as if he'd uncovered a secret, the kernel of experience. It was all right until one of them stood up and they needed to speak again.

'Of course you have,' she said flatly.

She stood in the doorway doing her teeth just looking at him. He used to do that to her too. Watch her all the time. She could feel his semen between her thighs. He was smeared a hand-span beneath her crotch. She watched him picking at his belly button, her irritation travelling across the expanse of pale cream carpet. Then pastey drips began to fall from the bottom of her chin and she retreated and locked herself into the en suite bathroom.

'You will be here, you will try to be here a little when my parents are staying?' she said from behind the door.

He heard the pleading in her voice and was irritated by it.

'You chose the worst moment in the last three years to have them to stay, and then tell me it's too late to change it. What am I meant to do, Julianna?'

She re-entered, having tied up her dressing gown very, very tight. She was aware of how little there was in her life that this should matter so. But that wasn't her fault. They had once been so recklessly besotted with each other. Their marriage her deliverance. How could she have known that it wasn't enough? It was meant to be enough. Everyone had always said it was.

Bob sat on the 10.30 train into London, open to everyone else's sensations better than his own. He held himself still, listening to people confined. His reflection diffused him out beyond the train even, into sunshine on stubbled, harvested fields. He wasn't a man who attracted much attention, despite his attractiveness, his pale cherrywood skin. A dilution of his Brazilian father. Was that why he'd learnt to exist so shapelessly in public? He didn't give his mixed-race parentage much thought, but occasionally a drunken gob-shite would fling a weakly offensive word at him. But he never even looked at the mouth which uttered the abuse, so arguments had never developed. But perhaps he had been avoiding the issue, avoiding himself for years. His reflection, transposed on back-sliding scenes, as insubstantial as he felt.

Matthew had told him that Silver's had been bought and all debts transferred to AFH. He'd heard of AFH of course; unlike Silver's they had enough money to advertise in the Sunday tabloid magazines. They were the reputable face of unsecured loans. But this transference gave Bob the feeling that his own injustice was being moved on and away from him. Into large impersonal buildings on unknown city streets. If he wasn't careful his name would be locked away in an archive, and it would be harder than ever to prove that he had been robbed of his life. With the instinctive, repeating insight he used so effectively at work, he understood that he needed to keep himself visible, and the injustice alive. So today he was on his way to do some research on AFH at Companies House, soon to learn of Stephen Harvey's son Jack. A new name and involvement in his life, someone who Bob would be able to deem responsible for his loss.

Bob doesn't yet have the self-importance, the self-examining imagination, to call this a quest. He has never thought of his life as a cumulative adventure, internally dramatising his past, considering the impact of his story so far on a potential listener. He does not consider his life a story in which he is the hero, or even a story in which he takes the decisions.

But as a woman sitting on the other side of the aisle has

noticed, he is an attractive, dreamy-looking, gentle man, who wordlessly helped her put her case on the rack, who doesn't flinch at the truanting gang who enter the carriage with an explosion of noise. He's not tall but made of solid matter, just as the watcher likes them. Not reading car magazines, not plugged into headphones, just facing the rush of landscape.

Compared to everyone else in the carriage, the woman notices, he seems happy to let go, to suspend himself while the train charges on. Everyone else is holding on to something, shouting into brand-new breaking-up mobiles, not on a train unless they've told someone, shuffling CDs in and out of Walkmans, reading novels about different continents or magazines that offer new identities to choose from. The woman over the aisle, who is training to be a yoga teacher, thinks she sees a crucial question answered in Bob; here is someone who has learnt to let go. The other essentials, she knows from the Buddhist workshop she has just left behind, are therefore within him – the ability to love and the knack of living in the fullness of time.

Ironic then that Bob is on a mission sparked by the loss of a job he didn't *want* to let go. But his anger at the injustice is stronger than his anger at being deprived. He doesn't recognise this as a mission, only a natural progression. But the fact that he doesn't ask, what is going on, where am I going? is both his engine and his armour. He is driven, not given to analysis, and, at this moment, simply pleased to be off that bloody sofa.

Jenny sat in the car in the dark waiting for Matthew. She'd parked just before the road curved, a couple of hundred yards from Stephen Harvey's front door. It crossed her mind as she smoked one cigarette after another that something bad could happen to him. But somehow she couldn't see it with Matthew, the little prince. Richard . . . he caused trouble, it hung round his head like flies, but Matthew was blessed by charm and innocence. He'd be all right.

When he finally opened the door and got in, he looked sheet white.

'That bad?' she asked.

'I think I need a drink,' he said cautiously. 'I think I need several drinks and I think I need you to drink with me.' She laughed shortly and took him to a pub on the edge of town, where she could leave her car, get drunk and still make it home on foot.

He bought them a pint each and a shot and sat at the table and drank the latter in a single breath. Then he picked up the pint and began to drink. Stephen Harvey had refused to even ask Matthew in, but had stood on his doorstep obliquely answering questions about Silver Services, about his retirement after AFH's offer. He had said nothing of particular interest but his hard, sneering manner and the cruelty of his language had shocked Matthew. The fact that he knew Matthew's parents' names too, that had freaked him. He thought of them as a self-contained unit that almost only existed through him. The thought that their limited lives had rippled as far as people like Stephen Harvey was new to him.

He put down the pint glass and looked at Jenny. It had been one of the more peculiar hours of his life, and he felt as if he had nothing to lose. Jenny had reapplied her lipstick several times in the car. She was surprisingly sparkled and wet-lipped. She wore a pink shirt, stiff-collared and unbuttoned to show the freckled, gathered skin of her breastbone. He wanted to reach between the starched and slitted edges and touch the gully from which he could see her breasts rise. The skin would be soft and a little loose he thought. There were two lines bracketing her mouth, markers for her smile, and gathers beneath her eyes. He liked the lines, it was like knowing what someone looked like naked. This is the shape of me, they said.

She never covered her birthmark these days; it slid down her right cheek, below her shirt, down her neck, and it looked as if it were made of softer skin than anywhere else so clearly on show, and Matthew reached out to touch it with his fingertips. She flinched slightly. 'Sorry,' he said. Then looked straight at her, and said, 'I feel a bit distracted by you, sitting opposite me like that.' And she realised he meant it by the strength of his attention.

She felt at the centre of things under his stare. She grinned broadly at the unexpectedness of his concentration, and drank watching his sand-splattered face, hair uncut and falling, blue darting eyes. He was like confectionery; he made her want to put her tongue to his eyelids, nose, fore-head, bones and lobes. She was sure he would taste of frosting. Tart lemon and sweet.

'What was he like?' she asked. 'What did he say?'

Matthew crossed his legs, focused back on the story and looked away from her. He settled into his characteristic folded-up, curiously camp pub-pose – his elbow resting on his knee, cigarette in his hand, shoulders rounded in conversation.

'Put it this way, he was one of the meanest-looking men I've ever seen.'

'I've heard that.' She wrinkled her nose, and waited for him to light her second cigarette of her first drink.

'He didn't tell me much. I don't know, I suppose it was a bit optimistic just turning up on his doorstep. But I mean, what else are you supposed to do? Anyway, he says he's retiring, since he's been bought out by AFH.'

'Oh poor Bob,' said Jenny, with a deep inhalation. How often she'd said that. Gathering meaning and richness in its resaying. Old sympathies billowing over the sticky, circle-stained table.

Matthew kept forgetting about Bob. As a person that was. 'Yes.' There was a pause. 'Why? I mean obviously because he's lost his job, in a sort of dodgy-looking way. But ...'

'Because he doesn't stand a chance, does he? Fighting AFH over a lost job is like ... spilt milk ... you know, they're big, aren't they?'

'I don't quite know what AFH are,' Matthew said with a middle-class grimace to denote a frightfully lucky ignorance.

'No, well, you wouldn't. Not with your background. It's like a bank for people who can't get ordinary credit any more, a place where they can get loans and mortgages that high street banks wouldn't give them.'

'Like Silver Services then.'

'Sort of, but not really. They can lend you more money, for a longer time, and I don't think they'll come and beat you up for it. But the interest and the charges are still high. You've still got to be careful.' She finished her drink.

Matthew inclined his head, serious in his neon naivety.

Jenny continued. 'It's a trap, isn't it? A cycle. Once you start borrowing you can't stop. Not unless more starts to come in from somewhere else. I've been tempted, you know. We haven't had a holiday for two years, took me a few months to buy a new telly last year. The kids don't get to go on all the trips they want. And I have a salary, you know, I'm lucky.'

She stopped. She didn't like herself like this. She tried hard not to be a moaner. She found that by keeping a cheerful front against each day obstacles fell away more easily. She was surrounded by complaints, working with the sick, coming home to children. Brightness was deflective. And anyway, she was lucky. Look at her brother. Look at Bob.

292

'Another drink?' she asked. 'Mum's at ours all evening.'

'I'll get them,' he said, finishing his pint. 'That man's left me rather on edge.' And he got up and went to the bar again, leaving Jenny smiling. He talked like a 1930s woman in a TV drama. She liked it, it was something different from her usual brand of masculinity.

Matthew had never had sex like this before. They hadn't been able to wait long, so he wasn't even entirely inebriated. Which was just the first of many differences. They'd kissed downstairs then he'd followed her up to the bedroom. Spontaneity had to be contained in a house full of children, he realised. When she'd undressed he'd watched more carefully than ever before, because it was more interesting to him than ever before. Her body had obviously been used by her and others and by her children. She had tan marks, and a tiny tattoo of a butterfly, and stretch marks like snail trails along her belly and over her buttocks. She had thin limbs and a soft belly, and the slight waistlessness of her figure, the contrived girlishness of the bows on her bra and knickers, made her seem like a rather overgrown, decorated child. He found her underwear surprising; he'd have thought older women graduated beyond pinks and flowers and sheer panels with delicate touches, but perhaps not. She smelt warm and boozy and smoky and sweet.

He'd got under the covers immediately he was undressed, but she told him to get out and let her see him. She was standing up, shutting the curtains, her full front exposed to the street as she did so, the light from the orange lamp coming round her and through her legs in a way that prefaced something exotic, that made him nervous and excited as if he were meeting sex for the first time, as if it were actually a person.

When they met and kissed, naked and upstanding, at the

foot of the bed, their alert, chilled skin laid the length of each other, Matthew was shocked. Shocked by how this seemed more intimate than encounters in bedrooms ever had before. The undulating feel of her – fingertips and legs cold, breasts and breath warm – all that flesh against him was almost rude. Like meeting and embracing himself.

He felt almost unbalanced. Because whatever this evening was, and Matthew would struggle later to define it, he'd never lost himself so in a physical state. From frustration, ants-in-your-pants, comes sex, but from disorientation comes lovemaking.

Jenny had closed him off, kissing him till he was on the bed, beside and beneath her, manoeuvring him slowly inside her body, angling herself so that they both gasped at the peculiarly personal penetration. They moved very little, the slightest of repetitions, one coming soon after the other. And they stayed locked like that, swivelling on that axis for cigarettes and glasses, until the sensation became less raw and more urgent once again, and then he moved her beneath him, and she was pleased to be beneath a man again, even one whose chest was so bare. He stopped and watched her and kissed her. They hadn't touched their mouths to each other for some minutes and it made her open her eyes. They glistened, make-up smudged around them, her face pink with exertion.

She has gone beyond looking appealing to him and now, by this stage, with her demonstrativeness and her certainty, is simply the source of the sexual grip he's in. She is old enough, meanwhile, to know that her looks have nothing to do with it by this stage of the night. What matters is the way her body behaves and interprets what's going on in her head. She tells him bits of her mind, and just like the first arrival of sex in the room, it's a bit embarrassing and his first response is faltering, until she laughs a little and shifts

294

the words to accommodate him and he is emboldened to try again.

They fell asleep at three a.m., their limbs muddled, him so exhausted and sense-drained he couldn't tell what was his anyway. His last sight before closing his eyes was the top of her blonde head on his ribcage, her clothes draped on a chair by the door. The bright thin line of light from the landing. A washing machine working through its programme somewhere downstairs.

Chapter Twenty

Just a few days before György, Éva and Tamás arrived in London (and just three weeks before the flotation of AFH), a new series began on television called *Freak Family.* Six real families were sent off to a remote part of the countryside, to start a commune. Within five days arguments thundered, sides had been drawn and by the end of the first week they had become stars. With hindsight it would look like a gentle exploitation, although seditious. But for Jack it meant nothing, he had long ago given up on being able to recognise the faces on the front of tabloid newspapers. He didn't mind. He'd met the editors of the *Sun* and the *Mirror*, one at a drinks party at 10 Downing Street for what the invite had grandly called 'innovators', and whom the Home Secretary had insisted on calling in*nov*ators, to rhyme with barometers, and the other at a corporate England rugby team dinner. He thought of the tabloids as comics, play papers. The real world could be glimpsed on the back sheets of the broadsheets, on the front of the *FT*, and he valued the fact that the majority of the population were entirely unaware of who was really in charge of the country and their lives. He wondered sometimes how the editors of such newspapers, who knew the facts of life as much as he did, could hold back from blowing the fiction away. He saw no entertainment in footballers' shortcomings, saw only pacification and distraction.

Matthew, however, had no choice but to care about the new television series because one of the stars, a small, unassuming young woman called Rosie Mason, came from Westington. Once she had shown herself to be capable of Mata Hari levels of seduction and destruction and had become a tabloid favourite, Matthew had been relieved of all responsibilities except Rosie Watching. Anything he could dig up on her through local sources could be profitably syndicated by the *Gazette*. Matthew's mother took an amused, anthropological stance at this development in her son's career; his father simply snorted. But for Matthew it granted him his first reason for professional cynicism because it meant that nothing more had been done on his Silver Report (as he called it) in the last few weeks. Despite, or perhaps because of, the indefinably threatening undertones to his meeting with Stephen Harvey, he was still determined to shape a story out of the man. His colleagues had taken to calling him MatthewGate after a session in the pub when he had promised that his story would eventually blow Westington District Council away. 'You're scaring me,' his editor had said, standing up, already undoing his waistband on his way to the gents.

Katie Flood and her aunt were addicted to *Freak Family*. Rosie Mason had grown up five minutes away from Jenny, who had once gone for a drink with Rosie's uncle's best friend, and as everyone in the family, everyone in the King's Arms too, knew for a fact, Rosie had always been a bitch. (The word was not however permitted on Katie's nine-year-old lips, only in her ears.) This fact guaranteed a whole other level of ownership and excitement in Westington.

Jenny hadn't seen Matthew since that night and didn't expect to. She day-dreamed of him, but she wasn't wasting hope on a twenty-five-year-old.

*

Julianna watched *Freak Family* every evening with horrid fascination. Unlike Bob's mother, who felt it a shame that Westington should finally be put on the map due to a young girl with a filthy mouth (she was sensitive although realistic about young women and the way one night can bring a lifetime's sexual reputation), Julianna found the people in the programme totally alien. Where did they get their confidence to lie and show off so? To inhabit the box of the screen with such totality. They seemed to think it entirely natural and right that they be on television for three hours a night. Who were they? These pale-faced idiots, the same age as her, showing their pants in public.

She longed for Kisrét these days. Even for her own family, muted and sidelined by the village as it was. Due to János Kiss's involvement with certain revolutionary figures, neither his son György nor Éva had ever been able to work in the local stoneworks, not in the offices where they ought to have been, given their white-collar backgrounds, or in the quarries, where they would have been part of the union, and part of the workers' community. Instead Éva had had to do two shop jobs and György was employed in the administrative offices of the local hospital. But even then, there had been an awareness of the neighbourhood, of the fortunes and orders at the quarry, of the problems of certain families and marriages. There had been the stoneworks-sponsored children's days and mothers' days, all organised by the Communist Youth League. Neither Julianna nor her friends had belonged to the league, but the days always brought food and drink and celebratory atmosphere. A break in the routine. Now she looked back to an un-lavish childhood with affection. She missed the place, the people. She dreamt of their small, mended home, the allotment of land, the horses on the ridge, as she slept in this large, insulated house. But the serial, repetitious, entrapped nature of her dream life had two effects. First it made her aware that she was forgetting. Unlike many émigrés she had no one to remember with, neither the country, nor her home, nor her life before England. It had transformed into nostalgia, a stagnant romance. Second it made her aware that she was living in a limbo. A lifestyle created by circumstance, someone else's lifestyle in fact. She could not see a way around this, however. She wanted all that she had. But apart from her son, none of it seemed to belong to her.

She veered between apathy and fury and longed for some clarity of mind. Instead she had her family's first visit. And anything less simple than the arrival of her father, step-mother and Tamás was hard to imagine. But she invested hope in them, that they would bring on the air of their arrival, in the disturbance of the stillness of 36 Leicester Gardens, some of the rigour she had lost.

Which was why when they all first arrived at the house, late in evening's fading light, silenced by the odd familiarity of a different European country (traffic lights, cars, win-dows, dogs, how different had Tamás thought it could be?), tired after the same hinterland journey that takes place after each airport arrival, Julianna was shocked to see Tamás point to the television and say:

'*Freak Family*, they have it here too, Mum.'

György, Éva and Tamás had arrived in London just a few days from the summer solstice. As they circled Heathrow the sky turned silver and violet, day bleeding into night, a northern European palette. Tamás, who was sitting by the window, wearing his favourite sweatshirt which said *PUNK*, sat in the emerging mercury gleam of the summer moon. He could not tell where the city began, but he saw a river, which pleased him, because it gave him a place to start, a thing to ask. There were patches of empty greenness, but mostly the land looked full and densely organised. Not obviously ordered but nevertheless packed with people and planning. This struck Tamás as noticeably different to the air-scapes of Hungary. Tamás had watched Budapest from the air with awestruck fascination. It was the first time he or his parents had ever been on a plane and the ascent into a brand-new realm, a world *above* his own, which was proving so complicated and unsatisfactory as a teenager, struck him as such a magical, massive trick that he couldn't believe his sister had visited and arrived with such languor. In fact he couldn't understand why anyone who had ever flown would ever talk about anything else at all. He knew now what it was he was waiting for. What these years of growing were for. His body was solidifying, his head expanding so that in the end, he could be a man who flew.

Julianna had arranged to meet them at Heathrow. She stood behind the silver barriers in the arrivals lounge. Around her others waited, leaning on walls or barriers, shifting weight, everyone struggling to hold their body load by that time of day. Taxi drivers held pieces of A4 printed with names as false-sounding as characters in a play, arms hanging heavy as lead. Julianna, beyond anxiety now, pushing Luke back and forth. He was awake, but happy, with the noise and passers-by, the lights and shop signs to absorb. People began to trickle through and the sparse crowd moved forwards. Julianna walked further down, near the exit. A woman came through, with a raincoat and briefcase, then several more men dressed for business. A young woman in a short baby-blue skirt suit and matted blonde ponytail came through trailing a white fur coat. She looked confused. Unmet. As if she wasn't sure she'd got off at the right country.

Julianna watched the woman, worried for her, hoping someone was waiting to gather her sour-smelling hair and clothes into a bundle in their arms, fearing that this girl had travelled to meet a man with no gentleness in him, on whom colours like baby blue were wasted. Julianna looked away (the empathy came too easily) and waited still for her family. There was a gap in passengers. The noise of planes landing and taking off, the shush of the automatic doors. The business of leaving and arriving such a very big business that most people filtered through looking cowed or aggrieved or at the very least tired. Julianna had stopped having to fear airports and the immigration questions years ago, after much money had been spent and strings had been pulled. But it still remained with her, and she thought airports were full of uncertainty and sadness. Something about the way people came round the corner into arrivals was like a delivery of goods, a production line of faulty persons, all the rumpled ones and grubby ones, and flaky faces. No one arrived feeling up to the inspection. The eyes of some searched anxiously for their own people, while others blankly focused down, as if they expected to be stopped.

The next man coming through was alone and purposeful, short and carrying a small tatty suitcase. But he had excitement and light in his eyes, an expectant stance. And she formulated the idea that this man was a good man, a funny man, someone who ought to be welcomed, before she had worked out that he was her father. She watched him, for perhaps just five seconds, before he saw her. He must have walked ahead of Éva and Tamás. It was only five seconds, but they were sharply demarcated from the fuzzy months and years that had gone before, as if she had finally arrived at a previous prediction. Here were a few seconds of the clarity that she had so wanted. It seemed one of the most important meetings in her life so far.

Why though did he come as such a surprise to her? Here he was, fresh off the plane journey they'd planned for months. She'd seen him twice in the last five years. He hadn't changed a great deal, his hair shorter and whiter, a full-length overcoat she'd never seen before. A suitcase which hadn't come out often. Was it just that he was here? Carried eagerly, finally, from the world she'd abandoned to the one she'd landed in. He was real here too. Here, standing still, at the end of the funnel of barriers, looking around, flickering from one face to another through the crowd. The way he looked for her made her catch her breath, pause with pain and affection, the way he stood, modest suitcase clutched, a small man ready for the next big adventure, impatient, rising on the balls of his feet a little, a slight smile on his face. It was the way he looked for her that made her cry.

Trying not to, she waved and said Dad. He dropped the suitcase, raised his arms and spread himself into a crucifix of celebration. Above, his face radiated pleasure, to find her, now, again, just three-deep away in the crowd. Then they came together and he hugged her with such vigour that it hurt.

It wasn't until they had disentangled their greetings, redistributed the luggage and set off towards the car that Julianna got a proper look at Tamás. The first impression had been purely of his height. But in fact, he looked like a boy who had been taken and stretched, played with and molested. He was thin like a larch tree, lightweight but obstinately supple. He had unfeasibly dark hair on his upper lip. The darkness of it seemed obscenely manly. A bit pubic. Julianna was almost embarrassed to look at him. Ashamed also because his transformation was so dramatic that it just highlighted the extent of her absence. They hugged, and she talked to him carefully, but still, by the end of that first evening, she felt they were peculiarly strained.

Luke was the focus and gift of the situation, though. Both Julianna and her stepmother herself were surprised by the intensity of Éva's pleasure at the boyishness, the characterfulness, of what was still only a thirteen-month-old baby. She was more effusive than Julianna ever remembered was possible, although no less blunt. 'He has a very bad shaped head, we just have to hope it changes,' she said with a broad smile, as Luke reached for her necklace with a fierce greed. By now he was a miniature boy more than a newborn, and when György took him from Éva's hands with a nervous little lift, Julianna felt the gentle satisfaction of seeing her parent holding her own child.

Julianna and her stepmother looked similar, which given that every man has certain proclivities, wasn't surprising. But it was disturbing. When Julianna was fifteen, she'd been allowed to let her hair grow long, and it gave her a new lushness, and her youth had begun to hold greater charms than Éva's dehydrated, if fine, face. Éva was both thinner-skinned and thicker-necked than her stepdaughter, but she was blessed with eyes of the most extraordinary deep blue. The irises had the vivid purity of an Adonis Blue butterfly and lent every one of her exchanges a significance. Because of this her presence had always been noted, remarked upon, in the manner of a black cat or a priest. So, while she was an ordinary woman, she was unusual in that she was treated mostly with respect.

Julianna and Éva had a restrained relationship and both recognised the effort that had been made over the years. Éva had the good manners to never use Julianna's mother's death from pneumonia as a reason why Julianna should necessarily love her as a parent. As a young girl Julianna had been too uncertain of the etiquette of transferring affections as quickly as her father to ever fall in love with Éva. But both were grateful for all the arguments that remained un-had, for the loyalty each showed to György, Julianna's father.

Jack came home that night in time to catch them at the table. If not for the meal itself. György stood up, opening his arms for Jack to enter. He was so moved and proud at the sight of Julianna the mother and his first grandchild that he wanted to thank Jack for this home he was seeing for the first time, to atone for ever having doubted him. But Jack, having kissed Éva briefly, shook György's hand instead and settled himself with a glass of wine at the opposite end of the table.

'Julianna says you are busy,' began György, interested, nevertheless, by what successes might be being planned.

'All rather crucial right now,' Jack said with a slightly strangled laugh, as if it should have been obvious to everyone, the whole damn world, as far even as Hungary, that something extraordinary was going on. Which somehow capped the possibilities of further enquiries from György.

The first few days of their visit passed slowly. They were years out of practice as a family, and it showed. Each one peaked in energy or moved past their best at a different point in the day. There was never a consensus of mood or move-ment. György or Julianna waiting for half an hour in the hall with bags and pushchair packed. By the time Éva was ready to leave the house for a sightseeing trip Tamás had wandered back to the telly. By the time Luke had settled for a sleep her father wished to hold him. By the time they were finally gathered at the table Luke was hungry and Julianna had to watch her plate grow cold. And by the time they had all taken themselves to bed Jack returned.

By the end of the fourth absent evening Julianna was beyond anger. She was humiliated. György and Éva had stopped asking when they might see him, and György had begun to talk about the safety of the house and the area rather a lot. 'Since you are alone a great deal, and London is dangerous.' She stayed up until Jack returned, trying to find – somewhere in the unimaginable drama of his days – a space to talk to him. She had waited in the sitting room, pulling herself back from sleep, nauseous with tiredness. She felt the weight of her visiting, sleeping family upstairs. The reversal; her home, their suitcases, their dithering before cupboards, insisting on assisting when it would be simpler without, was sometimes more of a responsibility than she could bear. Caring for and feeding her own child seemed lightweight, slow, tenderly ecstatic, sometimes tedious, but housing her father and brother and stepmother reinforced nothing more than her youth and incapability. The ways in which she was failing. In such lush sur-roundings too.

When he finally arrived home, past one o'clock, she was awoken by the click of the front door. He walked into the sitting room to pour himself a nightcap. (He was the one who had arranged the layout of his home, planned the drinks cupboard by the window, the elaborate stereo in the alcove. Julianna had only been encouraged to play with cushions and china. He had rightly surmised that she wouldn't have known how to clothe, how to feed a house of this size and history. It needed butch sofas and self-confident chairs. 'You haven't learnt how to live yet,' he'd said three years ago, with a kiss and a gesture that was meant to encompass all the wealth and ease he could dispense.)

He poured himself the drink, and sat down without even noticing his wife on the sofa. His head was racing, and he had encouraged it, fought off the descent into the taut silence of his house, by playing Bruce Springsteen loud in the car on the way home.

'Jack,' she said softly. She didn't want to shock him. Knew

somehow that a sudden voice from a corner would provoke an outburst rather than a laugh.

'Jesus,' he said and put a hand to his heart. 'What are you doing up? Hiding there.'

'I was waiting for you to come home.' There was silence and then came the exchange that they both knew the rhythm and lines to. Practice making the accusations perfect. He was never there and she was incapable of understanding the need for sacrifices. His sentences were longer than hers and his patience shorter. Her words better chosen, his repetitious and overbearing, so that as she sat listening to them in the corner of the sofa they wrapped their way round her, trying to bind her and silence her. Her trying to communicate, him trying to silence. Yet tonight she shocked herself by suddenly feeling something new – the humiliation dissolving into boredom like a suspension clearing into purity. His words were predictable, and entirely meaningless in her day-to-day life. In his office they might have some weight, here the carefully modulated but lazily constructed sentences twisted above his head, where daisy-chains climbed up the curtains to the ceiling. But then something he said snagged in her brain.

'I won't keep having this conversation,' he said.

To which she responded, 'It is the only way to have *any* kind of conversation with you. Unless I provoke you, you would forget I was here.'

'Don't be so ridiculous. The house is full of your fucking relatives,' he spat.

There was worse even than boredom, than the thought of an unending future of this. When he spoke like that she didn't like him, and she didn't like anything he stood for, his rudeness, his coarseness, his arrogance, his lack of empathy for anyone without his success. His customers, in fact. The ones who made him all that money. She sat on the sofa, watching him unbutton his cuffs, retreat into his head, resettle himself after the disturbance of her presence, and felt a burst of contempt. That ugly sofa had cost thousands. Even she knew it was vulgar, and yet he didn't.

What had she felt back then, when she'd first walked through London with him, when she had first drunk rich red wine and slid to the floor with him? Back then she had felt lust, and gratitude, and since love is a combination of different ingredients it was reasonable for her, so young, to have called it that. But as she was beginning to realise, happiness was not necessarily a question of ultimates or finite endings. Different people fell in love in different ways. Life had taught her that if nothing else. The thing would have been to find someone who returned her own mix and rhythm of love.

The area that Jack and Julianna lived in was an expensive one and nearly everyone passed through it in order to get to somewhere else. Their road, Leicester Gardens, was one of the alternatives to the Chiswick access routes to the M4. A Friday-night run to the instant, blissy country fix of the Cotswolds. The houses were big and set back far from the road, but it wasn't really a neighbourhood. Not like other parts of London that Julianna had known or visited. There were no shops nearby, it was not populated in the way the roads of the East End had been. You couldn't get anywhere worth going to without first getting in a car. She wasn't sure that it was really London. It was as if one had fallen through a wormhole at the Hammersmith roundabout and ended up on a lush, residential planet.

She often thought about the girl she'd been when she'd arrived at Dover five years ago, and her sense of herself and her feeling towards that era were enmeshed with her memories of the Westington landscape. She could still see the gracious collision of hills in her mind. She remembered turning that corner out of the Woodland Mile and seeing the line of the land, the carved folds in the Downs, the farmhouse sitting at the base of a depression. The freedom that she had felt, the delight at her escape, it was all there in that landscape. Her feelings for Matthew still lingering in the cracking woods, in the caravan planted below the shifting branches of the oak trees. (Had she been in love with Matthew? She wondered about this often. There weren't that many men to occupy her nostalgic dwellings. She didn't know. She found it hard to trust her emotions, especially from the untranquil distance of the present.)

Then the city had happened. Living and working in a way that now seemed brave but proactive, now she was stuck behind her heavy front door, at the end of a gravel drive, surrounded by rhododendrons, fenced by roads. Marooned in comfort. Julianna thought that Mila's life, though hard, could never, ever have been this lonely.

On the other side of the road from their house was a bench. They'd never really noticed it. Even Julianna, with years of time to hand and a child in a pushchair to walk, wouldn't think to crunch out of their gravelled driveway, wait for a gap in the traffic stream, tip the chair down to the surface, cross the road, lever up and trundle over the bank of grass, simply to sit and observe her own home. So neither she nor Jack had ever noticed the bench. On it was a plaque, in memory of a woman who had loved to sit there, in what must have been a quieter auto-era. Perhaps she had enjoyed watching the lush hedges grow in front of the grand houses, had imagined climbing the steps to their front doors, standing at the base of the wide stairs, graced with the fall of midday light, thick carpets running up to small attic windows where servants once lived. Sitting rooms that ran the length of the house, and trees regarding each other through the large windows at either end.

But that week a man, rather than a woman, arrived to sit. No one noticed him at first, neither the drivers flashing past nor the inhabitants of Leicester Gardens, all of whom, except occasionally Julianna, arrived and left by car. If you were going at anything faster than a pram pace it was hard to make his figure out. A mile-long stretch of sycamores gave the Gardens its secluded, expensive feel. They shaded the pavement and grass bank, making each passing a brown-green blur. In autumn winged fruit spiralled down, flicking off the bright lacquered cars.

Julianna didn't notice the man on the bench until the next day, when she slowly pulled into the road, once again carrying the load of her family alone. She had known that her argument with Jack would have made no difference and was unsurprised when he began his excuses at nine the next morning, a Saturday.

'*Nem jön el?*' her father had said to Julianna. 'Are we not going to see Jack's parents today? Does he not even want to appear for that?' Jack let the foreign language swill round him as he took the last drag of coffee. He couldn't have looked more indifferent if he'd been a teenager.

Jack didn't notice the man on the bench when he pulled out fast, five minutes later, wheels screeching slightly, turning left towards the city, foot down, gear change, change, change until he was cruising, long past the man who was sitting watching his home.

But when Julianna turned right out of the drive a few hours later, her father in the front, Tamás, Luke and Éva in the back, she noticed the unusual instantly. She hadn't known there was a bench there, so it was almost as if the two elements had arrived overnight together. It even crossed her mind that it might have been a sculpture. A rather unassuming sculpture but a false creation none the less. You never knew in cities these days; the parks were full of pink shapes and metal people.

The new element in her daily view made her stop and stare. Her father followed her eyeline.

'Strange place to sit,' he said. 'Too many cars for me.' Julianna nodded and then he said, balanced as ever, 'Unless he likes cars.'

A shriek from the back refocused Julianna's mind. It wasn't an unhappy shriek from Luke but had a warning edge to it that made her think he should sleep. So she pulled out quickly and the man on the bench passed from her mind.

'How is the car surviving?' said Julianna to her dad. He had always been a tinkerer.

'It's not a car, it's a Trabant,' said Éva sharply from the back.

Chapter Twenty-One

Pigeons shimmied beneath the six-legged tableau. It was a soft, unnoticeable day. The air and the ground served only to hold the scene, the season brought nothing to it. He was very still and, apart from Julianna, the people that passed him noticed him no more than the gentle gradations of grey in the sky, the minutely varied greens in the cat's-tongue leaves of the hawthorn bush.

The bench was a still centre. Cars flashed by to the same frequency as his breathing. He was surrounded by a loud, flat noise. It was that point in the road where people changed up a gear and got a sudden rush from actually driving, no longer merely waiting. Most of the cars were silver. Some black, some red. The odd police car, surprising as a display of independence in a machine.

It was the third day. He remembered being able to remember how many hours he'd spent here. Pigeons lifted into the air in front of him. How did they do that? Suddenly rise. What invisible displacement was caused by their wings? He berated himself for never having noticed the unlikeliness of it before.

It's like a job, he thought as he took out his sandwiches. Only with greater rewards.

Julianna watched him from her son's room. Now it was the eighth day. He had arrived just after her family, at the same time as the envelopes had begun to arrive. They came every morning, delivered by hand and addressed to Jack in neat, rounded handwriting. Julianna had noticed them – she sifted what was left of the post after Jack had gone – but she refused to stoop to either asking him about them or steaming his letters open.

Something was bound to rise to the surface here in the house. She knew that. Her despair veered between a stubborn anger and a desire to disintricate herself from everyone. The letters, this man, her arguments with Jack, Éva's tension and, unspoken, or perhaps just assumed, resentment at Julianna's comfort. Previously Julianna had felt that above all she needed to hold tight on to the security of marriage and their home. But after the last week, when for the first time she'd begun to wonder whether she couldn't have survived in something other than this particular arrangement, she now felt as though she were walking across the widest of frozen water, waiting to hear the cracking begin. She had no idea what would happen then.

She and her father met and reminisced and laughed in subsidiary rooms of the house. Her pleasure in his company apart from Éva was a guilty one. But Julianna absorbed his affection and praise like rain into dry earth. She stopped him when he began to ask when the three of them would visit, whether she was happy, why Jack was never at home. One time, when they'd accidentally found each other in the utility room (he was mending a broken door handle that he alone had noticed) they stayed closeted, laughing like secret lovers for a few moments.

It seemed to Julianna that something had thinned in her father and Éva's relationship. Twice this week Julianna had interrupted low-toned arguments. Éva referred constantly to György's recurring unemployment and Julianna could feel her father's pride stretched as brittle as spun sugar. Julianna was finding it hard to sleep with all of them lying around her, in rooms above and beside her, each breathing air warmed and hung by their own bodies, each pushing, worrying and dreaming, beyond what seemed to be their lives.

She had come to assume that the man on the bench was the one writing letters to Jack. They'd arrived at the same time, like a poltergeist, a manifestation of the blame-full failure of affection in this house. Yet she didn't find his presence threatening. He obviously wanted something. She was used to hearing Jack refer to his opposition, his enemies in the world, and used to think he was exaggerating. Now she'd lived with him longer she didn't. She was surprised one of the neighbours hadn't phoned the police.

Her son began to cry so she picked him up out of the cot. She guessed he'd been asleep for two hours. Too long probably. She'd fallen asleep at the kitchen table on her arms. Hair in her soup. She gave him a bottle of milk and then afterwards, as he lolled fat, heavy and intoxicated in her arms, an adorable troll, she stood to look out of the windows again. He was still there. Even though the light was going. She felt suddenly sorry for him; the warmth and company of her boy felt luxurious in comparison. The comforting sound of the telly, being watched by her half-brother downstairs. She watched the man and put her lips to the top of her son's head, thought for the thousandth time how odd to be holding something male, made inside me. The allure of men's difference had paled when she witnessed the truth that they came from women. How different could they be when they were made by women? It made Jack's impenetrability even less forgivable.

She held her child, whose distinct, aboriginal personality had so surprised her, up, to the window and pointed out the watching man to him. Glad to have an independent viewer in the room.

Outside, on the other side of the road, Bob watched the woman in the top window, framed within an arch. In her blue jumper, holding something red, she looked like a painting – an altarpiece in oils whose piercing brightness had survived the most tremendous stretches of time and distance. He was discovering that there was a privilege in having the time to wait for things. Now that he had found the individual responsible for the abortion of the trial and his own suspension he was happy to wait for as long as it took to get under Jack Harvey's skin. He was here when Harvey left each morning and when he returned at night, and every day he hand-delivered a new letter explaining his position. He didn't quite know where this static campaign would take him (back to his desk, into the *East Kent Gazette* or even a police cell?) but, he told himself when his backside and knees began to ache, it was worth it, because he was no longer prepared to remain invisible. Something would surely happen soon. (How often have I thought that? he asked himself.)

Suddenly, as Julianna stood watching from the nursery window, the grey fuzz of the evening seemed to lift and sunlight came seeping through from a low angle. It landed at the man's feet. Cars blocked and then revealed him, mirrors winking, drivers slowly raising the backs of their hands at the direct sun.

He stood up slowly, still looking at the nursery window. He couldn't see her face, just the shape of a body, but the stillness of the form made him suspect he was being watched. He waited, eyes up, but no longer seeing. This, the most naked moment of his persistent demonstration, this asking to be watched by someone his equivalent of a placard.

The woman at the window disappeared and thus he was dismissed for the night. He walked over the verge to the pavement and gave a weary exclamation as he realised he'd trod in the same dog turd as yesterday.

The next morning Julianna finally caught Jack opening one of the letters. She stood halfway down the stairs, Luke on her hip, watching him open the brown A4 envelope, saying *BY HAND* heavily underlined four times. She saw him read it briefly, not properly; within only four seconds he'd ripped it up and put it in the fireplace in the sitting room. She began walking down the stairs so that when she reached the bottom he was opening the door.

'Goodbye,' she said, breezy and polite as if he were a visiting doctor. Something about the irritation in him, the paper pursual of him, amused her and it made her tone light.

He responded with a similar levity (whole eras of marriage can be maintained by the careful modification and replication of tone) and gave her and Luke a brief wave goodbye.

He left, crunched into the car, accelerated hard on to the road and Julianna turned and walked straight to the fireplace.

Later that day Éva sought out Julianna alone. György and Tamás were packing their bags upstairs, ready for the early start to Heathrow the next morning.

'Can I speak,' Éva began, then stopped and looked to the ceiling, as if for support, 'to you alone? In confidence?'

The answer was obviously yes, but Julianna hesitated. It made her feel instantly (and this after having run to the far end of the continent to raise his grandchild) disloyal to her father.

Éva didn't wait for the answer, though; she had no patience with the routine of permission. She ran her hand through her short, red-highlighted hair, and drew herself up straight.

'We need to borrow some money. But I don't want your father to know.'

'Why?' said Julianna.

'Because we owe money and it has been hard to make any.'

'No, I didn't mean that,' said Julianna. 'I mean why can't he know?'

'Because he won't accept it.'

'Why?'

Éva looked a little exasperated. 'Because he doesn't know how much I've had to borrow. I deal with the money in our house.' The emphasis on the *I* was intended for Julianna, who absorbed this and paused, and then simply said, 'Of course.'

In her head she saw her grandmother, walking down a street, a shopping bag in each hand, tins like lead weights, straining the thin plastic, almost scraping the ground. 'I'll give you whatever you need.' But some fragment of child-hood made her carry on, keen to be seen as fair, like a child ostentatiously sharing. 'I did try to give Dad something when I came last year, but he wouldn't accept the cheque. Doesn't he know anything about the debts?'

'Do you think I've been buying clothes and luxuries for myself alone?' Éva looked at her with hostility. This was perhaps more defensive and more honest than Julianna had ever seen her stepmother. 'Do I look like I have been treating myself like a woman with money?'

Julianna shook her head with irritation. Éva wore the colours and patterns of a dowdy woman making an effort. There was no more to it than that.

'What shall I do?' she said. 'Will you need an overseas cheque or something? Shall I give it to you or send it to your bank?'

'I can take it but it needs to be made payable to them.

316

It's not a bank, it's a company, a . . .' she paused, 'in the end they are just people who lend money. They are called AFH. A cheque in forints for them will do. They'll be waiting for us when we get back and if we don't pay they take us to court. Maybe we lose the house.'

Julianna stood immobile. AFH. They were in debt to Jack's company.

Éva shrugged. 'I should never have taken the first loan. Because once you can't repay, and you're worse off than ever, they simply lend you more.' She stopped and looked into Julianna's pale face. 'You are that shocked?' She made a small sneer out of her mouth. 'You wouldn't know, it's been very hard. We've gone from one disaster to another. We aren't fighting in Hungary, so why would anyone know? It's not of interest. Sure, it was fine to be rid of them, but I didn't vote for it. Your father was furious that I didn't vote. The worst argument we've ever had. But I knew it would make no difference. Make things worse in fact, certainly for people our age. We lived through one disaster. We don't have the energy for this next one. We don't even have jobs any more.' She talked on and Julianna heard nothing.

She would give Éva a cheque that would draw from the money that AFH had made out of her family themselves. She felt sick. A little scared. She wondered if Éva knew. Might she know? No, just like her, they'd never felt it relevant to know the details of Jack's company. They would never have learnt its name. Again, like a child, she thought fearfully. They mustn't know. She thought she really might be sick. She needed to get out.

'Let me go now,' she said. 'I'll go now to the bank. Tell me the amount,' and she buttoned her jacket with shaking hands. I didn't know, she thought. I didn't know they were operating in Hungary. But then, walking away from the house, she thought how she did really. She knew that they were expanding into Eastern Europe. Looking at America. I didn't want to know, she thought to herself, just didn't want to know. And I should have done.

She left the house, saw that sorry man still sitting there. That letter had been full of sober, heart-rending accusations, Stephen as violent, Jack as corrupt. Him as a small, redundant man stuck in their machinations. What she felt more strongly than anything as she walked down the road was as if a sword had finally fallen, a punishment had finally come, for the indolent ignorance she'd chosen to live in.

Éva was left behind, playing with Luke, wondering at how little shame she felt. Compared to the weight of distaste in her stepdaughter's face. Had she grown so grand the very mention of debt made her run as if from a plague? Such fastidiousness, she thought, would do a woman no good in the end. She stroked Luke's sticky cheek, kissed the top of his head, where his hair licked round into a crowning circle. Thinking how he, like all men, would no doubt be blessed with petting and protection to the end.

PART 4

Summer 1995

And did you get what
you wanted for this life, even so?
I did.
And what did you want?
To call myself beloved, to feel myself
beloved on the earth.

Raymond Carver, 'Late Fragment'

Chapter Twenty-Two

Bob had begun to find, in the passing of the cars, in the slow arc of the day's progress, in the space that waiting brought, something vital. It was the most publicly private way to spend a day: sitting alone, facing a road, opposite gated driveways. No one came near him. Distractions were thin on the ground, and movement and events were never for his benefit. A sniffing dog, a pigeon, a sudden braking car, the postman. Weather was the most affecting element, rain unavoidable, a rainbow like an escapee from a cartoon. Weak sun was encouraging but full sun gave him his first taste of the pumping heat and mole-ish vulnerability of a spotlight.

When he saw the woman emerge from the driveway, he thought she must be going for one of her walks. He had assumed she was a nanny or an au pair. She had long dark hair and a tall woman's loping walk. She seemed suitably exotic, even in her jeans, for a rich man's servant.

So when he saw her stop at the edge of the pavement, look left and right and begin to cross the road, he had to resist the urge to run and hide. He assumed he wasn't the purpose of her road-crossing and he didn't want to be stumbled across. He wanted to be acknowledged and, in a way, feared. He couldn't have her just walking past him. It made a mockery of everything. After all this . . . they still hadn't even registered that he was here, waiting for an answer, right outside their house. His protest too peaceful to even be noticed. Had Jack Harvey even received, let alone read his letters? Suddenly his confident, deliberate patience evaporated and Bob felt foolish. Foolish and frozen as awaking from a sleepwalk. He picked up the paper he brought with him each day and hid behind it.

When he was a child he'd believed in the unanimity of women. That all little girls grew to be women like the ones around him. Wearing make-up and smoking cigarettes, wearing pinnies over skirts as they cooked, rationing and bargaining with the contents of their kitchen kingdoms. He liked to believe in this feminine union – one which held his mother close to its bosom – because it made him feel as if he and she belonged. His paternal situation was so blatantly wrong that his mum's outward normality was crucial. Where a dad should have been, silent with masculine concerns, watching football and drinking beer, tussling suddenly with his son, mowing the lawn beneath washing lines of generous-sized Y-fronts, there was none. The mystery of it was that his mother, despite the accident of his birth – he assumed it was a disaster that she'd made the best of – was almost *more* normal than most. At *pains* to prove her normality. She was less prone to anger than many of his friends' mothers, less given to tipsiness than others, was disapproving of betting and supportive of Sunday schools. So the mystery as to the collision that created a child but not a father was all the more. At the age of fifteen he was every bit as aware as a middle-aged child psychologist of all the things he was missing out on. He could have told anyone who cared to listen, in full sentences, of the deprivations of this male-less-ness. In a way it wasn't a father he needed so much as a man in the house. He knew that Carole King and Nana Mouskouri albums were for girls. He needed someone to teach him to shave properly. (It was unaccountably hard.) And he knew painfully well that making friends had been harder for him because of it.

This level of perception, a clear-eyed awareness of the benefits of fathers and the effects of their absence, had not extended to mothers or women. Even now it still came as a genuine shock to him to come across women who thought and looked differently to what he expected. That was why Alison in the office had been such a relaxing body to be with. Perhaps too relaxing, she had said last week, perkily. She'd popped round in her lunch break to let him know that she was happy to continue their weekly pizza night but that it would have to be '*sans* sex' from now on.

He was surprised how little he'd minded. He couldn't have agreed more when she'd said their relationship had always lacked dynamism. It would do, wouldn't it, since it had involved him? Nevertheless, he'd recognised that Alison belonged, and when he was with her, he had too. It wasn't that he really thought they should all still look like his mother; more that there was an attitude she had always carried, a valiant respectability, an unnoticeable dress code, a neatness of hair and accessories that he somehow believed all reasonable, decent, lovable women would be programmed with.

It meant he hadn't been a bold or experimental man when it came to women, hadn't ever sought out the unusual. Had, truth be told, been scared of women who seemed unfamiliar. So what he felt when he saw Julianna crossing the road was that here was a whole other kind of person from the ones he knew. Here was someone who might or might not belong, and he would be none the wiser.

Julianna saw him register her approach and then pick up a newspaper. She smiled slightly. It reminded her of seeing her husband petulantly rip up that letter and chuck it into the grate. She wondered fleetingly where this energy that was making her so fearless came from. Nothing would scare her today, she felt. She could feel it pulsing the ends of her fingertips. She crossed the second tarmac lane like it was a slip of beach and arrived on the grass a little breathless.

She'd wept again as she kissed her father goodbye, but it had cleansed her and she paid the same close attention to his eyes, his person, his age as she had when she'd watched his arrival ten days before. She promised that she would bring Luke over in the summer, and György had seemed relieved. Tamás she had told to come and visit again, later on in the holidays, and that she would pay for his flight. Then, just as she'd felt connected again, a longing to be part of the family (a low-lying guilt at her moments of full-house loneliness, relative desperation, seeping through her), she'd waved them goodbye.

In the car on the way home, she'd descended again into regret and self-recrimination. But when she slowed to turn into their driveway she saw the man was still there, and the permanence of him, like an icon in the alcove of a church, gave her the urge to confess, and an odd hope of absolution.

Julianna arrived in front of him. Just a few feet away. Something was happening. He could hear her breathing quickly. Very slowly he lowered his newspaper and looked up. She towered above him. He saw her flushed features, understood her face to be wide, felt the energy in her concentration, the acknowledgement of him. She was breathless and watching him, as if waiting for something to happen. It made him feel uncertain, woolly in his reactions. By accident almost (how else would he have dared?) he looked her in the eye. It was a peculiar convergence, like being offered something entirely new to eat. The best thing, he thought, is to make space for her.

He behaved with the most extraordinary calm. He slowly lowered his newspaper and looked up at her. She couldn't interpret his movements or his eyes. But, she thought, he seems so unsurprised. For a man who has been waiting for some notice for nearly a fortnight his movements are reluctant. What kind of man? she thought. Maybe only a madman or a drugged man. I know no other man with that patience, she thought. But his letter hadn't seemed exactly mad. By the time Julianna had finished it, she had seen that sitting outside their house was almost logical, and certainly one of the few peaceful, affordable actions available to him. What else can a single man do against a force-field of courts and companies? A history of unstoppable money-makers, a strata of rulemakers beyond an ordinary man's reach?

Then came a gesture Julianna had not expected from someone so close to obsession: he simply shifted up and made space for her alongside him.

'Do you work for him? For Jack Harvey?' he asked, out of touch with his own voice. She laughed. 'I'm his wife,' she said and Bob apologised. Then he waited for her to be threatened, or threatening, or worse just dismissive. He wouldn't move, though. He had decided that. He couldn't sit and wait for Matthew Woods; he would do anything to draw this corruption out of its house, its fortified car, its glassy offices. To make them pay attention to his anger's potential, to ensuring the wrongdoings were somehow recognised and the council gave him his job back. But she said nothing, and, noticing the familiar peach-grey tinge to the lower sky, reminding him of time's progression, for want of anything else he said, 'I've been here for nine days.'

'I know that,' she said, in a distinct accent which he was surprised by. She really was foreign, it wasn't just him assuming distances.

'I've been here for five years,' she said.

What *is* she doing? he thought. 'What? Here?' he pointed to the ground below their feet.

'Not here.' She swirled her arm round, reckless suddenly. 'In England.'

He shifted on his haunches to look at her, changing the shape of their side-by-side start.

'Where are you from?' He felt it was wrong to ask that somehow, impolite, not something you needed to ask one of those women from his childhood. But then he'd never needed to ask them, they all came from Kent.

'Hungary,' she said, and then laughed, as if she were as surprised and nonplussed by a strange country's arrival into a conversation on a bench as he.

He moved his head back, eyes wide, a picture of surprise. 'Wow,' he said. And laughed. 'I've never met anyone from Hungary,' he said, and then caught the sound of himself and wandered what the bloody hell was going on. It felt like play-acting. How could an encounter he was half of feel so surreal? He wasn't surreal. He was the least surreal person he knew. He was very ordinary. Wasn't he? Except this, of course, this ... this sitting, this could probably never be described as ordinary. And then, for the un-ordinary, this kind of conversation would be natural. For the first time he drew some solace from the idea of abnormality, and it made him feel a little giddy.

Perhaps it was the light. It was that time in the late afternoon when everything softens and alters. Lasting hours in the summer, only minutes in the winter. But this was the

328

summer of Julianna and Bob's lives and this evening, near the middle of the year, the changing time began slowly and would run and run until everyone had eased into a different state, so that the fall of darkness came like a treat, far from the biblical punishment of winter nights.

'What do you see from here?' she said, hard edges draining from the daylight.

He watched her as he spoke. Bravely. Eccentrically. 'I've seen more cars than I think I've lived minutes. I've seen bicycles too. They worry me. The lorries, they make cyclists shake and wobble, you see.' He paused, breathed through his mouth, once, self-consciously. 'I've seen you. You're the only person I've seen coming out of these houses on foot. But I've seen you in the car too.' He realised he did now sound like a stalker. 'Foxes, dogs, pigeons, squirrels, cats, babies. Well, your baby. Cats, a squashed cat once in fact.' She twitched into a smile. 'Rainbows, rain, blue sky, white clouds, grey clouds, pink clouds,' he stopped to follow her movements as she pointed upwards, 'and yes, now, strangely . . . clouds the colour of my mother's bathroom.' She looked at him, puzzled. 'Peach.' There was a pause. The traffic slowed, stilled, started again. 'Peach,' he said again, the word surprising him as they sometimes did.

She listened to him talk. He had the slight sludge of a provincial accent. Playing with words. She thought of the letter; precise, heartbroken. The voice of someone trying to stanch what seems to be an unending loss. At the moment she was curious about him, listening to him dropping words about the place, and curious of the situation she'd put herself in. She'd left Luke asleep over the road and she'd felt defiant about it until she heard this man describe the sky and it made her think of small boys in fields, overheard in serious discussion. She wondered if he was crying.

'I've left my son asleep, in the house,' she said. It just came out.

She looked less strong to Bob, more frail, when she'd said that. It struck him that she looked very young. Mid-twenties maybe. She had a wide mouth that she didn't seem entirely in control of.

'I expect he's fine,' he said. 'How loud does he shout?' he asked.

'Pretty loud,' she said.

'Then we'd probably hear him,' and just as he said that, a lorry went past, rattling its bodywork, its chuntering insides so loud that it took their voices with it.

After a minute they laughed.

'Maybe not,' he said.

'I've read your letter,' she said, aware now that her time was running out.

'Has he?' he asked. That was what mattered to him.

'Yes, and no. Yes, yes, he has.'

Bob watched her. Suddenly irritated. This wasn't a game.

Julianna sensed his discomfort and she wanted to be liked, admired by this man.

'I want to help,' she said, 'but I need to try to talk to him again.' Then she stood up, saying, 'I have to go now. I'll come tomorrow,' and then she re-crossed the road and ran up the driveway into her house.

Bob watched her go, his mouth slightly open. Within the space of four minutes he had gained a whole new compli-cation. She had just walked right over. He was astonished by the irrationality of it all. It made a change, though. He could feel the quickening in the tempo of his pulse and his thoughts. To discover something for once rather than end-lessly losing both people and places.

Matthew sat at his desk in the far corner of the *Gazette* offices, picking at a scab on his chin and staring out of the window. This was what the Rosie Watch usually consisted of. Death Watch they'd nicknamed it in the pub on account of how long Matthew sat still doing bugger all. (They went to the pub a lot at the moment; there were long evenings to fill and a summer mood of desperation in the office.)

The phone rang.

'Yeah,' said Matthew. Over the last week his professional manner had slipped so far it would probably only ever re-find itself in the gutter.

'It's Jenny.' Matthew sat up and made the face of a man submitting to an electric shock. He'd never phoned after that night.

'Jenny. How are you?'

She paused, they waited, both knowing there were vari-ous answers and that the degree of chill she would subject Matthew to was entirely within her own control.

'OK,' she said.

Matthew couldn't believe he'd ever had the luck and courage to make love to her, let alone pursue her for a date. He defaulted into hyperbolic charm.

'Good? Great! Well, that's great. Been quite busy here, well, busy enough for me anyway. I'm really sorry I haven't been in touch, I'm stuck on this wretched TV series . . . it's extraordinary how much . . .'

'Matthew,' she interrupted him. He stopped. 'You are twenty . . . what? Twenty-five? Yeah. I am thirty-six. I have been round the block more often than you've had hot din-ners. Just shut up.' She could almost hear him deflating. Like an escaping balloon.

331

There was a silence in which they both considered what an immature prat he was. 'I loved that night,' he said in the end. Nothing to lose, after all.

'I need to tell you something,' she said. 'I think you'll want to know.'

His mind flickered 'You're not preg . . .'

'Oh Jesus Christ,' she spat at him. 'No, Matthew, I am not.'

'Sorry.'

'Can you meet me in the King's Arms in an hour?' she said.

He saw her arrive that evening, in the pub, before she'd noticed him. He watched her body, he couldn't help it. She was wearing a pale yellow V-necked top made out of a soft fabric that caught on her breasts, then dropped sheer over her ribcage and stomach. She walked past him at first, looking down the back of the pub. Her arms thin, pale and reedy down the side of her chest's swell. She wore dark blue jeans and several gold bracelets. He hadn't noticed how long her neck was. He was used to her birthmark now, saw it but thought little of it. He was frightened of her capacity. Now she knew the extent of him.

None of the girls at college had ever given him this sexual charge before and no one since Julianna had made him feel this exposed. Every other one of the women he'd slept with he'd been able to play with, like a cat that is spoilt with toys.

It was quiet that night so she spotted him quickly and he got up to buy her a drink at the bar. They stood side by side, not speaking. Him feeling awkward, her inscrutable. Who knew what she was thinking? He didn't. He kept thinking of the moment when he'd first seen her with no clothes on. Her belly and the butterfly. He wondered who was looking after the kids.

'I haven't got long,' she said when they sat down. He put his pint on the table too hard; its legs were uneven and the beer slopped all over. He swore and moved beer mats around in the puddle. She got up, impatiently, and came back to the table with a red towel bearing the name of a lager, and mopped the beer up.

He felt overheated and messy.

'This is about Richard.' Matthew looked a little blank. 'Richard, my brother.'

'Right. Right,' he said.

'Do you always say everything twice?' she said.

'Yes,' realising it for the first time. 'Yes. My dad does too.'

'Must be great round yours. Four answers when one would do.' He smiled sadly and took a drink.

'Now listen,' she said, and seeing his face she tutted and said, 'You'll be pleased. I promise.' She took a large drink of gin and tonic.

'I talked to Richard tonight, on the phone,' she said. 'He says he'll talk to you, for Bob's sake. I told him about Bob's job and everything.'

'Is he all right? Richard?' asked Matthew.

'He'll survive. He's got a job in a garage. He's drinking too much, I think. But anyway . . .'

There was a long silence. Matthew continued to rip his beer mat into hundreds of tiny pieces.

'What's the matter with you?' she said, exasperation in her voice. She only had so long before she had to get back to the kids; she was telling him something she thought was important. For his sake. For Bob's sake. Sometimes her shoulders ached with the weight of carrying it all. Wide awake for everyone.

'I don't know,' Matthew said. He looked at her with a half-smile. 'Nothing I'm sure you couldn't make go away. You seem to me,' and at this point he shunted forwards in his seat so his torso stretched over the table, to take him closer to her face, 'someone who can make the bad things all go away.' She listened to the child, aching to touch him and furious at his limitations.

Chapter Twenty-Three

The handbook, *Going Public*, that stood on Jack's shelf said that the crucial thing was to keep both emotion and ego out of the process. If I'd done that with AFH from the beginning, thought Jack, I'd have nothing at all. These days he looked sort of grey. Everyone in the office had noticed. But they understood. All of them, except those who had worked with him longest, accepted it. Why was it with Jack that he felt the people who knew him least understood him best? The flirtatious receptionist was more perceptive when she said in the lift, 'Mr Harvey, you'll need a holiday when next week is over.' Rather than David, his commercial director, who had said this morning, 'Jack, you're looking really very stressed. Is everything all right?'

Of course he was looking *stressed*. This was the summit which everything had been building to. Everything that had gone before was low-lying, misty flood land, compared with the castle on the pinnacle of these crystalline days. Now, more than ever before, everything had to be kept clear. So was it any wonder he looked tired?

Because the problem was, just when everything should be getting crystal clear, like the castle on the hill in the perfect morning light, things seemed to be growing more and more fogged.

When he'd been in his final year at university in Hull

he'd passed out after a lecture. It had only been a few weeks until the exams began. It was his last ever possible lecture, and this huge wall of definitive, non-negotiable change – the end of his university life, the expulsion into a larger world, the challenge of maintaining his reinvention outside of the protective walls of lecture rooms – combined with overwork and sleeplessness and a diet of toast, had made him pass out after a single pint. He'd been raving afterwards. They'd called a doctor. It had stilled the busiest student pub in town and embarrassed his friend.

He'd always looked back at the incident with affection. What a hardworking, intensely determined boy he'd been! The first in the family to get A levels, let alone a degree. You don't get anywhere, he thought, without touching extremes. Yet as the days slid forwards towards the flotation, he had an overwhelming desire to hold on to them, slow them down like a strong man stopping a runaway train, wheels screeching and sparking. He began to taste the familiar bitterness of fear. He kept remembering more and more about his revision tactics, his endless timetables, multicoloured charts, fixation on dates.

At least then he'd had only himself to worry about. He felt scorn for that panicky undergraduate. What did it matter if he got a first or a second in Business Studies? It mattered to no one except him. Now he had a company of 300 staff, his own family, a son and a wife, and his old family hanging on to his coat tails for dear life.

What was it his dad had always said? Money comes, money goes. Like a little prayer. He knew the truth of it. But he just couldn't help feeling uncertainty in his body. He had to remember to disassociate. He knew. It wasn't always going to be good. The flotation was only the beginning. There would be worse to weather ahead. He was only as good as his mind. He was a man who won things more often than he lost them. This was the thing to remember – he was someone who could bully the elements to ensure that he survived.

It was a Friday night and he'd decided to leave the office at 6.30, earlier than he had for months, years even. They had completed the roadshow, the presentations to potential investors were all done, and he needed to be at his best for the next seven days. Today he'd been told the book was now filled, the offering fully subscribed, and all he'd felt was an urgent need for sleep. He would obviously be working all through the weekend, and he was a little scared by the way his mind kept swinging from one subject. His thoughts seemed to be very loud in his head.

He drove himself home listening to Classic FM, in a sorry attempt to unwind. It didn't work because they were playing an aria that he recognised vaguely, which reminded him of a night at the opera, last month. He had walked into the gala opening night with his wife on his arm. He'd liked her black dress and thought that she was becoming an impressive-looking woman, someone whose looks made you take her seriously (which was not always the way with an attractive female). For the first time in over a year he'd felt her presence and grace as a blessing, a benediction of light that illuminated the two of them in this room of grey-haired snobs and tax-evaders. For a moment he and she were above all of this.

But then they'd entered the auditorium and on their way up to the back of the stall he'd passed a woman with blonde hair and a shortish skirt. This woman had looked at him, in his expensive suit and choice seats, with such a bold come-on that he'd suddenly realised he was with the wrong kind of woman. Not just the legs and the blonde hair and the knowing in her eyes but the way you could tell that she knew the way the world really worked, a woman with a perspective, for Christ's sakes, a world view and an education. And a humour in her choice of skirt. He'd sat in his seat with heart pumping fast and furious, the terrifying enlightenment that he had the wrong woman at his side glowing through him as blood does in the face of a drinker.

That night he'd found it hard to concentrate on Mozart. He'd drunk wine too fast in the interval, looking every which way but Julianna's. He'd seen a man two rows below apply lip balm carefully and repeatedly throughout Act 3 and he'd had to stuff his fist hard into his mouth so as not to laugh and laugh and laugh until he brought the nonsense to a halt with his noise.

He reached Leicester Gardens at seven. It was gloomy inside. Julianna was always there when he got home, but it seemed, this time, when he felt weak with tiredness and hunger, that she wasn't. He wondered when she'd be back. If she'd be back. There was nothing that didn't require cooking in the fridge, so he got back into the car and drove to a shop in Hammersmith that he knew was always open. Last night Julianna had accused him of ruining the family that slept soundly on the second floor of his house. Were they beyond irony in Central Europe? he wondered as he drove into Hammersmith in a temper. Thank fuck they'd gone. Julianna had paid Éva the money they owed AFH, so what did it matter now? It was, if you looked at it one way, funny. To discover her family had been starving themselves to pay their own daughter's supermarket bills. But he knew it was no more than ironic, that their pennies and pounds and forints and florins no more went into her pocket than Slobodan Milosevic's. The world was not that simple. It was up for every manipulation, and available for any excuse you needed.

338

Julianna, of course, drawn by some immature, ghoulish curiosity, had been reading the madman's letters. The ones he'd ignored, and accepted as a further occupational hazard of being his father's son. He'd given David a copy of one. And David had rightly counselled him to ignore it. Said this man was a harmless by-product of a problem already solved. Why shouldn't a madman sit on a bench if he wanted to?

Last night she had cried and cried in front of him and he hadn't felt the slightest flicker of pity. She seemed to think he had the time to resolve her funny little world, her crazy family, with their bad shoes and cheap toiletries and unfamiliar smells. A man on a bench with a bee in his bonnet about some job.

He and his wife no longer belonged in the same sphere. They'd always shared a peculiarity, their aloneness. He saw it in his head, with the synaesthesia of unhappiness, as her pulling wilfully against him, refusing to budge from her place, as he tried to pull them both in another, westerly, direction. He wondered if she had gone. If he should be worrying about her. About his son in her care.

An hour later Julianna let herself into the house. She dragged Luke's pushchair up the stone steps with heavy jolts. He was half asleep and jerked floppily within his harness. She had assumed Jack would still be at the office and had been surprised to see his car in the drive. She wondered, hopefully, whether he'd been as upset by their argument last night as she had and had come home early to talk. It seemed unlikely but she was still brimful of her encounter with Bob and some vague idea of redemption, for all of them, stimulated her.

It was colder in than out, and there was a sour smell to the air. She let Luke out of his pushchair, and rubbing his eyes, tentatively at first, then picking up speed, he went into the sitting room, found a toy of his and wobbled back, delighted at the way things he recognised had waited for him. Julianna carried him down the stairs (he was getting so heavy that she had to lean far to the right to support him on her left hip), turning on lights as she went. Judging by the smell, the bins needed emptying, and she focused on this domestic urgency. She stepped down on to the cold stone and saw Jack. Sitting at the kitchen table. A bottle of whisky and a half-eaten sandwich in front of him.

He looked old.

Luke seemed surprised at this apparition. His father being a less reliable object than the furniture and even less accommodating. So he walked uncertainly, offering up the toy truck he'd found on the floor, quietly trying a generous-sounding syllable. Julianna watched Jack take the toy, and bend to look peculiarly closely at Luke's face.

'Where have you been, Luke?' he said. As if he were normally home at this hour, ready to bath his son and read him a story.

Julianna had never seen him look this ill-kempt and exhausted. She felt chastened. She had become so used to thinking of Jack as a self-absorbed, tunnelling force that the full truth of the pressure her husband was under, even of the vulnerability in his lonely determination, hit her. An unnerving thought crossed her mind, and would sit, niggling, unsolved for weeks. How complicit had she been in their familiar dynamic, him distant, her ignorant? Him effective and stimulated, her passive and longing to be as adored as before. A rush of emotion went through her – she had met him and they had loved each other in a place quite far from the monstrous demands of his business. Perhaps they could again, when everything was over.

'I'm so sorry,' she said, sitting down, placing her hands on his. 'I didn't realise you would be home early. We went for a long walk by the river. Luke, he'd been in the car so much today, taking my parents to the airport, you know.'

They sat for a little while in silence, watching Luke play with the house keys on the table. She wanted to talk to him, properly, calmly, after the anger of the night before.

'I was so angry last night, you know. I was shocked about "my family", and that letter from the man. I realise how little I know. I have never tried to understand. I have never really understood your world, the business . . . That man, I wish you would read his letter properly. Talk to him. I have, just this afternoon. He is very calm. Reasonable.'

'You spoke to him?' Jack asked, negatively entertained by the idea. She nodded. 'What the fuck did you do that for? Don't you have any idea? About anything?'

Julianna began to talk over him, fast. 'The things we said last night. I understand that my family's problems are not your fault. And you have helped me by paying all their debts. It is weird, though, you must see. I don't feel like anybody should be making money out of my home, out of my people, but I know that is naive. We have helped them anyway. I just want us to find some time later, to be together. Perhaps after next week, when all the offering is over, you will have more time. Maybe there's another business. Something new, which will be different for us . . .'

'Julianna.' He held up a hand to stop her. 'Julianna. I came home, and you weren't there.'

She stood, fighting the sinking hurt of an offer made and ignored. She picked up Luke. 'We were out for a walk, Jack, you never . . .'

'No, you're not listening. I came home and you weren't there. And I thought you'd left and I didn't care.'

She turned to look at him. Luke played with his mother's hair. Twirling it around his finger as he sucked his thumb.

No one said anything until Jack picked up the remaining

341

half-sandwich and said, 'I bought some food. I went to that shop round the corner, with the poncy name. It's a fucking rip-off, by the way.'

Then he left the room.

Once Luke had gone down, she went to look for Jack. Again she thought of her home in Kisrét. Impossible to not know where people were in those houses. She found him in his study, asleep. Unusually there was music on the sound system – some kind of ballad. It was unlike him to choose such a downbeat enhancement. It sounded like a lament. She turned it off and sat in a chair opposite and watched him sleep.

His breaths were deep and fast, greedy. His face lit from above. In this light, she could see just how he would look in twenty years, a grooved, puffed, sinking version of his face. Extraordinary that they slept and ate and did so little in the face of their disintegration.

The phone rang and Jack opened his eyes. Julianna picked up the receiver.

'Julianna? Oh, you are there, I'm ever so glad.' It was Jack's mother Rose.

'How are you?' said Julianna softly, picturing Rose hunched over the phone, trying to have a moment unheard by Stephen.

'Oh, you know. Fine. Just a little worried about Jack. I haven't heard from him since he came down that evening.'

Julianna said nothing, and to fill the gap Rose continued.

'But you're there, so the three of you are there. That's what matters, isn't it?'

'Rose . . .'

Then Julianna heard voices in the background and Stephen came on to the phone saying, 'Jack?' Julianna was silent as she tried to connect the violence she'd read about in Bob Shillabeer's letter with the man who was her father-in-law, who she kissed on greeting and leaving. Whose jokes she had tried to enjoy and whose cruelty she had chosen to ignore.

She handed the receiver over to Jack, who held it to his ear without saying anything.

Julianna watched him. She could hear the tone of Stephen's voice, loud and aggressive, although not the words. Jack remained impassive for a few moments then said, 'I've got to go,' and put the receiver down.

'What did he say?' Julianna asked.

'He wants to get himself some shares in AFH,' and Julianna began to laugh at the persistent insanity of it all. Even Jack smiled, and poured himself another drink.

Julianna took a breath, then tried one final time to stem the loss of hope from her marriage. 'I was thinking, Jack, about my grandmother and how she and János survived so much, and stayed strong together. And how, even though he'd died so early on, in such a way, she'd managed to convince me, when I was a child, that her life had been a lucky one. I was thinking how hard she worked to . . .'

'Julianna,' Jack said, looking rather more alert than he had at any point that day, 'would you like to hear a story?' He finished his drink in a swallow and said, 'So this is the story of an old woman, living alone in a cold country, in a cold house, who has nothing to control except a little girl. Who tells her how her grandad died in the streets of Budapest, fighting in a revolution, full of heroism, when in fact he was knocked over by a car after drinking too much wine in a bar.'

Julianna felt a cold front of sadness travel through her, but did not betray her family with any flinch, or sign of surprise. What he said assimilated itself all too easily into the emotional map of her family. 'Then what happens in your story?'

'The girl came to England and met a wealthy man who wanted to rescue her. She liked him and his money well enough, but never enough to try and understand where he was in the world, where he came from, and how the money she spent was made.'

'And then what did she do?'

'I've absolutely no idea, Julianna,' he said. 'It's not a fairy tale. It's up to you.' Then he got up and walked out.

'I think you have already made your choice,' she said, much, much later, colliding in the hallway. Arguments picked up from where they had left off, just as the endearments used to be. 'I think you would be sad not to see Luke so often, but I think you would rather be without us.'

He tugged hard at his hair, like trying to rip something out.

'I just don't think I can do all this, Julianna. My dad couldn't. I don't think I can. I think I haven't got the skills. I think no one gave me them.' And then again, 'I've just got to focus. I just need to focus. I can't deal with you. With this.'

His face was stretched with tiredness. He hadn't been so honest with her for years; now he was summoning everything to try and see the future clearly, trying to push her and Luke far enough away so that he could concentrate on the inhuman once more.

'I've just got to narrow it down,' he said.

'You're giving me away,' she said. 'I cannot believe you're giving us away.'

'I've just got to focus. I could say it's just this week, or this month, or this year. But it's not. I don't have . . . I can't keep you with me. You'll be all right. I'll make sure you're both all right. You'll have more than enough to live on.' He rubbed his face, and tried to smile.

'I'm not interested in the money.'

He raised an eyebrow, then his face dropped again as he remembered. 'No, clearly. You never did seem to learn to live with it.'

She felt herself begin to cry at their creep into the past tense. The finality that their language had developed, without her being ready for it at all. 'You want us to go. You've just chosen your business. Instead of us,' she said.

'Look, you can stay, I'll go.'

'I can't believe you don't want us.' Despite herself, her hands instinctively opened towards him. Such surreal, banal words.

'I can't, Julianna. I can't make it all work.'

Julianna watched motionless, and thought that men like him, who didn't know how to cry, must be rigid inside.

The next day Bob arrived at his bench at the usual time, 7.30 a.m. Having caught the 5.45 train. He sat with cold tea from the station café, watching the day bloom. Julianna Harvey had ruined it for him, of course; there was none of the usual pleasure in the stillness of his situation, or in the space to watch the way events unfurled and clouds grew and gathered, soft marching across the skies. She had ruined the peace for him by having arrived and left once before. Leaving him wondering if she would, as promised, make her way over the road once more. The vigour that the bold oddity of her had briefly given him had seeped away into his mattress overnight.

The sun climbed slowly. Beginning invisible, somewhere in a different part of the city, emerging late morning from behind, starting with a surreptitious, suspicious warmth on the back of his head. Like someone putting their hands in front of his eyes and playing guess who.

Now someone was finally paying attention and he wasn't

at all sure if he didn't prefer it before. Did he like it better, he wondered, as the heat of the sun licked at his ears, did he actually like it better when he was kept obscured? When no one turned up, so no one could disappoint. Was that why he had stayed in that same job, in that same office for so long, never having a wife or a child to celebrate, because it was less risky to hold on to what he'd built for himself?

By eleven he loathed her, in his most reactionary, provincial way. For her wrongness and foreignness. For interfering. For taking him seriously. For approaching such a very particular, delicate English issue as a redundant man sulking on a bench in entirely, entirely the wrong way.

He put his head in his hands. Sick-feeling and hot-full of recrimination. Dredging through the past and through each muddy decision and each stagnant year, until he suddenly wondered what on earth he was doing here, on the edge of the road and the city. On the edge of everything. He picked up his cup, paper, jumper, and just as he stood up he saw her come down the drive.

Julianna looked like all the colour had been blotted from her lips and her skin, into some other absorbent, now crimson fabric. She was muted and matt, her hair tied back. The draining made her look calm, but insubstantial, as though she might evaporate if you tried too hard to hold on to her.

Bob sat back down again, and gestured for her to sit next to him. This was no place for a grown man, he thought. He had some savings, and all the time and space in the world, he thought. He should be walking through a park with a guidebook in his hand and that interested, self-amused expression of people who aren't scared to look out of place.

'I am afraid I have tried and failed, or, actually, I failed before I could even try.' She looked up at him and suddenly her eyes came into bright focus. 'I don't know why you lost your job. I realise I know very little about where the money for our life has come from.

'I'm sorry,' she said finally. 'There is nothing I can do. It is too big for me to solve.'

Bob said nothing, trying to measure the guilt he felt at having so easily been persuaded to put his problem on the floor and have it carried up to her door. What kind of man would allow a woman to end up holding a stranger's burden?

She rubbed her eyes, trying to hold off helplessness in front of him. She looked down at the ground, an empty squashed packet of Rothmans, a grubby piece of tissue paper, and realised that after all these years it was easy to step out again, back out there, into the reality, the fall-out of a city.

Out here, it occurred to her, she was free to suggest things that she might never if she spent the rest of her life cloistered in that house.

'But can I help some other way?' she said. 'Can I help you? What can I do? My marriage is no use to you. But I want to try and make something right. I want to help.'

Bob listened and wondered how she might be made to recur in his life, and felt only pleasure at this slight prospect of change.

Chapter Twenty-Four

It rained during the night. Julianna left early with three bags balanced on the pushchair. She refused to take more, even to take the car. She intimated to Jack that they were going straight back to Kisrét for a while, and that they could talk about possessions later. He felt a sense of relief, as if things might finally be returning to a decent kind of order. Something permanent would have to be sorted out, eventually, but he didn't have the time for it now. Ordinarily, he knew, a wife and child would stay in the house; the man would leave for a hotel or a small flat in town. But Julianna had only ever inhabited this house like an au pair. This was his house, not hers. He was trying not to think too hard about Luke, his anxiety glancing off the image of his son in his head. Luke belonged with his mother, as boys always did. As he always had.

He watched her turn out of the bottom of the driveway, the sturdy sound of the pushchair's wheels disappearing behind the wall. He stood still, until they'd definitely gone. Breathed deeply, to clear his mind and suppress an image of Luke with his thumb in his mouth, and went in.

Julianna took the long walk down Leicester Gardens slowly, the massive, grey-trunked trees and their branches making a hazy tunnel along the red-brick wall. Wrinkled eyes burst through the bark. Ahead and far into the distance, leaves fell to the ground, pummelled by rain, frequent as births in cities.

*

When Matthew was with Jenny – and after that night in the pub when she'd worn the egg-yellow jumper he'd seen her in almost every day – at certain moments, or given certain gestures, he would feel an expansion in his chest. A rush of sensation. Once even it was just the way she put on a sweatshirt, talking through the fabric, flushed on emergence, impatient with her body for holding up talk.

Early on Saturday morning, he and she were dozing greedily, the children staying at her mother's. Matthew was disturbed from his dreamy contemplation of a hidden pulse in their intertwined limbs by the phone ringing. It was Bob. They hadn't spoken for over a week; for an unemployed man Bob had been remarkably hard to get hold of.

'Are you busy?' said Bob. 'I have someone I want you to meet. Jack Harvey's wife.'

Matthew's heart quickened as he made arrangements, and once the phone was back in its cradle he sought Jenny's chest with enthusiasm. A woman's body was an easy route to pleasure, but the exhalations of affection that kept on overtaking him meant, just as this journey with Bob Shillabeer did, that he was beginning to implicate himself into other lives. He was beginning to have his own form of effect. He'd always backed away from action before, scared of women's fickle tempers, of other men's dismissal. But he knew, just as he knew deep down that falling in love with Jenny would be more like rising, he knew he should gather his yearning for action inside him, the one that had led all these others to exposed places, and carry the full weight of it like a man.

Julianna sat on the bus. She felt very odd. Unable to grasp things in her head. And cold, even though the sun bore down on her shoulders as the bus swayed past Hyde Park. Luke sat in her lap and she hugged him tighter for warmth, but he pushed through, needing space to play with her keys. She still had the keys to Kisrét, she noted. How extraordinary it was that her marriage was over, and she was in the process of leaving it behind – while travelling on the bus, with a pushchair, looking for all the world as if everything were fine. She was on her way to a café with a bag full of pieces of paper with which she intended to betray her husband, and she couldn't muster even a flicker of anger. She felt anaesthetised, interested rather than involved in what she was doing.

Luke would now never have the proof of his father in his day-to-day presence. Just as she hadn't had her mother's. What sort of patterns did people live out unknowingly? Without Jack, Luke would not have existed. But it was hard to attribute Luke's existence to anyone other than himself. His distinct solidity was deceptively independent. Jack also seemed to have forgotten that both she *and* him had called Luke into being together. It was hard not to believe in some kind of baby bank, a cloud of unformed amoebic people, so that when cells began to divide in yet another womb a soul-child was handed down and the woman took what she was given. It would surely take more than two such unfinished people as his father and I, thought Julianna, to create as definite a baby as Luke.

She could picture Kisrét at this time of year, the green fields and hot, uncertain weather, clouds fast like rabbit scuts. They went beneath the shadow of the army barracks and felt suddenly cold. It was purely physical, reactive remembering – she was too tired and numb for more – until she saw a window display of emerald-green lingerie. Then came the memory of a nightgown made of impermeably glossy cream fabric, edged everywhere with lace. Her mother's nightgown. Wearing it blatantly, deliberately, around the house for a whole weekend, simply to remind and upset her father. Simply to make him unhappy with his second wife.

She wondered why she had still minded, after all that time. He and Éva had married when she was five. Would she forget today in a decade or two? she asked herself, disturbed by the vengefulness she'd shown. (And she always thought of herself as gentle . . .) The day she travelled to meet a stranger with papers of her husband's in a plastic bag? The sun broke through again, a blast of white light direct on her face, just as rain strangely began to beat the windows of the other side of the bus, so that it seemed to be cutting through two great weather fronts. She felt something other than a procession of tangled thoughts, something simpler – a sense of movement, and in that there was relief.

Bob walked fast across the Charing Cross concourse towards the Villiers Street exit. He had arranged that they would all meet in a café, but he was hurrying to make sure he was there with her first. He wore a new navy long-sleeved T-shirt and jangled his car keys. Around him people waited to catch the train to the countryside, arrived to visit shops and galleries, outfits and money set aside for the weekend. Bob was full of anticipation, and anxious. Julianna Harvey was only bringing them staff lists and contact details, whatever papers she could find in his office at home. He wasn't using her – she had offered to help him in any way she could, because, she had said, Jack would listen to nothing. 'But I want you to get your job back. I want to make a point, I want to rescue something,' she had said. 'I have had my eyes closed,' she had said in the end, quietly, and Bob had understood what she was feeling, if not her situation.

Julianna had also asked to come to meet the journalist he'd talked about. She said she wanted to try to understand what had happened, what kind of company her husband ran. And when she'd said this it gave Bob the impression of a child with a balloon floating just within reach, trying to clasp it and pull it down.

The café she had suggested meeting in was in the back streets behind the Strand and had once been a straightforward place that made breakfast and sandwiches, things peeled out of packages to create warm, plasticky platefuls. Now it had declared itself an art gallery as well as a wholefood café. What that meant was that it served brown pastry quiches instead. Flaccid spears of broccoli trapped in yellow custard, served alongside cappuccinos with hefty wedges of foam. Julianna liked it here, though; it was quiet. On the wall, a painting of a yellow sunflower bloomed, radiating purple Rasta slogans.

Bob arrived and they ordered coffee, then fell into silence.

'This'll be the first time you've seen me without a bench stuck to my arse then,' he said.

Julianna didn't quite react; she seemed heavy and subdued, so he started to explain, until he realised that it was his brand of levity that was inappropriate, not the complexity of his English.

Matthew walked in from the rainy street, straight from one warm watery atmosphere to another – a café hot and moist with steaming milk and microwaved falafels. He dried his face with the crook of his arm, a newspaper in one hand, a fresh packet of fags in the other. A young man, at the weekend, arriving for a strange sort of assignation. He stood at the bar and ordered his coffee and cast his eyes around for Bob. And then he saw Julianna. Sitting with Bob.

He turned away, then immediately back again. She hadn't yet seen him. She was smiling faintly. She looked older, more serious, but as he saw her Matthew thought, this is

352

how she *would* look five years on. As if he'd known it, without knowing it, all along. This is obviously how she would look, and it was like looking at an alternative reality, as if he was watching the back of his own head, watching himself sitting at a table five years on.

What was she doing here? And what was Bob doing with her? What the fuck was going on? He felt there must be some kind of trick in hand, that Julianna had come looking for him, and once again, the familiar reaction in his legs, the fidgety desire to run and shut the door. Until he saw Julianna see him.

At that instant he could see she had long ago given him up for good and that the sight of him filled her with nothing other than dismay.

Bob also saw Julianna's face change – at the sight of something behind them. He turned his head and saw Matthew. For a few seconds Bob watched Matthew, watching his effect on Julianna. They obviously knew each other, this was a chain of revelations. Bob knew instinctively that no one was watching him, and this was always the way it had been, and that he could get up and leave here and now, and no one would run after him. With Julianna there was a heat of action, emotions given and taken and words exchanged, that he had never built up with anyone. Except, perhaps, Richard.

Bob looked down at his hands. The thrum of his heart in his head, until he heard the chair next to him being scraped back and Matthew sat down.

No one said anything, and with a surge of irritation at the unruliness of everyone and everything around him, Bob said, as you would, as one should, as normal people do, 'Matthew, this is Julianna.'

'I know,' he said, still staring at her. Julianna was now swivelling her cup in its saucer. 'We used to be friends.

Years ago.' Matthew noticed Luke, asleep in his pushchair, for the first time, and gave an uncomfortable half laugh.

Still nothing was said, so in the end Matthew, with the trick of nonchalance, something taught at his school, that allowed him to talk evenly in even the most sacred of places, said, 'So this is odd, Julianna. All this time.'

Julianna could hear all the sounds around them with peculiar clarity. A table next to them with two women snorting with laughter. Luke snoring a little. A woman behind the counter singing. A cab outside, its engine making a low bubbling noise. For the first time since Jack had told her he didn't care if she wasn't there, she felt herself engorge with anger. An urge to unleash a tirade of reality at the lot of them, to turn over chairs and tables as she left this whole city to stew in on its fetid self. She dug her fingernails into the back of her hand, focusing on nothing but the strength inside her. She had never, ever felt quite so powerful. Capable of breaking and ruining anything.

'What are you doing here?' she said harshly. Matthew Woods was a boy; Matt the journalist, she had assumed, was a greying man, with experience in these things. 'I don't understand. How do you know each other?' The two of them could hear a woman who had reached the wall of her limits. Bob because he sensed these things, Matthew because he had never heard her sound like that before, had been so scared of this potential in her that he'd never spoken to her again after that summer.

'Matt is the journalist I was telling you about,' said Bob flatly.

She wanted to say, no he's not, don't be so stupid, you stupid soft man, he's a schoolboy not a journalist. She looked at the two of them, the hopeful radiance of Bob in his neat T-shirt, the childish familiarity of Matthew, and began to laugh. They were intending to take her husband on? Heaven help them. She could see how entirely ridiculous, dismissible these men would be to him. To his partners and associates and lawyers and staff. At which point she began to care less. They could all take care of themselves. She owed nothing to anyone. Just her son.

They waited until she stopped laughing. 'So you got married?' said Matthew, and without meaning to there was an accusatory edge to his voice.

'And I have a son,' she said, pushing back hard on his eyes, inclining her head towards Luke, fat and flushed inside a navy sweater.

Suddenly Bob stood up, and said, 'I'm going to go and ... get something. Leave you to talk.'

They watched him struggle to find his coat and manoeuvre chairs, and Julianna watched the discomfort in their faces without care.

Then Matthew said, 'So tell me. What did you do? I always thought you'd have gone home. I imagined you back in Hungary.'

'You were wrong.' Important to say that early on, and then again, wherever possible. 'I met Jack when I was working in a restaurant,' she said simply. 'We got married and we have a son.'

'Are you happy?' he said, and she snorted in response. Why did he think she was here? That was the sort of rubbish he'd always talked. She felt about a hundred and one. He, on the other hand, looked no older than twenty-one. Carrying the same presumptive amusement in his bright eyes and smooth-skinned face, but slightly thicker around the torso and the jowls. She could see he looked a slightly more serious, substantive prospect than he once would have done.

He lit a cigarette, offered her one, and inhaled with concentration. There was silence, almost as if he were listening for the nicotine.

355

'You can't be happy,' he said in the end. 'You're caught up in all this.'

'All what?' she said. Define your terms.

'This . . . story I'm investigating. Corruption and violence and loan sharks.' He wasn't showing off; he was confused, but activated.

She didn't like his presumptive tone. 'Bob told me a journalist was helping him, because of the way he lost his job, because of AFH. It wasn't fair. So I offered to help, and bring what I could find. I don't know if there's anything useful . . . To be truthful, I don't care much any more.'

'Julianna,' he said, ignoring her words, looking down at the mug-ringed table, provoked by her irritation, 'I'm sorry that I never came.'

She said nothing.

'I didn't because I was pathetic. I was scared . . .' He stopped. 'I wish I had. I've always wished I had.' He raised his eyes again and saw her face settle a little. Her head moved just once or twice, from left to right. Here she was, sitting with men who wanted to do damage to a husband who had finished with loving her, and still Matthew's abandonment felt like the worst betrayal she'd ever known.

Then with a swiftness that was disarming, he moved on. 'What are you doing here? This family, your husband's, they're your family too. I don't understand. I was just told by Bob, like he'd found some bloody murder clue, that he'd found this woman who might help us.'

Quietly she said, forcing herself to inch forward, 'I've said. I thought that I wanted to help. I wanted to help you teach my husband that not everyone can be thrown away. They put my father into huge debt. I wanted somebody to fight back.'

'Julianna, have you grown *very* mad since I last saw you? I don't think you understand what you're dealing with. It's

356

not like people don't choose to use AFH. He's not a criminal. His father might be, but he's not. This is business. Big business.'

She gave a derisory laugh, something Matthew had never heard from her before. 'A year ago and I'd think you were right. But . . .' she paused and thought of how to say this, then shrugged a little; less was probably better, 'now I know how much damage he causes.'

'Does he hurt you?' asked Matthew.

Again Julianna laughed. 'No, he doesn't hurt me like that. Matthew,' she leaned forward, and looked at him hard, 'I think I had to grow up quite quickly that first winter. And I think that one of the most important things I learnt was that life is more boring *and* more shocking than you and I had ever dreamed in that little caravan.'

She shunted her long mouth aside and bit the inside of her cheek, then said again, 'No, he doesn't hurt me like that.'

'You shouldn't have married him, if you dislike him so much.'

'Who knew?' she said, dancing her hands a little, the ring catching the light, her gesture suddenly old-fashioned, melodramatic, feminine. 'We were in love. Who knew what would happen?'

It suddenly occurred to Matthew that she might not be a lost girl that he had found once in a farmyard, now again in a malodorous café, but a woman actually enjoying herself. A woman aware that, for the first time, she holds some power beyond attraction. That was, after all, why he had fallen in love with Julianna, because he'd felt the future in her.

Matthew felt a breeze at his neck and Bob, with plastic composure, walked back in. He sat down and said, 'Right, let's get going,' and Julianna, to his relief, emptied her plastic

357

bag of brown files on to the table. Matthew thought, very distinctly, marking it as it passed as a new emotional experience, that this moment he was participating in was perhaps not so much about him.

When they stood up to go, Julianna's limited knowledge exhausted, dates and names noted, the papers examined, Bob noticed the bags. 'Where are you going?' he asked. She said, exhausted now, beyond a fight, that she didn't know. That she'd left him. And Bob, for the second time that week, made it clear that there was plenty of space alongside him.

On Monday night Jack once again opened his heavy front door to a dark, empty house. He wondered briefly if there had been a power cut. He shut the door behind him, dropped his jacket and briefcase where he stood and exhaled. Until he felt himself sag, then inhaled. Then out again, then in again, until the business of breathing began to feel joined up. It was a relief to be alone. In the end David had told him to go home; everything, he had said, would settle, and tomorrow would be better.

He poured himself a drink, the day's scenes flashing before his eyes like cue cards. The calls had started at midday. Direct lines rang, as they do in every office around the world on a Monday morning. Each staff member receiving a call from an unfamiliar colleague who needed to know something they should either have remembered or probably shouldn't need to know. Just one slightly odd call per person, but not enough to mention. Tiny snippets of information gathered about AFH's internal workings, its communication systems and passwords, the flotation details, and, in particular, the buy-out of Silver Services. It wasn't until David overheard a trainee in the legal department that they discovered something was on the move. He had demanded to know who she was talking to, grabbed the phone, then heard it hang up; and then discovered the accountant she had thought she was talking to was in hospital with acute appendicitis.

Jack felt hollow. He presumed this was what happened. He didn't know. Information-gathering wasn't unexpected at a time like this. Attention was on him and his company. He knew that. But the combination of the calls and the news that three large investors had today pulled out, leaving the shares undersubscribed, had rendered him nearly speechless with panic, until the decision to borrow the money and buy the remaining shares himself galvanised him again. He turned on a table lamp, and another, and another until the sitting room blazed.

He went downstairs to find something to eat, and as he reached the tiled floor, his carpet-muffled footsteps suddenly ringing loud and lonely on their way to the fridge, he remembered that Julianna had gone and taken Luke with her.

He reached for the fridge door and found an opened packet of salami. He ate the thin slices methodically, leaning on the counter, his right foot lifting to rub at an itch on the opposite calf. He stood for a second with the empty, greasy packet, unsure which cupboard the bin was hiding in. He bore the surroundings of his office like a lifetime's indent in an armchair, and he struggled to expand into other spaces.

He walked up three flights of stairs to Luke's room. It looked much the same. There were perhaps fewer toys in his cot than normal. Though he couldn't be sure. There was an elephant he liked to hold by its trunk that seemed to be missing.

He went down and looked in her wardrobe. The sparse line of clothes rippled as he opened the double doors.

He sat on the floor in the doorway trying to work out how he felt. Leant against the wall, looked at his substantial home from a new angle. The carpet had been badly fitted in one corner. In his head scenes from the day continued to repeat. He tried to move his thoughts on, to think about his son, and when he might next try to see him, but his nerves were too frayed to get a grip. He pushed at the bulging carpet in the corner, and it struck him that it was at moments like this, in places like this, the small corners of buildings, that men usually found God. Wasn't it that, that they'd find themselves face to face with the toilet cistern, or the dirt beneath the cooker, and say, enough, enough, enough of all this, I shall devote myself to the work of the Lord? Jack found himself waiting in the clicking quiet of his home. The silence far from absolute.

He waited there for a few minutes until he felt his eyes closing, and then went to bed. Sleep came on heavy. Dreams thundered in his head with submerged power; a cathedral sinking beneath the waves.

Chapter Twenty-Five

In the papers that Julianna had taken from Jack's desk at home was only the barest information, nothing that an experienced financial journalist couldn't have drawn together with a few calls. Most useful, however, because people are always the weakest link in any security system, was an entire list of staff, and a list of all office direct lines, private numbers and home numbers. The date of the flotation, the Thursday of this week, had given Matthew and Bob their deadline. On Monday Matthew presented his editor with the background and sources so far. They agreed the story would need to run on Wednesday, the day before the flotation, to have the most impact. This story which suddenly seemed to be coalescing into a headline with all the editor's regional favourites, violence, local business, and corruption in the council, should also be picked up by the nationals.

Matthew's brain was galvanised as never before. Bob Shillabeer was brought in, taken through meetings with lawyers. A hungover Richard Flood was interviewed over the phone about the assault, but the editor then forgot to pass on a message of stilted regret to Bob. Subs were sent to examine court records, reporters to the council, where they stalked Bob's boss Frank. A disgruntled councillor revealed that funds from Jack Harvey had covered the cost of a new health centre, an annual firework display, and a brand-new set of Christmas lights for the high street. From both silences and accusations deductions were drawn. Work-experience boys were sent down to the paper's archives; one even showed an interesting initiative and hacked into AFH's email system, and late on Tuesday night the threads were all drawn together: Stephen's past, his jail sentence, the trading standards warnings, the assault on Richard, the prosecution, the sale of Silver Services, Jack's rise and Bob's fall and the flotation that was due to happen tomorrow. SCANDAL IN CORRUPT COUNCIL ran the *Gazette*'s headline on Wednesday morning. Matthew thought he could have done better, but to his surprise he wasn't asked.

Wednesday morning and the first editions sold out fast. A sense of outraged community flickered in Westington in a way it hadn't since the *Gazette* had revealed plans for a refugee holding centre in the old army barracks outside the town. Silver's was not, after all, an affectionately thought of local firm. Wednesday evening saw the story on the business pages of the *Evening Standard*; by Thursday morning it was the lead business story in every paper.

The opening share price of AFH, touted as the retail offering of the year, was 8p compared to the 75p expected. Having remortgaged his house and sold all his investments to buy thirty per cent of the shares himself, Jack Harvey, once again, found himself owing millions more than he owned.

Late on the Thursday afternoon Bob came into Jenny's kitchen carrying a pile of national papers, high on the visible success of their exposé. He stopped still when he saw Julianna and put the papers down. He placed his hand on them, almost as if to keep himself, so heady with activism, still and steady. She looked tired and the child was crying.

'Are you OK?' he said. 'Shall I leave? Is this too much?'

And she gestured at the papers and looked at him as if

to say, what do you think? Then Luke began to cry again, in a way that made Bob think he might be the problem. So he popped out again, leaving the door on the latch, deep-breathing the wet air, trying to settle his head with the earth-iness of it, so packed with the smell of geraniums and rain.

Julianna held Luke's bucking head and rigid, flailing form very tight, and began to pace back and forth across the small kitchen.

She had half wanted to go home to Kisrét, but was too ashamed to be seen returning in need, too aware that she would never be able to tell them how little she had under-stood their life, or how much she had betrayed her husband. Not prepared to admit to them that their home only appealed when life was at its worst. She had therefore been staying with Jenny since Monday. Bob had volunteered Jenny's house as a refuge – knowing she'd be prepared to help – and had then wondered why Matthew had looked quite so disturbed. Bob wished he'd had the courage to insist she came to stay in his spare room.

How had it come to this, Julianna asked herself, her hus-band's name all over these papers? All of them spread out over Jenny's kitchen table. She felt physically sick at her part in it. A wrenching sense of guilt and pity for a time in the past which she had betrayed. She could no longer remember what had driven her. Had she just wanted to help a stranger get his job back? How could she not have drawn the line at publicly ruining the man she'd married?

She had helped betray Rose, and even Stephen, whose table she had always been prepared to sit at. Whose com-pany she had grown accustomed to, if carefully – she'd recognised early on the hardness of Stephen's heart in Jack's increasingly impenetrable carapace. Luke held on to her neck, quiet now but unnerved by her unhappiness, so she unclasped his hands and looked into his small, wild face and tried to smile. 'It's a mess, Luke,' she said to him. 'But it'll be OK. We'll be OK.' *I just never knew*, she wanted to carry on; wanted him to understand. Trying to justify herself to a toddler. Never knew what? She wanted to pin it down. Which turning had led to this? Then she wondered if the fact that she couldn't ever remember having taken a conscious direction hadn't been the trouble all along.

Luke whimpered to be let down and Katie, who'd come round for tea with her cousins, came into the kitchen and said shyly, 'Can I take him?' Julianna watched her lead Luke up the step. Katie was involved too. Even that overgrown nine-year-old implicated and her father departed. Katie's appearance served to remind Julianna that there was someone at fault, and it wasn't just her. But this . . . her eyes swept helplessly over the print. All such small, flawed people, and here making great stories, shouting of money, great sums of money, such sums that she would never imagine, and now she came to read again, sums that she found quite obscene. All because of Jack.

But hadn't she helped make all this happen, hadn't she abandoned her marital allegiance? Her grandmother hadn't run the moment she'd found herself alone, the wrong nationality in a foreign country run by yet another nationality of soldiers. Mila had remained loyal to her marriage, even after János had failed as the hero she thought he should have been. Even thirty years later, when the statue removals began, Mila was still propping up János's memorial alone.

Julianna could remember when she'd believed that her life would be a cumulative, controllable procession. She wondered what had ever given her that idea. Mila, she supposed, yet it wasn't as if Mila would have chosen the life she ended up with. Julianna had been seduced by Mila's storytelling, into believing that her grandfather's death as a hero, their unending love for each other gave everything a rightness in the end. Julianna realised she had always thought of their marriage as the one truly successful one she knew of. Yet János had been dead for fourteen years before she'd been born. And he, clearly, had found the fragile balance of existence in an era of technologically aided brutality too much to contemplate in the end.

Now Julianna had a son, and that bond was proving to be the one reliable essential. This whittling down, to essentials and compromises, must be the important thing. She'd always thought Mila had been trapped in Hungary by politics alone. Yet Julianna, possessor of a valid passport and a healthy personal bank account, was free to leave and did not yet know how to make an independent decision. Like a Victorian heroine, fated by social history, she had bound her story to the decisions of men. But why? Because of her faith in what, exactly? In love? Which had done nothing to help her orient *herself*. She'd been waiting for someone to come along and release her into the full realisation of her own story. She stood, looking out of the window at the garden, as if the simplicity of greenness had gone, revealing the parasitic structures beneath. Could she accept that she'd long ago arrived at the reality of herself?

Bob returned with a pint of milk, but so quietly that Julianna didn't register him standing at the top of the kitchen step. He wavered before stepping down, absorbing the warmth and the smell of food in the kitchen, the familiarity of standing on the edge of a woman's domain. The shining oddness of it, though, was Julianna, placed in the middle of Jenny's kitchen. The most desirable woman he'd ever known, standing here in this scene, so familiar that Bob could have told her where to find the instant coffee, how to make the kettle button stay down, why the lino in the corner was ripped, which child had been bathed in the sink. Here in this uncoordinated kitchen, full of the once new and often mended, the cast-off and happily fingerprinted, stood Julianna. Around her the surfaces were cluttered with hamburger gifts and rude mugs made in Taiwan, thin comics, cheap pink bracelets and small red plastic monsters moulded in Korea. There were leaflets pinned to the fridge listing Indian and Chinese takeaways, pizza deliveries and jerk Jamaican chickens. A jar labelled *Biscuits*. A tin labelled *Tea*. And Julianna standing looking out of the window. Beyond description to Bob. Simply the most extraordinary thing to have ever landed in this limited little town, which had never before repaid his diligence or propriety.

'Julianna,' he said suddenly, and she jumped, put her hand to her heart.

'I didn't see you,' she said, and there was a small pause in which she wondered what it was that he was going to say, what it was that made his face joyous. Then she watched his smile smooth out to nothing, and heard him offer her a cup of tea.

That night Matthew took Jenny out for a meal and Bob and Julianna babysat. Bob, in an entirely excitable frame of mind, chose to forgive Matthew his involvement with both the women in his own life. Jenny looked happy and he got to spend the evening with Julianna. It was a peculiar arrangement, but then this week was beyond surreal. Julianna and Matthew found each other's company problematic, and avoided each other's eyes. She could recall his love very clearly, now that they were often in the same room, yet she felt there were only so many things she could hold in her head. Her failure within her marriage mattered more.

Jenny opened Bob a beer as he told her how he was thinking of redecorating. He'd begun to hate his wallpaper and the fussy, old-womanish look of his kitchen. His white leather sofa had developed the irritating habit of expelling air whenever one sat down – a high-pitched, long-winded whine of protest.

'Hard to believe,' said Jenny, 'but some of us have ordinary jobs that go on and on. Why don't you come and be my cleaner if you're that restless?'

'I think I'm going to get it back. The job, I mean,' said Bob. 'They've scheduled the tribunal.'

'Well that's good, isn't it?' she said.

'Not sure.'

'Oh for Christ's sake,' she said.

'I don't know if I want it now, Jenny,' he said, looking amused.

She just shook her head at him, and then said, 'Men.'

Jenny drove Matthew towards the town centre, but he suddenly suggested a detour, then directed her until they were parked outside his parents' door.

'Where are we?' she said.

'My parents',' he said.

'Blimey,' and she guaffawed. 'You sure?'

He escorted her to the door, trying to ignore the pounding in his ears. Determined to get this over with, only the second, perhaps the last, and definitely the most unsuitable of his girlfriends ever to step through the door.

In the soft light of the kitchen his mother was hunched over the week's newspapers, and stood up in surprise at his entrance, confused by the re-emergence of her past, by Stephen's name all over the papers, and by the sudden display of energy and action in a son she'd always had to push so hard. Too shocked to do more than offer this woman, his girlfriend, a stiff drink and a chair. Then, when they were all seated, nervous of her son's gaze, Miriam realised that to bless them would ultimately bring her more.

Chapter Twenty-Six

Mila had written weekly letters to her sister throughout the war, never knowing whether they'd arrived. There was no chance of a rhythmic exchange; her sister's replies came so rarely and assumed knowledge that had long gone astray. Even through the most terrible seasons Mila's letters conveyed an infuriating superiority, won through experiences that her sister would have never even wished to share. But after the events of '56 Mila stopped writing. She was effectively separated from her past and her family in England for ever more. So when Julianna was born, so too was a new avenue for Mila's living. Julianna had been just a few hours old when Mila began to tell her tidy stories of her past. The first time she held her granddaughter she had seen only János in her features, the carved, prehensile upper lip, and in the darkness of her flat whorls of hair. This was fourteen years after János's death, and it felt as close to resurrection as humanly possible. She didn't believe much in God, but she believed in prayer, which had brought this sign of his presence to her eyes. How then could she not tell the child of her origins? It was a way of keeping him alive, of fighting the pervasive politics which had tried to infantilise its people into believing the past had gone.

It's hard to tell an old woman that she is making things up, hard to see how they are absorbed into a child, so that any later revelations of truth settle like a new layer rather than a correction. Mila felt, quite distinctly, as the keeper of her own body and past, that some things should and some things simply shouldn't be graced with remembering. Salvation came in the alchemy of living, the way good could come from bad. Leave the bad behind: the soldier who forced his way into her one night, the sadness that ate into János with the drink. Redemption lay in willed acts of creation, she was sure: new stories, new love, new lives.

Yet before she died Mila had begun to wish she'd been able to explain things in clearer detail to Julianna. She had waved her off to England, then worried, as her health finally failed, that she'd done wrong in not telling her the nasty paradox of life, before she stumbled into its trap. The paradox that it had taken her years to discover – that you had to live and fight as if others didn't have the ability to remove every-thing, to pull the ground from under your feet. You had to live as if it wasn't possible to be knocked down by a car shooting fast around a corner, as if it wasn't possible to be raped by a soldier wearing the colours of a liberator. You had to live with the practicalities in hand, as if you your-self were in control. Then switch your priorities to riding out the storm when you weren't. It took confidence and humility to survive. And will, sheer, primeval strength of will.

Once Julianna had gone, Mila had let go of her simpli-fied, glorified János. It was almost a relief. She had held him in their house, in front of their very eyes for years, until the effort of trying to keep her and György and her family alive, as well as raising the dead, had exhausted her. He had not been able to ride out the storm; he had found his inability to protect his wife too much to carry. Mila knew women could lower their expectations better, could survive loss to still find hope in the smaller things. And look, hadn't their love remained to comfort her? Even at the age of eighty she had been able to remember the weight of his eyes as they rested on her, from the opposite side of a train carriage, resting on her as the land slid back like fabric rolled in fast. The feel of his body curled within hers, in a room lit orange by firelight, within the forests, listening to a storm cross the continent outside.

We're such small people, she had wanted to tell Julianna at the end. Trust the land to survive, and nothing else. Find a lover who clarifies your instincts, whose lovemaking will connect you to the revolutions of the earth. Because everything else will pass.

The airport was busy, an average summer season of holidaymakers, salesmen and photographers – flights to Ibiza, Delhi and Belgrade all leaving within ten minutes of each other. Julianna, Luke and Bob had arrived ludicrously early and sat in a café watching them go through the gates.

'She's going to see her boyfriend.'

'She doesn't look happy about it.'

'Maybe she's late.'

'Maybe she's making a mistake.'

'Well, you can tell her that. I'm not.'

'Will you call to say you've arrived safely?'

'Of course. And I'll write.'

'Are you excited?'

'God, yes. Why didn't I do this before?'

'Good. That's good.'

'What about you? You going to be all right?'

Julianna nodded; she was wearing a bluebell-coloured T-shirt and looked just as young as she was. 'It's a relief, to be going back to a place that I know, to a house without tension, a house that isn't so big that you lose people in it.' Bob laughed.

'I want to make the garden nice,' she carried on, playing with sugar packets on the formica table, pulling Luke's pushchair back and forth with her foot. 'So we can be outside all summer. The wall, by the yellow rose, where the sun collects, it's pretty. I just want to sit there with a cup of coffee, all summer long.'

Once on the plane, studying the route, Bob found it hard to understand the scale of his journey. He was too amazed to find himself there. He couldn't imagine how it had actually all happened. His neighbour already slept deep as a drunk man, as if the aeroplane air were doped, and Bob just watched the land spread and spread. Bowled over at the impetuousness of himself.

The clouds were succinct, infrequent. Through the inadequate fish-can-shaped window, he could see Britain stretch far into wild distances he'd never explored. Below him was Westington, where his mother, Julianna, Jenny were ranged. He and Julianna had swapped places, him travelling, one land mass to another, her choosing to hold still at the foot of the Downs. Renting his house for the month he would be gone. It brought him warmth, knowing that she was protected by the walls of his house.

There was so much that he loved in that small town below. It was precarious in its wonder. The Bükk hills surrounding Julianna's homeland, they too were somewhere far below, just a short distance round the earth's curve.

The screen ahead of them showed the map of the journey. Slashes showing the pattern of their progress, the science and engineering of it so assumed that they used shorthand to demonstrate the progress of the great white Boeing 747's arc across the ocean.

Where do you go when you discover the multitude of reactions in your head? He's using his credit card to take the trip he once tried to win in a raffle. A holiday he's always held back from, in the killing hopefulness of a woman he loves to accompany him. He's decided to take a trip to America by himself, leaving Julianna and Luke with space and freedom, in the moderate shelter of his own home.

He fills out his complex green slip, which will allow him immigration into the smallest, highest city of them all – New York. For the first-timer, New York hides the whole of America behind it.

He thinks again of Julianna. Extraordinary how his head can be there, here and also in the future of New York. He knows that he would never have made Julianna love him by clutching at her, or thinking too much on security. It has brought him nothing before. He has made space for her in his heart and his house and he will earn her through adventure, he thinks.

Seven hours later the air hostesses will begin walking and, one by one, men pull blankets from their heads. People will queue to brush sleep from their teeth. Everyone will have shared their air and space for too long. The window shutters will slice up and an unbearably bright, yellow-white light flood across the rows of legs. Together the travellers will witness the sun, a magnesium flare and the fast-gradual emergence of an orange disc, and in the distance the city will wait for its arrivals to finish waking and prepare their proper excitement.

He will hear Manhattan being spotted, look and find the tiniest grey outline, a huddle of uprights in amongst a sea of habitation. A collection of tiny grey monoliths against a yellow-streaked morning.

Yet the true depth and height and power of this, the greatest man-made landscape he has ever seen, will only be revealed by coming face to face with its shining granite flanks. Will only be revealed when he walks the streets, from uptown to downtown, for the first time. That first-day, sixty-block stretch. When he will understand how those around him are feeding their lives, just how they are experiencing, tasting, witnessing their own narratives in the most dramatic of backdrops. The skyscrapers like crude clocks for the progress of the sun, the streets full of dark falling shadows.

In its island definition Bob will sense every fraud, every crime, every generosity, every sweetness, every isolation, every experience to be found on its crowded crossways and its tunnel avenues, down to its fringes where the buildings and roads run down to cold waters. Where the wind that has streamed from the heights runs out, wraiths on the water, swirling at the feet of the financiers' two highest towers. Curling around the exact, glassy corners of a landscape built with passion and money. The energy of this boiling city will both frighten and exhilarate him. Will keep him exploring, until love roots him to the earth once more.

What more could he want, after all, beyond witnessing America, beyond the locating of his own voice, than the determination of love to find him? The discovery of the sublime in quiet words, in the calm of his heart – in connections made, and left like droplets in the air, for those who come later to absorb.

As Bob's flight made its journey towards the no-man's-land of immigration controls, Julianna was, as promised, sitting very still in Bob's back garden, her eyes closed, face to the setting sun.

On the lawn Luke resided in a small, bright green, plastic paddling pool that Bob had bought him. He brought the flats of his hands down on to the water hard and shrieked at the splash. He kicked at the patterns of shells and fish on the side. It was by far the brightest thing he had ever sat in.

Tomorrow Jenny was going to take Julianna shopping.

Julianna wanted to buy some plants for the garden and Bob had asked her to choose a new sofa. She wanted to ask Jenny about finding a part-time job, until Luke was old enough for her to finish her training. She thought she'd like to teach after all. Necessity had brought about the expansion of Julianna's will. She had only the contents of her bank account to rely on for now. Jack was badly in debt, a development that she was shocked and confused by at first, until she discovered that it somehow didn't seem to be impacting on his life in the way a smaller debt would have done to a less ambitious man. He insisted he would support her in the end; there were plans for a new start-up altogether, he'd said, sounding far too wired, but Julianna would refuse it, would only allow him to contribute to the upbringing of his son. Julianna felt she had forfeited his money by giving his papers to Bob. So now she was both forced and free to start again. A redemption of sorts.

She was immoderately content at her small plans. It wasn't the scale of the choices that mattered, it was the act of making each one for herself. Acting through her feel for the moment, not her demands of the future. There was pleasure, and liberty, in these very mundane and logical steps. After the disgrace of the last months, she was moved by the practical salvations of her small circle of family and friends. She did not want these moments in the sun to be consumed by her back-story so far.

In the end, it's quite an ordinary garden, except for the unique oddity of her and Luke's presence. She's not looking for epiphanies, just watching how things grow. There's a soft yellow rose climbing above her head, a multitude of blooms, mingling with the smell of jasmine from over the fence. There's a burst of noise from a garden a few doors down, music and kids shouting. A white leather sofa sitting transient and incongruous against the back wall and Luke's plastic paddling pool, its green vibrant and vamped, bulging in amongst the long grass.

She closes her eyes again and her face settles into the lines of a woman who has already lived a little. What happens next is a matter of chance and reaction. In the air there is a peacefulness that comes from an openness to its interruption. The wind picks up and she inhabits herself fully in these momentary conditions. The warm stone at her back. Her son in his green pool. Her pulse quickening. This whole plot of land alert to what might now astonishingly unfurl.

Acknowledgements

Many people took the time to help with my research on the flotation process, the Consumer Credit Act 1974, the Office of Fair Trading, student farm workers and immigration law. Thank you to Liz Harris, Vicky Doran, Christine Lumb, Angie and Thomas Konrad and many others. I also want to thank László Kũrti for his excellent book *Youth and the State in Hungary*. Thank you too to Time Warner Books, Ebury Press, Vivien, Jeremy, Hannah, David, Eve, Debs, Jane and, in particular, Paul. And thank goodness for Victoria Hobbs, Emma Parry, Sam Kelly and Jo Dickinson, whose advice and support has been invaluable.

'Late Fragment' from *All of Us: The Collected Poems of Raymond Carver* © Tess Gallagher, published by Harvill Press. Reprinted by permission of the Random House Group Ltd.

'Letters 2' by M. R. Peacocke from *Speaking of the Dead* © Peterloo Poets 2003

Imre Kertész Nobel Prize acceptance speach © The Nobel Foundation 2002

'Sliding on Loch Ogil' from *Landing Light* by Don Paterson, reprinted by permisssion of Faber and Faber Ltd.